LAST
SEEN
ALIVE

LAST
SEEN
ALIVE

A Mystery

Ioanna Schaffhausen

MINOTAUR BOOKS
New York

First published in the United States by Minotaur Books, an imprint of St. Martin's Publishing Group

LAST SEEN ALIVE. Copyright © 2021 by Joanna Schaffhausen. All rights reserved. Printed in the United States of America. For information, address St. Martin's Publishing Group, 120 Broadway, New York, NY 10271.

www.minotaurbooks.com

Library of Congress Cataloging-in-Publication Data

Names: Schaffhausen, Joanna, author.
Title: Last seen alive : a mystery / Joanna Schaffhausen.
Description: First edition. | New York : Minotaur Books, 2022. |
    Series: Ellery Hathaway ; 5
Identifiers: LCCN 2021037781 | ISBN 9781250249678 (hardcover) |
    ISBN 9781250249685 (ebook)
Classification: LCC PS3619.C3253 L37 2022 | DDC 813/.6—dc23
LC record available at https://lccn.loc.gov/2021037781

Our books may be purchased in bulk for promotional, educational, or business use. Please contact your local bookseller or the Macmillan Corporate and Premium Sales Department at 1-800-221-7945, extension 5442, or by email at MacmillanSpecialMarkets@macmillan.com.

First Edition: 2022

10 9 8 7 6 5 4 3 2 1

For #TeamBump.
What a wild ride it's been.
How lucky I am to have you with me.

LAST
SEEN
ALIVE

Prologue

Her mother had warned her not to go to the window. Abby hadn't questioned why. At first, she hadn't found the breath to question anything. Her throat swollen and raw from lack of water, her skin burning from the ravaging infection, she'd welcomed the tether of the IV pole and the deep recesses of drugged sleep. Doctors and nurses prodded at her from time to time. Her mother flitted in and out. When Abby did finally ask questions—*Is it over? Can I go home now?*—her mother floated back nonanswers like a Magic 8-Ball. *Reply hazy. Ask again later.* Abby had started to wonder if the hospital was for mental problems, if maybe she'd dreamed the monster. Or worse, maybe she was dreaming now and her body still lay trapped inside the closet.

When Abby opened her eyes on the fourth day, she found herself alone. She held out her arms and catalogued the cuts on her body. She smelled like antiseptic. The angry red slashes around her wrists made her look like she'd tried to kill herself, and the deeper wound on her left arm had been stitched closed. Her jaw ached from where he'd struck her. Tiny scabs covered her legs from where the splinters were removed. The skin she'd worn off her fingers clawing at the walls had started to grow back, tight and itchy. She tried not to think about the searing pain between her legs, but her body mourned for her, tears stinging unbidden in her eyes. Furious, she swiped them away.

Her watery gaze slid to the cheap beige blinds covering the window. *Don't look,* her mother said. Abby hadn't seen daylight in a week. She hadn't moved two feet on her own, hadn't made a single decision by herself since she'd stopped her bike next to the man's car. With a determined breath, she forced herself upright and then paused, her weakened limbs shaking from the effort. She let her legs dangle over the edge of the bed so that they hovered above the cold tile floor. *You can do it. Just one step.* She had coached herself through three days of hell. She could make it fifteen feet to the window. Gingerly, she eased onto her bare feet, her toes spasming, her hands clutching the side of the mattress until she could be sure her knees wouldn't give way. She swayed as she relinquished her grip but did not fall. Using the rolling IV pole for support, she dragged herself to the window. *Please be out there,* she told the world as she yanked up the cord.

She gasped from the shock of bright summer sun. *People,* she noticed. *Lots of them.* They stood around on the Chicago sidewalk like they were waiting in line at a club, like they were expecting some celebrity, until someone saw her and one man pointed up at Abby's window. They swarmed toward the building, moving like one creature, like a flock of birds swooping in the sky. They shouted up to her and some of them had cameras. Abby dropped the cord and shrank back from the glass. Maybe they were all still looking for him. Maybe they were waiting outside because they figured he'd return. Her heart pounded and she thought she might be sick. Why did they want her picture? Would they show it to him?

She lurched to the bathroom, but her stomach had nothing to yield. She turned the faucet on with trembling hands and splashed cold water on her face. When she raised up her head, she saw her reflection and her mouth fell open at the sight of her new face. Terrible dark circles ringed her eyes. A chunk of her hair was gone. Her upper lip was split and swollen, and she had a six-inch scrape down the side of her face. She'd become the monster. *I'm your god now,* he'd sneered at her when she'd prayed aloud for relief. He was God and he had made her in his own grotesque image. She stared at her face until all the features blurred together, until she was numb to the abomination. It moved, she noted with some detachment as she watched her reflection. Her image wavered with each intake of breath. *You'll die when I say so,* he'd screamed in her face, but this part had not come true. His power had limits.

She shambled back to bed and crawled under the sheets. Someone knocked at her door and called her name. She did not answer because she was exhausted and also because she'd learned her answer made no difference. People came inside whether she wanted them to or not. A man in a dark suit stuck his head into the room. "Abby?"

She tried not to recoil. It was him. The other him. She hadn't seen him since that night.

"My name is Agent Reed Markham," he said as he slipped inside. His voice was gentle, with a slight Southern accent. "We met the other night."

She snorted and turned away. "I know." She'd been naked and delirious at the time, but she remembered his face. It was the first one she'd seen since the monster took her.

"I don't mean to intrude. I wanted to see how you were doing."

"How do you think?" She shot venom at him, and she didn't know why. He'd pulled her from the closet.

He retreated at her fire, his back against the door as if poised to flee. "You look—better."

You're a shitty liar. She did not give him the satisfaction of an audible response. She fixed her gaze at the bathroom door, not looking at him. In her peripheral vision, she saw him fumble for something in his suit pocket. "We're heading back to Virginia tonight," he said, "but I wanted you to have this. In case you need anything."

He stretched out his hand and placed a business card on the sheet by her knees. It had his name, phone number, and the embossed FBI logo. *What?* She wanted to yell at him. *What can you possibly give me?* She knew she was supposed to thank him. That's why he'd come, right? To see her be grateful. She felt like if she opened her mouth, she might never stop screaming.

"I'm sorry," he said gruffly. "For what happened."

Again, she did not reply. He got the hint.

"I'll leave you alone now. I—I only wanted to see that you're okay." She stared at him as he struggled to find more words. He'd gotten a haircut, she noticed. Maybe it was for the cameras. He was younger than she'd thought at first. Or maybe she was just older now.

Only as he moved to leave did she realize there was something he could give her: a straight answer. "Wait," she blurted, and he froze like a trapped animal. "What happened to him?" Her mother only said, *He can't hurt you now,* and Abby already knew that was a lie.

"We got him," Agent Markham said with obvious relief.

"He's dead?" Her heartbeat seemed to hang on the answer.

Markham's face darkened. "No, we arrested him. Coben's in custody. Don't worry, you're totally safe—he's under heavy guard, and he won't get out. Not ever again."

Abby sank backward into the pillows, reeling with the news. The FBI man didn't understand what he was saying. The monster was still out there breathing the same air. No wonder there was a huge crowd at her door. Of course, everyone wanted a picture.

The story wasn't finished.

1

Reed's mistake was to stop for a cup of coffee. Or rather, his error was in the routine, stopping as he did at the same coffee-house every morning on his way to work, a habit he counseled others against when they asked how to stay safe in a world full of human predators. *Vary your patterns. Be vigilant.*

Reed heeded neither as he performed his morning shuffle in a long line of caffeine-hungry patrons. Outside, a fierce wind swirled snow through the air like a conductor on the stage, bowing and weaving with the symphony. Winter blasted in with a crescendo every time someone new entered the front door. Through the windows, the bare trees looked like X-rays of their summer selves, skeletons clattering in the breeze.

Reed felt like a skeleton himself. The dead followed him around, their eyes on him as he waited to place his order. Eight ghosts had trailed him for years, sometimes whispering, sometimes howling as loud as the wind outside, reminding him always of his unfinished business. These lost young women never showed up in the movies or books or glossy magazine articles written about Francis Michael Coben. They had no happy ending, or indeed, any ending at all. They remained in limbo as possible victims of the infamous serial killer, not included in his body count. Only Coben himself knew the truth, and for nearly two decades now, he'd remained as silent as their graves.

"*Weed!* Grande coffee here for Weed," hollered the barista, forcing Reed to step up to the counter to retrieve his poorly named caffeine order.

"That's me," he said, and her amused glance raked once over his serious dark suit.

"Enjoy," she replied as she handed over the hot paper cup. "Weed."

Reed ignored the dig and threaded his way through the crowd to the milk and sugar station. He fumbled a yellow packet and bit back a curse as white crystals sprayed everywhere. "They do that on purpose, you know," said a voice at his arm. He looked up from his cleaning to see a well-manicured woman about his own age, dressed to stand out in a cherry-red pantsuit and stacked heels.

"Pardon me?"

"They write your name down wrong for their own amusement. The cretins over there." She jerked her blond bob in the direction of the coffee bar. "They get off calling Manny 'Fanny' or whatever juvenile epithet their air-brains can generate in the time it takes to pour a venti latte. Honestly, my fourth-grade nephew has better put-downs."

"I'm sorry, do I know you?" He did, but he didn't remember how. His brain scrambled as his mouth tried to buy time. *A fellow parent from Tula's school? A lawyer he'd seen in court once?*

Her laugh carried over the din as she turned her own cup around so he could read the scrawl. *Kate.* "I'm Kate Hunter, and you, Agent Markham, have been dodging my calls." She wagged a red-tipped finger at him as though he were a naughty schoolboy, and her identity clicked into place.

"You're that TV woman."

She laughed again. "I've been called worse. You've seen the show, then?"

"In passing." His ex-wife, Sarit, had detested this woman but sometimes flipped on her show, *On the Hunt,* to hate-watch it. Kate

Hunter yelled her outrage nightly into the camera, demanding justice for the victims. "You talk up famous cases," he said to her.

"Honey, they're not famous till I get there."

Reed recalled looking up from his book one night to ask Sarit, *Are all the victims on this show female?*

Yes, and also young, Sarit had answered. *And always white.*

"It's nice to meet you, ma'am, but I'm late for a meeting." His boss and the FBI director planned to huddle today to determine what to do about Coben's offer.

"The meeting isn't until ten," Kate said, checking her Rolex. "We have time."

"You presume to know my schedule?"

"I'm attending the meeting." She flashed him a smile and pointed at him. "Which you would know if you'd taken my calls. Shall we sit? I snagged a table in the back."

He noticed then that people were looking at them—at Kate, really—with accompanying whispers and stares. He'd gotten used to the looks and murmurs when he was with Ellery, adapted to the constant "titterati" as she called them, but it had been months now since he'd seen her and he'd receded into anonymity. "I don't give interviews anymore," he said. He hadn't done any press since he'd reconnected with Ellery a few years ago and seen what the media hunger did to her, how the public appetite for Coben's story left her without one moment of peace. On the hunt, all right. Survivors like Ellery got stuck in the crosshairs.

"You're not the one I want to interview," she said, and nodded her head again in the direction of the table. "Come sit."

Not him. Someone else. There was only one other person it could be. "Not Ellery." He hadn't said her name in public in months, and the words came out sharp. "You leave her out of this."

Kate considered this as she sipped her coffee. "Agent Markham," she said in a reasonable voice, "I'm not the one who invited her to the party. Coben did."

Reed followed her to the table she'd selected and watched as she took her seat and scanned her phone for messages. She texted a reply while he lowered himself into the chair opposite her. "What is it you want, Ms. Hunter?"

She looked up and smiled. "The same thing you do—justice for those poor girls Coben cut up and killed. He's indicated he's willing to talk, right?"

"I wouldn't put it that way." Coben had mailed Reed a bunch of dark hair and suggested it belonged to Tracy Trajan, one of Coben's suspected victims. Tracy's body had never been found, and her hands were not among those recovered at the farm where Coben was captured, leading to questions about whether she had been one of his targets. "Also, Francis Coben is a narcissistic sociopath. You can't believe a word he says."

"The FBI director believes it. That's the point of the meeting today."

Reed opened his mouth to reply but she waved him off.

"Save it. I happen to agree with you. Coben's got an eye-popping resumé, but he's not as special as he thinks he is. He's a weak man who kills women to feel better about himself. I've run across a bunch of these guys, men who buried their wives in a hole somewhere so they could carry on with a younger, prettier version. Every single one of them cries about how they're the real victim. 'It's not my fault, Judge.' 'She ran around on me, Your Honor.' 'She drank or used drugs or was a shitty mom.' 'She hit me first.'" She leaned across the table toward him, her blue eyes intense with fury. "'She made me do it.'"

She banged the table, causing Reed to flinch.

"The only thing that makes Coben special is his body count," she said, easing backward. "He knows it, too. Why do you think he's refused to give up the other girls? It's the only power he's got left."

Reed let out a slow breath, reassessing her. Her insight was dead on the money so far. "Then you see the quandary," he replied. "He's been locked up for seventeen years now. Life on death row in Terre Haute is torturous in its isolation and tedium. Coben's decided to cook up a little excitement for himself. So he whips out his pipe and plays the one tune he knows will bring us all to the dance. *I'll give up the missing girls,* he says. The problem is, if he follows through, his power is gone, and he knows it."

"He's never admitted to the murders, right? He was convicted on the strength of the evidence found at the farm, on the DNA analysis from the bodies. He never said he killed them. Getting him on record, getting him to talk about what he did and why he did it, that could help us understand where he came from and how to stop others like him in the future."

"You think we haven't tried?" He'd visited Coben a dozen times in those early years under the rubric of trying to understand him. Coben had requested Reed by name, and back then, his ego puffed, Reed had been happy to oblige. The biggest, baddest criminal since Ted Bundy knew his name and demanded his presence. Reed's boss back then took note, too, as did the publishers. Reed soon had a promotion and million-dollar book deal. For all his training and his fancy education, Reed had been slow to notice that any power he'd received in this exchange came from a sociopathic murderer. When they met, Coben had only wanted to discuss his art, his legacy, and Ellery, as though she, too, belonged to him. Reed left these winding conversations exhausted, frustrated, and diminished. He'd long ago stopped going. But there was enough ego left in him to wonder if Coben's recent letter was another mindfuck, an invitation to renew their special pas de deux. After all, the envelope had Reed's name on it.

Inside, though, the letter had contained the dark hair, the titillating reference to Tracy, and an offer of information. The price was in the name Coben did not use. *Bring me what I need,* he wrote. Reed didn't require explanation. Coben hungered for the one thing they'd kept from him as much as possible: any mention or glimpse of Abigail Ellery Hathaway.

"Listen," Reed said to Kate, "Francis Coben is happy to talk nonsense for as long as you'll listen, but we never get anything useful. As you say, he's never fully admitted to one murder, let alone the sixteen we've pinned on him. You could send me in there to talk to him a hundred times, but he'll never give up the bodies."

"Ah, but that's where I come in." She wrapped both hands around her coffee. "I can give him what he wants. A bigger audience."

The full meaning of her words dawned on him. She wasn't planning the usual rehash of Coben's story with some cheesy reenactment. "You want to put him on television."

"You look so shocked, Agent Markham. It's not like the public doesn't know the details. You wrote a book, as I recall. And then there were movies about it?"

"They were a mistake."

Her eyebrows lifted. "Oh, a mistake. Then you must have returned the advances and royalties from the projects, right?"

Reed felt his ears grow hot. "That isn't the point."

"Sure, it isn't," she said dryly. "Here's my pitch, okay? For real. This project has been in the works for a year now. The producer, Ben Lerner, has a blank check from Marquee Productions to make this event happen. They plan to stream it to a hundred million eyeballs, but money is not Ben's motive. He's like you and me, a crusader. Maybe you've read about him? His kid brother was murdered years ago and they never caught the guy who did it, so Ben understands what those poor families are going through. He wants to bring those girls home, and he plans to beat this asshole at his own game. Coben wants the spotlight? Okay, bring it on. Shine the lights on him so bright he has nowhere to go. Make him melt down."

"The authorities at the prison will never go for it."

"They've already agreed."

Reed sat up ramrod straight. "You're not seriously bringing a man who murdered two dozen women into a TV studio?"

She looked offended. "Of course not. All filming with Coben would take place within the concrete walls at Terre Haute. He'll wear shackles and there will be guards standing by. It will be totally safe."

He shook his head at her as she calmly sipped her coffee. "You don't need me, then."

"Oh, but we do." She widened her blue eyes. "You know him better than anyone. You're the ultimate consultant. Ben said we had to have you."

"Then why isn't Ben here making his case?"

Her lips curved in a half smile. "We've researched you enough to know you might be more receptive to a woman's touch." She reached across and put her hand on his forearm. Reed glanced down at her perfect manicure before yanking his arm away. She sniffed and leaned back in her seat, her tone becoming businesslike once more. "Of course, we'd love to have you on camera."

"No way."

"And we'd love to have you bring Ellery along."

"Double fucking no way." He saw it now. They didn't give a crap about his opinion. He was being used, as always, to get to the bigger players in this drama: Coben and Ellery. He was merely the conduit, the go-between, the link that made the magic happen.

"You don't think she'd want to help find those girls? That she'd want to show Coben how she's thrived since her abduction?"

"Thrived?" Ellery had lived for years with her closets nailed shut. She bore scars on her body that attracted the stares of strangers every time she wore short sleeves. The press, the public, they never stopped hounding her to tell the story one more time. "I think Ellery has earned the right to be left alone. She doesn't owe anyone a damn thing."

"Not even Tracy Trajan? What about Cathy Tyler or Alicia Arnold?" She named more of the suspected victims. "What about their families who have been waiting twenty years or more for an answer? Alicia's sister still has wrapped Christmas presents from the year Alicia disappeared. That was 1998, Agent Markham."

"I know when it was," he shot back, more harshly than intended. These were his private wounds she slashed at, the names he'd carried all these years. "I was there in the living room with the Christmas tree. This was my case, my business. It doesn't concern you and it definitely doesn't concern Ellery."

"Ellery's a cop now, right? I'd say she made it her business."

"Leave her out of this. Leave me out of it, too." He stood up and started for the door. He felt like Superman trying to halt a runaway train. If he could get to his boss Helen, maybe he could make her see reason. Just because Hollywood liked to make movies about serial killers didn't mean they should tangle with the real thing.

Kate grabbed her designer tote and scrambled after him as he pushed out into the frigid air. The snow, only a few inches deep, swirled like frosting at his feet. "Don't you want answers?" she shouted over the wind. "You can help bring Tracy Trajan back to her family. You can be the hero again."

He whirled on her. "You don't get it. You have no idea what kind of man you're dealing with. Francis Coben is not your garden-variety wife beater. He's a killing machine who started plucking young women off the streets at will when he was barely out of his teens. His IQ is one hundred and fifty. He's talented at appearing normal for long stretches of time. He laughs, pretends to cry, minds his manners, and speaks like the educated man he is. It's an act. Or at least only part of the show. There's a second Francis Coben who lies hidden underneath, a monster who needs to feed, and he hasn't been let out to play in seventeen years now. You want to throw him a party. Make him a star. You want my expert opinion? Well, here it is. You're out of your ever-loving mind. You cannot call up the devil and ask him to dance."

The air fogged with his breath. Ice crystals caught on her thick eyelashes, and she blinked them away, thoroughly unchastened. He turned on his heel, disgusted, and stalked toward his car. "An impassioned speech," she called after him. "Maybe you'd like to give it to Maxine Frazier's mother."

Reed halted with his back to her. The cold seemed to whoosh down his spine. "What did you say?" he asked as he turned around again.

"Maxine Frazier. She deserves the truth, don't you think? And a proper burial."

"Maxine Frazier isn't on the list of Coben's victims."

"Sure, she is."

"She's not," he insisted, bearing down on her. "Who do you think would know?"

She dug out her cell phone and swiped around on it. "I think he would," she said, turning the phone for Reed to see.

Snowflakes dotted the screen and turned to water, making the image appear as though it was crying. Reed saw a list of handwritten names in familiar dark printing. Eight names he recognized, and at the bottom sat the new one, Maxine Frazier. He'd received enough mail from Coben over the years to recognize the man's handwriting. Either Coben wrote the list or it was an excellent fake. "Where did you get this list?" He had to stop himself from shaking Kate. "Tell me where."

"From him. Coben wrote it."

Heaven help him. He'd comforted himself for years that at least there were no more. Sixteen known dead, with eight outstanding potential victims. One survivor. Coben's damage had been limited. Contained.

"That meeting's coming up soon," she said. "Are you going to be there or not?"

Had Coben offered other names to the producers? What the hell else had they not been telling him? He had no hope of putting this case to bed if he didn't have all the facts. The truth kept shifting and slipping away from him. *Be the hero again,* she'd said to him. She didn't understand that he never was, not for Ellery. Not for any of them. Snow swept into Reed's collar and started a freezing trickle down his back. *A cold day in hell,* he thought. Aloud, he said, "I'll be there."

2

Ellery jabbed the elevator button as if it were a suspect and she was trying to make it talk. She checked her phone again but there were no further texts from her neighbor. The one from a half hour ago read, *Can't you make your dog be quiet? It's after 9p.*

"I'm sure he's fine." Evan gave her arm a sympathetic squeeze. "Sometimes basset hounds like to sing."

"Not mine." Bump only sang to tuba music or to protest his empty dish, and she'd filled him up before leaving for the evening. He'd barely looked up from his nap on the couch when she went to meet Evan.

The elevator ground to a halt and Ellery sprang through the doors the moment they parted. Rounding the corner with Evan on her heels, she stopped short when she saw Reed Markham in the hall. Her heart, which had been thundering in her chest, lurched in confusion. "I—what are you doing here?" She had not seen him since their breakup five months ago.

He glanced behind her to Evan. "I need to talk to you. I rang the bell. I called your name, and well . . . that happened." He waved at the door in a helpless gesture. On the other side of it, Speed Bump yowled his unhappiness at being denied one of his favorite people.

"You couldn't have called?" She opened all three locks on the door, keenly aware that Evan was watching her. He didn't consume a lot of pop culture or social media, so he didn't know the details of her history. She liked it that way.

"If I'd called, would you have answered?"

She'd deleted his number so she wouldn't be tempted to contact him. She'd packed away his gifts and hidden his pictures in an unnamed album on her phone. Only at night did she lay awake in bed and poke at the memories like a kid shoving her tongue through the window of a lost tooth. Measuring the emptiness. *I love you so much,* she'd told him that last night. *But I can't do this anymore.*

When she wrangled the door open, Bump surged into the hallway with a joyous bark, streaking right past her to Reed. He jumped up with both front paws on Reed's expensive suit, wagging furiously, but for once, Reed didn't shove him back down. "Hey, boy," he said, his voice almost tender as he rubbed the dog's giant ears. "I've missed you too."

"Boy, he sure likes you," Evan remarked with a hint of envy.

"We have a long history," Reed replied to him, but he was looking at Ellery. She stared back, drinking him in. She caught a whiff of sandalwood cologne and the wet wool of his dark coat. He smiled at her attention, not with his mouth but with his eyes, the brown growing soft and warm under the intensity of her gaze. "I've missed you," he murmured again, ostensibly to the dog, as he gently disengaged.

We aren't supposed to be doing this, she told him silently. One brief visit in the hallway and she would have to recalibrate her whole existence again. "You shouldn't have come here."

His face fell. His jaw tightened. "I'm sorry. I had no choice."

His genuine regret got her attention. Fear washed over her like an icy wave. Whatever it was, it was bad. She could think of only one name that would make Reed hop a plane at night and show up unannounced on her doorstep. "Tell me he's not free."

Instantly contrite, Reed started toward her. "No, no," he began, but Evan stepped up to cut him off.

"Hey, man, the lady said she doesn't want you here. Maybe you should go."

"Evan, it's okay." She put a hand on his arm to forestall him. "He's—he's a friend. Evan Anderson, this is Agent Reed Markham from the FBI."

"FBI?" Evan's expression turned puzzled as he accepted Reed's handshake. She couldn't blame him. An hour ago, they'd been having dinner at the new Cuban place downtown and debating the greatest Talking Heads album. "Is this about work?"

"In a way," Reed said, his tone cautious.

"I'm sorry," Ellery said to Evan. "I have to cut the evening short."

He peered past her to the open doorway, nakedly curious about her apartment. They'd been out together four times, but she had not let him inside. "Um, okay. I'll call you?" Bump ambled over and Evan leaned down one hand for a scratch.

"I'll call you."

He hesitated and then gave a short nod. "Okay, beautiful. I'm here if you need me." He kissed her cheek and then walked down the hall, casting a periodic glance over his shoulder as he went. When he disappeared around the corner, she let out the breath she'd been holding and stalked inside her apartment. Reed followed with the dog.

"He seems nice."

She leaned against the kitchen island and tossed her keys down on the granite. "Don't even start with me. What's going on?"

Reed took off his overcoat and placed it across one of the tall stools, like he was planning to stay awhile. Ellery remained in her black leather jacket. "Recently I received a letter at my home, postmarked from Boston but sent by Francis Coben. He included a bunch of what looked like human hair and suggested he might be willing to give up the location of Tracy Trajan's body. The dark color of the hair matched Tracy's known color at the time of her disappearance."

"And was it hers?"

"We found no viable roots to do the DNA test. The hair had been cut off. All we can say is that it's human."

"That's awful, but I don't see what it has to do with me."

He rocked on his heels like he didn't want to say anything more.

"Reed? Tell me what this has to do with me."

He gave a long exhale. "There's a price for Coben's cooperation. He's willing to give up information on the missing girls if we bring you to him."

All the air went out of her lungs. He'd given voice to her nightmares. She could smell it all of a sudden—the stinking, blood-soaked closet. Her eyes watered and she swiped at her nose before rubbing her palms on her jeans. The motion made the cuffs slide up, revealing the scars at her wrists. Coben always kept the hands and dumped the rest. "What does that mean, exactly? Bring me to him."

"It doesn't matter," Reed replied, his voice steely. "We're not doing it."

She chuffed a humorless laugh. "You're here. You didn't come all the way up here to tell me some plan you're not doing."

"There's more. A big-time TV producer is involved, as well as Kate Hunter."

"The woman who yells about crime on TV?"

"She yells about it in person, too. Trust me."

"So, they're going to do another program on him. Big whoop." She rubbed her forehead, where an ache had begun to form.

"It's not just any program. They're going to interview Coben."

"What?" She looked at him sharply and he gave a small nod to confirm.

"It's happening with or without me."

"But they want me," she guessed.

"Coben wants you. My guess is, they want the ratings. My bosses would welcome the positive publicity that closing these final cases would bring. Not to mention that dragging Coben out of his hole is like parading the giant shark from *Jaws*. 'Look what we caught.'"

The celebrated catch, she recalled, was the wrong shark. She shook her head and paced the length of her kitchen. Bump followed on her heels, whining as she approached his dish and then flopping down with a noisy sigh when she turned away again. "So, what's the plan, then? Put us all on stage together like an episode of *Dr. Phil*?"

"They've assured me that Coben doesn't leave the prison. According to Kate and this producer, Ben Lerner, you wouldn't have to go in. They'd loop you in remotely."

"But he would see me." She stopped and swallowed. "And I would see him."

"You don't have to do it. In fact, I don't think you should. But it's your choice, obviously."

She searched his face. In her dreams, when the closet opened, he was one of only two people she saw on the other side. She had a thousand other memories of him now, to the point where that young FBI agent from years ago seemed like a different person. She knew only Reed, her friend who always told her the truth. "You're going ahead with it."

He ducked his head. "It's different for me. Coben's my job."

Always a stiff upper lip. Always willing to shoulder whatever the world threw at him. "Maybe. But he's not your responsibility. Reed, I . . ." She came around the island to him and he stepped backward swiftly, as though she meant him harm.

"I never told you," he said, a catch in his voice. "I never told you how Willett found you."

"I—what?" Willett was the killer who'd followed in Coben's footsteps. He'd hunted down Ellery a few years ago, determined either to impress her with his crimes or finish what Coben had started. "What are you talking about?"

"He used my book," Reed said tightly, his gaze fixed on the ceiling. "It didn't matter that I created a pseudonym for you. He got the information from it about your basketball ability, that you'd played in high school. He used that to figure out you might play in college too, and from there, it wasn't hard to find you and learn your name change."

Her legs felt shaky and she lowered herself to the nearest stool. "So, he used the book. He could've found me a hundred other ways. I was mostly counting on nobody ever looking."

"But he did." He looked at her with anguish in his eyes. "And he used me to do it. Me and that animal we've successfully kept away from human view for more than seventeen years. Now they want to give him a platform and broadcast his exploits to a hundred million eyeballs. What if one pair belongs to another Walt Willett?"

She shuddered. "There's still time to stop them. Maybe they'll listen to you."

"They haven't yet. I spent four hours arguing with them today." His shoulders sagged and he sounded exhausted. She knew she should offer him food and drink, but a niggling thought surfaced in her brain at the mention of Willett.

"Reed."

"Hmm?"

"You said the letter was postmarked in Boston."

"That's right." He ambled over and leaned against the island. "When I saw it, I had hope it might be from you."

"How did Coben send a letter from death row in Indiana that was postmarked in Boston?"

"He clearly had help." Reed's tone was grim. "His lawyer, maybe. That guy's as nutty as his client, mark my words. Plus, there are legions of true believers, as you know. Coben has a small army ready to take up for him. That's my primary worry." He paused. "That, and the families. If we get their hopes up that the missing girls will be found and returned, only to have Coben devouring their pain like an opiate . . ."

"There's eight of them not found," Ellery murmured. "I remember."

"Maybe more." He moved aside his coat and took the stool next to her. "The list of names he gave to the TV people listed one I didn't recognize. Maxine Frazier. I don't know what to make of it. We went back through the files, and there was no record of a Maxine Frazier being reported missing in Chicago at the time of the other abductions. In fact, there are only three Maxine Fraziers listed in all of Illinois. One is four years old, and the others are in their fifties. All are alive and well."

"Maxine Frazier," Ellery repeated as she turned the name over in her head. "I know that name."

Reed tensed, on alert again. "A friend of yours? Someone from back home?"

"No, I heard it recently." She struggled to place the connection. "Oh, no," she said as it snapped into place. "No."

"What? What is it?"

"My partner, Dorie, got loaned out to missing persons when three of their people came down with the flu. She mentioned they'd taken a report on a missing young woman named Maxine Frazier. Attempts to locate her turned up nothing. The brass said to put a pin in it because Maxine's a sex worker with a drug habit, but Dorie was worried."

"When was this exactly?"

"During the Christmas holidays or right after, I think. So . . . around five weeks ago."

Reed grabbed his coat. "We need to talk to Dorie. We need everything you've got on that case right now."

"You really think they could be connected?"

"I don't know. But that letter I got from Coben? It was mailed five weeks ago."

3

Outside, Boston was deep in its midwinter freeze. The subzero air crackled her lungs while the full moon shone bright as a pearl against the black sky. A thin coating of ice encased her SUV and she had to yank hard to get the door open. The leather seats squeaked in the cold. Ellery hit the power button and the big car roared to life like an angry bear awoken early from hibernation. Reed reached for the seat warmer and cranked it to high.

"Still got that thin Southern blood, I see," she remarked as she pointed the SUV toward Dorie's condo. The cold and late hour may have kept everyone indoors, but Boston's narrow streets remained jam-packed with cars, parked as they were with snowbanks on either side of the road.

"I'll have you know it was snowing in Virginia this morning. Four inches."

"That means we'll get ten when it shows up here."

"And to think I didn't pack my boots."

She felt a smile tug the corner of her mouth. "You never do." Half the time in their whirlwind relationship, one or both of them jumped a plane with only the clothes on their back. Later, when it was just the two of them, the clothes fell to the floor. She pushed the thought away and cleared her throat. "How are you? How's Tula?"

"She turned eight last month. Sarit threw her a spa-themed party and all the girls got sparkly pedicures."

"You attended?"

"My toes are still purple."

"You know, that stuff does come off, or so I've heard." Ellery's mom had raised her to look down on salon styling as excessive, prideful, and vain. As an adult, Ellery understood they couldn't afford it.

"I know, but I like the sparkles," Reed said as he looked out the window. "They remind me of Tula when I can't see her."

Ellery wondered if he'd kept any mementos of her. She'd cached away what she could but there was no hiding the marks on her body. She wore her history like armor and he'd been forged with her. Neither of them would be the people they were if not for Francis Coben. He was their origin story, the man who'd given them rebirth as characters in a saga that never seemed to end. Reed the rescuer. Ellery the victim. Coben was the beast who'd set it all in motion. There was no escaping him as long as they were together, which was why she'd had to leave.

"Tell me about the guy," Reed said, turning back to look at her.

"There's not much to tell. I met Evan at the dog park, where he was hanging out with his Goldendoodle, Ollie. Evan's an EMT and plays guitar. He and his buddies have an Eighties cover band that plays in some bars around town. They're not bad."

"And he thinks you're beautiful."

She squirmed in her seat but kept her eyes on the road. "He doesn't know me."

She felt his surprise. "He doesn't know about . . ." He trailed off, apparently unable to pick just one part of her explosive past.

"He's not on social media and doesn't follow a lot of the news. He cares about medicine and music." The winter temperatures meant she looked normal in her turtlenecks and long sleeves. Evan didn't have reason to question her. Yet.

"Ah, well." Reed settled in his seat, contemplative. "He gives you what you wanted."

"What's that supposed to mean?" Anger flared in her, hot and quick. She'd been the one to break it off, but it didn't feel like her decision. Nothing in her life ever did.

Reed regarded her with serious eyes. "Anonymity."

The best thing about Reed was the way he understood her. Sometimes it was the worst part too. He broke away from her gaze and glanced outside. "Isn't that Dorie's place?"

The tires screeched as she hit the brakes. She found an illegal parking spot half a block up and they walked back on the icy sidewalk. At least the lights were on in Dorie's unit so they wouldn't be waking the household. A chorus of loud barking erupted when Ellery hit the bell, followed by her partner's instructions to shush. Dorie opened the door wearing plaid pajama bottoms and a faded BPD sweatshirt. She had her glasses on rather than her usual contact lenses and her gray-blond bob looked shaggier than Ellery remembered it from earlier in the day. Dorie clenched her teeth as she held back a tide of eager Labrador retrievers. "Hathaway, you know it's past ten."

"I know, but it's urgent."

"I had guessed that if the Feds are involved," she said, turning her gaze to Reed. She inclined her head. "Unless Agent Markham is here for a social visit."

Ellery ignored the note of hope in Dorie's voice. "No, it's about a case you worked a few weeks ago. Can we come in?"

"Sure, of course," she said, corralling the dogs behind her as best she could. "What's up?" The chocolate one, Grover, burst free and came barreling straight for Ellery's legs.

"Maxine Frazier," Ellery said as she helped Dorie herd the animals to the kitchen. "She was reported missing when you were working the desk after Christmas, right?"

"Yeah, she was. I checked in last week to see if there'd been any updates in the case. Nada."

"Dorie?" Dorie's wife, Michelle, appeared in the doorway with a mug in her hands. "Who was at the—oh. Hi, Ellery."

"Sorry, it's about a case," Dorie said.

"I guessed that."

"Ma'am," Reed said. "Apologies for the late hour and the intrusion."

"You're not the worst we've had," she replied with a deep sigh. "Can I get anyone coffee? It's decaf." She waved her mug in offering.

"Thanks, hon, but could you take the dogs upstairs?"

Michelle hesitated a beat and then gave a short nod. "Come on, boys. Let's go see what's on Netflix." With some urging, the dogs followed her out of the room, and Dorie turned impatient eyes to Ellery.

"What's your interest in Maxine Frazier? Did she turn up?"

"Not as far as I know. Tell me more about the case."

"Maxine Frazier, age twenty. Caucasian female, one hundred and thirty pounds, five feet, four inches tall. Her driver reported her missing right before the new year."

"Her driver?" Ellery said.

"Well, the rideshare guy she used most often to travel to 'dates.' His name is Lester Gibbs, I believe. He got worried when she didn't contact him for over a week, so he texted her. I guess they sometimes did business off the books. She didn't answer his texts. He drove by her place, knocked on her door. A neighbor walked by and said she hadn't seen or heard Maxine in days, and that's when he went to the police."

"What did you do?" Ellery asked.

"We sent patrol by for a welfare check. They knocked, got no answer. So, we raised the building manager on the phone and got him to let us inside for a look-see. The place was messy but not ransacked in any way that suggested foul play. No sign of Maxine. No money, wallet, ID, or phone. We ran her through the system and she's got an armful of priors for solicitation, drug possession, for which she received mostly fines and/or a suspended sentence. Small-time stuff."

"And?" Ellery pressed.

"There is no *and*. I talked to McCaffrey last week, and he said the girl came out here from a small town out in western Mass, and they figure she went back there or someplace just like it down in warmer climates."

"Did they follow up?"

Dorie shrugged. "You know how it is. She's an adult. She's allowed to leave town whenever she wants. As McCaffrey put it, 'The Uber guy is probably mad he didn't get to take her to the airport.'"

"But you were concerned," Reed said, reading Dorie's expression.

"I figure if she's going someplace long-term, she's going to take her suitcase. Instead, we found it sitting in her closet." She folded her arms over her chest. "I've told you what I know. Now you tell me what's your interest in this case."

Reed filled her in on the latest missive from Francis Coben. Dorie's face, usually smooth for a woman pushing fifty, took on wrinkles of confusion. "But he's locked up in Indiana, right? He didn't do anything to anyone last Christmas. What's his play here? You think he heard some rumor about Maxine and he's jerking your chain about it?"

"It's possible," said Reed. "He's got nothing better to do at the moment."

"Can you take us to Maxine's place? I'd like to check it out."

"I can, but . . ." Dorie pulled out her phone and swiped around on it. "It might be more helpful if we caught a ride."

Twenty minutes later, Lester Gibbs rolled up in a black Chevrolet Tahoe, a big cruiser of a car that housed an equally large man behind the wheel. Gibbs looked like he could have played defensive tackle for the Patriots back in the day. He wore short sleeves despite the frigid temperatures, showing off faded tats all the way up both arms, but his glasses were granny-style, round lenses with slim wire frames. "Detective Bennett," he said with a warm smile for Dorie as they climbed in the car. "It's nice to see you again. You saying you want to go past Maxine's place. Does that mean there's been some news?"

"No, I'm sorry. Nothing yet." Dorie took shotgun, forcing Reed and Ellery to sit in the back together. "This is my partner, Ellery Hathaway, and FBI Agent Reed Markham. They're looking into the case as well, so I was hoping you could answer some of their questions about Maxine."

"I sure as well can," he said as he put the car in gear. "Lay it on me."

"When was the last time you saw Maxine?" Ellery asked, leaning forward in her seat.

"Day after Christmas. She called me to take her to a job at the Pineville Inn up in Woburn. It's right off of Ninety-Five but farther out than she usually goes, so she gave me a nice fat tip. I had a Christmas surprise for her—a cherry-red popsicle. I stopped at Joe's corner store special before I picked her up because they're the only place that sells 'em loose like that. You see, Maxine, she only likes the cherry ones. She buys them multipacks sometimes and gives me the grape and the orange because she won't eat them. It's kind of our thing. She ate it while I drove, and we talked about our holidays."

"About what time did you drop her off?"

"It was nine thirty p.m. exactly when I left her at the parking lot." He shook his head in sorrow. "I didn't watch where she went. It's one of those places where the rooms go right outside—you know, like a Motel Six? The dude gave her the room number and she started walking on back. I had another call for a pickup, so I left right away."

"She didn't tell you the room number?"

"If she did, I don't remember. I'm sorry."

"It's okay," Ellery assured him. To Dorie, she said, "Do you know if McCaffrey pulled her cell phone records?"

"I don't think so. No cause. He still thinks she left on her own."

"Without telling nobody?" Gibbs scoffed. "No, Maxine wasn't like that. She'd tell me if she was packing up for good. And then why wouldn't she be answering my texts?"

Ellery knew that the missing persons detectives could answer this question a hundred ways based on the cases they'd worked. People got offended over nothing at times, cutting friends or family off. Or maybe Maxine lost her phone. Maybe she went home to western Massachusetts and vowed to leave everyone from her old life behind. When Ellery first went missing, the cops had initially marked her down as a runaway. "Tell me more about how Maxine seemed that night. Was she worried about anything? Did she say anything about the client she planned to meet?"

"Nah, she wasn't worried. She was laughing because he was willing to pay her two Gs to spend the night with him. Her usual overnight rate was two hundred. She called him her Splenda Daddy. All the sweetness but none of the calories. I think I remember her saying he was from out of town, but I don't know where from. I'm not sure Maxine did either."

"Did Maxine have someone who arranged this meeting for her?" Reed asked delicately.

"No, she was in business for herself. Put up her picture and advertised on the internet. She screened the dudes by phone ahead of time. She showed me her work photo once, the one she used as bait. I liked to rag on her that the joes wouldn't even recognize her when she showed up because that picture looked nothing like her except for the red hair. She'd run her face through so many filters she looked like a damn hologram."

"We need those phone records," Ellery murmured to Dorie.

"I'm on it," Dorie said, pulling out her own phone.

"Here you are. This is Maxine's building." He pulled to a stop in front of a boxy old house that had been converted into apartments. It lacked the cute trim and architectural details of some of its neighbors. "She's got the basement unit, but I guess those windows are all blocked by snow right now."

"I texted the owner, who lives a few streets over," Dorie said. "She's meeting us here."

As if on cue, a red Camry pulled up and a petite woman in a huge coat got out. Lester gestured at the house. "You want me to hang around and take you back when you're done looking around?"

"That would be great," Dorie told him. "Thanks."

Ellery looked to Reed as they walked up the narrow path that had been shoveled to the front door. "What do you think?"

"Too early to say for sure," he muttered back. "But no one offers an escort ten times her going rate unless he very badly wants her to show up. Whoever called Maxine that night, he wanted no doubt that she'd come."

The building owner, Mercedes Kim, appeared irritated as she let them into Maxine's apartment. "She's late with the rent now two months. If you find her, tell her I'm boxing up this stuff and putting it out in the snow."

Ellery flicked on the wall switch and was relieved to find the power still on. The naked bulbs in the overhead fixture revealed a cramped living room and a Seventies-style galley kitchen. The place was cold and smelled faintly like rotting garbage. Ellery looked in the fridge and found three half-drunk bottles of different red wine, milk so old it was threatening to burst the plastic bottle, a carton of eggs that expired a month ago, and a dozen takeout containers. Junk mail piled on the narrow counter. The living room featured an old futon with a black-and-white striped cover on it, but the design did little to hide the ass prints worn into the cushion. A cheap bookshelf housed at least a hundred paperback titles, mainly mysteries and romance with some self-help diet books thrown in for good measure.

Ellery pushed open the door to the bedroom and saw an unmade bed, rumpled clothes on the floor. The bedside table had a framed picture of a redhead she presumed was Maxine alongside a blond girl about the same age. There were empty cans of Diet Coke on almost every surface. The trash can overflowed with used tissues. Ellery double-checked Dorie's assertion that the suitcase was in the closet, and yes, there was a little black roller bag sitting to one side. A stuffed white cat with long hair and green eyes sat atop the dresser, an enigmatic expression on its face. Ellery paused to smile at it and touch its nose. "Where's your momma?" she whispered.

Reed poked his head in. "Nothing in the bathroom except a year's supply of hair products and the entire beauty aisle of your local drugstore."

"See?" Dorie said. She hadn't moved from the front door. "There's nothing obviously out of place."

Ellery returned to the kitchen and searched listlessly through the mail, hoping for some clue. She found only bills and catalogs. "I don't see any signs of a computer around the place, so she must have used her phone for internet access. We really need those records."

"They're working on it," Dorie told her. "It will take time."

Reed put his hands on his hips. "I don't think we can get anything more here."

"I guess not," Ellery said, turning away from the mail to face the fridge again. Maxine liked popsicles, Lester had told them, and Ellery felt a kinship in this. Popsicles were the ice cream treat of the poor, cheap and easy to make or buy. Growing up, she and her brother, Daniel, had consumed hundreds of them over the hot Chicago summers. She reached for the freezer, wanting to see Maxine's collection, hoping to extend her moment of connection with the missing woman. The door swung open, the burst of cold smacking her in the face, and Ellery shrieked in horror.

"What is it?" Reed flew across the room so he could see.

She turned to him, unable to look again. She didn't need a second glance because she would never forget. "It's her hands."

4

At quarter to three, Reed found himself again lingering awkwardly under the garish fluorescent lights in Ellery's hallway as she handed off Bump to her neighbor Liz, who lived a few doors down. Ellery murmured her apologies about the ungodly hour as Bump wagged an enthusiastic greeting to his best buddy, Liz's dachshund Daisy.

Liz accepted the bag of food and the leash with equanimity. Her greeting was for Reed. "Hey there, Agent Markham. It's nice to see you again." She directed this last bit to Ellery, and Reed wondered what Ellery had told her neighbor about their breakup, if anything at all. Ellery guarded her few remaining secrets with the grim determination of a 1970s KGB agent. He'd argued with her last year about her logic, insisting they could forge their own path and that Coben didn't need to define their relationship to one another. Yet here they were again with another missing girl and a pair of severed hands, and Reed had to accept that maybe Ellery was right.

He pushed away from the wall as she finished up with Liz. "You don't have to stay," Ellery told him. "It's not your case."

"It is. It always has been."

"Coben didn't do this."

"We don't know what his role is. But we can be certain you have a violent predator on the streets with a keen interest in Coben's handiwork." He paused. "And in you."

Her face darkened and she started off down the hall. "Don't drag me into it."

"You think this guy picked Boston by accident?"

Ellery didn't get a chance to reply because her cell phone rang. "Yeah? Okay, what have you got?" He saw her fingers tighten on the phone. "I'll meet you over there."

She started moving again for the elevator, and Reed hurried to keep pace. "What is it?"

"Dorie got the first part of Maxine's cell phone records since the case is priority one now. The last transmission pinged off a tower that is less than a hundred yards from the Pineville Inn."

Reed followed her into the elevator without a word. He thought of Lester Gibbs, who'd had tears in his eyes when he'd dropped them off earlier after their ghoulish discovery at Maxine Frazier's apartment. They couldn't give him details, but he'd lived long enough to know what it meant when the crime scene tape went up. "It's gonna be in all the papers now," he'd said. "They're going to call her a prostitute, a hooker, and people who read the news will call her something worse. They didn't know my girl Maxi. She didn't want this life. Her mama was always fragile—you know, upstairs." He'd tapped the side of his head. "But it was okay because her daddy took care of both of them. He had a good job at the post office. Reliable pay. Good bennies. But, to hear Maxine tell it, he also had epilepsy. The doc gave him this drug, the only one that seemed to help, and everything was fine until the government decided to reclassify the drug as illegal. Maxine's daddy got busted. Can you believe that? They arrested him for takin' pills that a doctor done prescribed for him? Of course, he didn't get the medicine in jail. Two months in, he had a seizure, fell on the concrete, and got a brain bleed. His family wasn't even with him when he died. Maxine, she was all of fifteen when that happened. Her mama started wandering during the day so Maxi quit school to take care of her. One day while she was in the shower, her mama wandered off where nobody found her for three days. It was the middle of January and she got pneumonia. Just like Maxi's daddy, her mama checked into the hospital and never came out. Now I ask you: What chance did that girl ever have?"

Reed looked across the elevator to Ellery, who in her own way, had been as vulnerable as Maxine the night Coben had grabbed her. Just turned fourteen years old. Father fled the family. Brother sick with cancer and her mother overwhelmed. Ellery didn't choose this life either. "Are you okay?" he asked her softly.

She met his eyes with a hard gaze. "Are you?"

He said nothing as the elevator slid to a stop.

Ellery did not break her stare. "We have the same nightmares, right? Yours are from a different angle. Those hands in the freezer are about you as much as they're about me."

She brushed past him into the lobby and Reed waited a moment before following. He found her in the car, letting it idle. She didn't look at him, but she didn't prevent him from getting in with her, either. They drove in silence out of the city and off the ramp that led to the Pineville Inn. Dorie and a couple of cruisers had beaten them to the scene. Reed stepped out of the car and the snow crunched under his foot like the first bite of a crisp apple. His eyebrows froze as he took in the landscape. The Pineville Inn was shaped like a long rectangle that sat alongside a large parking lot. There were two rows of rooms, each with a door facing an outside sidewalk, one up and one down. A couple of pine trees near the front accounted for the name and all the landscaping. The orange neon sign in the window of the lobby boasted a rate of $39.99 PER NIGHT.

Dorie waved to them from behind the glass doors of the lobby. She indicated a balding man behind the front desk. "This is the manager, Norm Rivera. He's pulling video for us from December twenty-sixth. They have two cameras on the parking lot and two that cover each row of rooms, so maybe we'll get lucky. The motel has a hundred rooms total, but only forty-seven were occupied that night.

Mr. Rivera is going to provide us a list of the registrants. When we get the full cell phone dump, we can cross-reference those names to Maxine Frazier's calls."

"Here it is," Mr. Rivera said, gesturing at the screen. "This is our main camera from the night of December twenty-sixth, starting just before nine thirty."

Reed crowded with the manager, Dorie, and Ellery behind the counter so that they could all look at the computer monitor. The camera's image was slightly grainy, with poor lighting, but it was enough that Reed recognized a familiar Tahoe pull up at 9:29. It stopped near the mouth of the parking lot, and after about twenty seconds, a young woman with red hair, a purple leather jacket, and knee-high boots got out of the vehicle. She turned to say something to the driver and then began walking across the parking lot. Within a few strides, she disappeared off-screen.

"That's her," Ellery said. "That's Maxine. Do you have the other angle?"

"I figured you'd ask. Here it is." He hit a few keys and the video switched to a camera from the side of the parking lot, near the slim row of trees that separated the Pineville Inn from its neighbor. The video showed nothing for a few moments, but then Maxine strode across the screen, a confident sway in her hips. She had her phone out, its white case visible in her right hand, and she looked down at it as she walked. Maybe rechecking the room number? She once again vanished off-screen when she walked out of view of the camera.

"What about the cameras for the rooms?" Dorie wanted to know. "We should be able to see what room she went into."

"Here's the first floor." He hit some buttons and the camera showed a long cement sidewalk and metal railing. The snow hadn't hit yet, so the pavement was all clear. They watched as a woman came out in bare feet and scampered down the presumably cold walkway. She reappeared a minute later with a soda in her hands. "Vending machines are down that way," Mr. Rivera explained.

The video rolled on, but Maxine did not appear.

"Let's check the upper camera," Dorie said.

"Sure thing." He cued up the video from the top row of rooms. The camera angle was from the back, farthest from the lobby, in the direction that Maxine had been walking. If she was going to one of the second-floor rooms, they should get a good look at her. An old man came out with a tiny dog and took it down the steps. A male and female couple came up the steps, laughing and shoving each other, and disappeared into Room 88.

As the video rolled past 9:36, Reed frowned. "She should have arrived by now."

"Is there another camera?" Ellery asked, frustration evident in her voice.

"There's one by the pool, but it's only on when the pool is open during the summer." He shrugged. "Maybe your girl never got here." The relief was plain on his face. "Like I was telling Detective Bennett earlier, nobody got murdered in any of these rooms. The cleaning staff would have mentioned finding a body or a mess of blood around." He halted, obviously struck by some unpleasant thought.

"What is it?" Ellery asked.

"Uh, probably nothing." He licked his lips and ran one hand over his bare head. "But my cousin Solly works construction, and he's part of the crew putting up the new office suite over yonder." He pointed to the three-story building going up on the adjacent lot. "A few weeks ago, they arrived on the job to find one of the ground-floor rooms covered in blood. They called the cops and the cops said it was most likely a deer who got hit by a car and ran through the building."

"When exactly was this?" Dorie demanded.

"Geez, you'd have to ask Solly. But I think it was after Christmas."

"Let's check it out," Reed said, heading for the door.

Rivera called out after them, sounding helpless. "Solly said they cleaned it up!"

They paused to grab flashlights from Ellery's trunk before crossing the mounds of plowed snow and line of bare trees that comprised the barrier between the two lots. Construction on the new office space appeared nearly finished. It now sported doors and windows, as well as a finished roof. Ellery ran up to the doors and tugged at them. "It's locked. I don't even know who we call—Cousin Solly?"

Reed didn't answer. His gaze slid to the tall copse of pine trees visible at the back of the lot. Trudging through the icy landscape, he went around to the back, where he found a dumpster and a pile of cement blocks partially covered in snow. The woods he'd glimpsed from the front appeared substantial, the equivalent to several uncleared lots. He waded in for a better look, his flashlight trained at the ground. He saw animal tracks—small squirrel prints and larger indentations likely made by deer, as the cops had surmised. He sank in past his ankles, stumbling in the drifts as the cold air stung his nose and numbed his fingers. He heard only the sound of his harsh breathing as he staggered deep into the woods. *What the hell are you even looking for?* The snow would have blanketed any evidence. He shone the light around, interrogating the trees.

He spotted one low branch that had been snapped off and paused to study it. Possibly a deer broke it off. Or a winter storm. He swished his light around in dismay as the woods yielded no secrets.

"Reed?" Ellery called for him from a distance.

"Here!" he yelled back.

"Did you find anything?"

He turned to go. "Nothing."

"Dorie's got Cousin Solly on his way."

He picked his way back through the trees, his heel skidding on a patch of black ice as he rejoined the pavement. Ellery appeared just in time to grab his arm and prevent him falling on his rear into the snow. "Thanks," he muttered as she released him.

"You need to bring boots if you plan on mucking about New England crime scenes in February."

"We don't know this is a crime scene. Not yet."

The sound of a large engine pulling up out front, like from a light truck or work van, caused them to exchange a look. "Cousin Solly," they both said at the same time. Returning to the front of the building, they found instead the crime scene investigation van.

"Dorie Bennett sent us," said the first of two men to emerge. He was young, slender, and on the shorter side. "I'm Alan Liddle. The joke is that makes him Big." He jerked a hand at his companion, who had gray bushy eyebrows and hulking shoulders.

"Ryan McCaffrey," he said as he shook hands with Ellery and Reed in turn. "What've you got for us?"

"Not sure yet," Ellery replied. "We're waiting on access now."

A pair of high beams cut her across the face and she shielded her eyes. Reed turned and saw a red pickup truck pulling into the lot. A balding man dressed in jeans, a Patriots jersey, and work boots got out. Cousin Solly had arrived at last.

They followed him inside, which was no warmer than the parking lot as the heating system had yet to be engaged. "Electricity is fully wired but there are no lights installed yet," Solly explained as he used his own flashlight to show them to the back of the first floor. He waved his beam in a rear corner that was not far from one of the back exits Reed had glimpsed in his exploration. "This is the spot," Solly said. "This is where we found most of the blood." He indicated the door. "We had plastic sheeting nailed up over the frame, but the storm must've blown it loose. We found it flapping in the wind when we got here. That's how the deer got in here."

"Any hoofprints?" Ellery asked as she shone her light around the floor. "Deer droppings?"

"Nah, just a lot of blood. It was pooled over there like I said, and some was smeared by the door."

Reed crouched down where Solly had indicated the blood had been. They had done an excellent job with the cleanup. He could find no visible traces. "Do you carry luminol?" he asked Liddle and McCaffrey, who had suited up with coveralls and booties.

Liddle seemed offended. "Of course." He knelt down to consult his kit. They waited while he sprayed the area. "Okay, kill your lights," he instructed. They all turned off their flashlights and the concrete floor glowed in a splotchy pattern that stretched nearly two feet wide.

"There," Solly said excitedly. "See, I told you. The stains went partway up on the walls, too, but you can't see them on account of the drywall we put up." He paused. "You don't have to tear that out, do you?"

"It could still be animal blood," Ellery said. "Right?" She turned to Liddle, her form barely visible in the dark.

"Right. Easy enough to confirm if it's human, though. Let me get a swab."

"Wait," Reed said. "Can I see that spray bottle a moment?" He extended a hand in Liddle's direction and the tech pressed the luminol into his palm.

"Go nuts, man."

Reed switched his flashlight on and turned it up toward the steel beams overhead. The walls had gone up but the ceiling had not been finished. He consulted the dim glow of the stain, used his flashlight to aim an arc over his head, and then followed up with a spray of luminol along the same trajectory. When he'd finished, he switched off the light again. All the heads around him tilted up to see the fresh illumination: a splatter of dots across the beam.

"That's cast off," Ellery murmured, pulling out her cell. "I'm calling Dorie."

"Tell her to bring the dogs," replied Reed. They would need to search the woods out back.

"Wait, what's that mean?" Solly asked, his tone anxious now. "What did you find?"

Reed backed away, tugging the man with him so that the techs could take over. "This isn't the scene of some animal's unfortunate accident. It's a murder."

5

It took the dogs less than five minutes to find her. Whoever had put Maxine Frazier in the ground, he hadn't hidden her well, found as she was in a shallow grave in a wood sparse enough to glimpse the neighboring highway. Only the intervening back-to-back snowstorms that laid down a thick blanket of cold and ice had prevented her previous discovery. Ellery watched from afar, across the road and inside the warm safety of a Dunkin' hut, as the state troopers descended to take control of the scene. Outside of Boston city limits, the Staties had jurisdiction: ownership of Maxine Frazier's case would be decided by where she died, not where she'd lived.

The morning rush was on and commuters streamed in and out of the donut shop, everyone murmuring to one another and peering out the large windows at the circus of blue flashing lights that surrounded the construction zone on the other side of the street. Ellery and Reed had a tiny table to themselves in the corner, him with coffee and her with hot tea. Dressed in their regular clothes, they could have been any of the anonymous onlookers, stealing glances through the steamed-up glass.

"Dorie's going to be running point from our end," Ellery said, her hands wrapped around the paper cup but her gaze fixed out the window. "Depending on how much they let us share the case. Everyone's waiting on the full dump of Maxine's cell phone to find out who her last client was, but there's no way it's going to be that easy. The guy who planned that—" She paused to gesture at the chaos at the construction zone. "He didn't use his real name and number."

"No, I think not. But he did do one thing to give himself away."

She looked at him. "What do you mean?"

"His bit of theater, putting her hands in her freezer—it's a tell. If he lured her here through her internet business, he shouldn't have known where she lives, but clearly he does have this information."

"Maybe he got the address from her purse when he killed her."

Reed shook his head. "Remember the video. She wasn't carrying a purse."

"A wallet then, inside her coat."

"Maybe," he replied, sounding unconvinced. "But I still think this wasn't a random attack. He picked Maxine for some reason. That means their paths had crossed before the night of December twenty-sixth, which is helpful because if we can find that contact, there's good odds he may not have been as careful at the time."

"He could have been a past client."

"Definitely worth checking out."

They would need to interview Lester Gibbs again, she realized. Maxine had talked about the client and mentioned he was from out of town. Maybe she had also said whether he was repeat business. Ellery suppressed a shiver as the coroner's van pulled out of the lot across the street and drove away. At the morgue, Maxine's hands could be reunited with the rest of her. Ellery put her own hands over her face, shielding her eyes. She couldn't see the scars. Most days she didn't feel them. But times like this, they seemed to burn. "Dorie says the captain may pull me off the investigation at any time," she said, dropping her hands and spreading them on the laminated orange table in front of her. "Because of the Coben connection. What is the Coben connection, Reed? Is this just another wannabe? How the hell do these homicidal maniacs with a hand fetish keep popping up everywhere like weeds? You chop one down and two more spring up in their place."

"I don't know what Coben's angle is. I promise you I aim to find out. Whoever did this, we'll catch him."

"Sure. And then there will be another him." She pulled back. "That's your real fear, right?"

He sat back with a weary sigh. She'd long admired Reed's shoulders. He had a swimmer's body, lean but broad at the shoulders and tapered at the waist. At that moment, though, he appeared hunched, like a man with a guilty secret. He glanced outside across the street before answering her. "Do you know why mass shootings often seem to come in spurts? The copycats, they already have the fantasy. They have stockpiled the weapons. They've selected targets. They dream at night about committing the murders, excite themselves with the imagined screams. Then someone else acts on their specific fantasy. They bring it to life and make it seem possible. The same way that watching someone achieve a good dream of yours can make it seem like a reality, like completing a marathon or graduating from medical school, so can these dark dreams propagate among people who harbor similar thoughts. So if they put Coben on the screen, they risk making more of him."

"Then we can't let them do it."

"I've tried to stop them."

"Maybe they'll listen to me."

He gave her the same look Dorie had, the one that said she shouldn't be near this case. "Ellery—"

"They think they know him. But they haven't seen him with the mask off. They haven't seen him wild-eyed and holding a bloody knife. He licks it, you know. The knife. He cuts you open and then he licks your blood."

Reed's kind eyes welled with sympathy. "I know."

"You don't," she cut him off impatiently. "I mean, you know it here." She touched her head. "But not here." She yanked down her collar to reveal the scars by her neck. "And not here," she continued as she pulled up her sleeves. "All those girls he killed, they knew the real Francis Coben. He killed them all and figured he'd take his secret self to their graves. There was only one girl left who could tell the truth, and she's been scared silent all these years. Well, not anymore."

She waited for him to argue. Instead, he pulled out his cell phone and started tapping on the screen.

"What are you doing?" she asked finally.

He didn't look up. "Booking you a ticket."

On the plane, she leaned back and briefly closed her eyes. Reed traveled business class, meaning roomy seats and the opportunity to board first. She knew she should try to take the opportunity to sleep since they had been up the entire night, but her body flickered with nervous energy. When her phone buzzed, she grabbed at it, hoping to see news from Dorie. It was from Evan. He'd sent a cartoon of a grinning golden retriever with two tennis balls at his feet. In front of him, a genie rose up out of a lamp. The genie was saying to the dog, "I want you to think *really hard* about your third wish."

Evan added: *My wish is to have dinner again with you this week. Maybe Thursday?*

She wondered if he would see the news and start to piece the story together. It would be easier if some talking head broke the story to him than if Ellery had to tell it herself. This was partly why she had spent most of her life refraining from dating. When men saw the scars, they wanted answers, assuming they didn't already know who put them there in the first place.

She risked a sideways glance at Reed, who had his nose buried in a book he'd picked up at the airport. She didn't believe in fairy-tale romance, recognizing it as bullshit from the start. Her father had walked out on her mother when Ellery was still Abby, just ten years old. She'd grown up on the streets of Chicago where men yelled and whistled at her even before her boobs came in. She did not expect any of them to turn out to be a Prince Charming, but neither had she been afraid of what they could do to her. Not back then.

With Reed, she'd never had to explain the scars or anything else about her peculiar existence. He'd accepted the nails in her closets and the locks on her doors and even the iron wall around her heart. He had fixed her dinners and held her hand and calmed her nightmares in the dark. He'd said "I love you" and waited patiently for months for her to say it back. She'd managed the words only once, when she was already out the door. The hurt on his face when he realized she was leaving him felt like a betrayal of every wonderful moment they had shared together. *Coben has already stolen so much,* he'd argued with her. *Don't let him take this too.*

But it wasn't up to her. Coben was locked up but he never went away. The public appetite for the story saw to that, with a new book, TV show, or movie almost every year. They all had their roles to play. She would be locked in the closet. Reed would play a hunch and liberate her. Of course, Hollywood wanted a happy ending. They didn't understand. If Reed was perfect for her, it was because a madman had made it so.

She swallowed the lump in her throat and texted Evan back. *Had to leave town unexpectedly for work & not sure when I'll be back. I'll call you.* She tucked the phone away as the flight attendant came through to make a last check before takeoff. "What are you reading?" she asked Reed.

He tilted the cover to show it to her and she saw the big bold title read *All In.* "Know your enemy," he said as she recognized the author as Ben Lerner, the writer/producer determined to put Coben on the air. "It's his bestselling memoir."

"I've heard of him. He's the guy behind that cable series, right? The one that won all those Emmys a few years ago?"

"*Rockheed Mountain,* yes. It's apparently loosely based on the murder of Ben Lerner's little brother, Andrew, when they were kids. Andrew disappeared from the family campground and was later found a mile away, drowned in a creek. He'd been bludgeoned over the head and then weighted down with rocks in his clothes. He was six years old. Ben was ten."

"God, how awful."

"Lerner also wrote that gritty cop drama from ten years ago, the one about how they all turned into terrorism hunters after 9/11. Then last year, he did a rom-com for Netflix. Apparently, he's got range. He's also got three million Twitter followers, where he does takedowns of inept politicians and campaigns for criminal justice reform."

Ellery took the book and studied the author photo on the jacket. Ben Lerner was about Reed's age, mid-forties, with chestnut-colored hair and bright blue eyes. He was smiling for the camera, showing an array of expensive white teeth, but his outfit was pure everyman: jeans and a basic black T-shirt. "Did they catch the guy who murdered his brother?"

"No, and I gather that's an animating force in both his work and his life."

"Maybe he'll listen to reason then." The thick book felt heavy in her hands. Ben Lerner sure had a lot to say for himself. She handed it back to Reed with a yawn. "Wake me if he reveals the meaning of life in there anywhere."

The plane lifted into the air, and she closed her eyes to rest. She didn't expect to sleep, but she jolted awake again when the plane touched down in D.C. She smiled briefly when she noticed that Reed had covered her with a fleece blanket. He had a caretaker's heart, mending the world in every small way he could. She loved this about him, even if it was part of why she'd had to leave. *You're a project to him,* Sarit had said to her last year. *His favorite crusade. He'll never fix you but he won't stop trying.*

He moved to grab her carry-on from the overhead compartment, but she stopped him. "I've got it."

He had no luggage. He wore the rumpled blue suit he'd shown up in the day before. Brooks Brothers would be appalled. "We have a couple of hours yet before the meeting with Ben, Kate, my boss, and Coben's attorney. I can change and we can grab something to eat."

She wasn't sure she could force down any food. "Sure, whatever."

They grabbed sandwiches and sodas to go, and she ate hers standing at Reed's kitchen counter, not tasting the turkey and mustard as it went down. His condo looked much like she imagined it did the day he'd moved into it—the same renter's beige walls, mostly bare, with no curtains at the windows or throw pillows on the leather sofa. He had an upright piano against the far wall and a pricey stereo system to go with it. She'd browsed his music collection on her previous visits, short as they were. They had a shared love of Beethoven and Chopin, but his classical collection ran much deeper than hers, into odd names like Shostakovich and Moszkowski. To see that this was Reed's home, you had to look to the kitchen with its six-burner stove and the extensive collection of pots that accompanied it. His spice rack contained at least one bottle for every letter of the alphabet. Ellery had never stayed with him longer than a single day, not indelible enough to leave a mark. He'd carved out a dresser drawer for her but she'd never moved anything into it. Curious now, she crept upstairs to the master bedroom, where Reed was showering in the en suite bath. She went to the mahogany dresser and slid open the bottom drawer. Her heart squeezed when she saw it still lay empty.

It's probably for the best, her mother had said on the phone when Ellery said she'd broken off with Reed. *He's got his work and his family in Virginia. You need someone who can give you his full attention.*

Ellery stared at the drawer, feeling as empty as it looked, until the water stopped on the other side of the door and she had to disappear again. She was surprised to find her cheeks wet and she wiped at them with both palms. Her mother didn't understand. Yes, there were other men who cooked fancy meals or who played the piano, men who didn't have a young daughter to care for or a time-intensive job. Maybe, somehow, Ellery could even convince one of these men to love her. But the same Reed who stubbornly held an empty drawer for her was also the one who had refused to follow orders and then found her in a closet all those years ago, after most of his squad had written her off for dead. Reed Markham lived in a state of perpetual hope. When she was with him, she felt its glow, and now her life was colder for its absence.

The meeting was scheduled at the Four Seasons Hotel downtown, where Ben Lerner and Kate Hunter were staying. To Ellery, the boxy, redbrick building looked more like a 1930s factory than a modern luxury hotel, complete with a looming clocktower to dismiss the workers at quitting time. Inside, however, the lobby shone with a sleek black-and-white marble floor, an ostentatious vase of flowers, and stylish contemporary lighting. Reed stopped to check the directory and a male voice called out behind them, "Agent Markham!"

Ellery turned with him to see a man and a woman rise up from one of the long white couches. They were supposed to be meeting a flashy television star and a big-time producer, but these two didn't seem like the jet-setting Hollywood types. Ellery pegged them in their mid-sixties. The man wore a blue cardigan sweater, and the woman had a flowery dress on that reminded Ellery of the kind her mother used to wear to church on Sundays, back when the Hathaway household still believed in God. She glanced to Reed and saw him working his jaw back and forth the way he did when he was thinking hard or extremely nervous. "Mr. and Mrs. Trajan," he said. "It's nice to see you again."

"Yes," said the man in a tone that suggested he didn't entirely return the honor. He shook Reed's outstretched hand once and then dropped it. "You look well."

Trajan, Ellery realized with a start. That was the name of the girl whose hair may have been in the letter that Coben sent to Reed.

"Mark and Janice Trajan, please allow me to introduce my colleague," Reed began, gesturing to Ellery.

"We know who she is." The woman cut him off, her gaze flicking over Ellery. "She's the one who lived."

Fire burned across Ellery's cheeks and her mouth went completely dry. She tucked her hands in the back pockets of her jeans out of habit, hiding her scars.

Janice Trajan stared at her for a long moment, her mouth set in a thin line. "I've written you a hundred times inside my head. Ever since your story went public a couple of years ago. I even started a few letters but I never managed to finish one. I guess I figured that the answers I want, you can't give me, and the ones you can give . . ." She broke off and shook her head slightly. "Maybe I don't really want them."

"I'm sorry," Ellery whispered.

"Don't be sorry," the man broke in. "We need to know before the meeting starts: Are you going to do it?"

"You're here for the meeting?" Reed said with surprise.

"Kate Hunter called us," Mark Trajan replied steadily. "She said Francis Coben has made contact."

"That—that's true, but . . ."

"She said that he's willing to say what he did with Tracy." He looked to Ellery, who took a small step back. He raised one shaking finger and pointed it at her. "He'll give up Tracy as long as he gets to talk to her. So, we need to know: Are you going to do it?"

6

Reed felt Ellery stiffen, heard her sharp intake of breath. "It's not that simple," he said to the Trajans as he eased sideways to put himself between them and Ellery. "Francis Coben is a sociopath and a habitual liar. We have no reason to think he's telling the truth now."

"So send her in there and call his bluff," Janice argued. "At least then we'd know."

They didn't even know for sure that Tracy Trajan counted among Coben's victims, but at nineteen years old and with nicely shaped hands, she fit the profile. She was last seen alive in 1998, on a cold Saturday night in Chicago. Tracy had been out dancing with friends at a club for several hours. She had wanted to leave and they wanted to stay, so off she'd trekked to the nearest L train at just past one in the morning. No one ever saw her again.

"Please. It's been more than twenty years. Waking up every day not knowing what happened to her . . ." Janice blinked rapidly as tears filled her eyes. She stepped around Reed to plead with Ellery. "He's locked up, right? There would be guards present so nothing would happen to you. Just—just talk to him. Ask him what he did with Tracy. Get him to tell us where she is."

"I promise you we're doing everything we can to bring Tracy home," Reed said.

"You've been saying that for twenty-three years!" Her cry rang through the lobby, echoing off the marble. People turned their heads to stare. "We still don't know where she is! They talk about Coben on TV all the time, but no one ever mentions Tracy or the other girls who went missing. It's like they think it's over because he's locked up and she got to come home." She glared at Ellery. "It's not over! He still has to answer to us. He still has to answer for Tracy."

Her husband put an arm around her and squeezed tight as Janice began to sob.

"I'm sorry," he said to Reed, color high on his cheeks. "But you have no idea what kind of hell we've been through."

"I don't. You're absolutely right." He felt Ellery rigid behind him, trapped between him and the wall. "And you have no idea what Ms. Hathaway has been through or what you're asking of her. So why don't we get some water, sit down, and we can talk about this."

"Agent Markham!" A familiar voice called out to him from across the lobby, and he saw Kate Hunter sweeping in the door with a broad smile, coffee in hand, her heels click-clicking across the tile floor at her approach. She halted when the Trajans turned around and she caught sight of them. Irritation flashed across her perfectly symmetrical features before she reined it in and rearranged her features to a warm, welcoming smile. "Mark. Janice. You're a long way from home. What brings you to town?"

"You invited them," Reed reminded her.

She looked taken aback. "I mentioned the meeting happening today, yes. . . . Goodness, y'all didn't drive down from Indiana just for this, did you? I'm so sorry. This isn't the show, darlings. This is boring preproduction stuff."

"It's about Tracy. How could we not come?" Janice replied. She took out a tissue from her purse and dabbed at her eyes.

"Yes, if *she's* here, then we should be, too." Mark pointed again in the direction of Ellery, where she remained behind Reed, and Kate's eyes lit up as she noticed her for the first time.

"Well, as I live and breathe," she murmured, snaking around the Trajans to admire Ellery like she was a crown jewel. "Abigail Ellery Hathaway. I hoped you'd come but I never quite believed it would happen. You haven't ever sat for an interview."

"And I don't intend to." Ellery eased out from behind him. "I'm here in a law enforcement capacity."

Kate laughed, a melodic tinkle that somehow held no humor. "Oh, that can't possibly be true. We're not breaking any laws here."

"She's here to talk to Coben, right?" Mark cut in. "She's going to find out about Tracy."

"The situation has changed," Reed told Kate. "We need to speak privately." He didn't want to be spilling details of the new murder out in the middle of a hotel lobby.

"You promised us." Janice grabbed his arm and held it in a vise grip, her fingers white as they bit into him. "You promised you'd bring her home."

Shame flickered up inside him, hot as a flame. He'd been naïve at the time, on the job less than a year. He'd found one girl by following his instincts, and Coben's farm had yielded new bodies every day thereafter. It stood to reason that Tracy would be one of them. When she didn't turn up in the first search, or the second one at Coben's residence, or the excavation of Coben's mother's home, Reed knew he'd misspoken. But it had been too late. The words were out there and he couldn't take them back. "I know what I said and I meant it. I mean it. I have never forgotten Tracy, not for a moment."

They frowned, clearly disbelieving him. Ellery cleared her throat. "It's true. He's talked about her a lot."

Reed looked sharply at her because this wasn't true, at least as far as she knew it. He'd decided long ago not to ask Ellery to work this case with him in any fashion, even if it meant leaving some potentially valuable information untapped. Ellery had given her statement at age fourteen. She'd given her DNA for a match to that found in Coben's closet. He would not let the case take anything further from her.

"You know what?" Kate said, putting an arm around Janice. "I'm actually glad you're here because I have my researcher here with me. She's helping us put together the show, and I've been meaning to have her sit down with you to get a full background on Tracy. Farah? Could you come over here? This is Farah Zardari, my intrepid assistant for this project."

A slim young woman with a long dark braid materialized as if out of nowhere. She clutched a large tote and nodded in Reed's direction. "Agent Markham. I read your book." Her tone gave nothing away as to her feelings about it.

"Farah graduated top of her class from Yale Law," Kate said, proud as a mother hen. "She thinks she might follow in your footsteps one day, Reed. Join up at the FBI."

Reed eyed her. "We'd be lucky to have you, I'm sure."

"Farah, could you take Mark and Janice here into conference room B and get that background info we talked about?"

"Of course," Farah said, but the Trajans were not so easily swayed.

"You said it was important we have a voice," Janice told Kate. "We didn't come here to be shunted aside like usual."

"This is about making your voice heard. About making sure the audience gets to know Tracy. We want to tell her story and we need your help to do it. You know her best, right? Come on, I'll walk you in and we can call up the kitchen to order some pastries and coffee. Whatever you want."

She was good, Reed had to admit as he noted her soothing tone and her use of the present tense to refer to Tracy. The Trajans allowed Kate to lead them away and Reed turned to Ellery. "You didn't have to lie for me."

She regarded him with a level gaze. "I didn't lie."

"I've never talked about the missing girls with you. I've never mentioned Tracy."

She nudged his hand with hers. "You didn't have to. I know you."
She turned her head away.

He clenched his jaw, holding back a surge of emotion. "We're in
conference room A downstairs," he managed after a moment.

Ellery set her shoulders and rolled her neck. "Lead the way then."

Inside the quiet of the elevator, he squeezed her hand. "I'm sorry
for that ambush. I had no idea Kate Hunter had been in contact with
the Trajans."

She shrugged. "It's not the first time."

"What?" He looked at her aghast.

"Not them. But other families have written me with questions
about Coben. Some of them known victims, some of them not. I feel
bad for them but I don't reply." The elevator dinged as the doors slid
open. Ellery paused at the threshold and looked back over her shoulder. "Mrs. Trajan is right. They don't really want to know."

The conference room turned out to be a square windowless room
with a thick carpet and modern chandelier. But instead of the usual
long table with chairs, it was arranged almost like a living room, with
a pair of gray sofas dotted with fuzzy white throw pillows, round
glass end tables, and multiple low-slung armchairs covered in flaxen-
colored velour. Reed's immediate supervisor, Helen Fields, sat in one
of the chairs, and to her left was a casually dressed man Reed recognized as Ben Lerner. Two additional men whom Reed had not met
personally rounded out the group. He recalled seeing Elliot Pritchett,
the latest mark in Coben's parade of lawyers, during Pritchett's recent TV appearances on Coben's behalf.

Helen and Ben rose to stand as Reed and Ellery entered the room.
"Agent Markham, glad you could join us," she said.

"Yes, well, we would have been here sooner, but we got waylaid in
the lobby by Tracy Trajan's parents."

Helen's pale eyebrows shot up to her white fringed bangs. "Tracy
Trajan's parents are here?"

"Apparently Kate Hunter tipped them off."

"Hey, I'm Ben Lerner," Ben said, leaning in to shake Reed's hand. Then Ben gestured for one of the other men to join him—this one a blonder, shaggier version with squarish glasses and a goatee. "This here is Jack Reeves—he's the head writer on this project. Jack and I go way back so I know he's the right man for the job. We appreciate your taking this meeting." Up close, Reed saw the Ralph Lauren insignia on Ben's sweater and the thousand-dollar Tom Ford leather sneakers on his feet. Ben put a hand to his chest in apology. "Listen, that's my bad about the Trajans. I told Kate to loop them in. I just feel for them so much, you know? All these years without knowing what happened to their daughter, and now finally, a break. I don't know how much longer they can hold out. Mark had heart surgery last summer, did you hear?"

"I didn't know that." Reed had initially kept in close contact with all the families, but years with no news meant there was nothing more to say. He'd brought a bombshell with him to this meeting, though, and it was time to give her the floor. He stepped to the side so she could take prominence. "Please allow me to introduce Ellery Hathaway."

Ben put his hands to his cheeks like a kid on Christmas morning. "Wow, Ellery. What an honor. No one told me that you were coming."

"I didn't know I was."

"Jack Reeves." Jack extended an eager hand to her, and after a pause, she took it. "I'm a big fan. Huge. I can't wait to tell your story—with your help of course." He twisted her arm slightly and Reed saw him looking for the scars. Ellery noticed too because she yanked her hand back.

"I'm not here to tell a story. I'm here to try to make you see the truth."

"Yeah, rock on, man." He nodded enthusiastically and made an approximate "hang ten" gesture with his hands. "I'm all about the truth."

Kate came sailing into the room behind them. "Hello, darlings! Sorry to be late. I hope I didn't miss anything important."

"Ellery Hathaway is here," Ben replied, holding out both arms to her like he was introducing her at the Oscars. "Can you believe it?"

"Yes, it's amazing," she replied, giving Ellery a little squeeze as she breezed past to the sofa. "Especially surprising after Agent Markham rather forcefully told me to leave her out of it."

"Does this mean she's agreed to do the interview?" Elliot Pritch-ett, tall and thin and dressed in an ill-fitting suit, stepped forward. The rumor mill said he was a true believer, not in Coben's innocence but in the power of God's forgiveness to erase mass murder. Coben had sinned but there was hope yet for his soul to come back into the light. Any headlines that came with representing the country's most famous living serial murderer would be a mere bonus.

"I'm not going on television," Ellery told him flatly.

"I mean the interview with my client."

"Why don't we sit?" Reed said, gesturing at the sofas.

"Great," said Ben. "I can't wait to take you both through my vision for the series. I know this is a story that has been told a dozen times already, but I really believe we have a fresh angle."

"What we have is a fresh body," Reed said, cutting him off.

Helen frowned. "What are you talking about?"

"The list of names that Coben gave them, the ones he said he has information about—it had a new name on it. Maxine Frazier. Maxine was not among the missing young women in Chicago in the late Nineties or early Aughts. She was murdered outside of Boston on or about December twenty-sixth of last year. Her hands were cut off and removed from the scene. They turned up in her freezer."

"Why didn't you tell me this immediately?" Helen demanded.

"It's all unfolded rather quickly," Reed replied. "We just found the body this morning."

"We," she repeated, looking to Ellery.

"My partner is working the case alongside the state police," Ellery replied.

"But Francis Coben couldn't have done it," Kate said.

"That's obviously correct," his lawyer Pritchett interjected. "He's on death row in Indiana."

"He has some knowledge, or Maxine's name wouldn't be on the list," said Reed. "Either he's working with someone on the outside or someone is committing his crimes in his name and feeding him the details."

"So he heard some prison talk," Pritchett replied with a shrug. "They all do."

"Wait a minute, wait a minute," Ben said, looking troubled. "Are you saying we've got a copycat on our hands?"

Reed scowled, tamping down his flash of irritation. There was no *we* here.

"This thing just blew up big-time," his buddy Jack replied. He rubbed his palms together and sat forward with relish. "A real-time murder mystery and we've got an exclusive."

"Yes, but once this gets out, everyone will want a piece of the story," Kate told him. "*Dateline, 20/20*, Oxygen. Even the daytime shows will turn out for this. The news trucks will be stacked three deep by noontime, and *poof*, there goes our edge."

"Not if we have him." Jack gestured at Pritchett as a proxy for Coben. "Or her." He pointed at Ellery.

"You don't get it," Ellery said hotly. "You can't put Coben on television. Not now, not ever. Whoever this new guy is, he's following a script that Coben wrote. They're communicating somehow. You really want to give him fresh material? You maybe want to get a third guy to jump on in there too?"

"Hold on," Kate said. "If there's another killer out there, and Coben knows about it, isn't that more reason to talk to him? We're not only worried about past victims anymore."

"It's reason for law enforcement to interview him, yes," Reed replied. "Not a TV anchor."

"Great, you talk to him. Absolutely." She spread her hands in magnanimous fashion. "But I don't see why that would preclude our interview. If anything, it gives you more leverage to get the truth."

Reed shook his head. "If you think turning the bright lights on Coben will get the truth, you're misguided."

"I don't like the implication thrown around here that my client is involved in any ongoing criminal enterprise." Pritchett rose to his feet and hitched up his pants. "He's cooperating. He wants to help."

"He wants to drag his last victim before him like a cat with a mouse," Reed snapped. Beside him, Ellery flinched. He softened, immediately contrite. "Sorry," he murmured to her.

She held ramrod still, her eyes on her lap. Eventually, she gave the tiniest shake of her head. "No," she whispered. Then louder: "Let's be real. I have a badge, but that's not why I'm in this room. I'm here because Coben put me here. I'm his victim. There's no changing it, ever." She got up off the couch. "Agent Markham is the profiler. He can tell you about these guys, how they wear human masks most of the time and keep the monster inside them carefully hidden. But the monster comes out in private. I've seen him because he's the one who did this to me."

She yanked up her sleeve and showed off the raised white scars, first to Helen and then to Kate. Helen looked away but Kate remained riveted.

"He carved me up over a couple of days," Ellery continued. "First smaller slices, then bigger ones, each carefully positioned so that I would scream and bleed but not die. You want to show America what it was like? Here, take a good long look." She got right up close to the men and pulled down her shirt so they could view the scars on her neck. "The trouble is, each time the monster comes out to play, it's harder to put him back in the cage. The violence feeds the beast and the beast gets stronger. The mask slips. Coben was beginning to unravel when Reed followed him. He was getting careless, more erratic. The art gallery putting on his show complained he missed a meeting with a big buyer and that they'd found a bloody smear on one of the photographs."

"We have some of his artwork," Jack told the others. "Nothing with blood on it though."

Ellery took two steps until she stood right in front of him, stood over him as he sat on the tailored sofa with a bottle of Perrier in his hands. "And do you know what art he's produced on the inside? He's sent me some once. It's hands." She held up her own, showing him how they trembled. "Because he's still the same guy who carved up at least seventeen women. There's no reforming that. Sure, he's been lying low, being a good boy. There's nothing to feed him but fantasy and pencil drawings, and so the mask is back in place for now. He'll show you whatever you want to see."

"With all due respect, Ms. Hathaway," the lawyer said, "you haven't seen or spoken to Francis Coben in almost seventeen years now. Who are you to say what he's like now?"

She whirled on him. "You're the one who hasn't spoken to Francis Coben. He's the man who did this." She lifted her shirt to reveal the largest scar, a jagged one across her lower ribs. "He did this to me and all the others, and he only stopped because he got caught. You actually believe he's sorry?"

"I believe God is the only one who knows the human heart."

"Great. Then let him be judged by God. Leave me the hell out of it." She shook her head, disgusted with the lot of them. "For years, people like you have sold my story and packaged my pain as entertainment. You set it to scary music and surround it with ads for toothpaste and luxury cars. You justify it by saying there's a lesson here. We can learn about him. We can protect ourselves better in the future. Well, the fact that we're here now, that you're talking about giving him the stage and making him a big, big TV star . . . that proves you haven't learned a fucking thing at all."

She stalked out of the room, slamming the door behind her. Ben jumped at the noise. Jack ducked his head, appearing chastened. Helen grabbed her water bottle and drained it in one go. Kate, however, had a grin on her face. "I love it." She looked to Reed. "Please tell me she'll repeat that for the camera."

Reed didn't bother with a response. He went out into the hall, where he found Ellery leaning against the wall, still breathing hard. "Sorry," she said when he approached. "I lost my cool."

"I thought you were rather restrained, actually."

She gave a short, dark laugh. "Do you think they heard anything I said?"

Reed opened his mouth to reply when he caught sight of Ben Lerner emerging from the conference room. "We're about to find out," he muttered.

Ben sauntered over to them, his hands shoved in the pockets of his designer-wash jeans. If the Hollywood asshole dared to utter one offensive word to Ellery after she'd just laid herself bare for them, Reed might actually deck him. The FBI had suspended Reed before, and they could do so again with his blessing. But Ben surprised him. "Are you okay?" he asked Ellery, his brow furrowed. "Do you want some water or anything?"

"No," she said, shoving off from the wall. "I want you to stop this whole nonsense with Coben."

He searched her face, his eyes solemn. "Yeah, I got that." He scratched the back of his head with one hand. "I hear your concerns. I do. I just think we have a rare opportunity here to make some good from this mess."

"But—"

"Just hear me out, okay? When I said I empathized with the Trajans, with all the families going through the hell of not knowing, it's because I've lived it. I am living it. My brother, Andrew, was murdered when we were kids and they've never caught the guy who did it. At first, it was terrifying. My parents pretty much locked me up, thinking I could be next. I was ten and wet the bed that night in total fear. Every noise, every footstep in the hall, I was certain that the killer was coming for me. But as days went by, then weeks, then months and years . . . no one ever came. The boogeyman never arrived, but he never got a face either. All we got was silence. Silence in the house, as Andy's room was shuttered with his toys still on the floor. Silence from the cops who had nothing useful to tell us. All I remember from that time was my mother weeping on the other side of her bedroom door and my father's unrelenting anger. He put two holes in the wall with his fist, like he could bust the house open and find the guy hiding in there somewhere."

"I'm sorry," Ellery said. "Truly."

"I may not have scars like you. Neither do the Trajans. But we're changed just as much, just as unable to be made whole."

She'd locked eyes with him, both of them staring so intensely at the other that Reed felt his face go hot. "Coben can't make you whole," she said finally. "Not you or me or even the Trajans. He's—he's empty. He's a pretty face on a black hole. Maybe that's why we keep telling stories about him. We can imagine him into whatever we want. Pritchett wants redemption. Kate wants a villain she can parade for ratings. The FBI wants to relive their big success story. But Coben doesn't change, no matter how much we might wish it. He wants only one thing—dead girls with their hands chopped off. So if you go looking to him for answers or forgiveness or justice, you won't find them. You'll get only more of the same."

"What do you want?" he asked her, seeming genuinely interested in the answer.

Ellery faltered. "It doesn't matter."

"It does to me."

She licked her lips and glanced to Reed, remembering he was there. "I want it to be over."

Ben nodded as if to himself. "What if . . ." he said slowly. "What if we run a play on him? We send in the cameras and tell him the special is on, but we don't broadcast it."

Reed's skin prickled at the possibility. "You could do that?"

Ben grinned. "With my budget, I can do anything."

"I can't imagine Kate will go for that," Reed replied. Her schtick involved performative outrage, and the cameras only mattered if they came with eyeballs attached.

Ben glanced back over his shoulder to the conference room. "Then let's not tell her."

On the plane to Indiana, Reed came awake with a sudden seize of his muscles, twitching so hard that the heavy book on his lap slid to the floor and landed on his foot. "Easy there," Ellery said from the neighboring seat. "You can't be waving lethal weapons around like that." She bent to retrieve Ben Lerner's book and handed it back to him. "It must be scintillating reading. You've been dead to the world for the past hour."

"Just tired." The plane was dark, the sky black outside, and most people were quiet around them. He wedged the bulky book into the mesh flap in front of him. Ellery had returned her focus to the phone in her hands. "Texting the boyfriend?" he asked, keeping his voice casual.

"Duran Duran," she replied as she took out the earbuds he'd failed to notice in the low light. "'Girls on Film.'"

"Ironic," he noted.

"I knew you'd appreciate it." She tucked the phone away. "Also, he's not my boyfriend."

"I don't care if he is."

She snorted. "Oh, yeah, I can feel how much you don't care. It's like, beaming off you in giant rays of nonchalance."

She settled back in her seat, her shoulder pressed against his. "You were a revelation today," he told her, changing the subject. "Telling them the truth when they didn't want to hear it."

She made a humming noise that neither agreed nor disputed him. "It's a truth," she said at length. "Maybe we all have our own personal versions." Her head leaned on his shoulder. He didn't dare move. "I was thinking . . . I want to do it. I want to talk to Coben."

"What? No."

She sat forward and twisted to look him in the eyes. "I meant what I said earlier. I'm his victim and nothing will ever change that.

But it's not all I am. I'm also a detective and if Coben's mixed up in Maxine Frazier's murder, then this is my case."

"Ellery . . ."

"I know. I know what you're going to say. But he's been put away a long time now, living with his memories and not much else. He wants me back to show he's won, that he still gets to call the shots. I think—I think when I go in there, he'll be expecting Abby. He thinks I'm still some terrorized fourteen-year-old girl. But he had his chance with that girl and he didn't finish her. She grew up when the others didn't. Became someone else. I think if I talk to him, that's what he's going to see."

She swallowed hard. He took her hand and waited.

"He didn't win," she finished finally. "He lost."

7

Reed designed a crash course in Francis Coben and presented it to the others in the conference room at the Wyndham Suites hotel. He had discouraged Ellery from attending. *There's nothing I'm going to say to them that you don't already know.* She ate an early dinner alone at the bar and then went for a run in the frigid midwestern air. The dark didn't bother her even though she jogged through unfamiliar streets. Terre Haute was a small city and the wide streets were mostly quiet on this bleak Tuesday night. She took comfort from the rhythmic slap of her sneakers against the cold hard pavement and the bitter wind rushing past her ears. Her shrink had probed once about Ellery's need to run and how it had sprung up in her teen years after her ordeal with Coben. At the time the shrink took issue with her, Ellery had sprained her knee and been restless to get back to her routine. She'd felt trapped, crawling out of her skin.

When you run, does it feel like you're running from him? the shrink wanted to know.

It feels free.

Free from the closet, from your past?

Free from the sausage pizza I ate last night. Can't I even have one simple hobby without it being all about Francis Fucking Coben?

She halted in the street at the memory, her rapid breaths visible in the night air. A trail of stars shone overhead, scattered like sugar at the bottom of a cauldron. She couldn't see half of them back in Boston because of light pollution from the crowded city, but out here, they would be visible all the time, these constellations that blanketed the nearby prison. She shivered as she looked in the direction of the Federal Corrections Institute a few miles away. This was as close to Coben as she'd been since it happened, and for a moment, she swore she could feel him, rumbling like an awakening volcano. She ran twice as fast back to the hotel, where she purchased a bottle of water from the hotel lobby and slipped inside the conference room to catch the last of Reed's talk.

The lights were dimmed and the large TV on the wall served as a screen for the presentation. Reed had the rapt attention of everyone at the long table, and so no one else noticed her entrance. His gaze met Ellery's briefly, the corners of his mouth turned down at her appearance in the room. She stared right back at him, defiant. He wouldn't dare kick her out. On the TV behind him, Michelle Mendoza's picture smiled out from beyond the grave. "Michelle is Coben's first confirmed victim," Reed continued. "She disappeared twenty-one years ago this May. Her body was discovered in Busse Woods several weeks after she was first reported missing, and her hands had been removed. They were later found in Coben's collection at his family's farmhouse."

"How did he remove her hands? With one of the farm tools?" Jack was taking notes on a laptop.

Reed was slow to answer. "Yes. He had a set of large garden shears."

Ellery clenched the plastic bottle in her hand and swallowed hard against a sudden surge of nausea as she pictured the shears.

"You say Michelle is the first confirmed victim," Kate said, "but Tracy Trajan disappeared a year earlier."

"Yes, it's possible she was his first. There may be yet others we don't even know about."

"Do we know how he picked them?" Ben Lerner asked. "Tracy or Michelle, I mean. Did he select them ahead of time or was it more of a random chance kind of thing?"

"A bit of both, I think," Reed replied. "He and Tracy both attended a special exhibit at the Art Institute of Chicago the week before she disappeared. We think that's where he first saw her. With Michelle, we don't know how their paths first crossed." He continued on about how Coben would select particular targets but pivot to others if the opportunity arose. The TV images changed, flashing through the young women's faces. Ellery had seen them before, years ago when the girls first went missing and many times since, but looking at them now she felt shocked by how young they were. How it was the same pictures every time this story got told. The families had offered their most treasured ones, the shots that showed their girls' best smiles and proudest moments. A high school graduation picture for Margie Rose, still in her cap and gown and grinning in triumph as she held her diploma. A night club picture for Michelle, with the bright lights behind her catching her big hoop earrings and showing off her amazing talent for eye shadow. The pictures never aged.

Michelle would be in her forties by now, Ellery realized. Maybe she'd be a mom with kids. Maybe a fashion designer or a singer like she'd hoped. There were so many maybes.

Kate turned to her assistant, Farah. "Michelle has a sister, Luisa, who is willing to be interviewed for the piece. Isn't that right?"

"Yes," Farah confirmed. "She's done interviews in the past."

"We have reps from nearly every family," Kate continued, "even if we don't end up using them all. The Trajans, of course, are camera-ready. Also, Cathy Tyler's father will be especially effective, I think. Cathy's mother killed herself on the five-year anniversary of her daughter's death, and the dad blames Coben for it, too. Raw, powerful stuff. Plus, we've just confirmed Caroline Hathaway. That's huge. She's never done anything on camera before."

"What?" Ellery blurted, and everyone turned to look at her, surprise evident on their faces. "You talked to my mother?"

"Of course, we contacted her. We're talking to everyone." Kate blinked guileless blue eyes at her. "Caroline's a tremendous 'get.'"

"And she just . . . agreed?" Ellery said unsteadily. Her mother never wanted to discuss what happened with Coben. "She said she'd talk to you?" *It's over now,* her mother said whenever Ellery broached the subject. *You're safe. Let's put it out of our minds and not think about that awful man.* Like Coben was a book she could close after the last chapter, then put on a shelf to gather dust.

"We don't have her on camera. Not yet. But she's said she'd be happy to be interviewed."

"Happy," Ellery repeated, the word like ashes in her mouth.

"She knows it's important work we're doing," said Kate. "Trying to bring the missing girls home."

Ellery could never go home. Her mother had seen to that. She refused to move from the apartment they'd been in when it happened, across the street from the scene of Ellery's abduction. *All of Daniel's memories are here,* she'd told Ellery numerous times. *The last place he ate. The last pictures he drew. I can't leave him.* She lived with Daniel's ghost while her living daughter had to fend for herself.

"My mother can't tell you where those missing girls are," Ellery said when she could speak again. "There's no need to interview her."

"She's there for contrast."

"Contrast to what?"

"To the Trajans and the other parents," Ben answered mildly. He looked to Kate. "Right?"

Kate nodded and regarded Ellery. "Caroline is the happy ending. Her daughter came back."

Ellery stared at her, mute, for a long moment, hardly believing what she heard. Then she left without a word. Kate had obviously written the ending in her head. *Justice delivered, TV-style.* Everyone had a role to play, and Ellery's never changed. She was the ray of hope. The one who lived. All those other faces, the lives lost, all those maybes that would never be answered—Ellery bore the weight of them, and the universe wanted her to be grateful for the chance.

She went outside again, seeking the bracing cold air. She walked down the path until she came to a wooden bench, where she sat and took several deep breaths. The hotel had added some evergreen bushes for landscaping. One leafless tree even still had twinkling white lights left over from the holidays. The parking lot held few cars. The tall trees beyond rose up like a castle wall, shielding the hotel from the road beyond. There was no traffic noise and no people about, no animals or birds chattering from the trees, and in the utter silence, she felt a creeping sense of dread, as though someone was watching, totally still, from the shadows.

He's like an animal, always watching you even when it seems like he's not. The words sprung, unbidden, a fragment from Reed and Sarit's book. A college girlfriend of Coben's had testified at his trial. Coben had never hurt the woman, but he'd unnerved her nonetheless. *One time I walked behind Francis where he was reading on the couch, and I reached for a candy dish, and right away he said, "You'll get fat if you don't watch out." But he never even looked up from his book. How did he even see me?*

"It's a bad habit."

Ellery jerked in surprise and found Kate's assistant, Farah, had appeared silently beside her as though walking on little cat feet. She had a cigarette in her hand.

"I should quit, I know."

Right at that moment, Ellery wished she smoked. She wanted something to do with her hands. "I should get back in there," she said, rising to leave.

"They're on a break," Farah told her, and Ellery stopped. "An argument erupted between Kate and Agent Markham after you left. Ben's playing peacemaker."

"Your boss is a piece of work."

Farah smiled and took a drag from the cigarette. "Kate's a ball-buster, as my father would say. But he'd say it with pride." She clearly caught Ellery's sense of disbelief. "It's true. You know how I ended up with this job?"

"Graduating top of your class from Yale Law School," Ellery recalled.

"Nope. Fifteen years ago, my father was arrested for murder." She let that sink in for a moment, taking a puff and then turning her head away from Ellery to blow out a long exhale. "He didn't do it. But that didn't matter to the cop on the case. See, my parents owned a little corner grocery store. One night, these two guys came in while my father was alone in the store. They held him at knifepoint, cleaned out the register, and made off with the cash and an armful of candy. But Papa didn't just let them go. When they turned to leave, he got his gun from under the counter. He chased them down the block, but they were younger and faster. Only here's the twist—two days later, one of them turns up dead. Shot in the chest."

"And the detective thought your father did it."

"They had him on tape, chasing the guys with a gun. The bullet was too damaged to make any kind of match. Plus, this cop got lucky. He found a witness. She ID'd my father in a lineup, saying she saw him leaving the parking lot where the shooting happened. We didn't have money for any kind of fancy attorney. The legal aid lawyer told Papa to take a plea—twenty years. She didn't care if he was innocent. So, I wrote to Kate Hunter." She gave a thin, flinty smile. "I was a kid. I saw her on TV, talking about justice all the time. I thought she might want to take the case."

"I haven't seen much of the show, but it doesn't seem like her usual style."

"It's not at all. I see that now. But here's the thing—she read my email. She wrote back. She said she'd make a couple of calls. The next thing I know, she's got an investigator from Pittsburgh willing to do twenty-four hours of pro bono investigation. That's all it took."

"They dropped the case?"

"Turns out the convenient witness was sleeping with the investigating officer. She'd witnessed about a half dozen other crimes over a two-year period. His whole caseload came up for judicial review, all because Kate put her manicured thumb on the scale. So yeah." She paused to crush out the remnant of her cigarette. "Papa sends her a crate of champagne every New Year's."

"Nice story. Maybe she should put it on TV instead."

Farah looked amused. "Papa has a big nose and thinning hair. He talks with an accent and wears the same brown shirt every day. He's not, as Kate would say, 'camera-ready.'" She looked Ellery over from head to toe. "He's not like you."

Ellery held out her arm. "Do you need me to show you the scars again?"

"The scars are a bonus. They're your proof."

"Proof of what, exactly?"

"That you're the one. You survived." She waved off Ellery's next protest. "I'm not here to lobby you on Kate's behalf. I want you to know there's another side to her. She cares about all the victims, but she's realistic enough to know which ones belong on television. I've watched her up close for a year now. Men think she's pretty and vain so they don't see how smart she is. She plays the network game to give her access and power, but ultimately, she follows her own rules." She narrowed her eyes at Ellery. "I've read enough about you to know you operate the same way."

"You don't know me."

Farah shrugged one shoulder. "You're here, aren't you?"

Ellery stared at her. This woman was a few years younger than her, just out of Coben's age range at the time he'd been stealing girls from the streets. Maybe she thought that made her safe. Another person who'd read the books and thought they knew the ending. "I'm leaving now," she said, pushing past Farah and striding toward the door.

"Wait," Farah called. "I came over here because I have information that might help you. For when you talk to him."

Ellery backtracked. "What information is that?"

"There's a woman named Hope Herndon who lives outside of Indianapolis. She says she's Coben's girlfriend."

"A lot of women say that."

"Yes, but she's been to visit him. They correspond, at least according to her. She has a vlog where she talks about their adventures. Some of it is clearly fantasy, but other parts may be real."

"If she's been to visit him, then she's already on the radar."

"It's not her I'm worried about. I mean, she's mentally ill. Vulnerable to manipulation. She spent part of her twenties in a cult that believed vaccines were designed to create an alien race that would bring about the end times. Ten members attempted suicide to save themselves from the injections they knew were coming, and three people succeeded. Hope was one of the survivors and the cult was ultimately disbanded. But she's been looking for a new master to follow."

"And she found Coben," Ellery concluded.

"She's willing to die for her beliefs, for a sense of belonging. If I can see that in her, I'm certain Coben can. What's more, Hope has a younger brother, Tommy. She talks a lot about saving his soul because he's been so troubled by the devil."

"Troubled how?"

"He abducted a seventeen-year-old girl, raped her and strangled her. She lived so he only got fifteen years. That's when Hope took a liking to writing people in prison, it seems."

A prickle broke out across the back of Ellery's neck and she glanced once more in the direction of the prison. "Is Tommy at Terre Haute?" Coben was housed in the Special Confinement Unit, often called death row, but other parts of the complex were medium-security facilities devoted to regular offenders.

Farah gave a thin smile of satisfaction, evidently pleased that Ellery had pieced the story together. "Not anymore. Tommy served just five years of his sentence. He was released eight months ago into the waiting bosom of the Herndon family. Hope talks about him on camera sometimes. She claims he's seen the light and is one of God's own angels now."

"Okay, we'll look into it." Ellery paused and offered a grudging, "Thanks."

"Of course. But you have to keep in mind—Hope says the same thing about Francis Coben."

8

R eed sat at the bar with the remnants of a bourbon and a plate
of fries. He'd brought along his old file on the Tracy Trajan
case, which he had committed to memory years ago but nonetheless
dragged out from the archives to reexamine in case he had somehow
missed the one piece of evidence that would reveal her whereabouts.
Tracy was a practicing Catholic. Coben's mother was Catholic too.
Maybe a connection there? A different sort of burial for her? Reed's
own handwriting taunted him, written as it was by a younger, more
confident man, one who was sure he would find her.

"Last call," said the bartender. It was quarter till midnight.

Reed looked again at his case notes. "Don't I know it," he muttered.

He caught movement out of the corner of his eye and looked
up to see Ellery sauntering toward him. Her hair was down, loose
around her shoulders, and he had a flash of memory—brushing aside
that hair so that he could kiss her neck. She took the stool next to
him and stole one of the fries from his plate. "Those are cold," he
warned her.

"Since when does that ever bother me?" She snatched a second fry
for good measure.

"You eat like a raccoon."

"Hey, not all of us grew up worshiping Julia Child. Pardon me if I don't make coq au vin for me and the hound every night." She leaned in to look at the file. "What are you reading?"

"Old news."

She leafed through a few pages until she came to Tracy's picture, which she took out and studied for a long moment. "She doesn't look anything like me," Ellery said as she studied Tracy's picture. "Not her or Michelle or Renee or any of us. We have different hair color, skin color, height and weight. Have you noticed that?"

"Coben's focus is the hands." All the girls had beautiful hands.

"It's more than that, I think. He didn't have a type. He wasn't trying to remove one kind of girl from the world. He wanted us all." Ellery placed the picture gently back in the file.

Reed sat there with the knowledge that they'd be confronting him in the morning. He wished they had something more to challenge him.

"Dorie called me a while ago about the progress on Maxine Frazier," Ellery said, as if reading his mind. "They got the records from her phone and traced the number of her last client. The name he gave her—Jean Rennbimler—is likely fake and returns no hits in any database. The phone was a burner. Dorie is trying to trace the sale now, and they've had forensics go through every inch of Maxine's place since we know the guy was in there."

"Anything?"

"Not yet." She eyed him sideways. "Well, one weird thing. Maxine had your book."

"Of course, she did." He scrubbed his face with both hands. "Coincidence or do you think it means something?"

"Who knows? It was a used paperback copy like most of her books. No way of knowing when she bought it or what it means. Dorie just thought we would want to know." She bit off the end of another one of his stale fries and then made a face. "You're right. These are terrible."

"I told you."

She moved on to the last dregs of his bourbon, which she finished in two long sips. "That's good stuff, though."

The finest he could buy. "If you want one of your own, we might be able to sneak it under the wire here."

"Nah." She regarded him. "I do miss your cooking, you know."

"And I miss your eating." Cooking for one was a joyless experience.

She laughed and his ears warmed with reflexive pleasure. He hadn't heard that sound in months. "You just miss trying to trick me into eating vegetables."

"Don't think I didn't notice when you tried to feed them to the hound."

She gave a happy sigh. "He's like me, a meat-and-potatoes type. We're simple folk."

"There is nothing remotely simple about you."

Her smile vanished and they stared at each other. She inched closer to him from her stool. "You know, Agent Markham, I may also miss some other things about you." Her voice dropped as she slid her hand over his thigh. His leg twitched like a fish at her touch.

"Ellery. You said no more." He squeezed his eyes shut but made no move to stop her.

"Yeah, but these are special circumstances." Her hand took up a slow caress and his skin tingled wherever her fingers went. She leaned her cheek against his shoulder. "I can't sleep, Reed. I can't sleep and there's a closet in my room and I'm tired of thinking about him. Don't you get tired of thinking about him?"

"God, yes." His voice was strained, hoarse. "So much."

Her lips found his ear. "Then let's go."

They started kissing in the elevator and continued in the hallway, his hands cupping her firm, round bottom. He didn't care if anyone could see. Rumors and stories about them flew so fast that he half expected to get a news alert the moment she yanked him inside her room by his tie.

Adrenaline sang in his veins, matching her intensity. Time was short. They weren't supposed to be doing this, not anymore. Every bit of restless urgency poured out into their kisses and he moaned with lust into her mouth. He fell backward on the bed and she crawled on top of him, her nimble fingers already fumbling for his belt buckle. He surged forth into her hand, his hips arching. "Ellery, wait."

"Hmm?" Her tongue was busy at his neck.

"Slow down a second. We don't have to rush." They'd told themselves this wasn't about Coben, but Reed felt his presence anyway in her desperation. Her need for control.

"You seem ready to me." She stilled his protests with her mouth and hand. He'd wanted this for so many months now and he couldn't muster further argument. His palms slipped under her T-shirt and he mapped the bone and slope of her, reveling in her hot, sleek skin. She hissed against his lips as his thumbs found her nipples.

He let her strip him, take him. The bed moved with her rhythm and he held back his rising tide of need. She rose and fell with an increasing pace but didn't seem to be getting anywhere. Her face showed determination, grit, like this was an act of defiance. Gamely, he kept with her, trying to help her make it happen. When they first started sleeping together, she'd said she couldn't experience orgasm and so he need not bother to attempt it. She'd tried on her own a few times and gotten nowhere. The doctors had told her years ago that the infections from Coben's abuse left her damaged, and she'd assumed this was part of the price she'd paid. But one rainy Boston Sunday, they'd been fooling around in bed, kissing for the better part of an hour while one of his hands played in her hair and the other slipped lazily between her legs. The unexpected climax came almost from nowhere and knocked her over like an exuberant puppy, making her laugh with surprise and delight. They'd repeated the process a hundred times since then, but not like now. Not when she was hunched and tense atop him, trying to force pleasure like it was a literal fuck-you to the man who waited for them in a cell three miles away.

She fell forward, spent from the effort. He felt her cheeks wet with tears against his face. "I'm sorry," she whispered near his ear.

He kissed her and turned them so they mirrored that old position from her safe bed back in Boston, her leg hitched high over his hip. "It's okay." There was only one part of them Coben could never own, never guess. He would never even imagine. Reed used one finger to tilt her face to his. "I love you," he whispered.

She closed her eyes, denying it. But her lips were soft, her mouth open and clinging when he kissed her again.

"I love you," he repeated as he moved again inside her. She answered with a sob, her arms tight around him, her face buried in his neck. Her eventual moan as she came for him sounded ripped from her soul and he followed her into blessed release.

After, she lay cuddled with him, relaxed and sleepy, a rare moment of quiet contentment. He threaded his fingers through her long, wild hair and pressed his lips to her warm head. He should just enjoy this but his brain wouldn't let him. "I can't believe you willingly gave this up."

"And I can't believe you ever thought it would work."

He squeezed her. "I believe it was working fine a few minutes ago. Better than fine."

"Sure, in here. Here, you're you and I'm me. But the minute we leave this room, I'm the girl in the closet and you're the big bad FBI agent who nailed Coben." She eased away from him, drawing the sheet up over her breasts.

"What about Evan?"

She grabbed a T-shirt from the floor and slid it over her head. "I never made him any promises."

Reed lay naked in the bed as he watched her disappear inside the bathroom. He realized then she'd never promised him anything either.

The bedside phone rang, jangling his nerves, and he reached for it out of habit. "Hello?"

He heard breathing on the other end but no reply.

Reed struggled to sit up against the headboard. "Who is this?" he demanded with authority. More breathing, followed by a hissing noise. A voice mumbled something, slurred, maybe coming from a drunk. Reed couldn't be sure of the words but they sounded like *I know where you are.* "Tell me who this is."

He heard a click, followed by silence.

Ellery poked her head out of the bathroom. "Was that the phone?"

"Yes, but there was no one on the line," he said as he replaced the receiver. "Probably a wrong number or some sort of switchboard error with the hotel."

Ellery went back into the bathroom and he heard the shower turn on. This was her room, he realized anew. Not his.

The phone call was meant for her.

9

Reed woke alone, as he usually did when sleeping in Ellery's bed. Poets nicknamed death "the long sleep," and this was close enough to the truth that Ellery surrendered only in fits and spurts when her body demanded it of her. This time, she'd not stopped at leaving him amid the sheets; she'd fled the entire premises. The strange phone call from the middle of the night continued to gnaw at him even in the light of day. If it was truly meant for Ellery, then someone knew not just her location but her room number. Reed returned to his room, took the world's fastest shower, and slipped on clean clothes to go after her. His concern grew with each passing second until he finally found her sitting around the corner in the breakfast room. She had a cup of tea and a bagel in front of her and was reading something on her phone.

She did not smile as he sat down across from her. "You missed a spot of shaving cream," she said, fingering her own jaw by her right ear to illustrate, not reaching over to touch him.

He wiped it away as a waitress appeared to turn over his porcelain coffee cup. He nodded to her to fill it and she pointed him toward the breakfast buffet. He could smell the sausage from where he was sitting. That Ellery had access to a thirty-foot buffet spread and had only returned with a bagel, barely touched, told him more about the state of her nerves than anything she might say. Maybe there had been other disturbing phone calls. It wouldn't be the first time she'd kept secrets from him. "I need to ask you: who all knows you're here?"

She lifted her eyebrows at him. "Like, right here in this room?"

"Here in Indiana, with Coben."

A shadow passed over her face at the name. She took a deep breath. "Outside of the people with us on this little boondoggle, not many. Dorie, of course. My captain. Apparently, my mother's in the loop too, thanks to Kate. Why?"

"What about Evan?"

A frown appeared on her face. "What about him?"

"What have you told him about where you are?"

"Just that I'm out of town. He doesn't know the details."

"Are you sure? Because that phone call last night suggests someone knows you're here."

She drew back. "You told me it was a wrong number."

"Maybe it was. But what if it wasn't?" The more he thought about it, the more it made sense. If Evan called Ellery's room expecting to hear her voice and got Reed instead, maybe he'd flipped out. Maybe he'd known all along who she was.

"We're leaving to see Coben in one hour. We don't have time for 'maybe' games right now."

"Coben didn't kill Maxine Frazier."

"And what? You're saying Evan did?" She leaned across the table and lowered her voice. "Last night doesn't change anything. It damn sure doesn't give you the right to play profiler with my boyfriend."

"So, he is your boyfriend now."

Her cheeks turned pink and she pushed away from the table. "I'm done with this conversation."

"Wait." He grabbed her wrist. "You've been seeing him how long? A few weeks, you said?"

"It's none of your business."

"You told me you met him in early January. That's right after Maxine was killed."

She jerked loose from his grasp. "This case is making you crazy, Reed. Listen to yourself. I met Evan at the dog park, where he was already playing with his dog before I got there. Bump and I had never been before. You're saying this man waited at a dog park, hoping I might stop by one time so he could meet me and pretend not to know who I was."

"We've seen it before," he replied, his voice even. He hated to throw Willett back at her, but circumstances gave him no choice. "Your face was on the news almost every night a couple of years back." Her unmasking as Coben's living victim had made national headlines. News vans followed her for weeks. "Never mind the newspapers, the magazines, and the TV specials. It strains credulity that this man doesn't know who you are. Was he recently released from a bomb shelter? Unfrozen as a cave man?"

Ellery turned her head away from him. "Monsta X," she said after a beat.

"I beg your pardon?"

She pinned him with a hard stare. "Monsta X. Tell me who they are."

"I have no idea what you're talking about."

"They're a K-pop band. Huge following around the world, with tons of media coverage and worldwide tours. How do you not know them?" At his silence, she gave a satisfied nod. "I get it, Reed. You see this case everywhere because it's all you've ever known. I guess to you, it's all I'll ever be."

"That's not—"

"I ran his name through the system," she cut him off, swallowing hard. "Evan's. He checks out a hundred percent. Give me some credit at least." She blinked back angry tears, maybe because he'd questioned her judgment, maybe because she lived in a world where she had to run her dates through NCIC. "We're spending the day behind one of the most impenetrable walls on the planet," she said at last. "If some idiot wants to take a run at me there, well, I wish him luck."

She stalked off, and Reed didn't see her again until it was go time and they were waiting in the lobby for the Hollywood brigade to show their faces. She leaned against the wall farthest from him, her clothes completely black and her expression much the same. He did not approach her.

"There you are!" Kate's voice sang out across the lobby, as though she'd been waiting on them and not the other way around. "Ready to go?"

Ben emerged from the elevators a moment later, a paper cup of coffee in his hands. His buddy Jack was with him, wearing dark shades and yesterday's beard. Reed barely nodded at them. His attention lasered in on the two new people standing behind Kate holding a bunch of camera cases. One was an older man with shaggy gray hair that peeked out under his Phillies hat. He wore large-framed glasses and a plaid shirt with a black vest over it. Next to him, clutching the top part of a lighting rig, stood Farah. Reed zeroed in on her pink nails. "What's this?" he asked Kate.

"Oh, them?" She turned as if surprised to find them there. "That's Marty Sanders, and you already know Farah. They'll be operating the cameras today."

Reed had briefed everyone on the visitor instructions from FCI Terre Haute. No weapons, no revealing clothes, no orange-, khaki-, or maroon-colored clothes that might blend with inmate gear, no jewelry outside of stud earrings or a wedding band, no sunglasses, purses, wallets, or other personal items would be permitted into the visitor area. He had not realized he needed to mention that women who looked like Coben's victims should not be allowed either. "Not her," he said of Farah.

"What do you mean, 'not her'? She completed all the forms. She's been cleared."

"Not by me."

Reed's job didn't often put him in physical danger. He showed up after the violence happened and tried to explain who had done it and why. He scrutinized crime scene photos and provided advice to the men and women who would actually hunt the predators, trying to point them in the right direction. He had only been terrified a handful of times in his career. The first was the night he'd shown up at Coben's farm and pulled Ellery from the closet. She was soundless on the other side and he was sure she was dead. Then, when he discovered her still breathing, he'd had to scoop her up and run off into the nearby woods to call for help before Coben could return to find them both covered in her blood. Crouched in the bramble, summer bugs stinging his skin and Ellery silent across his feet, Reed could barely hold his cell phone. He'd felt like he was sitting atop an atomic bomb. *Tick, tick.* How long before she'd be dead? *Tick, tick,* the monster could already be here with him among the trees. Reed had called for backup and an ambulance and then waited in agony for the sirens. He hadn't known then that he'd been hiding with a bunch of corpses buried all around him.

He had felt a different sort of fear the first time he'd talked to Coben. Coben hadn't yet been convicted, wasn't even yet on trial, but by then, they'd already assembled a complete dossier on him, from his kindergarten teacher's glowing assessment ("Verbally advanced, plays well with others") to the high school girlfriend who had perhaps glimpsed the other side ("He only ever wanted to have sex in the cemetery"). Reed should have known better than anyone at that point how Francis Michael Coben hid his true self from the world. Some advantages were obvious. His family had money, and in America, money lent you the appearance of success and smarts. If you had money, people believed you had earned it, you were deserving. If his riches weren't galling enough, young Francis had also been blessed with the other American currency: good looks. He had thick, dark hair with a mischievous wave to it, a curl over his forehead that suggested a playful attitude. Harmless. A grown schoolboy. His nose was unremarkable, as all the best noses are, but he had a strong jaw that housed a row of even white teeth. It was his green eyes, rimmed with charcoal lashes, that got him called "movie star handsome" by the reporters who breathlessly rushed to cover him. The actors eventually cast to play him in the bigger budget productions were leading men. George Clooney, in his prime, expressed disappointment that he'd missed out on the role because of other commitments. These men knew what Reed hadn't yet grasped: becoming Coben, a man who had raped and dismembered a girl as young as fourteen years old, would not tarnish their reputations. Americans loved a serial killer.

That first day, Reed had let Coben control the conversation, asked him questions like he might do on a first date. Coben, having been locked up for months at that point with only his attorneys for company, thrilled at the visit. "A real-life FBI profiler," he had marveled. "Sent just to talk to me." He was relaxed, at ease, smiling often and stretching his long legs out under the table. They'd chatted about Coben's upbringing and how he'd loved to go to the ballet with his mother because the dancers were so graceful on the stage. Coben had asked about Reed's education and been delighted they were fellow Ivy League graduates. Coben hungered for pecan pie and Reed had found himself admitting he made bourbon pecan pie that won blue ribbons at the county fair. "Your momma's recipe, I'm betting," Coben said, pointing a knowing finger at Reed. "Passed down from her momma before her. The secret is cold butter that makes the crust so light and flaky."

Reed had left the visit buoyant, self-satisfied. He'd connected with his subject and Coben swore he looked forward to a return visit where they could "speak of deeper matters." Reed felt sure that he'd established a dialogue that would eventually lead to a confession. At his car, he'd tossed his bag over the passenger seat with zest, and his forceful enthusiasm had caused the messenger-style leather tote to upend, spilling folders out onto the floor. Reed had still been humming when he picked up the papers and the photographs. Michelle

Mendoza stared back at him and the image drew him up so quick, it was like a shiv between the ribs. He'd forgotten about her as he sat with Coben. Not a single internal alarm went off, nothing to remind him that he sat in the presence of a killer. Gooseflesh pimpled across his arms as he'd hurried to pick up his mess. He'd known about the trap and fallen right into it nonetheless. *He'd wanted the murderer to like him.*

Reed no longer cared about his personal popularity or level of influence with the man to whom he owed his fame. He focused on limiting any further damage. Ellery could stand across the room shooting daggers at him with her eyes. Kate could pitch a fit in front of the whole lobby. Reed wasn't standing down. "No, Farah doesn't enter the room with Coben," he said to Kate. "If the camera can be controlled via computer, that's fine. But she does not go inside with him."

Farah herself stepped forward. "That's sexist bullshit. Marty gets to go because he looks like someone's homeless grandpa, but I'm a woman so I have to stay home and bake cookies or something."

"I'm with Farah," Kate said, folding her arms. "She's young, but she's talented and she knows exactly what I want from this shoot."

"And if you want any chance to get anything useful from Coben at all, you don't send her in there. He'll be distracted and agitated."

"He'll be cuffed. He can't touch her."

"I'm telling you, it won't matter. He'll be thinking about nothing more than what he wants to do to her."

Farah jutted out her pointed chin. "And that makes him different from every other guy how?"

"With all due respect, miss, most men aren't fantasizing about raping you with blunt instruments, severing your hands, and then using them to masturbate themselves." He kept his voice low so as not to attract even more attention, but his tone was deadly serious.

"She gets to go in," Kate said, nodding in Ellery's direction. "And we all know what he'll be thinking about her."

"Yes, and he's been thinking it every day for the past seventeen and a half years. No need to give him any fresh material."

Kate opened her mouth to object further, but Marty nudged her arm. "I can work both cameras. It's no big deal."

"I'm still coming," Farah insisted.

Reed checked his watch. They were overdue to leave for the prison. "As long as you're not there when they bring him in. Let's go."

Outside, a blank white sky greeted them, cold and expressionless. They walked the flat, wide parking lot and climbed into two black SUVs. Reed thought Ellery might prefer riding in the other car after their earlier exchange, but she took the passenger seat next to him. She stared straight ahead as they drove.

"Did you mean that?" she asked finally. "Did you mean what you said about how he's been thinking of me all these years?"

"He asked for you. No one else."

She leaned her head back, considering this. "I have dreams where he screams my name. I can hear him but I can't see him. I run but the screams get louder so I know he's getting closer." She turned to look at him. "But it's 'Abby' that he's yelling. Not 'Ellery.'"

Reed understood what she was saying. Meeting Coben now would show him the person she'd become. He would have a new name to haunt her dreams. "You don't have to do this. It's not too late to back out."

"No," she said, sitting up straighter. "I'm going. In fact, I think I should go in first."

"What?" The SUV swerved across the double yellow line. He yanked it back as he recovered his shock.

"He'll be expecting you. He's prepared for that." She glanced his way again. "No offense, Reed, but he's talked to you a dozen times already. He's seen your every move."

He gripped the wheel tighter. She had a point about the benefits of taking Coben by surprise, but if they led with Ellery, they gave up all their leverage. "If you talk to him before he's told us anything about Tracy Trajan or Maxine Frazier or any of the others, then he has no incentive to cooperate. You've given him what he wants."

"I said I'd talk to him. I didn't say I'd give him what he wants."

She held up a pair of black winter gloves to show him and then slipped each one in turn over her hands. Reed watched as the scars at her wrists disappeared from view. She flexed her fingers and then balled them into fists. They rode that way in silence the rest of the journey to the prison.

10

The two-lane prison access road—one in, one out—was optimistically named Justice. It snaked alongside the Wabash River, which churned, flecked with winter ice, just beyond the thick rows of trees. Beyond the river lay Illinois, Ellery's birthplace and the land she had not returned to since she'd left home at age seventeen. As they drove past, she felt it tugging at her, a million tiny magnets zinging in her veins.

The Federal Correctional Institution was a hulking redbrick structure with few windows and a bunch of vents sticking out of the top. A skinny man with a gun at his hip arrived at the gate to be their escort. Ellery guessed he was barely into his twenties. He had a buzz cut and close-set eyes that gave him the look of a shaved ferret. Just driving onto the premises with its high brick walls and barbed wire fencing set off Ellery's claustrophobia. She couldn't imagine coming to work here every day. Kate had similar questions. "You must have some mettle, deciding to take this job. This place houses men who raped schoolgirls and murdered their own grandmothers."

His cheeks wrinkled with his easy grin. "It's not so bad, ma'am. The USP—that's the United States Prison—has the worst of the lot. I work over on this side at the FCI, which is medium security."

Ellery knew they planned to move Coben from death row to the FCI to do the interview. She imagined him, strapped Hannibal Lecter style on a stretcher for the transport.

"Still," Kate said, craning her neck around as they passed the high watchtower, "desperate men do desperate things. I imagine there are plenty of inmates who would kill to get out of here."

"Maybe so. But ain't one of them managed it yet."

"Have they tried?" Kate obviously sensed a story. Ellery wished she would just shut up.

"Ma'am, not on my watch." He smiled again as he stopped the van. "I'll tell you what, though—I make sure my will is up-to-date. Watch your step there getting out."

The mention of a will seemed to give Kate pause. She hesitated before sticking her low-heeled pump onto the pavement. Ellery, Reed, and the others followed her into the security room for processing. It took longer than check-in at an airport. Each of them had to be verified, recorded, their pockets emptied and excess clothing stored away. No coats, sweaters, or hats. After some debate, Ellery was allowed to retain her gloves. The camera equipment was thoroughly examined.

"Hold your arms out like this," said the corrections officer assigned to search her. He was older, a jowly man with a pale face. The flicker of recognition in him when they locked eyes told her that he knew who she was.

"Why?" she asked even as she complied. "Are you afraid I'm going to bust him out with a stick of gum or something?"

"It's procedure. For your safety and everyone else's."

She gritted her teeth and looked at the ceiling, trying to ignore the feel of his hands as they roamed over her body. This would be a bar story for him later, she knew. *Guess who I got to pat down today? The Coben girl.* That's how people referred to her most often. *The Coben girl.* Like they were family.

When he stepped back, when she could breathe again, she unclenched and found Jack Reeves watching her, a speculative look on his face. "What?" she demanded, her face hot. "Did you enjoy the show?"

"It would be something, wouldn't it?" he asked. "If Coben got free."

"You saw the men with guns outside. The acres of bare land surrounding this place. Even if he broke loose somehow, he'd be shot dead before he reached the road."

"I'm just saying, from a story standpoint, it would be incredible."

She gaped at him, this man who sported a tan in the middle of winter, with his soft hands and his designer jeans and the four-hundred-dollar sunglasses they'd locked away for him. Here, she realized, was the problem of constantly remaking Coben's exploits for entertainment. You started to think he was a character from a horror story, something you could control.

Jack started to grow uncomfortable under the weight of her stare. "Hey, it's not like he'd come after you, right? He'd have to be—"

"Insane?"

Jack shut his mouth. Reed finished his conversation with the liaison from the SCU where Coben was held and returned to give everyone their marching orders. "Okay, we're ready. We can go into the mess hall to set up the equipment, but then everyone has to leave the room while Coben is transferred. Following that, Marty and Ben can reenter. Ben has agreed to work the second camera."

Ellery's gaze searched out Kate across the room. She was deep in conversation with Farah, going over notes. "But it's just for show, right?" Ellery asked him under her breath. "We're not live or anything."

"Ben assured me that nothing gets on air without his say-so. He's the producer, and it's his money that's backing the whole thing. The cameras are to convince Coben that the special is proceeding according to plan."

Ellery shot Kate another look. "I'm not so sure it isn't," she murmured.

They entered the belly of the beast, deep inside the concrete walls.

Ellery smelled the sting of disinfectant and fumes of fresh paint. Maybe someone had spruced up for their arrival. In the dining hall, she barely listened to the liaison as he described what would happen. Instead, she walked the waxy floor, curving around the stainless-steel tables and stools that were bolted to the floor. On the right-hand side, women in hairnets peered out with curiosity from an open pass-through window. They were unloading no-name bags of chips from boxes marked AR-ROWMARK FOODS. The scent of mayonnaise and tuna told the tale of the coming lunch.

"That's her," one of them said to the other two. "They said she was coming today. They're doing the interview right out over there."

"Do we get to watch it?"

"Nah, warden says we got to clear out by eleven."

"But I want to see him. Eight years working here, and I never got one glimpse."

Ellery turned away from them and let her eyes travel up the concrete walls to the observatory at the top. It was shaped like a theater box, but the man inside held an automatic rifle. He met her gaze and gave her a short nod, as if to reassure her. Ellery repressed a shudder and went back to join the others. She avoided the wide, unblinking eyes of the cameras now trained in her direction.

The warden told her not to touch Coben, not to get near enough that he could reach her. No contact. The words triggered a flashback so intense it took her breath away. Coben's face leaned into hers, close enough that she could smell his sweat, the stink of alcohol radiating from every pore. *Please,* she begged him in her memories. *Water. I'm so thirsty.* He'd laughed and imitated her plea. Then he'd tossed a glass of water in her face, cup and all.

"We can get you some water," the warden said, and she realized she'd spoken aloud. He crossed to the pass-through and called to the women inside. "Alma, get me a cup of cold water."

Reed regarded her with a troubled gaze as she sipped at the edges of the paper cup the warden provided. *I'm fine,* she told him silently. She drank down every drop to prove her point. The warden's walkie-talkie crackled to life, and he snatched it up. "Roger that. Give us five minutes to clear out before you bring him in." To Reed and Ellery, he said, "He's here."

For once, she was grateful for the cameras. They allowed her to watch on Kate's and Farah's laptops from a different room as two guards escorted Francis Michael Coben into the dining hall. Ellery kept her arms folded tight around her, her eyes trained on the screen, scanning continuously for any sight of him. Finally, he shuffled into view with a guard on either side of him. The shackles at his ankles slowed his progress. His hands were chained together in front of him, the silver bracelets obscuring the ringed tattoos at his wrists. *He looks so small,* she thought. In her dreams, in her memories, he was a giant. A total eclipse of the sun. Now, he looked like an ordinary man, both shorter and slighter than the guards who took his chains and locked him to the stool.

Reed touched her shoulder, making her jump. "Sorry," he said. "You okay?"

"Stop asking me that." He had to know the effort it cost her to say yes every single time.

The warden poked his head in. "Ready when you are."

Ellery felt them all turn to look at her. She rolled her shoulders to loosen them. "I'm ready."

She started to move to the door when Reed spoke again. "Remember the outside may look prettier now, but there is no hidden vein of empathy you can tap. He's capable of mirroring human emotion but he does not feel it."

"I think I know that."

"Yes, but . . . he will try to make you forget."

Ellery held his gaze a moment and let him remember the truth. They were sending her in because out of every person on the planet, she was the one Coben could never fool. She took the gloves from her back pocket and slipped them on. "Let's go."

Marty and Ben trailed her as she followed the warden out and down the windowless hall to where Coben waited. She took a deep breath as he unlocked the door. "There are guards posted at the rear of the mess hall, and I'll be right out here should you need anything."

"Thanks."

The door opened, and somehow, she made herself walk through it. A buzzing started in her ears and her mouth took on the metallic taste of a nine-volt battery. The presence of the two men behind her faded away as Coben looked up, his face shining with anticipation, and met her eyes. "Abby," he whispered with wonder, the word almost tender on his lips.

In her head, he screamed it. She saw his features not as they were now, placid and friendly, but twisted by rage and spraying spittle on her open wounds. Fear crashed over her, an ocean wave from behind, nearly taking her off her feet. How could anyone not be afraid of him once they knew what he was? "It's Ellery now."

"Of course. Ellery. Come, sit down. Let me have a proper look at you."

Her body wanted to flee, already turning back toward the door, her heart beating so fast it became a constant flutter in her chest. She halted her retreat and jerked in his direction, forcing herself along. She crossed in front of the camera and took a seat on the stool opposite him. The bright beams from the lighting rig shone down on them, giving him an ethereal glow. The heat from the lamp spread sweat across the back of her neck. *So hot.* She'd been burning up in that closet.

He looked her over, his gaze traveling slowly from her face to her chest to the shiny metal table beneath which she covered her hands. "I knew it had to be true but it's hard to imagine you as a grown woman now. Well developed. No longer fourteen years old."

"Does that disappoint you?"

He sucked in his bottom lip, a gesture she remembered from before, and her stomach spasmed. *Do not be sick. Do not be sick.* She swallowed hard and forced the bile back down. "It does disappoint you. I can tell. You like them young."

He smiled and peaked his fingers together in a contemplative gesture. "The female form is remarkable no matter what the age. But I confess a certain wistfulness at the sight of a fresh young beauty. It goes so quick, you know. Wrinkles, liver spots. If you don't take good care of yourself, the sun will slowly cook you alive. You, though— you've maintained yourself well."

"And you look scrawny and underfed." It wasn't quite true. He had become leaner but also more muscled, hardened to the bone. Up close, she could see the blue-black tattoos that ringed each of his wrists. They had faded with the passing years, a reminder that he, too, was older now. Human like the rest of them.

"You didn't come to the trial," he said, his tone reproachful. "I kept expecting you to appear but you never did." He stretched his manacled hands across the table, but he was nowhere near enough to touch her. She kept her hands in her lap where he could not see them.

"I didn't need to be there. The DNA tests and grotesque discoveries from your farm were enough to hang you."

He chuckled as though this were an in-joke. "Not yet," he reminded her. "Although the noose hangs perpetually above my head. What do you think, hmm? When the government finally straps me down and puts a needle in my arm, Abby, will you be there? You're my living witness, after all."

"Your condition, alive or dead, means nothing to me."

"That's a lie. I don't believe you." He leaned back to study her again, from her face to her chest to the table beneath which she held her hands. "You think of me as often as I think of you."

She leaned away. "Not really. I mean, I'm pretty busy chasing other criminals who haven't been caught. But I realize you don't have much else going on right now. That's why we're all here, right? You got bored and decided to play the only card you have left."

"I have several cards." He was coy now.

"They're all the same one. Tracy Trajan. Alicia Arnold. Cathy Tyler. You took them and you killed them, but the irony is that now they're the only way you get some attention. You have to use their names to get anyone to show up here and talk to you. On your own, you're boring." Ellery looked pointedly around at the bare concrete walls. "This has got to be your biggest outing in more than ten years, right? And all you did was move next door from one prison to the next."

His eyes darkened like a midnight sky. Even the smell of him changed; a predator who couldn't hunt.

"And let's not forget," Ellery continued with studied ennui, "I'm the one keeping you here. When I dismiss you, it's back to the hole for you."

He forced a flinty smile. "Meaning what?"

"Meaning you should be working hard to keep my interest up. So far, this whole experience is a bit tedious."

The chain between his hands clanked against the metal table as he shifted. "Begging your pardon, Madam. I'd tap-dance for you but I'm afraid my overseers have made that impossible. Shall I tell you a story, then? Which one would you like to hear?"

"The one about Tracy Trajan."

He tilted his head like her dog did when he was trying to calculate whether he should obey her command. "I don't think you'd like that one. It doesn't have a happy ending."

Another flashback. She lay half-conscious on the dirt floor in the woods, brambles scratching at her skin. Reed's voice on the phone. *Send help. Hurry.* Her last thought before the world disappeared was that she had held on long enough. She was saved. Her tongue slid out, moistening her dry lips. "Tell me anyway," she said to Coben, hoping she sounded like she meant it.

He made her wait. "You have to understand, the person who did this, it wasn't me."

"You're saying someone else killed Tracy?"

"The beast," he said, his voice tinged with regret. "Once he saw her, there was nothing I could do to change his mind. He had to have her. I tried to argue with him but he doesn't see reason. He'd followed her home that first day, you see, so he already knew that she lived in this tiny studio apartment on Maryland Ave. It's an old building. You know the kind. Sturdy, prewar, with a metal fence around it and just a hint of grass around the outside." He sighed to himself. "I think about that grass now. It's funny, what you miss."

Ellery kept her expression as neutral as possible to hide her revulsion. She imagined Tracy riding home on the L train with Coben across the car, maybe reading, maybe listening to music, never realizing she was being hunted. "You followed her home," she said. "Then what?"

"Not me," he corrected her. "Him."

"Okay, him. What did he do then? Did he grab her?"

"No, no, not then. Once he knew where she lived, it was only a matter of time. He had to make plans. He hadn't had a girl before, not the way he wanted. He'd spent years doing drawings and making fantasies about how he would be with them, but he was too scared to make a move. What if he tried to talk to her and she laughed at him?"

More memories. That hot summer night, she'd been riding her bike aimlessly around the block. He'd pulled his car over to her and waved. The dark sedan was shiny, new, with a purring motor under the hood. Her mother had told her not to talk to strangers, but Abby knew a rich guy wouldn't hurt you. He could buy anything he wanted. Maybe, if she was nice to him, he'd give her money for a soda.

She blinked rapidly, forcing herself back to the present. "What plan did he make?"

"He remembered our grandmother's farm. Mother had inherited it, but she was no kind of farmer. It sat idle in the countryside—a kind of animal sanctuary as nature reclaimed the land. I'd driven out to look at it a few times, thinking I could sell it when it finally became mine. The beast had other ideas. He saw how the house was far from the road. He saw the unplowed acres that formed a wall around the place. He could hide for years there and no one would ever know."

A cold chill went through her because this part was true. Coben had eluded capture for five years, plucking women and girls from the streets at will and disappearing with them into the woods. The police only ever found the pieces he wanted them to find. "What happened next?"

"The beast watched her. He learned which bus she took to work and where she bought her cigarettes. Sometimes she took a sketchbook down to the Lake. She would sit in the sun and draw pictures of the people around her. Once, the beast took his notebook down and sat nearby, but he didn't dare open it. He watched her hands as she worked and I think maybe he hoped she would see him. That she would draw him. But she started flirting with a shirtless male jogger and then they left to get a drink together from a hot dog cart."

"Did that bother you? Seeing her with another man?"

"She wore a cross around her neck. She knew the sins." He twitched and the cords of his neck stood out. "Mother always said these were the worst kind of hypocrites, the ones who covered themselves with Jesus's imagery while sinning against his teachings."

"The beast is the sinner in this scenario," Ellery told him. "He is the one with envy."

"Thank you." He held out his chained hands to her in beseeching fashion. "I told him that, but he wouldn't listen. He'd built up the whole fantasy around her at this point. He knew what she would taste like, how she would smell, the way her eyes would roll back in her head when he cut her. The fantasy wasn't enough to sustain him any longer."

"So, he took her." Her voice came out coarse as sandpaper.

"She had a little place on the side of the building where she came out for smoke breaks. She'd stand flat up against the building, out of the wind, so that she nearly disappeared into its shadow. Her last cigarette was usually about midnight, right before bed. The beast parked the car on the street nearby long before Tracy showed up. He had his own cigarette ready for when she appeared. He went over to her and said something lame, like 'Nice night we're having,' and he thought it was all over right then because she would see what a pathetic creature he was."

"But it wasn't over."

He shook his head, his eyes fixed beyond her. "She answered him. She laughed and said, 'If you like them freezing.' She didn't recognize him so the beast got closer. She looked at him and said, 'Have we met before?' and he said, 'I don't think so,' but by that time, he'd dropped his cigarette and taken out the rope."

His arms shot out as he imagined strangling her, and Ellery jumped at the sudden movement. The room seemed to spin around her. She sweated under the lights and she knew he could smell her fear. Her voice came out as a croak. "What then?"

Coben shrugged. "He choked her until she went limp, and then he put her in the car. He drove her to the farm where he could be alone with her." He sat back, relaxed now that the story was out there. "I think you know the rest."

Her turtleneck clung to her skin and she could feel the dark rings forming at her armpits. He watched her, probably the way he'd watched Tracy, a tiny smile on his lips. "That's not the end," she said when she could find her voice. "Where is Tracy now?"

He spread his hands as wide as they could go. "Who can say?"

"You, dammit!" She banged her hands on the table in front of her. "You made this deal. I leave my life and come back to see you, and for this privilege, you tell me what happened to Tracy—that's the agreement."

He wasn't looking at her. His gaze had lasered in on her hands, still in the gloves but above the table for the first time. "You're holding back," he said, nodding at her hands. "Then so am I." He looked up with a winsome smile. "Tit for tat, Abby."

She took a steadying breath. She could hear Reed's voice in her head. *You don't have to do this.* "Just so we're clear: if I take the gloves off, you'll tell me where Tracy is."

He grew serious. "I will tell you."

"Tell me first then."

"Ah, ah. You're not playing fair."

She tamped down the urge to scream at him. This was not a fucking game. "Only one of us is wearing a prison jumpsuit, you asshole. Why should I trust anything you say?"

"Why indeed?" He gave her a sly look. "I've kept tabs on you,

Abby. I've followed your story. People like to send me all your news. Like you say, I'm the one in prison, but I'm not the only one who's taken a life. Isn't that right, hmm? Maybe I'm the one who shouldn't be so trusting."

The gunshot rang out inside her head. She saw the man dead on the floor and the look of horror on Reed's face. *Look what you made me do.* "You don't know anything about me."

"Oh, I do." He lowered his voice, made it soft, almost like a lover's. "I know you inside and out."

She jumped up from her stool. "That's it. We're done." She shielded her eyes from the bright lights and looked for the guards. "You can take him back now," she called. "This was a waste of time."

"Wait," he said as she turned to go. "Wait, you didn't get what you came for."

She held up her gloved hands like she was flipping him off. "Neither did you."

"Okay, just wait a minute. I'll tell you what you want to know. Better yet, I'll tell Agent Markham." He strained to one side to look behind her, past the cameras into the shadowed corners of the mess hall. "I know he has to be here. He goes everywhere you go these days, isn't that right? Even to bed." He wagged his tongue and then laughed at his own humor. "Go get him. I want to see his face when he hears the truth."

She took any excuse to get out of there, even for a moment. She strode to the door to summon the warden, but when she reached it, Reed was already on the other side. He must have been listening over the microphones. The warden scanned his security card and the heavy door unlocked. Reed's face, lined with worry, searched her over. "Are you okay?"

"What did I tell you about asking me that?"

He nodded. "You can leave now if you want. I'll handle him."

"Not bloody likely." She swallowed with effort. "I want to hear him say it."

They returned to the table where Coben had reapplied his cheerful demeanor. "Agent Markham, it's good to see you. You're looking fit as ever—and those suits! The ladies love a tailored look, am I right?" He winked at Ellery. "I have to tell you, though, back when we met, I never dreamed we'd end up sharing the same woman. Of course, I had her first—"

Reed cut him off. "You have five seconds to tell me where Tracy Trajan is or we send you back to your cell."

"Okay, okay. No more pleasantries. I thought you might want to catch up a little, seeing as how you haven't visited me in ten years. You have a daughter of your own now, I heard. Maybe you'd like to show me a picture."

"Guards!" Reed called sharply.

The men at the opposite end of the hall came forward. Coben held up his shackled arms in mock surrender.

"Tracy Trajan," he said with his eyes closed, his brow furrowed like he was trying to summon her psychically into the room. "I remember now."

Reed put a hand to his hip. "Remember fast or the cameras go away and you go back to your cell."

Coben's face broadened into a smile and he regarded Reed with a twinkle in his green eyes. "You're going to love this. Really. I can't wait to see your reaction when you learn the truth."

"Where is she?" Reed leaned over the table, his face flushed with anger.

"The farm!" He grinned and made his hands into fists, which he bopped lightly on the table. "She's been there the whole time."

ll

Reed heard the words and registered his failure. Coben chuckled, thoroughly amused with his trick, and Reed lunged across the table at him. "Where on the farm? Tell us where!" Not normally a violent man, Reed had to restrain himself from wrapping his hands around Coben's throat and squeezing with all his might. No more conversations. No more psychological tests. No more attempts at understanding. *People will need to know where he came from,* the editor had said when Reed turned in his book. *They'll want to know the reason he killed all those girls.* Reed had interviewed serial predators and talked to neuroscientists who'd looked at their brains. He'd read research about how psychopaths didn't show normal reactions to physical pain, how certain variations in their neurochemicals might make them more aggressive. None of it explained why, when two men had similar backgrounds and brain chemistry, one might become a celebrated surgeon while the other started carving up people for sport and burying them in his backyard.

The closest Reed could offer as an explanation was the thread of callousness that appeared to wind like a vine up the side of Coben's family tree. His father was a banker who had carried on a years-long affair in public, humiliating Coben's mother, Cora, and turning her into a misanthrope who despised even her own son. Her own father had been a popular town mayor for sixteen years until he was caught embezzling funds and had to resign amid scandal. He avoided jail time by paying restitution, but when he died, the family found half-assembled bombs in his basement workroom. Sociopathic behavior wasn't all or nothing; it existed on a spectrum. The mother who killed her children to be with her boyfriend was not far removed from the mother who merely abandoned her children for the same purpose. Roll the dice on this cluster of traits—impulsiveness, hostility, lack of empathy—and eventually they'd come up snake eyes.

Coben cast them a reproachful look, one to the other, and lowered his gaze to Ellery's hands, which were still encased in gloves. "I've told you where to look. I've fulfilled my end of the bargain."

"The land is almost eight hundred acres, much of it uncleared," Reed replied. "It's not possible to dig up every yard. We need specific information on where to look for Tracy."

Coben tilted his head, considering. "Matthew chapter six, verse thirteen. 'Lead us not into temptation but deliver us from evil.' The beast was tempted and I was not strong enough to fight him. That's my sin, and I've accepted it. What of your sin, Agent Markham? Do you know it yet?"

"We're not here to talk about me."

Coben looked to Ellery, a small smile twitching at his lips. "I bet Abby could tell you."

Ellery quivered beside him but did not yield. "No one cares to hear your thoughts on sin."

Coben threw back his head with unexpected laughter. "But why not? I'm so good at it. An expert, after all. He knows. He wrote the book on me. Maybe I should write one on him. Let's see . . . the poor sordid tale of a little boy whose teenage mother was dumb enough to get knocked up by a Virginian politician on holiday. Daddy-o then took him in when Mama got murdered, only he pretended Reed was adopted because that Latin blood didn't blend well with the rest of the family. How did that make you feel, Markham? Like a magpie in a nest of swans? You wanted to prove your worth, didn't you? You graduated top of your class, the best of the best schools, then joined up at the FBI with the noble purpose of hunting down very bad men like the one who murdered your mother." He heaved a regretful sigh. "Didn't quite turn out like that, did it?"

"I got you," Reed said steadily. "That alone would be enough."

Amusement vanished from Coben's face. "That's right. I made you what you are. Don't you forget it."

"Where is Tracy?"

"I told you where she is. This conversation is growing repetitive. I think I'd like to return to my concrete walls and solitude now."

He turned away from them and Ellery leaped forward like a panther, seizing him. "No, you don't." She grabbed his shoulder and spun him back around on the stool. "You got out of that hole because of me, and you'll go back there when I say so."

"No touching! Step back!" The nearest guard shouted at her, his hand on his Taser. Ellery didn't move. Reed could feel the thrill of the cameras watching them, recording every move. "Get back behind the table now!"

Ellery released Coben. She retreated, breathing hard, but her voice had no tremor when she asked, "Let's talk about Maxine Frazier. Or is she also too boring for you?"

A light seemed to brighten behind Coben's eyes and a slow smile spread across his face. "Maxine," he said, savoring the name. "I wondered if you would get around to asking me about her."

"She was on your list," Ellery reminded him.

"Not mine, no. The beast would never have picked her." He licked his thumb and then brought both hands to his face, smoothing back a lock of hair from where Ellery had shaken it free. "I added her name because the poor girl's fate had come to my attention and it seemed like no one was looking for her. Don't tell me you've found her."

"She came to your attention how?" Reed wanted to know.

"Oh, you have located her. Thank heavens. I can rest easy tonight."

"How did you learn about Maxine?" Reed asked again. Coben spent nearly all his time in isolation, far from the prison grapevine. His mail and email were monitored. Maybe under ordinary circumstances a chatty guard might have remarked on the case to Coben, niggling him about the severed hands, but Maxine had not been discovered until a couple of days ago. Coben had known about her in advance.

"You see, Maxine had a small tattoo, here." Coben twisted his right hand awkwardly to point at his left, indicating the fleshy ball at the base of his palm. "It was an infinity sign right at the end of her thumb. Barely visible to most people, but the beast wouldn't have missed it. Also, she wore those dreadful press-on nails." He shuddered in revulsion.

Reed recalled the severed trophies carefully preserved in Coben's freezer, each hand beautiful even after death. "You seem to know a lot about Maxine," he observed, "considering she wasn't one of yours."

"I know the man who did this," he said slyly. "Not personally, of course. How could I? I'm shut away here, alone up to twenty-three hours per day, and he's on the outside . . . with you. But I recognize him by his work. As I'm sure you do, Agent Markham. You're the expert profiler. Suppose you tell me about the man who took Maxine. I'll be happy to correct any of your misconceptions."

Reed glanced to Ellery. Her pale gray eyes had turned huge and dark. She gave him the tiniest nod. *Do it.* Reed licked his dry lips, felt the cameras bearing down on him. He started with the obvious. "He's a white male, physically fit, age is somewhere between twenty-five and forty-five. He's single and lives alone. He has a history of troubled relationships with women, probably going back to his own mother, who was either absent or neglectful."

"Amateur hour!" Coben scoffed. "Any *Criminal Minds* viewer could spout off that bland bunch of nothing without a second thought. Have some pride, man. Dig deeper."

Reed leveled him with a hard gaze. "He has comfort with sex workers. He's used them before. Maybe he even spotted Maxine as one straightaway, or possibly he used her services previously and knew he could lure her to the motel with no trouble. The use of the motel suggests he is from out of town, not native to Boston, although he has traveled there enough to be familiar with the area."

"Better," Coben said, nodding with enthusiasm. "But not yet impressive."

"He knows your work, of course. He's probably read every book, watched every movie. They played into his fantasies, the dreams he's had since adolescence. Your success is a road map to him. You give him freedom to act on his desires."

"No," Coben said flatly. "You don't yet see it."

"See what?" Reed's irritation flared. "If you've got something to add here, just say it."

"It's better if you see it for yourself. This man you mention. He's like me but he's not me."

"He doesn't share your hand fetish, for one. He left the hands behind, not kept them as mementos as you did. It's not about the hands for him. It's about complete and utter power over another human being. All the failures in his life, all the times he's felt small or useless or humiliated, he can erase them by killing her. This woman will never laugh at him or make him feel less than."

"You're getting offtrack," Coben replied, impatient. "You're right, he doesn't care about the hands. He could have killed Maxine in a hundred different ways. Gutted her belly like a fish. Hung her on a hook. Filled her full of bullet holes until her brains leaked out her nose."

"He did it your way," Reed said, musing. "He was . . . he meant to send a message."

"Yes. What does it say to you?"

"He's signaling. He's saying he'll carry on your work. He's mocking the police—and menacing Ellery by targeting a woman in her backyard."

"Yes, but no." Coben leaned as far as he could over the table. "All that is true, but it's not enough. Think, Agent Markham. I've been locked up like Rapunzel for the better part of two decades. You've chased a dozen killers in that time, each one following his or her own script. This one wants mine. Why?"

Reed's mind raced. Why indeed? He perspired under the heat of the lamps, his collar growing damp as the cameras zoomed in to catch his befuddlement. Coben stared hard at him with an expectant gleam in his eyes. Reed sensed Ellery to his left, holding her breath, awaiting his answer. The entire world was waiting. If this were being broadcast for real, he could imagine the whole of America leaning forward, hanging on his next words. Nothing he could say would appease them. Nothing would slake their hunger. They would tune in to the next Coben special, and the one after that, maybe hoping for better insight. Reed turned his head slowly and met the black eye of the camera. "It's the attention," he said. He returned his gaze to Coben. "Infamy. It's the one thing you have that he can't get for himself. Not easily, not without time and effort in building his own brand."

"Precisely," Coben replied, sitting back in satisfaction. "This man took a shortcut. He's pretending to be something he's not just to ride my wave."

"If that's true, how do we catch him?"

Coben scrunched his face in disgust. "Not by looking at poor Maxine with her ghastly purple nails. No. You'll have to find him at a time or place when he's being himself. When he's shown you his true face."

"And when is that?"

Coben wagged a finger at him. "Tut-tut, Agent Markham. The FBI pays you, not me."

"Maxine wasn't the first one," Ellery blurted out. "Was she?"

Coben grinned and pointed at her. "She's so clever. I can see why you're fucking her. Tell me honest now—do the pair of you talk about me in bed at night? Whisper my name across the pillow?"

"Who else did he kill?" Ellery demanded. "Give us a name."

"I gave you all the names I know. I can promise you one thing—Maxine won't be the last of them. Because this man you're seeking has the beast in him too."

"Your beast," Reed said, "how long have you known he was in you?"

Coben looked surprised, like this was the first original question he'd heard in years. "I can't remember a time without him. There was one summer picnic—I can't have been more than three at the time—and I was wandering through the bushes while Mother set out the food. A beautiful butterfly flitted past me, dancing on the air. It was a brilliant orange with a black fringe at the edges, bursting with color as it floated here and there among the leaves. Even as I admired its beauty, the beast imagined holding it in his hands and crushing it to oblivion." He squeezed his hands together so hard they turned white.

"And did you?"

"I don't remember grabbing it. I only remember seeing orange smear across my fingers and Mother scolding me for getting dirty. She tried to shame the beast for what he'd done. She said, 'Imagine tonight when that butterfly's mama is waiting for him to come home to her. Imagine how she'll cry over what you've done.' She was trying to make him feel the loss of a stupid insect, but the beast only heard her say that butterflies could cry. If they could cry, he reasoned, maybe they could scream. It took many more butterflies before he admitted Mother had lied to him. Butterflies die as silently as they appear, no matter what you do to them."

No one said anything for a long moment. The cameras kept rolling. "And now?" Reed asked finally. "What does the beast say to you now?"

The air in the room grew close and heavy as Coben contemplated a reply. At length, a physical change seemed to come over him as his skin tone darkened, his mouth thinned, and the veins in his neck bulged outward. He turned his eyes to Ellery as his lips twisted into a fun-house version of a smile. "I miss you," he said, and then he blew her a kiss.

When the warden came to let them out, Reed pulled him aside. "You need to search Coben's cell before you take him back there."

"Search it for what?"

"Someone has direct communication with him about Maxine Frazier's murder, and we need to determine who that is. Cards, letters, anything that might have slipped past the initial inspection."

"Okay, we'll take a look."

Reed found Ellery outside the visitors' room where the others waited. She had her back to the concrete wall, her arms folded across her chest. Her entire posture said *go away*. She glared at him as he eased toward her. He held up his palms in a gesture of peace. "I'm not going to ask if you're okay." Who could be, after that?

Her chin stuck out. "You believe what he said about Tracy Trajan? That she's been on the farm the whole time?"

"Yes. It makes the most sense. I'm not sure it will help us find her, though."

"But you're going back there to look."

He spread his hands. "I have to."

She pushed off from the wall. "Then I'll go with you."

A chill went through him at the thought of it. Both of them, back at their beginning. "It's not safe there. Coben set up hazards around the property—razor wire, bear traps, pits covered with branches. We've uncovered a bunch of them but there may well be others."

She stared at him. "You think the traps are what concerns me?"

"No, I just meant—"

"If it's safe enough for you, then it's safe enough for me."

His heart squeezed. She hadn't even been back to her mother's apartment, and yet here she was, volunteering to return to the scene of her torture. "You have nothing left to prove to him," he said, his voice soft. "Not to him or me or anyone else."

"That's good because I wouldn't be doing it for you. I'd be going there for Tracy." Her voice grew thick, her eyes watered, and she looked away from him so he couldn't see her tears. He remembered lying in bed with her on a warm spring night, the windows cracked and the hound, belly up, snoring loudly at their feet. Reed's fingertips, tracing lightly down her arm, found one of the scars and followed it. He didn't ask her about her time with Coben but he wanted to make sure she knew he would listen if she cared to talk about it. *You can tell me anything,* he'd whispered into her hair. *You know that, right?*

She'd curled into him. *You sound like the reporters,* she'd said. *Or my shrink.*

No, no. I'm not trying to analyze you.

Her hand crept up and she'd placed her fingers against his mouth. *Shh. Everyone thinks they want my secret. They think they want the truth.*

His heart had pounded. *I do, I do.* He'd kept the words inside, hardly daring to breathe as her fingertips explored his mouth. When she spoke again, her voice was barely above a hum.

The truth is it would be so much easier if I'd died.

Standing with her in a narrow prison hallway, his palms ached with the need to reach for her, but he knew she might never speak to him again if he tried. The warden appeared with a grim expression on his face and Ellery sniffed hard, wiping her eyes with her sleeve. Reed cleared his throat and stepped forward. "You found something," he noted, nodding at the paper in the warden's hand.

"This was stuffed in his Bible. It's, uh, graphic."

Reed took the paper gingerly and used a thumbnail to open it. Years of immersion in Coben's crimes had not hardened him to the sight of a fresh horror: recently severed hands lying on a cement floor, their purple tips clashing with the bright red smear of blood. Ellery looked over his shoulder. "Oh my God," she breathed. "Those are Maxine's hands."

"Get me Elliot Pritchett," he said to the warden. He could think of only one person who could get an image like this past prison surveillance.

As prompted, Coben's attorney ducked out from the visitors' room with a broad smile on his face. "Agent Markham, that was a remarkable interview. I think you'll agree my client has been helpful and responsive to your questions."

"What is this?" Reed asked him, holding up the printed photograph.

Pritchett shrank back. "Oh, heavens, put that away."

"Your client carved up at least sixteen women just like this." Reed shoved the picture closer to Prichett's face. "The warden found this recent souvenir in his cell, and from the looks of it, it was taken at the time of Maxine Frazier's murder. So, we're all wondering how it ended up in your client's possession."

"And you think I know this? Me?" He clutched his hands to the lapels of his brown suit. "I took on Francis Coben as a client with the firm understanding that this"—he waved fluttering fingers at the printout—"was all behind him. I have no idea where he got that picture, if in fact you found it in his possession."

"His mail is monitored. The only person who can pass paper to him uninspected is his lawyer."

"I never brought him this." He practically hissed the last word.

"What did you bring him?"

Pritchett raised his bushy gray eyebrows, perhaps realizing too late that he'd admitted to bringing something past the guards. He smoothed his shirtfront. "Legal papers, of course. Sometimes a novel or magazine to read, but nothing that wouldn't pass muster. I also bring him letters from his cousin Annabelle. She's a sweetheart of a gal, brokenhearted by what happened to Francis. She believes strongly in the power of forgiveness, as do I, and so it was my pleasure to facilitate their correspondence."

"His cousin," Reed repeated with an edge in his voice.

"Yes." Pritchett's tone took on a trace of impatience. "I met her about a year ago when she came to my office. She's got brown hair, about yea tall. She teaches preschool, and her husband doesn't approve of her writing to Francis. That's why she can't write him directly. So, she sends the letters to my office and then I bring them here when I visit." He looked Reed over once, his hand on one hip. "Look, I can see your skepticism, but I assure you there's nothing in these letters to be concerned about. I read the first few just to be sure. She writes him news about her children and talks to him about repenting for his sins. Bible quotes, and what have you. She's been good for him, as you probably saw in there today."

"I don't know who you met," Reed answered. He took several slow steps until he was nearly nose to nose with Elliot Pritchett. "But Francis Coben's mother had two sisters, neither of whom had any children. His father had a brother who died in a sledding accident at age nineteen. No children there, either."

"What is it you're implying?"

"I'm not implying. I'm stating facts. And the fact is: Francis Coben never had a cousin Annabelle."

12

Ellery had taken enough French in school to know that *Terre Haute* must mean "High Ground," but the view from the rental car showed her nothing but flat, colorless terrain as they left the prison. The voluminous gray sky met the horizon like in a child's drawing where all activity was confined to one narrow space at the bottom of the picture. Even the trees lacked perspective with nothing nearby to scale them. Snow coated most of the ground, with patches of brown grass peeking through, frozen and unmoving, looking for all the world like spring might never come again. Ellery, raised in Chicago and now living in Boston, was accustomed to the towering comfort of skyscrapers. This alien landscape felt open and exposed, with nowhere to hide.

Her unease grew as the hotel came into sight and she spotted two news vans in the parking lot. "Looks like we've got company," she muttered to Reed.

"Kate Hunter must have put out the bat signal." He banged his palm on the steering wheel. "I'm going to duct-tape that woman's mouth shut and tie her to a chair."

"Careful. You'll end up bunking at the FCI with Coben."

He parked the car, and as anticipated, a small throng of reporters descended upon them. "Ellery! Is it true you talked to Francis Coben today? What did he say?"

"No comment," she replied, brushing past the microphones and handheld tape recorders. Reed flanked her on the left and held out his arm to keep them at bay.

"Did he ask forgiveness? Did he tell you where the other girls are buried?"

"She said no comment," Reed snapped.

The lobby doors slid closed behind them and they met Kate Hunter, mad as a wet hen, on the other side. "You're FBI," she said, her heels clicking briskly on the tile floor. "Can't you make them go away?" She gestured at the press and the photographers still gathered at the windows.

"Me? You're the one who called them. Wouldn't want to miss even one headline."

Reed stalked off to the elevators, with Kate and Farah on his heels. Ellery followed.

"I didn't call them," Kate replied testily. "Why on earth would I give up my exclusive like that? Now that everyone knows Ellery is here talking to Coben, even the low-rent podcasts are going to come running."

"Well, we won't be here," said Ellery. "We're going to the farm to look for Tracy."

Kate brightened and grabbed Reed's arm. "Perfect. Oh, that will be amazing footage. We've been using the old B-roll from the initial searches, but this is a hundred times more dramatic. What are the odds, do you think, that we find her?"

Reed hit the elevator button. "We aren't going to do anything. This was never part of the arrangement."

"Oh, yes it was. This whole exercise is to bring those missing girls home. Now you're telling me I can't be there when it happens? Fuck that noise, as my nephew says. I have a right to be there. Maybe you've heard about a little thing called freedom of the press—you know, that pesky first amendment to the Constitution. You, Mr. FBI

Man, are the government, and you don't tell me what I can and can-not cover."

The elevator doors slid open but Kate blocked his entrance with her body. Reed, at six feet, towered over Kate when she wasn't dressed in her usual stacked heels. Ellery thought he might sweep her aside like an annoying housefly. "You're right. I can't stop you from stand-ing in the middle of a country road like a lost cow. However, I can damn well prevent you from trespassing onto a crime scene. Would you like your camera crew to videotape you being hauled off in the back of a police cruiser?"

A smile twitched at her big red lips. "You have to admit it would be great TV." She smacked his arm in camaraderie. "Don't worry. You're a man of reason. I'm a reasonable woman. I'm sure we can work something out. Farah? Let's go get something to eat while we talk tactics."

Reed shook his head as if to clear it and stepped into the elevator. Ellery joined him but stood as far away as possible on the other side of the car. She desperately wanted a shower, one hot enough to erase the feel of Coben's eyes on her. "I am going to call Dorie to see if there's any progress on Maxine Frazier's case," she said.

"Good idea." He held the doors back so she could step out first. "Please tell her to be careful."

She stopped in the hall to look back at him. "Careful of what?"

"Whoever the mysterious cousin Annabelle is, Pritchett said she'd first contacted him more than a year ago. That means that this plan has been in the works for a long time."

"But you said the killer is probably from out of town. That means he's unlikely to be still in Boston, right?"

He regarded her with solemn eyes. "Yes, indeed. So you be care-ful, too."

She watched him take out his room key and pause in front of his door like he couldn't face what was on the other side. "Reed?" His name escaped her before she could stop it. He looked over at her. "Are you okay?"

He touched the door with his fingertips. "Someone has to call the Trajans."

She thought of Tracy lying somewhere on the farm, the searchers walking past the body, maybe with their boots right on top of her, but never finding her. Even if they could recover Tracy's remains, she would be nothing more than bones by now. She supposed the Trajans would welcome the chance to choose Tracy's final earthly resting place. As it stood, she remained on Coben's land like another one of his family's rotting possessions. "At least her parents have been expecting this confirmation, right? They've said all along that he killed her." Coben's confession was one they'd been begging to hear.

"There's knowing and then there's knowing," replied Reed. "Tonight is the first time they can be absolutely sure their daughter is never coming home."

Freshly showered and dressed, Ellery lay on top of her bed, which had been tidied by the cleaning crew, its newly neatened corners and crisp, turned-down sheets erasing the mess she'd made with Reed the night before. Her current shrink, Dr. Sunny Soon, would have a field day with this development if she knew. *You used him,* she'd say. *You substituted sex for your uncomfortable feelings.*

Ellery held her own in the imaginary conversation. *Sex used to be my uncomfortable feelings. Look how far I've come, Doc.*

Yes, but the problem is that when the sex is finished, your feelings are still there.

Her phone buzzed with a text, and she glanced at the screen. It was from Evan. *A tech in my unit sent me the link to your Wiki page.* (He linked to it in case she somehow didn't know.) Ellery shut her eyes and let the phone fall down against the bed. This was it, then. The start of a million questions or the fetishization or just a straight, old-fashioned dumping. She steeled herself to look at the screen, knowing whatever he said to her, she would deserve it. The tiny bubbles worked and worked but no text appeared. Either he was writing a tome or continually erasing and revising his words to her. After what felt like an eternity, he sent one short sentence: *I hope that you're ok.*

She clicked the link, and sure enough, there it was: a breathless new update showing her visit to the prison in Indiana. "Hathaway is believed to have reunited with her captor at the FCI in Terre Haute, where he is awaiting execution on death row." *Reunited,* she thought. *Fuck it.* She shoved the phone into the back pocket of her jeans and slammed the door on her way out of the room. The loud reverberation might have been enough to startle Reed, three doors down, but he did not emerge from his room. She paused in front of his door, listening, wishing she could knock and see him and hear his voice with its gentle Southern accent.

He makes you feel safe, Dr. Sunny Soon had said, back when Ellery and Reed started seeing each other.

Doc still didn't get it. *Nothing makes me feel safe. Reed makes me feel less crazy.* He was the only other person in this melodrama who knew the truth of it. The rest of the world spun endless tales about Coben, some mythologizing him, some desperate to find his humanity, all of them with an angle or an agenda. Ellery sometimes felt like a character in her own life, manipulated by outside sources beyond her control. Other people decided that she was cold or warped or sexually frustrated. They called her unhinged, damaged, and lonely. Her opinion never seemed to matter. *Go ahead and judge me,* she thought when she caught someone staring at her on the T. *You weren't there.* But Reed was.

She brought her hand up to his door, poised to knock, but lost her nerve and dropped it again. Sunny's imagined voice rang in her ears. *You used him.* The best she could do now was keep her distance. She took the elevator down to the main floor, where she decided to grab dinner at the bar—dinner and maybe a bathtub-sized margarita. On her way inside, she met Ben Lerner and Jack Reeves headed out. Ben wore a black T-shirt, jeans, and his usual expensive sneakers. Jack had slicked back his hair, somehow acquired cowboy boots, and sported a black long-sleeved shirt ringed at the neck with a blue-and-orange feather design—rather like a cartoon bird had crashed into his face. He caught Ellery's arm as she tried to pass.

"There she is," he said, grinning. His face was red. He'd clearly been drinking. "It's the woman of the hour. You were a freakin' badass in there with Coben today."

She pulled her arm free from his hand. "It's easy to look tough when your opponent is in shackles."

"Naw, man. You got all up in his face, like 'I say when you go back to your hole.' I've known four-star generals who probably would've shit their pants, doing what you did in there."

"Really," she replied, deadpan. "You hang with many four-star generals?"

He threw an arm around Ben's shoulders. "We've got friends in high places." He peered past her at the quiet lobby. "Not much happening around here, though. We're about to catch a ride to Indianapolis, maybe hit a couple of clubs. You should come with."

She'd rather have her eyeballs scooped with a melon baller. "No, thank you. I'm just going to get a quick dinner."

"I'll join you." Ben disengaged from Jack, who threw him a wounded look. "If that's okay."

She answered with a half shrug. "I can't stop you from eating on the stool next to me."

"What about our plans?" Jack said. "The Uber guy just pulled up."

"You go ahead," Ben told him. He took out his wallet. "You need cash—or?"

"Please. Get off it with that shit. You don't actually own me, you know."

"I never said I did. I'm merely offering to cover my share of the ride."

"Yeah? Cover this instead." Jack flipped off Ben and strode off into the lobby, presumably to meet his driver.

Ellery watched him go and then turned to Ben. "That's your best friend, huh?"

"You'll have to excuse him," he said as he followed her to the bar. "He's wound a little tight."

"No, I'd flip you off too if you just ditched me like that."

"Believe me, he's done the same to me a hundred times. Especially when there's a chance to share a meal with a beautiful, intriguing woman." He smiled at her and she rolled her eyes. No one called her beautiful and meant it. Maybe this line worked on other women, those who hadn't been carved up like a Thanksgiving turkey. Her scars came with one superpower and that was to see right through men's bullshit.

"You're not eating with me. You're eating near me." The bartender appeared and she ordered a beer and a burger. Ben did the same.

"Fair enough," he said to her. "I did invite myself along, but honestly I didn't feel like partying Jack-style tonight."

"What is 'Jack-style'?"

"Noisy clubs. Lots of people. You've got to understand. Jack grew up the son of an airplane pilot. His dad was never there. His mom had gotten knocked up on purpose, thinking she could ground Jack's father for good, but he already had a family outside of Seattle. He wasn't looking for a second one."

"I know this story." Her father had skipped out when Ellery was ten and never looked back. She'd discovered only recently he'd had a second replacement daughter whom he was still raising.

"Yeah, well, his mom got depressed when she found the truth and then she tried to drown herself in the bottom of the bottle, if you know what I mean. Jack spent a lot of time alone as a kid, and now he compensates by never being alone. I tell you what, though. All that time inside his head made him a hell of a storyteller. Sci-fi, horror, rom-com, you name it—he can spin it like an Eighties DJ."

Ellery smiled in spite of herself. "I see. Take your crappy reality and shove it? Fiction's where it's at."

"Precisely." He lifted his beer bottle and clinked it against hers.

"Where's your other partner in crime tonight? You've got an even bigger ditch planned for her. I presume you haven't told Kate yet that there are no plans to use the footage from today."

He grimaced at the mention of her. "She won't be pleased, no."

"What do you even need her for on this project anyway? You put the money together. You've got the Emmys and the whole 'prestige TV' label already going for you."

He looked sideways at her, as if considering. "Truth?"

The glint in his eye made her stomach clench. She wasn't sure she wanted more truth. "Sure," she said, taking up her bottle again. She waited for him to say he was banging her like a screen door or some such Hollywood nonsense.

"I needed a woman." At her disgusted look, he clutched a hand to his chest. "Not me, personally. But for the face of the story. These days, you can't be some middle-aged rich white guy coming in to tell the stories of a bunch of slaughtered young women. Kate Hunter has a reputation of fighting for girls and women. When she tears up on screen, America cries with her."

"So, you wanted her because she fake cries real pretty."

"You think it's fake?"

She arched an eyebrow at him. "You think it's not?"

He dropped his chiseled chin to his chest as he pondered the question. "When you look at it through a camera lens, it doesn't matter where her tears come from. What matters is, people believe them."

"Then we're back to fiction again. The hell with the truth." She angled her body away from him as their food arrived. He shifted toward her, his posture conciliatory.

"I don't mean it like that. But don't be so quick to dismiss fiction. Humans have told stories ever since we evolved language, using words to share our ideas and emotions. To understand one another and the world we live in. Stories sustain us, entertain us, and reveal us."

"Spoken like a man angling for his own TV network."

"Right now, all I'm angling for is this burger." He picked it up with both hands and took a bite. She followed suit. The burger was cooked well but tasted rather bland. She missed Reed's version, which featured Worcestershire sauce, dry onion soup, and plenty of black pepper. Ben set his down after a few bites and wiped his hands on his napkin. "Jack was right about one thing," he said. "You were badass today."

Her shoulders went up around her ears. "I don't want to talk about it."

"Okay. I only meant—I know how much guts it took to face him like that."

"Oh, yeah?" She whirled on him. "You think you know me? How? Because you read a book about it? Because you saw a movie?"

"I know what it's like to be the one who lived."

His little brother, she remembered. The fight drained out of her and she shook her head. She had a dead brother, too. "It's not the same," she murmured.

"Not identical, no. But I know what it's like to have all that weight on you. You have to live your life not just for you, but for them, too— the ones who aren't here. You have to be twice as smart and strong and successful, and even if you are, it's not enough because that loss is like a hole you'll never fill."

She looked at her plate and said nothing. Maybe he did understand some of it.

"Look," he said, "if you don't ever want to air the footage we shot today, that's fine. I get that there is some guy modeling himself on Coben right now and that it's a risk to give him unfettered airtime. But I don't think you're considering what else people would see if we did show it. They'd see you. Surviving. Doing your job. Getting answers for Maxine and Tracy and all the others. Maybe there's some of us out there who could stand to see that. Maybe there's lots of us who need it. Because if there's one sick soul out there looking to Coben for inspiration, I can guarantee there's a hundred others who would be positively revived to see you." The small smile he gave her at the end suggested he might be one of these people.

Ellery shut her eyes. He said he understood the pressure, but here he was, heaping more upon her. "I'm not a role model. I was a dumb kid riding my bike way past my bedtime and I fell for a smooth line from some guy in an expensive car. He turned out to be the devil, I'm sure, because that farmhouse was hot as hell. In the closet, I thought about the girls who died before me. I assumed I'd meet the same fate and I mentally apologized to my poor mother for having to bury two dead children—me because of my own stupidity. Instead, by random chance, I survived. That's it. That's the whole thing. Everyone looking to make some big lesson of it is bound for disappointment."

He tried to apologize to her as she threw down money for her dinner. "Ellery, I'm sorry. Wait."

"I know," she said without looking at him. "The fictional version is better, right?"

"I didn't mean to upset you. At least let me pay for your meal."

"No." She met his eyes. "It turns out, Mr. Lerner, you don't own me either. Good night."

She strode out of the bar into the lobby, where she cast a longing look toward the front doors. She wished she could go for a run, but the creeping feeling she'd had last night along with the news vans potentially still camped outside kept her indoors. She saw a pair of swimsuits in the window of the hotel's store and remembered they had a pool on site. A dozen laps would take the edge off her energy as well as a three-mile run. She purchased a suit and headed in the direction of the pool.

The place was deserted due to the late hour, and she breathed a sigh of relief as she ducked into one of the changing rooms. She did not have to worry about being recognized or stared at because of the scars. She slipped on the one-piece, knotted her hair at her nape, and padded barefoot out to the pool. The large room was warm but dim and shadowy. High windows along the far wall usually provided most of the light, but night had fallen long ago. *Swim at your own risk*, read the warning sign. *No lifeguard on duty.*

She plunged into the water, welcoming the bracing shock of it, the chlorine spraying up to sting her eyes. She bobbed up with a gasp and looked about her. She'd heard a noise, like a door slam, just as she'd hit the water. No one else appeared. She waited, listening for signs of life, but heard only the hum of the pool filter and the lapping of the water against the sides. Her gaze slid to the brown door marked UTIL-ITY CLOSET. Surely it was locked. She watched it for a few moments, her heartbeat loud in her ears. *You're being paranoid,* she lectured herself. *There's nothing in that closet but a mop and pail.*

She pushed off from the wall and began her laps, turning her head to breathe as she'd been taught at the Y. Back before Coben. Before her father left and Daniel got sick. In her memory, the sound of chil-dren's laughter bounced off the hard surfaces. *Watch me, Mama! Watch me.* She completed five laps before the uneasy feeling grabbed her again. She halted at the pool's edge in the deep end, breathless, her feet dangling. The closet doorknob seemed to turn on its own. Or perhaps she was just dizzy.

Should have skipped the beer, she thought. She swam back to the ladder and exited the pool. Her wet feet slapped against the concrete as she went for the changing room. She ducked her head, prepared to hurry past the closet. No, she would look. She would show herself how silly she was being. It's just a closet. She repeated the mantra to herself as she approached, her arm trembling. *Just a closet.* She reached for the silver knob. She held her breath, closed her eyes, and yanked.

"Ah," she exclaimed, going weak with relief. Inside sat a mop and bucket, a bunch of rags, cleansers, and a stack of toilet paper. "See? It was noth—"

An arm reached around her throat, grabbing her tight and knock-ing her off-balance. *Help,* she tried to yell, but the word came out as a wheeze—a last breath as her attacker started choking her from behind.

13

The forearm across her windpipe held her tight, but it wasn't strong enough to keep her off her feet. Ellery clawed at the arm, trying to dislodge it as she lowered her center of gravity enough to regain traction. Her bare feet scraped against the damp concrete and then came up again as her attacker dragged her backward. "Stop it," the person growled as she struggled. "You can't have him. You understand me? He's mine!" The last words came with a hard twist that wrenched Ellery's neck to the side.

Pain exploded behind her eyeballs. Her lungs burned for lack of oxygen. She pushed backward with all her might, and the pair of them staggered sideways. *I'm stronger than you,* Ellery realized. She crouched lower, forcing the person on her back to follow suit. She felt the instant the momentum shifted and her attacker lost balance. Marshaling every bit of strength she had, Ellery took several punishing steps backward until she felt her heels hit the edge of the pool. Then she reared up to her full height while jabbing her elbows behind her like the flap of an angry rooster. She hit her mark and heard the answering painful cry just before her assailant pitched ass-first into the pool.

Ellery gasped several large breaths as oxygen surged into her lungs. She scrambled away from the pool and turned to see who had assaulted her. It was a woman with dark hair. She sputtered and bobbed, her jeans, boots, and sweater weighing her down in the water. Ellery ran the short distance to the changing rooms, where she retrieved her gun and her cell phone from her locker. She returned in time to see the woman reach the pool's ladder. "Don't move," she ordered. "You're under arrest."

The woman's dark hair clung like kelp to her sullen face. "You're not from here. You have no authority over me." She continued to climb out of the pool.

"Take one more step and I'll shoot you."

"You wouldn't dare."

"If you know who I am, then you know the answer to that."

The woman spat in her direction, but she stopped moving. "He doesn't want you anymore. Go back to Boston with your FBI boyfriend."

Ellery kept the gun trained on the woman with one hand while she dialed Reed's cell with her other. He sounded sleepy when she reached him. "'Lo?"

"We have a situation. I need you to come down to the pool."

"Should I bring my trunks?" He was more alert now, even playful.

"You should bring the local cops," she replied, her voice hard. "Tell them I've got Hope Herndon in custody."

The woman scowled and hugged herself, telling Ellery she'd identified her correctly.

"I'm on my way. Are you all right?"

"Peachy." Ellery switched off the call. Her neck hurt and adrenaline pulsed like fire through her veins, but she was otherwise unharmed. A quick scan of the area revealed no apparent weapon. Hope had figured to take her down with her bare hands. Ellery stood two inches taller and outweighed her by at least twenty pounds. "Just what was your plan here?" Ellery asked her. "Murder me and leave me on a deck chair? How far do you think you'd get?"

"Francis is saved. He walks in the light with me. You just want to drag him back into your world of sin and corruption."

"He walks nowhere except the length of his twenty-foot cell."

"You've chained his body but you can't control his soul."

"Yeah? His body confessed today to the murder of another nineteen-year-old girl. That makes his total seventeen dead, and those are just the ones we can prove."

Uncertainty flickered across her features. "You're lying. You—you want Francis to be wicked because you think it makes you good."

The pool doors burst open and Reed ran through them wearing only his trousers and an undershirt. "Ellery! My God, are you okay?"

"I'm fine." She gave him a short history of recent events. "So, if you're curious what kind of person would find Francis Michael Coben romantically attractive," she said, "here she is."

"You don't understand him," Hope shot back. "You only see what he's done, not what he could be."

"He could be executed for the brutal murder of seventeen young women," Reed informed her.

"Not if I have a say in it."

Ellery glanced at the doors to see a pair of uniformed officers coming through them. "Well, then it's good for all of us that you don't," she said. She explained what had happened, and the men handcuffed Hope Herndon and led her, still sopping, back through the doors.

"Are you sure you're all right? Did she hurt you?" Reed touched her arm, and she looked down with some surprise to see goose bumps there. Her throat ached where Hope had crushed it.

"I—I don't know." Her hand fluttered to her neck. The stress of the day crashed over her and she started shaking.

Wordlessly, Reed took the gun from her, set it aside, and enfolded her in his arms. He'd held her that awful night so long ago, but it was different then, when his touch was rough but necessary. He'd grabbed her up and run like hell into the woods. She'd known from the tightness of his arms and the fetid sweat around his collar that he'd been as terrified as she was. She let out an angry, anguished sob that she still had to carry that fear, that it never went away.

Reed held her tight, his desperate fingers at the back of her wet head. "I know," he murmured as though she'd spoken aloud. "Me too."

The doors opened and Ellery leaped back from Reed as if burned. "Ma'am?" The older officer stuck his head in the room. "We're going to need you to get checked by a medic and then come with us to make a statement."

"I'll be right there." She had to put on clothes first.

Reed stood guard while she changed back into herself, scars hidden and her hair combed back into place. The pair of them went to the lobby, which was now crowded with six uniformed officers and at least two dozen onlookers. "What are they, selling tickets out there?" Reed asked under his breath.

She spotted Ben and Kate at the back of the crowd, talking animatedly to one another. Kate caught her looking and answered with an excited wave. "Are you okay?" she mouthed, her expression concerned. "What happened?" Ellery ignored her and continued threading her way through the mass of people. Several had cell phones out, recording the chaos.

Elliot Pritchett appeared at her side. "Detective Hathaway. I heard the police sirens and when I came downstairs to see what the fuss was about, your name was on everyone's lips."

"Your client's girlfriend attacked me by the pool," she said without slowing down. He fell back, apparently stunned, but then scrambled to keep up with her. He caught her at the lobby doors. Outside, the parking lot was lit up like the Milky Way with flashing red and blue lights. A crush of cop cars plus an ambulance blocked access to the hotel. Ellery spotted Hope's sulky face in the back of a black-and-white unit. *At least she's sitting there in wet underwear,* she thought as she turned her head away.

"My client is on death row, which permits just one hour of time outside his cell per day. He doesn't socialize with anyone except myself and the prison guards. He can't possibly have a girlfriend."

"Tell that to her." Ellery jerked her thumb at Hope.

Pritchett followed her gesture and his eyes widened as he saw the woman in the car. "That's not his girlfriend," he said. "That's Cousin Annabelle."

Ellery walked to the doors, which parted automatically and she drifted outside into the frosty air. She ignored the calls from the medic to stop as she approached the car where Hope sat. Hope saw her coming and replied with a furious glare. Evidence suggested that "Cousin Annabelle" might know the identity of Maxine Frazier's killer. But maybe, Ellery considered as she rubbed her sore neck, Hope was Maxine Frazier's killer.

Hope broke her gaze as she spotted something beyond Ellery, and the flash of recognition on her face caused Ellery to turn around and look, too. It took her a moment to see him lingering in the shadows, just beyond the ring of cop cars. A young man in a black hoodie stood smoking, watching silently. His dark eyes and long nose mirrored those on Hope's face, and Ellery concluded this had to be the brother. Had he been waiting outside for his sister this whole time?

"Hey!" she called loudly, starting toward him. "Hey, you!"

The burly medic appeared in front of her and blocked her path. "Ma'am, we need to examine you now for the official report."

"And I need you to get out of my way." She stepped around him and halted, her breath fogging in the cold winter air. The man was gone.

14

Reed awoke with a headache, a relentless pressure behind his eyes, as though his memories had metastasized into a tumor that threatened to burst forth from his brain. He pinched the bridge of his nose as he lay in the half-light, Coben's words chasing themselves around inside his head. *What is your sin, Agent Markham?*

Reed grew up in the church. His mother had seen to that, checking his face on Sundays and rubbing any lingering dirt with the pad of her thumb. They'd lined up as a family in one of the first-row pews, tallest to smallest, which for years meant Reed the baby sat on the far edge. Early on, Reed had appreciated the certainty of the lessons. *God is good. Sin is bad. Read this one book and you shall know the difference.* He loved the old building with its creaky wooden floors and ornate stained-glass windows that transformed ordinary sunlight into rainbows on the altar. When the congregation stood en masse to sing, the whole structure would groan in harmony, echoing the generations that had worshiped within its walls. He felt a similar swell when he went with his father, state senator Angus Markham, to visit the Virginia State Assembly in Richmond. The strong white columns at the front and the burnished wooden desks inside were the stuff of history books, a reminder that this was the oldest deliberative body in the United

States, a veritable cradle of democracy. Reed, who had been just a few months old when his birth mother was murdered, had craved nothing more than belonging to something bigger than himself. Something righteous. Something lasting. Imagine, then, his shock and dismay when he learned both the church and the senate permitted such a liar and a cheat within their midst. His father had picked the front pew of the church not to be seen by God but to be admired by the rows of people behind them. The setting gave him cover, and what the church didn't provide, Reed and the rest of the family did. Behold this honorable man with his beautiful family—a loving wife of many years, three bright and blond young daughters, and look, there on the end, the mixed-race boy they adopted out of the goodness of their hearts.

His sisters had scattered and found their own churches; his parents still attended the one Reed remembered from his childhood. Angus Markham wouldn't dare stray at this point, not when he had so much to atone for. Forgiveness came easy for the church folk when the truth came out, but Reed still struggled with his end. Maybe this, then, was his sin.

He wished he could be like many of his colleagues, who found strength in their faith. There would be relief to know that the imperfect justice they had on earth would be made whole in the end, that the men and women who escaped Reed would eventually answer to a higher power. He imagined a needle slipped in Coben's veins, sending him to a great beyond where a choir of angels—too young, all female—passed a final judgment. The hazy dream gave him no peace, so he turned to the one earthly person who could.

"Hi, it's me," he said when his ex-wife answered the phone. "I know it's early."

"It's fine," she replied, perhaps sensing he couldn't take a fight right now. "Tula's having her breakfast. Let me get her."

His eight-year-old daughter came bounding to the phone. "Daddy! Guess what happened yesterday?"

"Your pony collection came to life and had a parade around the living room."

"No! Jeremy and I found a bird on the playground at recess. He had a hurt wing, so Mrs. Kennedy helped us move him off to the side where no one would step on him. After school, he was still there and Mama let me feed him some sunflower seeds. She called the Bird People and they said he wasn't special so just leave him there. I cried because what if a cat came and ate him? So Mama and I took him home in a shoebox and put him on the patio. She looked up on the computer how to fix him, but when we went to check on him, he was gone. We saw him in the magnolia tree for just a second, but then he flew off and didn't come back."

"I'm sure he was happy that you helped him feel better."

"Do you think he might come back to visit one day?" she asked wistfully.

"Maybe. But in the meantime, he's off living his best bird life, flitting over trees and eating big fat worms. He's alive because of you, even if you don't get to see him all the time."

"That's not as good."

Reed cast a glance at the door, imagining beyond it to Ellery's room. "No, darlin'," he replied with a sigh. "It's not."

Reed and Ellery left for the Herndon household under the cover of darkness, although the interstate freeway zipped along with plenty of traffic. The sun slept in, not bothering to roll into the sky until near eight o'clock, but the commuters around Indianapolis had no such discretion. Reed made a face as he sipped the pale coffee he'd taken from the hotel breakfast bar. There was no way this barely brewed brown water could power him through the day ahead. Beside him, Ellery chewed through her breakfast sandwich with short, mechanical bites. Periodically, she rubbed the side of her neck with her free hand. He knew better than to ask after her injury so he picked a different topic.

"What did Dorie have to say about progress on the Frazier case?"

"Not much. They are still tracking as many of her previous clients as possible, as well as pulling surveillance footage from around the motel and gas station before and after the murder."

"What are they looking for?"

"That's the problem. They don't know." She turned her head to look at him and grimaced from the effort. "There is one weird thing. She seems to have picked up your book fairly recently."

"Oh?" He cleared his throat. He'd long since disavowed the book, but the publisher kept churning out copies and now there were more than five million sold. These days, he took the checks they sent him and donated every cent to women's shelters, but it felt like throwing sand into the ocean.

"She bought it as a remainder because it's an old edition. The bookstore's stamp was inside the front cover—Ballard Booksmith. They can't say exactly when she purchased it because she paid cash, but the sale was running all through November."

"So, recently. At most, she picked it up two months before her murder."

"Maybe it's a coincidence. She had more than three hundred books stacked in that place, including a bunch of other true crime."

"Sure, maybe." He did not believe in coincidences. "Does Ballard Booksmith have surveillance?"

"Yeah, but it's turned over since then. No recording available." Her head lolled back against the seat and she let out a long sigh. "You know what's funny to me? All these people who read the books can't get enough of Coben. Kate Hunter, Jack Reeves, Ben Lerner all want to be in the room with him. Hell, even his lawyer, Pritchett—you think he'd be taking this case for free if it wasn't Francis Coben in the hot seat? Hope Herndon thinks she wants to marry him. All these people are so desperate to attach themselves to Coben . . . while I can't seem to get away."

The GPS told them to take the exit. By now, the sky was brightening and the streetlights had turned off. They drove until they reached Tuxedo Park. Rows of small, well-kept homes set close together gave way to ramshackle structures with peeling paint and boarded-up windows just one street over, the thinnest of lines between the haves and have-nots. A woman, bundled up and hunched against the cold, struggled to push her shopping cart full of belongings over an uneven sidewalk. "I think that's number fifty-seven up there on the right," Ellery said. Reed pulled over and stopped the car.

A records check said the squat, square house belonged to Morris and Darlene Herndon, although Morris was listed as deceased in 2002. The chain-link fence around the property had caved in on one side. Someone had spread kitty litter on the front walk to combat the ice. Pressing the doorbell did not produce any sound on the other side, nor did anyone appear, so Ellery rapped hard against the door. After a moment, the door cracked open and a slight woman with completely shaggy brown hair peered out at them, a cigarette in one hand. She wore house slippers, jeans, and an oversized pink T-shirt that said NOT TODAY, SATAN in fancy white lettering.

"Are you Darlene Herndon?" Ellery asked.

"Since the day my mama named me."

"I'm Detective Hath—" Ellery began, but Darlene waved her off.

"I know who you are." She eyed Reed. "Him, too."

"You've seen the news," Reed surmised, and Darlene snorted.

"I don't watch that trash. I've seen Hope's room. She's got pictures."

Reed and Ellery traded a glance, and he could tell she had the same fears he did about what kind of pictures they could be. "We'd like to talk to you about Hope if we could."

Darlene shot Ellery a dirty look. "You've got some nerve, coming around here after what you did to Hope last night, having her hauled off in handcuffs like some criminal."

"She tried to kill me."

Darlene barked a laugh. "Pshaw. Kill you? I'd like to see the day. Hope weighs little more than a hundred pounds. She couldn't hurt a fly. She just wanted to talk to you is all. To make sure you're not messing with her man."

"You realize her man is on death row for the murder of sixteen young women," Reed said.

"I know what he done." She took a long drag on her cigarette, turned her head, and blew the smoke away from them. "He's paying the price for it. It's not for me to judge him now."

"Ma, what the hell? You're letting all the heat out." A large man with close-cropped dark hair and a neck tattoo appeared behind her in the doorway.

"Watch your language," Darlene ordered as she slapped him across his muscular stomach. "We got company."

"You must be Tommy," said Ellery. They had looked him up, too. Since his release from the FCI, he'd been clean as far as anyone could prove. "I saw you at the hotel last night."

He held up his hands. "Minding my own business." He flashed her a grin. "Watching the show."

"You mean watching your sister get arrested."

"That's her crazy shit, not mine." He turned and walked away.

Darlene shivered and widened the door for them. "Come in 'fore I catch my death out here."

"You don't have to let them in without a warrant, Ma," Tommy called from the back of the house.

"What have I got to hide? Nothing. I got nothing." She spread her spindly arms out and indicated a threadbare sofa, large-screen TV, and a rocker recliner. Family pictures in cheap frames lined the wall. From the clothes and the fading edges, Reed noticed the photos mostly documented happier times from decades past, in which the curly-haired Morris was still alive. A hand-knit afghan lay folded at one end of the couch. A black-and-white cat sprawled across the back of it, snoozing, unimpressed with the visitors. Darlene wasn't so impressed herself. "Soon as Tommy gets paid," she said, "we'll get Hope out of jail and back here at home. I'll—I'll talk to her. Set her straight. She won't bother you no more." She snuffed out the remainder of her cigarette in a tin ashtray.

"If you know who I am, then you know what Francis Coben did to me," Ellery told her. "Hope could be in danger."

Darlene's jaw set. "I know, and I'm sorry for it. I'm sure he's sorry too. Either way, it don't matter. He's locked up till his dying breath and he can't hurt her none. If my Hope helps him find salvation, then he'll be better for it."

"What about the girls he killed?"

"They've gone to their reward. Nothing more's to be done for them now."

"Tell them they ain't searching my room," Tommy hollered.

Darlene rolled her eyes. "You better not have weed in there," she yelled back to him.

"Mind your own fucking business, Ma. They're here about Hope, not me."

Darlene looked embarrassed to be spoken to this way in front of company. Still, she made excuses for her son. "Don't mind Tommy. He's grouchy before he gets his coffee in the morning."

The girl Tommy had kidnapped and nearly murdered had spent a week in the hospital recovering from her injuries. *No wonder this woman needs to believe Coben is saved,* Reed realized. *She's raised a junior version of him right in her own home.*

"We'd like to see Hope's room," Reed said.

Darlene eyed him with suspicion. "What for? So you can rig up more charges on her?"

"We're interested in her correspondence with Francis Coben."

"Oh, that." Darlene snorted. "She writes him Bible verses, and he says she's the light of his life. Sure, the talk gets frank at times. Once he asked her for titty pictures, which I did not care for, but Hope knows better than to engage in that kind of smut."

Alarm bells rang in Reed's head. Francis Coben would ask to see her hands, not her breasts. "She's saved the letters?"

"They're in a box on her desk. Here, I'll show you."

They followed her down a dark, narrow hallway until Tommy's hulking frame emerged and blocked their progress. He pressed the fist of one hand into the palm of the other. "They got no right to be here," he said, locking eyes with Reed.

She slapped at him. "The quicker we cooperate with them, the quicker they'll be gone. You want to make more trouble for your sister? Go on with you. You've got to get ready for work."

He didn't move. Reed looked him over, from the black T-shirt stretched over his chest to the baggy jeans to the shiny new boots on his feet, searching for any sign of a weapon. Tommy caught him checking and answered with a thin smile. "See somethin' you like?" He turned to Ellery and licked his lips. "What about you, honey? You want to pat me down?"

"That's enough." Darlene gave him a shove. "You don't go making trouble where there is none."

He produced a pack of cigarettes and took out a fresh one. "Don't kid yourself, Mama. They knew 'zactly what'd they'd find when they knocked on our door. Hope's locked up, remember?"

"Ignore his fussing." He shifted and Darlene stepped around him. After a beat, Reed followed suit. He paused to let Ellery past, blocking Tommy as best he could. Tommy still made a kissing noise as she crossed in front of him. "This is Hope's room," Darlene announced as she opened the door. She folded her arms over her chest as they crossed the threshold. "You'll see she's a good girl. Just a little mixed up sometimes."

Ellery pulled out a pair of gloves from her jacket and went straight to the desk, where the stationery box sat. Reed turned in a slow circle, taking in the rainbow comforter, the lacy throw pillows, the Pepto-pink walls and gauzy curtains, yellowed with age and cigarette smoke. *Hope's a good girl*. That's what the room looked like to him—frozen in time when Hope was perhaps ten years old. There were a few faded 4H ribbons tacked on the wall. Pictures taped to the mirror that showed a younger Hope and some teenage girlfriends. The bedside table held a Bible and a raggedy stuffed dog with one eye missing. "How old was Hope when her father died?" he asked Darlene, who remained watching from the doorway.

"She was eleven going on twelve. 'Fore you get weepy on me, let me tell you—Morris had a steady factory job and he could fix up a car as good as anyone. But he had a temper that wouldn't quit." She squinted at Reed. "You see that broken window over there? He done that when Hope spilled her pop can on the front room carpet. Threw the can at her head where she sat on the bed right there, but he was so fired up he missed and got the window."

Reed looked at the cracked window that had a length of duct tape across it. "How come you didn't get it fixed?"

"I did fix it," she said, indignant. "Didn't you notice the tape?"

"Right," he replied mildly. "Of course." He crossed to where Ellery was paging through the letters from Hope's stationery box. "Anything?" he asked.

"A bunch of gross garbage. He doesn't care about women's bodies anymore, just the purity of their hearts. Prison has changed him. He prays every day for the souls of the dead girls. Hope is lovely, she gives him strength when he is 'at his lowest ebb.' They communicate mainly in Bible verses, it seems. I don't know this stuff, but in his handwriting it comes across as downright creepy."

"I did twelve years of Sunday school. Let me see." Reed scanned first one letter and then the next. Last spring, Coben had written: *For in hope we were saved. Now hope that is seen is not hope. For who hopes for what he sees? But if we hope for what we do not see, we wait for it with patience.*

Then later in the summer, his letter talked of being united with her in God's love. He included the verse *So then let us not sleep, as others do, but let us keep awake and be sober.*

Another letter described his loneliness and isolation, and how the letters from Hope kept him going. The verse this time sent a chill through him, given Coben's history. *You stretch out your hand against the wrath of my enemies, and your right hand delivers me.*

Coben wrote about how misguided the beast was to vent his fury at all women when those like Hope were good and pure. Hope had apparently urged him to forgive the beast, to answer his hatred with love. Coben assured her it was working. *If your enemy is hungry, give him bread to eat, and if he is thirsty, give him water to drink.* But then he had also added this, inexplicably: *You also must be ready, for the Son of Man is coming at an hour you do not expect.* Maybe he was concerned about his potential execution, the noose he'd referenced as hanging over his head.

The most recent letters urged Hope not to give up on him and perhaps hinted that they could be together one day. *And if I go and prepare a place for you, I will come again and will take you to myself, that where I am you may be also.* Ted Bundy had managed to marry a woman while serving on death row, so perhaps Coben had similar designs on Hope.

"I didn't see anything in there about Hope being Annabelle," Ellery muttered, a trace of frustration in her voice.

"Who's Annabelle?" Darlene demanded.

Reed read through the letters again. There was nothing in them that suggested the need to bypass prison security and use Pritchett as a go-between. Moreover, the woman who lived in this adolescent fantasy of a bedroom would not have had the inclination or the resources to travel on her own to Chicago and pretend to be anything other than herself. If she was using a script, then someone else had provided it. "Your daughter certainly knows her Bible," he said, turning to face Darlene once more.

"I told you she was a good girl."

Tommy appeared behind her, dressed now in a jersey that read ARROWMARK FOODS, with an arrow coming off the K in the logo. He leaned down to kiss Darlene's cheek. "Gotta go to work now, Ma."

She grabbed his face and squeezed it hard. "This one, he could stand more learning. But he'd rather sleep in on Sundays than go with me to church."

"I know the Bible, Ma. You remember the last chapter, right? We know who wins in the end." Tommy straightened up and pointed at Ellery as he quoted. "'And after the thousand years had ended, Satan was released from his prison.'" He lowered his finger, grinned, and favored them with a wink. "And to think I only did fifty-five months."

15

Ellery drove the long stretch of I-70 back to Terre Haute. A pair of ibuprofen took the worst of the pain from her neck, and she wanted something mindless to occupy her brain. The empty ribbon of concrete under her tires did the trick. From the passenger seat, Reed studied the pictures that he'd taken on his phone of the letters Coben sent to Hope as though they were hieroglyphics he could decipher if he just cracked the code. "Maybe he really did get religion," she said after a while. "Sitting on death row for seventeen years would give a person plenty of time to contemplate the afterlife."

"You saw him yesterday," Reed replied without looking up. "Did he look especially repentant to you?"

"No," she admitted. She chewed her lower lip in thought. "There's a lot of people who want to say God saved me, you know. My mom, just for starters. But I've had total strangers come up and say God was looking out for me, he must have had some plan, et cetera."

Reed did look up then. "What do you think?"

"I think it's bullshit. If God rescued me, then also he put me in that closet to begin with. If he saved me, he could've saved the others. He could've struck Coben down with a bolt of lightning the first time a murderous thought passed through his puny little head. People see God where they want to and disregard the rest."

Reed didn't say anything for so long that she thought he wasn't going to reply. Then he said, "I only got a glimpse of Coben when he left the precinct after questioning. The lead detectives and the SAC had cleared him. Later, when I had to explain why I followed him, I said it was the tattoos around his wrist, right at the spot where the victims' hands had been amputated, that made me get up and start tailing him. But that wasn't quite true. I didn't consciously register the tattoos until later. I saw him cheerily waving good-bye and a voice in my head said, 'Don't let him go.' I got up like I was having an out-of-body experience. I had no formal training in street surveillance. The voice said 'go' so I went."

She turned to look at him. "And what? You think the voice was God?"

"I don't know what it was. I've never heard it before or since."

All that praying she'd done in the closet, and she'd never heard a thing. If there was a God, she had no special relationship with him. Miles of road passed under their tires before she spoke again. "Let me tell you about prayers. First, I prayed to be rescued. Then I prayed for him to stop hurting me. Finally, I prayed for it to be over." She glanced at him, noting the grim set of his jaw. He squinted out the window at the barren trees.

"I see," he said, nodding to himself. "That's the crux of it, then. It didn't matter if God spoke to me or not. I showed up too late to answer your prayers."

An involuntary laugh escaped her. "I wasn't praying to you, you idiot," she said, giving him a playful shove. "But I was just thinking maybe it did help, imagining that someone was listening."

He softened and his hand stole across the seat to find hers. "Someone is."

When they pulled into the hotel parking lot, Ellery saw Jack Reeves huddled inside a leather jacket, smoking near the front of the building. "You think that's tobacco or something stronger?" she asked Reed.

Before he could answer, Ben Lerner emerged from the hotel. He crossed to Jack and said something that Jack didn't appreciate, judging from the flash of anger on his face. He argued back and Ben shook his head. The spat concluded with Jack throwing his cigarette at Ben's feet and stalking back inside the hotel. "Clash of the titan egos, maybe," Reed said as they exited the vehicle. "My advice is to steer clear."

Ellery had never heeded good advice. She let Reed go alone into the hotel and chose instead to approach Ben where he stood on the frigid sidewalk, still fuming. "Trouble in paradise?" she asked.

The dark cloud around him lifted at her arrival. "Just a difference of opinion about the direction of this project."

"Let me guess: he wants to use the footage."

Ben answered with a short nod. "We're going back today to shoot with the warden and some of the guards. Kate wants a sit-down with Coben herself, and Jack is for it."

"No way. The FCI won't want to go through the security protocol a second time."

He shrugged one shoulder. "You've got to remember, they've taken a ton of heat over the past few years from the media and civil rights groups. Coben is part of a class-action lawsuit alleging the SCU is cruel and unusual punishment. This is their chance to show their side, that he's perfectly healthy. They want to remind everyone who the good guys are. The ones keeping the monsters in the cage."

Ellery thought of Tommy Herndon and the menace in his smile, how he'd done just four and a half years because his victim had the temerity to live. The state had set him free thinking he'd learned his lesson. In reality, the probable lesson Tommy learned was to make sure the girl was dead next time.

"The way I figure it," Ben continued, "the warden and the others at the prison have the same stakes as the FBI in trying to get this story on the air. Sure, Agent Markham is here because he feels a duty to those missing girls, but why did his boss sign off on the cameras?

She knows Coben makes them look good. To the FBI, Coben's like a trophy head you'd hang on the wall. They want to show him off."

She let out a humorless chuckle. "You're even more cynical than me."

His answering look held genuine amusement. "I'm in television. It comes with the territory."

Hollywood had come for her story while she still lay in her hospital bed, and in the end, they'd decided to tell it with her or without her. Coben was public record and she had no particular existence outside of him. Sometimes it still felt that way. "There's one thing I don't get," she said to Ben eventually. "You have all this money. You're famous enough to pick your own projects. You could tell any kind of story you want. Why this one, when it's been done a bunch of times already?"

He looked off in the direction of the prison. "There's an end but there's no explanation. That's why we keep coming back to him, right? There's something still unsatisfying, even when the guys in suits descend on Coben's farm and put the handcuffs on him. Where did he come from? Was he already a psychopathic murderer at age two and we just didn't know it yet? Can he be reformed? Is he? What would happen if he got let out tomorrow?"

"More young women would turn up dead with their hands cut off."

He looked at her. "You believe that. He can't change."

"You heard him the other day. He's got something inside him, the thing he calls the beast. He can't control it. Maybe he doesn't want to."

Ben nodded and glanced again in the direction where Coben was housed. "I read his mother died during his trial. She had some kind of heart condition that she developed during pregnancy and then held over him during his childhood." He clutched his chest. "'Behave, Francis, or one day you're going to kill me.' I guess maybe she was right. You could add Cora Coben to his tally of victims, hmm?"

Ellery didn't hold out a lot of sympathy for the woman who had birthed and raised a human predator. "Maybe there isn't one place in his lifetime where you could go back and say, here, this is how it happened. This is what made him what he is. But he designed a guillotine for squirrels when he was ten years old. He clipped out descriptions of murders from the papers and drew the crime scenes for fun. If there was one person in the world who could have seen this coming, it was his mother."

"Sure, maybe." He shoved his hands in his pockets. "I guess the question is: what could she have done about it?"

The wind picked up, blowing her hair across her face, and she clawed it out of the way. They walked back to the lobby and a thought occurred to her. "You made a TV series out of your brother's murder."

"A fictionalized version, yes."

"Did you have it solved?"

"Of course. On TV, you can have any kind of ending you want."

Inside the lobby, she saw Jack Reeves hadn't gotten very far. He was chatting up the young woman at the concierge's desk. The deck of cards in his hands suggested he might be trying a magic trick, and the smile on her face said she was falling for it.

"The disappearing queen," Ben said when he saw her looking Jack's way. "It's one of his go-to moves."

"No offense, but your friend is kind of a jerk."

Ben laughed. "He'd probably take that as a compliment. He aims for memorable, and he doesn't much care which direction the opinion goes. But he's got a good heart. He was there for me when Andy died. I mean from the moment we found the body right until now."

"Jack was there?"

He seemed surprised she didn't know, as if, like her, every bit of his sordid history was public knowledge. "Jack was camping with us in Oregon when Andy went missing. We, ah, we were supposed to be watching him, but at the time we viewed him as an annoying little kid. We wanted to go looking for lava rocks and Andy couldn't climb the hills as fast as we could. We set him on an old stump and told him to wait there until we came back. But when we returned, he was gone."

Across the way, Jack made a show of demonstrating his empty

hands. *Poof. The queen had disappeared.* The concierge laughed and Ellery shook off the chill that went through her. "I'm sorry," she murmured. "That's awful."

"I know Jack can be crass at times, but to me, he's like a brother. The people who see you at the lowest points of your life and stick around anyway, well, they become part of you. They're like a mirror, right? They show you your true self."

Her eyes searched out Reed and she found him head down, talking on his cell phone. They were due to leave soon for Chicago, where they would organize with the CPD for another search of Coben's farm. Some form of their old telepathy kicked in and he raised his head to look right at her. Their gaze held. She thought of Coben and how he had seen the absolute worst of her. She thought of her mother, who'd cleaned her wounds but never soothed them. "Not always," she said to Ben. She broke free from Reed's gaze and regarded the producer, the one who believed he could choose any ending he liked. "Good luck at the prison today. I hope you get the answers you want."

"You, too." At her puzzled look, he said, "You're going to look for Tracy's body at the farm, right? We're heading up that way when we're done here."

"Don't hurry on our account."

"I'd like to be there when it happens. If Tracy Trajan can come home after twenty-three years, then maybe there's hope for the rest of us."

Reed drove the several hours to Chicago while Ellery curled up in her seat like the girl she'd been when she left, watching avidly out the window as the scenery grew more familiar with each passing mile. Wide open farmland, blanketed in snow, gave way to increasing clusters of homes, electronic billboards, concrete barriers, and green exit signs counting down the numbers like they were on a rocket preparing to blast into space: 127th Street, 99th, 64th, 59th. . . . Boston, her adopted home, had no straight lines and you could get lost trying to go around a single block. It was quirky and charming and endlessly confusing to someone who had grown up with orderly rows. Her hungry gaze devoured the jagged skyline in the distance, the prongs atop the Sears Tower rising to the sky like Neptune's trident. She knew that, like her, the famous building had a new name, but also like her, the world refused to use it. Eventually the L rose up alongside her, racing them like an iron horse, and she pressed her palm against the cold glass in greeting. She'd expected to feel terror or at least anxiety, but instead a painful wave of homesickness washed out of her, like she'd been holding it back for years. She smiled through her tears and traced an imaginary line across the window, mapping the buildings, apologizing silently to the city for the way she'd fled its borders. Chicago was merely a bit player in her personal horror story. Its broad shoulders held generations of artists and architects, creators, thinkers, dreamers. That it had also produced Francis Coben and the lone girl who would survive him could not be held against it.

They drove downtown to headquarters and Ellery continued to take in all the landmarks she'd never expected to see again—the grand old Chicago Public Library; the Art Institute with its regal lions standing guard; the opulent Buckingham Fountain, silenced for the winter. She remembered standing by the fountain on sizzling hot days, cooling herself in its windy spray. Some of the storefronts had changed names, a new skyscraper appeared here and there, but mostly the city looked just like she'd left it. There was one new element, though: the top cop at CPD headquarters was now a woman, and a Black one at that. First Deputy Superintendent Sharon West greeted them with a smile and a firm handshake, although her gaze lingered on Ellery. "Detective Hathaway," she said as they took seats in her office, "how does it feel to be home?"

"Strange." She did an internal assessment. "Like a case of déjà vu."

West's warm brown eyes assessed her. "You've got darker hair now and you've filled out some, but otherwise you're almost exactly the same. I know because I was one of the cops who turned out looking for you. I was a rookie back then, just coming up in the job, but the sergeant handed out flyers and we all had to memorize your face."

Ellery's spine stiffened and she had to force herself to relax. She had to convince this woman that she was competent, a grown woman who could handle the job. "I've got more wrinkles now," she said lightly. "Trust me."

West gave her an easy smile. "Don't we all. I just meant—I could still pick you out of a lineup. I bet every cop on the job back then could do the same."

Ellery leveled her with a stare. "Then you understand why I had to leave." Chicago contained nearly three million different people in dizzying combinations, but inside its borders, Ellery would only ever be one thing.

"I do." West took a breath. "And I appreciate why you came back. That took tremendous guts. So it pains me to say I can't let you come out to the farm tomorrow when we do the search."

"What?" Ellery and Reed both sat forward.

"It's a legal issue. You and Coben have, uh, you have a history. If we find fresh evidence, especially after all these years, his lawyers could argue that you planted it there."

"That's ridiculous," Reed said, but Ellery laid a hand on his arm. This was her fight, not his.

"Let me get this straight," she said, "you think I might have Tracy Trajan's remains stashed somewhere, and I've been waiting for the opportunity to plant them on Coben's farm?"

"I realize it sounds crazy. If it were up to me, I'd let you burn the place down if you wanted to, but it's not my call. The order came down from the state's attorney's office. Bringing a former victim back to the scene causes irreparable contamination that renders any future prosecution more difficult."

"What future prosecution?" Reed cut in. "Francis Coben is already on death row."

"You're looking to recover more bodies, aren't you?"

"Yes, but for the families and the official record. The odds that he stands trial for any of these additional crimes is essentially zero."

She threw up her hands. "Like I said, it's not my call."

Ellery didn't care what the procedural manual had to say. Coben demanded new rules. "I'm here because I'm pursuing another case," she said. "There's been a murder in Boston, which appears linked to Coben. It's for this reason I need to see the farm."

"In Boston," West repeated with emphasis. "You're far outside those city limits. And, like he just got done saying, Coben's locked up. He hasn't committed a murder in more than seventeen years now."

"But someone following his playbook has," Ellery persisted. "And whoever it is, they've been in contact with Coben. That someone could have been to the farm."

"You mean like some sort of pilgrim going to Mecca?" West looked skeptical.

"It's happened before," Ellery replied, frustration creeping into her voice. She sat back and examined the wall behind West, which proudly displayed various awards and merits she'd collected over the years. West had photos of herself with fellow officers, with the mayor, and, Ellery noted with a touch of envy, the World Series Championship Cubs. She didn't build this career by being dumb, but she also clearly knew her politics. "Listen," Ellery said, "you didn't get here by always following someone else's orders. Sometimes you had to use your own judgment."

West folded her arms across her chest. "And what makes you think I'm not doing that now?"

"Back when you were a rookie, when you were looking for me, what was your assignment?"

West looked taken aback by the question. "We were pulling over dark sedans and checking them for anything suspicious. Busted a few dope heads, but that's it."

"You were a foot solider," Ellery said. "You had no choice, right?"

"That's right."

"Agent Markham was green back then too. On the job less than a year." Next to her, Reed cleared his throat and looked at the floor. "He walked off his assignment to pursue Coben because he had a hunch. He broke the rules and solved the case. If everyone kept doing their jobs like always, I'd be dead right now."

West wasn't falling for the speech. "If we had a kidnapped girl and a serial murderer chopping off people's hands loose in the city, you might have a point."

Ellery pulled up her sleeve to show off the scars. "The man who killed Maxine Frazier in Boston cut her up just like this. Then he dumped her body, took her hands, and posed them in her freezer. He killed her in Boston, but we don't think he's local. He could be from anywhere. He could be here, now, watching girls go by on the street."

West's gaze slid to the big windows on her right. Outside, snow-flakes had begun to fall. Ellery waited, her arm still exposed, while West drew a long breath. "I'll talk to the state attorney. Maybe she would agree to let you come along with an escort."

"I'll escort her," Reed volunteered quickly.

West peered at him over the rims of her glasses. "With all due respect, Agent Markham, you're probably going to need one yourself." She turned her attention to Ellery. "You really think you're going to find anything useful out at that farm—now, after all these years?"

West's words made it seem like the farm existed far away and in another era; in reality, Ellery's nightmares only ever went one place, as though she'd never left. She lowered her sleeve and sat forward. "Please believe me when I tell you: I wouldn't be going back there if I didn't."

16

At her insistence, they ate supper at Portillo's, where Reed studied the fast-food menu with a frown. "If you order a salad instead of a hot dog, I'll have to move to another table," she warned him. The place still felt like magic to her. Whenever her father got a little money, at the start of his latest get-rich-quick scheme, he used to bring Ellery and her brother, Daniel, to Portillo's. *Order whatever you want,* he'd tell them with a grin as he took out his wallet. The Hathaways didn't eat out much, and when they did, Ellery knew to pick the lowest-cost item on the kid's menu. Grilled cheese. Spaghetti, no meatballs. But at Portillo's, her father always opened up the whole menu to them, even the chocolate cake, and they'd parade home with full bellies and the promise of a new future. The good times never lasted more than a week or two, but for Ellery, the smell of grilled meat and the sight of cheery checkered tablecloths brought back only happy memories.

Reed ordered a chicken patty with the works. "If I add on cheese fries, will that satisfy you?" he asked her.

"Depends on whether I get to share them." She ordered two Chicago-style dogs for herself, and when Reed tried to pay, she brushed him aside. "I've got it."

"We're going to need to get a hotel," Reed said as they ate. "Do you have any particular place in mind?"

"Actually, I do."

He quirked an eyebrow at her but she did not elaborate. She didn't want to say the words out loud or make any commitments she wouldn't be able to keep.

After supper, Ellery took the wheel because she knew the way. She'd spent years navigating by the weight of the Lake, always knowing whether it was to the right or behind her, its point anchored like the North Star. She felt it to her right as she drove through the darkened streets all the way back to her beginnings. Her family's third-floor apartment in the old brick building in Rogers Park stood as it had since before the war. Across the way, cold and silent, lay the small playground and the basketball court flanked by a chain-link fence. She parked the car but left her suitcase in the trunk. She did not know whether she would be staying. Reed got out with her, his gaze traveling across to the streetlamp, the site of her abduction.

He followed her to the front door where she paused to withdraw her mess of keys. She held her breath as she inserted it into the lock, but the key turned and they went inside. There was no elevator. As they mounted the stairs, she felt his eyes on her, felt his profiler's mind turning over the significance of carrying around the keys to a home she'd left more than a dozen years ago. She arrived at her mother's door faintly breathless, almost dizzy, but it had nothing to do with the climb. She steadied her hand and knocked.

The door creaked open to reveal Caroline Hathaway, already dressed in her robe and slippers, despite the fact that it wasn't yet eight o'clock. "Ellie," she murmured, shock coloring her features, then embarrassment to be caught like this. "My goodness, come in."

"Hi, Mom. You remember Reed Markham, right?" she said as Reed trailed her inside.

"Of course. But I thought—" She shook her head as if to clear it. "Never mind. It's good to see you. It's so wonderful to see you both.

This is such a surprise. I wasn't expecting company. Won't you come in and sit down?"

"I'm sorry. I didn't know we'd be in town," Ellery said as they took a seat in the front room. Her mother had a single table lamp on, plus the television. The green sofa was new but the paisley-patterned armchair was the same one that Ellery remembered from her childhood.

Her mother silenced the television and tightened the belt on her robe. "Let me go fix my face."

"Your face is fine, Ma."

She headed for the door as if Ellery had not spoken, then stopped herself. "Are you hungry? There are cookies in the kitchen, and instant coffee if you want it. I can put the kettle on."

"We're fine, thank you. We just ate."

"All right, then. I'll be back in a minute."

Her mother had always put on makeup to go to the corner store for milk. To her, appearance was foremost, especially for a lady. Ladies wore stockings and skirts that came to the knee. They neatened their hair and put on lipstick and made sure that there was nothing for anyone to criticize before they went out into the world. *We may be poor,* her mother had said once when Ellery tried to wear ripped jeans out of the house, *but we're not trash.*

Ellery rose from the sofa to look at the family photos her mother kept on the wall. Her and Danny at Loyola Beach. Danny beaming with a ribbon he'd won in fifth grade at the school's art fair. Ellery hanging upside down from a jungle gym, her pigtails nearly scraping the ground. Her father wasn't in any of the pictures but his presence hung over them nonetheless. He'd been the family photographer, and so she saw him behind the camera when she looked at the images. Then when he was gone, the pictures stopped. Her mother lived forever in this time, when they smiled big for the camera and making rent was the worst of all their problems.

From the end table, she picked up the one portrait that postdated their father's desertion: Danny's junior-year school photo. He had not lived to take a senior one. Ellery smiled to see his face again after all these years. Lightly freckled with serious blue eyes, he looked as he did in her memories, before the cancer had winnowed him to his bones. Reed came to stand by her. "That's Danny?"

She nodded. "Taken just before he got sick." She hugged the picture to her chest. "I wish we had taken more photos."

Her mother returned, dressed in slacks and a pale pink sweater and carrying a plate of cookies. "You wouldn't let me."

"I'm sorry?"

"The pictures. You wouldn't let me take any of you . . . after."

Ellery blinked. She didn't remember that part. "I meant pictures of Danny."

"Ah, well. I have a few more in my room. You're welcome to look at them if you like." The naked hope in her expression filled Ellery with a wash of hot shame. She'd left her mother here alone for years with only memories for company. Of course, her mother wouldn't fly to Boston to visit her, either. She was afraid to get on a plane and didn't want to drive all that way on her own.

"Maybe later," Ellery said to her mother as she put the picture back. "How are you? How's work going?" Her mother had worked for decades as a secretary at a small legal firm.

"Good. The partners got together to give me a spa gift card for my birthday, like for pedicures and hot oil massages. Can you imagine? Me, at a spa."

"I think you'd love it."

"Maybe." Her mother hesitated. "Maybe if you'd come with me. There's enough on the card for two and it's good for a whole year."

Ellery suppressed a shudder at the idea of a stranger massaging her semi-naked body. She barely tolerated getting her hair cut. "Maybe," she said in the same tone she used whenever her mother invited her home. Her mother recognized the canned response, and her mouth tightened.

"Sarit talked me into a spa treatment on our honeymoon," Reed volunteered. "It came as part of the package so I said yes. They said they'd wax my eyebrows to 'clean them up,' but they waxed one of them clear off." He touched it, remembering, and her mother laughed.

"That must have been a sight."

"Hurt like a yellowjacket's sting, let me tell you."

Her mother asked after Tula and his family, and they chatted while Ellery looked around her former home. The walls needed repainting; she could see flaking and chipping by the baseboards. The crack in the ceiling had been repaired and she had a late-model TV, but the rug was threadbare, worn thin beneath her mother's feet.

Finally, Caroline Hathaway asked the question that surely had been on her mind since she'd opened the door to them. "What brings you back to town?" It came out stilted, uncertain. She already knew it wasn't her.

"It's a case," Ellery said.

Her mother's brows knit together in concern. "Here?"

Ellery knew she may as well level with her. The press would have the story soon. "We're going back to the farm tomorrow to do another search."

"The farm." Her mother twisted delicate hands in her lap. "I don't understand why you'd go back there. I can't imagine what you'd hope to find."

"There are others who didn't come home, Ma."

Her mother scowled like Ellery had dropped a cussword in front of her. "I know that," she said, clipped and angry. "Don't you think I know that? When they did the news specials with all those other mothers crying their eyes out, begging for their babies, how do you think I felt? I could barely show my face in public. Even now, people say to me, 'You're so lucky. Abby lived. Your daughter came home to you.' And I make myself smile when I say yes, it's a miracle, because my child survived but . . ." She broke off and gulped down a breath. "My daughter lived but in the end it's almost the same because she's just as gone."

"Ma." Ellery got up and went to kneel in front of her mother. "You know that's not true."

"You left before you were even eighteen. You haven't set foot back here since. You think I don't realize it's because of me? I didn't protect you. I let it happen."

"You were with Danny at the hospital. He needed you more."

Her mother's chin trembled. "No, baby. He didn't." She reached out and held her palm to the side of Ellery's face. "I just didn't see it back then, not until it was too late."

A painful sob escaped Ellery, from deep in a place she didn't access very often, and she pitched forward to bury her face in her mother's lap. "I'm sorry," she choked out. "I knew I shouldn't have been out there. I'm sorry for the trouble I caused." Her brother was dying and she'd gotten herself kidnapped.

Her mother stroked the back of her head. "No, I'm sorry."

Ellery raised her head and let her mother see the tears. "I know you like to look outside and see the park. You see Danny and me playing ball and having fun and that's why you stay here. But I can only see one thing, one night, over and over, and that's why I had to go."

"You're wrong," her mother replied hoarsely. "I see it too, every time."

Caroline insisted they stay and Ellery was too weary to argue. She found herself back in her old bedroom, which had a fresh coat of sky-blue paint and several of Danny's paintings framed and hung on the walls. Danny's old twin bed, earmarked now for Reed, sat up against the far wall while Ellery's had the window as usual. She approached it cautiously, rounding the foot so she could see out but no one could look in and see her. The wooden floor creaked, making her jump, and she whirled to find Reed returning from the bathroom. "Sorry, didn't mean to startle you," he said.

"It's not you. It's this place."

He joined her by the window. She could smell the soap from his skin. "We could still decamp to a hotel."

She realized then that she should have insisted he go. Reed stayed in places that had Egyptian cotton sheets and thick towels, not the nubby Target specials her mother had kindly laid out for them. She curled her toes against the drafty wooden floor. "You can go. I don't mind." Her demons lived here, not his.

His phone buzzed from across the room. He picked it up and read the message. "They didn't get any interviews at the prison today. Some sort of food poisoning incident shut the place down. Ben says they'll join us here tomorrow anyway."

"Great," Ellery muttered.

"Let them bring the cameras and see how far they get. Sharon West means business. She'll have them filming from somewhere outside of Detroit."

Ellery dropped the curtain with a small smile. "Yeah, in a fight between Sharon West and Kate Hunter, I'll take the woman running the whole Chicago PD."

Reed pulled down the bedsheets across the room. He was already dressed in his boxers and a T-shirt, no longer bothering with any pretense of formality with her. When he turned to find her watching, he said, "I'd rather stay, if it's okay with you."

"It's okay with me."

They crawled beneath their separate sheets and turned out the light. Ellery's narrow bed had once felt like a coffin. After Danny was gone, it had been her alone in the room and her mother's restless footsteps pacing the house at night. Ellery had been sure if she sat up and looked out the window that she would see Coben under the streetlamp waiting for her. She sat up to check, pushing back the curtain. The street was empty. The snow flurries had stopped, leaving the night clear and cold.

Across the room, Reed let out a soft snore, and she dropped the curtain to look at his familiar shape, just visible in the murky light.

He could sleep anywhere at any time, like his brain had an on/off switch, no matter what kind of horrors his eyes had seen that day. She envied his ability to compartmentalize, to wall off his own troubled past so it didn't distract him all the time. For Ellery, the memories rose up like a creature from the depths whenever her body got quiet. They clawed at her chest so she couldn't breathe and set fire to her brain to the point where her skin felt tight across her face. She slept in fits and starts, whenever the creature grew too weary to torment her. It was wide awake now, roaring with old memories, so she retrieved her phone and her earbuds to shut it up.

She closed her eyes, listening to Pink Floyd's *A Momentary Lapse of Reason* and letting the atmospheric instrumentals dissolve the walls around her like they used to do. They took her back to the days when she'd ride around in the truck with her father, big-hair bands blasting on the radio, John Hathaway using the big steering wheel as a drum. He'd shout tutorials at Ellery over the din. "Roger Waters left and everyone said the band was washed up, finished . . . but just listen to that guitar sing. This album went double platinum." Her father had owned a guitar that mostly sat gathering dust in the corner of his bedroom, but she noticed he took it with him when he'd left. He didn't take his kids.

Her phone buzzed her hands with a text. Evan. *The band has a new cover, "Life During Wartime." Thought you might like a listen.* He sent a link.

She wrote back. *You're up late.*

Hey! He sent a smiley face. *Rode the late shift.*

The phone started a steady buzz in her hands. Ringing, she realized with a trace of panic. He was calling her. She glanced at Reed's sleeping form and rolled away from him to face the wall. "Hello?" she whispered into the phone.

"Hi. I hope you don't mind the call. I wanted to hear your voice."

She smiled in spite of herself. Evan sang backup in the band, not lead, but his baritone had a raspy edge to it that was undeniably sexy. "Your voice is pretty nice too."

"Oh, good," he replied with obvious relief. "I would have phoned earlier but I didn't know if you'd want to hear from me. You haven't answered my texts."

"I've been busy." That sounded curt, dismissive. "With work," she added lamely.

"Right. I, uh, I did my own search today. The news says you're out in Indiana." He paused and she swore she heard him swallow. "Talking to him."

"Actually, I'm back home with my mom right now in Chicago."

"Is that why you're whispering?"

She closed her eyes and curled in on herself. "Yeah," she fibbed. "Thin walls."

"No privacy when parents are around. I know exactly what you mean. So, what's keeping you up then? Have they got you stashed on a couch-bed with the springs poking you in the ass?"

She thought of home, of her comfy sofa where she slept as easily as anywhere, with Bump curled like a croissant at one end. "Couldn't sleep," she replied. "Too many memories, I guess."

She heard him breathing for a long moment. "Look, honey. I'm not going to pretend to understand what you've been through and I don't want to pry into your business with a bunch of nosy questions. What little I've read is enough for me to know—you're the bravest person I've ever met."

She rolled and blinked at the inky shadows on the ceiling. "I don't want to be the bravest person you've met," she said at length. "I just want to be someone you met at the dog park. Someone with better taste in Eighties bands than you."

"Hey, Whitesnake has hidden depths."

"Oh, they're hidden all right."

He chuckled low in his chest. "Did you click that link I sent you?"

"Not yet."

"Then let me get my guitar. I'll play it for you." She waited while he fetched one of his acoustic guitars, settling in as the notes began to play. He gave a stripped down, slower performance, exchanging the urgent beat for a gentler rise and fall. Her heartbeat slowed. Music tamed the memories, made her forget time and place, drifting her back to the days she'd been happy in this bed with her big brother in the same room and her mother and father together on the other side.

17

he dead of winter. This was Reed's thought as he waited under cold, gloomy skies for Ellery to emerge from her mother's apartment building so they could go search for more bodies on the Coben farm. His first visit had occurred in mid-July when the summer heat stuck to his chest and trickled down his neck. Sometimes just the whiff of his own sweat could take him back there and he'd be crouched behind the leafy brush with a dying girl at his feet, the blood rush in his ears so intense that he could barely hear the 911 operator on the other end of the phone.

Reed let his gaze wander across the boulevard to the park that was the scene of her abduction. There was nothing to mark the spot. No monument or memorial to say here stood Abby Hathaway, the last place she existed as herself. The sound of her footsteps made Reed turn his head and he saw the version who'd returned, dressed head to toe in black like God's own fallen angel. That she lived would never seem less than a miracle to Reed. "Do you want me to drive?" he asked.

"No, I've got it," she said as she clicked the lock on their rented SUV.

Once on the road, he took out the satellite image he'd printed of

Coben's farm. He studied it first from one angle and then turned it to examine another. It showed the main farmhouse as well as a couple of additional structures, including a large barn. Trees rimmed the property, and there was also a dense cluster of woods several acres wide in the middle. The fields were overgrown with grasses in the picture but now would be under a layer of snow. He marked the main entrance with his pen.

"What are you doing?" Ellery asked, eyeing his handiwork.

He frowned and rotated the picture again. "Hardened criminal sociopaths like Francis Coben generally have one of two relationships to religion, if they care at all. A portion become obsessed with it because their urge to kill feels like something separate from themselves, something that other people might associate with a message from God."

"What Coben calls the beast."

"Exactly. It lets them off the hook for their depravity. 'The devil made me do it.' Or God or some other supernatural force beyond their control. Coben's documented interest in religion, as far as it went, fell into the second category, fascination with the hypocrisy of it all. Religious people claim to be pious but commit sin anyway." *What's your sin, Agent Markham?*

"Everyone has sin. Isn't that in the Bible?"

"Yes, but it's the hypocrisy they see in religion that gives these men license to do the things they do. If everyone gives lip service to good behavior but acts venally—even revered figures like parents or priests—then why should these men feel guilty about killing? Why should they feel remorse for their victims, who, in their estimation, are equally sinful?"

"So, you're not buying his 'I've been saved' act."

"No." He scrutinized the image some more. "When we asked him where to find Tracy's body, he said, 'Matthew six, verse thirteen. "Lead us not into temptation but deliver us from evil."' Since Coben doesn't believe the words, I think it's probably a code of some kind. A clue as to where to find her on the farm."

"You mean like she's six paces in, thirteen to the left? Something like that?"

"Yes. Or that she's buried where they used to deliver the cows. It means *something*. I just haven't figured out what yet." He squinted at the pond located in the far northeastern portion of the farm. From above, it was shaped something like a six. It would be frozen over now. Plus, he was fairly sure they'd dragged it back in their initial search years ago and come up empty. They'd spent weeks on the property and recovered at least partial remains of sixteen young women. He'd stood in the shower each night to wash the dirt and sweat from his pores, but the stench of death clung hard enough that he'd had to burn his clothes at the end. *What's your sin, Agent Markham?*

While Ellery drove, he checked the more recent images of the farm against his previous notes on the case, trying to find any connection between birth/delivery and the numbers six and thirteen. Coben had been born on the farm, he learned. They had searched the farmhouse thoroughly, but he figured it wouldn't hurt to check it again. He'd been inside a hundred times but Ellery hadn't set foot there since he'd carried her out. The nails, he knew, still stuck out of the closet. He glanced at her and saw her knuckles white around the steering wheel.

"Don't," she said when she felt him looking.

"You don't have to take part in the search," he said, because he felt like someone had to say it. "I'd make sure to loop you in on anything that might pertain to Maxine's murder."

Ellery didn't answer him for a long time. When she spoke, her words came slow and even. "The worst thing already happened. Whatever we find today, whatever happens or doesn't happen, that place holds no additional nightmares for me. There is only the one memory, and it's forever."

They drove south, the roads narrowing, towns growing smaller and farther apart until they hit the Kankakee area. When Ellery made the last turn onto the narrow two-lane road that bordered Coben's farm, Reed sat up in his seat. A dozen cop cars lined the side of the street, accompanied by a forensics truck, an ambulance, and three news vans. "So much for a low profile," he murmured. "This is a circus already."

She flashed him a humorless smile as she parked. "That must make you the ringleader."

He didn't reply. He'd caught sight of Kate Hunter, dressed in a red wool coat and posed in front of a camera, sticking her microphone in the face of an older man and woman. The Trajans. She'd made good on her promise to bring them to the scene. Reed, meanwhile, had promised to bring their daughter home. He'd been so free and easy when he'd said the words. The search team had been pulling up body parts all over Coben's farm, and it stood to reason that Tracy's would be among them. *We'll have her back to you. I promise.*

He climbed out of the car and Janice Trajan turned her head at the same time so that they locked eyes. He saw the same pain in her he'd seen the night he'd made his assurances, when he'd thought it would be so easy to relieve her burden. Her mouth thinned and she looked away from him.

"Reed?" Ellery called from where she'd started up the road. "Are you coming?"

He gathered himself and pushed onward to join her. Coben might not believe in sin, but he surely knew Reed's because it shone in every taunt, every manipulative conversation that they'd had for the past decade and a half. He'd sent that letter to Reed in January knowing full well that Reed would answer.

Reed clutched his papers, the notes he'd taken and the photos he'd printed. He was following a half clue back to the place where he'd started, where he'd crisscrossed the property so many times that his steps could encircle the earth. How could he pretend this visit would be different?

What's your sin, Agent Markham?

"Arrogance," he muttered. Ellery pushed open the rusted gate and he followed her through it even as a herd of reporters rushed in pursuit, shouting the usual questions. Deputy Superintendent Sharon

West met them before they'd gone more than twenty steps onto the property.

"Detective Hathaway, Agent Markham. Nice to see you all this morning. Mother Nature has blessed us with a relatively mild day."

Temperatures were already in the mid-forties. Reed saw that the snow wasn't going to be as much of a problem as he'd feared. It was patchy in most spots, if drifting higher near the tree line.

"We brought ground-penetrating radar," West said as she saw him surveying their surroundings. "But it's only one unit and we can't cover the entire property. Much of the woods are too dense for the machine."

"We've used it before," Reed told her.

She shrugged. "This is your party. Use it as you like. I'm here to be your personal escort. The pair of you stick with me or I'll have you removed from the premises."

"You can't do that," Reed said. They were outside of Chicago. She had no jurisdiction here.

She stretched her body to one side to peer around Reed at an older man wearing a state trooper's uniform. She waved and he waved back. "That's Brad Hicks. He runs point in this district, and so technically we're all here by his invitation. Mine's engraved and yours is . . . well, let's just say the pair of you are my plus-one. Now, how do you want to get started?"

Reed laid out his theory about the Bible verse being a clue to Tracy's location. "I'd like to start the teams six acres in, thirteen to either side. Another team can search the farmhouse itself."

"I want to see the house," Ellery said, staring at it in the distance. The red exterior paint had faded with time and eroded under the weather, leaving it a muddy brown color. A classic weathervane on the roof, its arrow tip bent, pointed eastward.

"Then so shall we all," West declared. "Thanks to Brad, I even have the keys."

They walked up the sloping path and Reed noted the periodic shallow valleys around them, places where they had dug before. He also saw various boot prints. "Has Brad also paraded his buddies around the property?" he asked, pointing out a fresh imprint.

Sharon glanced down and sighed. "He tells me they get plenty of people coming by to take a look-see. Kids, often—teenagers daring each other to go up to the house and take a selfie. He says the town put up that fence around the front of the farm years back, but you can still sneak in from the side if you're willing to hike a while. It's a public nuisance, but there's nothing that the town or state can really do about it. The Coben family still owns the property."

The wooden porch sagged under their weight as they trooped up the steps to the house. Someone had pried off the house number, probably as a souvenir. Several windowpanes were missing, glass shards still visible on the ground; the vacant windows had been boarded up from the inside. His hand reached out, almost of its own accord, to touch the window he'd crawled through all those years ago. As Sharon West forced the key into the lock, Reed looked to Ellery and saw her staring at the closest tree line, perhaps fifty yards away. It was the place where they'd hidden until backup arrived. He'd wondered how much of that night she even remembered, given her delirium, but they had never talked about it.

"We're in," Sharon said as she shouldered open the door.

The chilly temperature inside matched the outdoors. Back then, the house had been an oven and stunk like blood and death, but now it smelled like nothing—a literal absence of anything alive or dead inside these walls for more than a decade. Even the inanimate objects had disappeared. No chairs. No lamps. No kitchen table or dishes by the sink. The walls had cracked and peeling paint that had sloughed to the floor.

They walked the rooms like one might traverse a cemetery, with silence and slow steps. The only noise was the creaking floorboards beneath their boots. Reed glanced up at the ceiling in what would have been the parlor or family room and saw a brownish stain. In any other home, it might have indicated water damage. But Reed knew the closet stood right above them. "I don't remember this part,"

Ellery said to no one in particular as she stood in front of the stone fireplace.

"What are we even looking for?" West said. "No one's been inside this place in years."

"Anything we missed before," Reed replied. "There was a shack on the property and a small hidden room in the basement, both of which are rumored to have been stops on the Underground Railroad. There may have been other hiding spots we didn't discover."

West looked up from where she was examining a loose floorboard. "Seriously? The same family that produced Francis Coben was part of the Underground Railroad?"

"Ted Bundy volunteered at a suicide hotline." Reed rapped his hand on the wall that bordered the kitchen. It felt solid.

"How many rooms are in this place?" Ellery asked, turning in a circle.

Reed did a mental count. "Thirteen total, I think, counting the bathrooms."

"Could one of them be considered the sixth room in any way?"

It was an interesting theory. "There are six bedrooms upstairs, but I don't think they have numbers assigned to them."

Ellery was already heading for the stairs. Reed hurried to follow her with West right behind him. His heart started pumping faster as he took the steps two at a time, but Ellery was quicker and she disappeared around the corner before he reached the top. Whatever else she remembered or disremembered, she found the room of her captivity unerringly. He caught up to where she stood at the threshold, her whole body rigid. There wasn't much left to see, he knew. The bloody mattress was gone, seized as evidence, leaving behind an old metal bed frame. They'd removed Coben's chains and ropes and garden shears. There was only an empty closet with bent nails sticking out of the frame and the circular stain of a bloody bucket left upon the floor.

Ellery inched into the room. He trailed her without a word. Even West fell silent as they watched Ellery catalogue the remnants of her cell. She stood over the bed frame with a blank expression. At the closet, she stretched out one finger to touch the sharp point of a nail. Eventually, she went to the curtainless window and regarded the farm below. "This part is exactly the same," she said without turning around. "He didn't put any shades or coverings on the window back then. When he took me out of the closet to . . . to hurt me . . . I could see sun or stars through the window and I knew then that no one would ever find me. If he didn't have to hide, if he didn't have to bother even with a curtain, then we were isolated enough that no one would hear me scream. No one could see what was happening."

Reed knew the house was set far enough back in from the road that it wasn't visible from the street. There wasn't a neighbor around for miles.

"He was a special kind of monster," West said, her voice tight.

"Yes," Ellery acknowledged, bowing her head. "And no." She turned around. "He looked perfectly normal the whole time he was killing these girls. He looks normal now. He's just a man, really, and if you start convincing yourself he's some other species, that's how he slips by you. That's how he did it for years."

Reed examined the walls and then crossed to the door so he could see into both this room and its neighbor. "There's no hidden panel here."

"Well, there's none in the closet, I can tell you for sure," Ellery said wryly.

He caught her gaze and held it. "Let's check the rest of the bedrooms, then."

One by one, they searched the whole house, top to bottom. The only hidden room they discovered was the one Reed already knew about in the basement. Checking in with the search teams outside, they learned nothing had turned up at either point—six acres in, thirteen in either direction. "Let's try thirteen acres in, six in either direction," Reed said. "And I'll take the pond."

He grew chilled trudging through the slush and mud. Coben's farm stretched at least a mile in all directions, much of it wooded terrain. Up close, the pond didn't resemble a six at all, and Reed wondered why the hell he'd dragged Ellery and Sharon West with him across the whole property to stare at a sheet of ice. West kicked at the edge of it so that a chunk broke free, revealing murky water underneath. "If she's under there, we're not getting her back today. By March, maybe."

A crow cawed down at them from a high branch, offended by their intrusion. Reed turned first one way, then another, searching for anything that suggested a thirteen. The surrounding woods were dense, comprising at least a hundred trees. The large rocks by the pond numbered only eight. Not far beyond the far side of the pond was the legal edge of the property. The nearest neighbor would have the house number nineteen, which was six plus thirteen. Could Coben have buried Tracy across the property line?

"Reed?" Ellery's voice jolted him from his thoughts. She turned her face to the gray sky. "I don't think he would have carried her way out here. I bet she's closer to the house."

"We looked there," he said, frustrated. Again and again, they'd searched.

She shrugged one shoulder. "I haven't."

She pivoted and disappeared into the pines. West eyed him for a moment and then followed. Reed looked at the crow, who sidled along the branch and leaned down to stare hard at him. "You win," he told the creature, and it spread its wings, flapping back at him with an angry wave.

He fell into step beside Ellery as they tramped backward through the woods. "Maybe six and thirteen have nothing to do with anything," she said. "Maybe he was just screwing with you."

"Maybe." Probably. Here was his sin again, thinking he could outwit a madman. As they came into the clearing, they passed some of the dig teams using shovels to overturn snow and dirt. They had been at work for hours now and the place looked like a dog had been trying to find his lost bone. Reed and Ellery, always monitored by Sharon West, circled the farmhouse from the outside, inspecting the foundation, edging around the previous makeshift graves. They passed a collection of rusted bear traps the searchers had collected on an earlier occasion. Coben had kept some bodies and dumped others, minus their hands, but they never got an answer from him about how he calculated which to keep and which to throw away. Reed tried six paces from the front stoop and thirteen to the side. Nothing. Then he tried the reverse and got the same result.

As the day wore on, a pair of uniformed officers arrived with sodas, hot coffee, and sandwiches to dispense among the search crews. Reed took a coffee and chewed through a dry turkey sandwich. The searchers dug and dug but turned up only rocks and the occasional small animal bones.

"Let's try the barn," Ellery said.

The large barn, like the house, stood empty and in disrepair. The loft had no hay. He couldn't guess the last time it had homed any animals. A patch of roof had opened up in the far corner, letting in the fading gray light from above. Ellery inspected each of the stalls in turn. One held an ancient saddle gone cracked with age. "We searched here too," Reed said, his voice echoing through the voluminous chamber.

"I know," Ellery called back. She'd disappeared from view as she continued her search.

Beside him, Sharon West shook her head in disbelief at Ellery's determination. "She's tough, your friend."

"You have no idea."

Reed looked up at the far end of the barn. A worn American flag had been tacked to the wall. Next to the flag was a clock that had been built into the barn, its numbers painted on the wall. It had stopped dead at 4:07, but who could say what year? "What time is it?" he asked absently, and West consulted her watch.

"Coming up on five."

It would be dark by six, and Reed stopped in his tracks at the thought. *Six thirteen.* Could it be a time? With nothing else to lose, he mounted the ladder for the loft.

Ellery's head poked out of the last stall. "What are you doing?"

He didn't answer. He edged his way down the loft to the point closest to the clock. He grabbed the nearest beam to steady himself and held his breath as he stretched bodily across the wall to touch the metal hand that indicated the minutes. He pushed it once, then again, until it reached the thirteenth position. Then he repeated the process with the hour hand. Six thirteen.

"Reed, wh—" There was a crashing sound and Ellery's voice broke off with a fading shriek.

"Ellery!" He scrambled down the ladder as West raced across the barn to the stall where Ellery had been standing. The floor had opened up under her, revealing a chamber beneath the barn. "Ellery, are you all right?" He fumbled for his cell phone to turn on the flashlight as West peered over the edge. She recoiled and the scent hit him a second later: death.

"I'm . . . I'm okay." Ellery's pale face, streaked with dirt, appeared perhaps twenty feet below them. "But I've found a body."

"Tracy."

"No." She glanced over her shoulder. "It's a fresh one. I think—I think it's Hope Herndon."

18

The skies dimmed from dove gray to dark slate before going entirely black, starless and oppressive. In the distance, Ellery could see the corona from the floodlights set up by the barn where the recovery team worked. Hope Herndon was the most recent victim, but Ellery had glimpsed at least two other skulls down in the pit before Reed and Sharon West found a rope and pulled her free. Now she was sidelined, a footnote in this fresh investigation, relegated to the edge of the property along with Reed, West, and the rest of the searchers who no longer had a job to do but stood around in the cold anyway, shifting their feet from side to side to keep warm as temperatures sank back toward freezing. Reed stood twenty feet away from her. He worked his phone, looking for a way back inside the circle. Now that there was actually something to see, the state troopers had backed the press up the road, so she did not expect to turn her head and find Ben Lerner on the other side of the chain-link fence. His buddy Jack stood with him, smoking a cigarette.

"How did you get in here?" Ellery asked him as she walked up to the fence.

He gave a lopsided grin. "Brad Hicks. Turns out he's a fan of my shows." When Ellery didn't smile, he poked a finger at her through the fence. "Plus, I told him I'm with you."

She looked at Jack. "And him?"

"He's with me."

"Did they find something in the old cistern tanks behind the house?" Jack asked with interest. He nudged Ben. "I told you those were sketchy as hell."

"Wait," Ellery said as she caught on to what Jack was admitting. The cistern tanks were not visible from behind the fence. She looked from one to the other. "You've been on the property."

Ben winced, chagrined. "We scouted it last summer and shot some footage. We had to have something to shop to the networks."

"No one needs six giant tanks like that," Jack said as if Ben hadn't spoken. "I bet that's where he put the missing girls. Am I right? Tell me I'm right."

"I'm not telling you anything."

He narrowed his eyes at her, took a drag on his cigarette, and then tossed it into the slush at her feet. "You want to keep it to yourself a little bit longer, that's okay," he told her with a thin smile. "The truth will come out. It always does."

"Just tell me one thing," Ben said, his brown eyes round with concern. "Is it her? Did you find Tracy?"

"I can't tell you that."

"Come on. Her parents have been freezing out here for ten hours."

"Whose fault is that?" she snapped. "I didn't bring them here. That was all on Kate. Maybe some on you, too. And for what? There was never going to be confirmation today. You get that, right? We're talking about a woman who's been dead for more than twenty years. There would be nothing left here but bones, and identification of those remains takes time."

"So, you did find something," Ben said, his gaze going to the lights behind her.

"Or someone," Jack added. He pointed up the hill to where the coroner's van was parked near the house. "Do they send a doctor out to pronounce the victims if they're a pile of bones?"

"I think you need to get back behind the yellow tape," Ellery replied evenly.

Ben unhooked his fingers from the fence and nodded. "Yeah, okay. But what am I supposed to tell the Trajans?"

Ellery looked back over her shoulder. The farmhouse itself stood draped in shadow, with only the bent weathervane on the roof illuminated by the light emanating from the barn. *I was supposed to be the last,* she thought. When she spoke to Ben, her voice emerged thin with fatigue. "Tell them to go home," she said, rubbing the side of her aching neck. "We'll contact them as soon as we know anything definite."

She turned and walked away before she could see whether they complied. As long as they remained on the other side of the fence, they were someone else's problem. She joined Reed as he finished up a phone call. "Tommy Herndon is in the wind," he said. "His parole officer checked and Tommy never showed up for work at the grocery today."

She shoved her hands in her coat pockets but found no warmth there. "Great."

"He paid Hope's bail yesterday afternoon. Apparently, Darlene didn't know anything about it. She thought Hope was still locked up for her assault on you. She swears she hasn't seen or talked to Tommy since yesterday morning."

"Yeah, well, whatever Tommy's involvement is, Coben has to be pulling the strings. He gave someone the combination to his little hidey-hole."

"Maybe Hope herself. After all, she's the one who's been in contact with him."

"She's down there with her throat cut. No way she did that to herself."

"No, but she could have led the person here. We know she's a student of the Coben lore."

"We need to talk to him." She forced the name from her throat. "Coben. We need to go back to the prison and sweat him until he tells us who else knew about the hidden chamber."

"About that." Reed's lips thinned, his expression flinty. "It seems we're behind on the day's news. That food poisoning outbreak at the FCI was no little case of stomach flu. A third of the inmates came down with violent stomach cramps, severe diarrhea, and vomiting. Several of the guards and food service workers are ill as well. The CDC is investigating but the early speculation is that this is some food-borne pathogen such as salmonella or *E. coli*."

"You're telling me Coben is sick."

"I'm saying he's not at the prison. He's one of more than four dozen inmates who have been taken to the hospital. He's in critical condition and we're not going to be allowed to talk to him."

Her jaw fell open. "They let him out?"

"There are guards at the hospital." He glanced at her. "So they assure me."

"I am not assured."

"Maybe this will help. The doctor said Coben was in such pain that he was begging to die when they brought him in. Skip the appeals. Just put the needle in him right there."

"I suppose there are medical ethics that prevent them from obliging him," she grumbled, and he rewarded her with a tight smile.

"He's unconscious at the moment. Sedated. We'll get nothing from him until tomorrow morning at the earliest. But I agree he's the first person we talk to, unless the Indianapolis police somehow locate Tommy Herndon. Coben didn't kill Hope, but he surely served her up to someone who did."

Nights like these, her scars felt like a burn. She could feel them hot against the sheets as she watched a black-and-white film through bleary eyes. If she tried to sleep, he would be there, so she propped her head in one hand and forced herself to listen to the rat-a-tat dialogue coming from the TV. It took her a moment to realize there was also knocking on her door. She silenced the movie, dragged herself from beneath the covers, and peered through the peephole. Reed. He was dressed in a T-shirt and sweats. Glasses, no contacts. She slid open the safety bolt and let him inside.

"Did my TV wake you?" she asked through a yawn. They had adjoining rooms at the hotel this time.

"No, I knew you'd be up." He held up a bunch of miniature liquor bottles. "Thought you might like a drink."

She smiled faintly as she curled up on the bed. "Do I have any secrets left from you?"

"I don't know." He looked at her. "Do you?"

She patted the bed next to her. "Give me a couple of those bottles and you might find out."

"What do you want? I've got bourbon, Tennessee whiskey, a red wine—that's all it says on the label, by the way. Red wine. Tequila. Vodka."

"Vodka?"

"I brought one of each."

She considered with a slow blink. "You know what? Give me the vodka."

He raised his eyebrows as he handed it to her. "See? You surprise me all the time."

He sat on the other side of the bed and it sagged a familiar amount under his weight. She crawled across the mattress and leaned over the side. Sure enough, the half-drunk bottle of orange juice she'd had with her dinner had rolled under the bed. She retrieved it and showed it to Reed, triumphant.

"Classy," he remarked as she added some vodka to the mix. He unscrewed the tiny cap on the whiskey.

"Cheers." She held up her makeshift screwdriver.

"What are we drinking to?"

She consulted the clock. "The end of this day."

"Good enough for me." He tapped his bottle to hers and took a swallow.

They both leaned back against her pillows and drank in silence while the TV played on mute. "My best friend in grade school was a girl named Krista Porter," she said. "We would play in the park together for hours, doing this pirate game that she made up. We rode our bikes to the corner store for candy. Slept over at each other's houses on the weekend. When my dad left, her mom used to drop by sometimes with a bag of groceries. She'd say something like, 'I accidentally bought two cartons of eggs this week' or 'They had a "buy one, get one free" coupon on turkey breast but we don't need both.' At the time, I thought she must be getting pretty forgetful in her old age, buying all this stuff she didn't need."

Reed smiled. "She sounds like a good neighbor."

Ellery scratched her chin with her free hand. "She was. Krista and I stopped hanging out as much when we got to junior high. She got into makeup and boys and I, well . . . look at me." She indicated her worn-out T-shirt and boy shorts. "I'd probably blind myself trying to put on eyeliner even now."

"You look plenty good to me."

"That's not the point of this story."

"I know. I'm just stating it for the record. Please continue."

She took a deep breath. "But we'd still do stuff together now and then. Krista had new friends but she'd still sit with me on the school bus and talk to me in the halls. If she got stuck on her math homework, I was the one she'd call. I liked going over there to help her because her apartment always had chips and cookies. Mom quit buying that stuff once Dad split on us. We ate spaghetti with ketchup and dented cans of Campbell's soup. Part of me was glad that Krista didn't come around as much anymore so she didn't see how empty our cabinets were, but I still considered her a friend."

"What happened?" he asked, his voice gentle.

She picked at the edge of the sheet. "After Coben, when I came back, I ran into Krista in the hall of our building. I could tell she was nervous to see me, but I was wearing baggy clothes and all my scars were covered up even though it was still summer. I said hi and she said hi with this weird laugh. I said maybe I could come over and we'd listen to some new CDs I got. People sent me stuff, you know? While I was in the hospital. Strangers sent money and candy and teddy bears. Finally, I had something I could show off to her. She said sure, come over after lunch. My mom was so excited that I was getting out of the apartment to see a friend like a normal girl that she let me take the new boom box. I carried it over there with a backpack full of different CDs because I no longer was sure what kind of music Krista was into. I heard the television playing and her little sister running around on the other side of the door right before I knocked. The noise stopped. No one came to the door. I knocked again. Then a third time. I think I must've stood there knocking for ten minutes before I accepted that they weren't going to let me in."

"That's terrible."

"It's not the end." She drew her legs up protectively in front of her and took a long swallow of her drink. She wiped her mouth with her bare arm. "When I returned and told my mother what happened, her face got all pinched and she said, 'You must not have knocked hard enough.' She took me and we marched back over to the Porter place. She banged on the door and called out Krista's mother's name, Martha. She finally answered it and I swear, the way she looked at me, it was like . . . like I was a dead animal by the side of the road. Like she felt sorry for me but she didn't want to look at me. She let my mother inside and they went into the kitchen while Krista and I stood in the front room staring at one another. She had a bright red face and blue painted nails. I remember that because I'd thought maybe she'd share the polish with me. Makeup, I could care less. But blue nails sounded cool." She almost smiled, remembering.

"What did your mother say to Krista's mother?"

"They tried to keep their voices down. My mom was angry. Krista's mom was upset, maybe even crying. It made my stomach hurt to hear it. This was who I was now—someone who could make random adults cry. Then, I heard her say it. She said, 'Krista's too young to know about such things.' I don't know if my mother answered her. A minute later, she came and dragged me back home. I never went back to Krista's house again."

"And the bus?"

"She sat with Debbie Stevens. I saw her looking at me sometimes. But she'd turn away if I looked back. I thought she was too good for me now. That she didn't want to be seen with a freak with scars on her arms. Her mom said that what happened to me was so terrible we couldn't speak about it. Innocent children shouldn't hear."

"She was wrong," Reed said gruffly.

"She wasn't. Eighth graders shouldn't have to talk about rape. Fuck, Reed, we had to get permission slips signed before the health teacher could talk to us about pubic hair and acne. No way anyone was teaching a class on what I went through. And my mom, at home, would urge me to put it behind me. It's over now. No point in dwelling on it. I survived. I got the message, all right—keep my mouth shut if I wanted to fit in. Don't say anything or my mother would start shaking. Being good meant staying quiet." She looked at him with wet eyes. "And I wanted to be good again."

"Honey." The word came out hoarse, broken, and he leaned his head against hers. "You're the best person I know."

She gave a watery laugh of disbelief and sniffed hard. "Agent Markham, you may need to expand your social circle."

"I like where I am right now."

She closed her eyes with a hum, sleepy now as she sat slumped against him. She might have drifted off for a moment, she couldn't be sure, but the piercing scream of a woman made her sit bolt upright. Reed leaped to his feet as well. "You heard that," she said. It wasn't a dream.

"Next door. The room that isn't mine."

On cue, they heard a thump and another scream, softer this time. Ellery took her gun and went next door. Reed followed. She banged as loudly as her mother had at the Porter's apartment, and within a few moments, the door cracked open and Jack Reeves appeared in his underwear. He reeked of alcohol and cigarettes and the left side of his hair stood on end.

"What do you want?"

"We heard a woman screaming. We came to see if everything is all right."

"Everything's fine," he replied, his irritation plain.

"We'd like to see for ourselves."

He looked her up and down. "You got a warrant?"

"No, but if you like, we can all stand right here while I phone up the local police and they can file one. It's two in the morning, though, so it could take hours."

"Fuck it." He flung open the door with disgust and spread his arms. "Look all you like."

His hotel room mirrored hers. He, too, had a supply of miniature liquor bottles, although his were strewn about the desk, the bedside table, and the floor. Half of a pepperoni pizza sat congealing on the desk. Discarded clothes scattered across the blue carpeting. And a pale young woman with dark hair wriggled around under the sheets, apparently replacing her skirt and tube top. "Are you okay, miss?" Ellery asked her as the girl popped out of the bed, redressed and looking as annoyed as Jack did.

"I'm fine. I'm leaving." She bent down to put on her high-heeled shiny leather boots.

"You just got here," Jack protested.

"Yeah, well, you didn't tell me it was going to be a group thing. With cops." She grabbed a pair of twenty-dollar bills from the desk as she walked past. Jack caught her arm and she shot him a stony look.

"What, I don't even get a good-bye kiss?"

She pursed her red lips and for a second Ellery thought the girl might comply. "Kiss my ass," she said, jerking free. She breezed past Reed and right on down the hall.

"Fucking great," Jack said as he shoved the desk chair. "You guys owe me a hundred and forty bucks for this."

"So you were paying her."

Jack flopped on the bed and folded his hands behind his head. "Paying for her time, sure. Anything else that happened here was purely coincidental."

Ellery stalked the length of the room and back again. It was a sad scene, pathetic even, but with the girl gone there was nothing illegal about it. Jack watched her with heavy-lidded eyes. When she looked at him, he rubbed his bare stomach and arched his back in suggestive fashion. She turned her head away.

He chuckled and thumped the pillows. "You mind hitting the lights on your way out? I'm going to crash for the night."

Reed nodded to the door and Ellery reluctantly followed him. "I need a second shower," she muttered in the hall. "Maybe even a third. That guy is as scuzzy as a week-old ham sandwich. I don't know why Ben keeps him around."

"Old friends, I guess," Reed said as he trailed her to her room. "Jack goes back to the part of Ben's life before his brother died. Maybe he gives Ben a way to access that time, to remember what it was like before."

"He was there with them, you know. Camping in Oregon when the brother went missing."

Reed looked at her with some surprise. "It's more than that. Jack found Andy's body."

Ellery halted from rearranging the pillows. "He what?"

"It's in Ben's book. The boys split up when they were playing in the woods—hide-and-seek or something. Jack came across Andy's body in the creek." He paused. "That must've been a terrible thing for a ten-year-old to see."

Ellery made a noncommittal noise as Reed pulled down the sheets on the other side of the bed. "You're sleeping with me?"

"That depends. Are you planning on sleeping?"

She put a hand on her hip. "I always plan on it. Just sometimes my body doesn't cosign the agenda."

"Then I'll stay up with you," he vowed. "We can watch . . . whatever that is." The black-and-white movie had turned into some creature feature, and a poorly costumed blob was rising from the inky depths to menace a pair of picnicking teenagers.

Ellery hid her smile as she climbed into bed with him. She turned the volume on low, but within ten minutes, the cheesy movie score was joined by Reed's snoring. She turned off the television and reached for her cell phone. Jack Reeves patronized sex workers, like Maxine Frazier's killer. Jack Reeves was familiar with the Coben property, like Hope Herndon's killer. Maybe these coincidences amounted to nothing, but Ellery sent a quick text to Dorie: *Check to see if Jack Reeves has been to Boston recently. Maybe even a former client of Maxine's.* She found a photo of Jack from his social media and attached it for Dorie.

Dorie replied immediately. *Why are u up?*

Ellery curled away from Reed so the light of her phone wouldn't disturb him. *Why are u?* she wrote back.

Hot flashes in February because menopause has a sense of humor. Who's this Jack guy?

Ellery gave her what little background she had on Jack Reeves. *Bottom line is, I don't like him,* she wrote.

That's enough for me. I'll check into him. You be careful.

No problem there. I've got Reed watching my back.

And the rest of you, I'm sure. Just watch yourself. I don't like how these murders keep following you around.

I'm fine, Ellery insisted. *Coben's yanking someone's chain and we have to figure out how he's doing it.*

Exactly my point. This person is following Coben's plan and Coben wants just one thing.

Ellery stared at the words for a long time before replying. *Me.*

19

In the morning, Reed called the prison about getting access to Coben and was informed he would have to wait until Coben was returned to the FCI. "He's recovering, then?" Reed asked.

"I don't know his present condition," the warden replied. "You'd have to talk to the docs about that. But some of the cases we treated here are recovered enough to return to their units. With beds opening up, we can transfer inmates back to our care if they are deemed medically stable."

"It's urgent that we speak to him."

"I understand. But I'm sure you can appreciate that we are severely limiting access to the ward right now—medical staff and guards only. You can have your conversation with him, but you'll have it when we can better control the environment. It's for the safety of all concerned."

"It's safety I'm concerned about. There's someone out here killing people, and Francis Coben knows who it is."

A beat of silence on the other end. "Can you prove that?"

"Not yet. That's why we need to talk to him."

"Call me back this afternoon, or if you get some proof of Coben's involvement."

Stonewalled by the warden, Reed and Ellery returned to the Herndon household to follow up on their only other leads—the victim, Hope, and her absent brother, Tommy. Darlene Herndon opened the door dressed in a nubby lavender bathrobe and holding a cigarette. "Please accept our condolences on the loss of your daughter," Reed said.

"Sure," she scoffed. "You're sorry now. You're the ones who got her locked up. Prolly someone she met at the jail got her and killed her." She took a drag and blew the smoke toward his face. "I know you think Tommy done it, but you're wrong. He'd never hurt Hope."

"We haven't drawn any conclusions yet," Reed told her. "We'd like to take a look around, with your permission, to see if there is anything that might lead us to her killer."

"You won't find that here," she retorted, but she widened the door to admit them.

Reed stamped the slush from his boots before crossing the threshold into the cramped kitchen. It smelled like bacon grease and cigarettes, and his gaze went to the overflowing ashtray on the table. "You say Tommy hasn't been here since the day before yesterday? Not even a phone call?"

She lowered herself into one of the chairs. "You mean did he drop me a line and say, 'Hey, Ma, I murdered my sister'? No, he did not. I'm telling you, he looked out for that girl. And she needed lookin' after."

"What do you mean?" asked Reed.

She tapped her ash into the tray. "I mean that girl was born searching for something she never found here on this plane. Always running off with someone who'd make sweet talk to her, from the time she was small and Dicky Witter lured her into his trailer by promising her a puppy." She held out a finger to Reed as a thought occurred to her. "Guess who pulled her out of there with her pants down around her ankles? Tommy. He looked out for Hope. No way he's mixed up in whatever happened to her."

"We're just going to look around his room for a few minutes," Reed said.

She shrugged, not eager to give them a tour. "Suit yourself."

Reed and Ellery put on gloves before searching the place. From the disarray, it seemed like maybe the local cops had beaten them to it. One of the dresser drawers stood open, the T-shirts inside riffled. The bed had been stripped. The footlocker beneath the bed had been hauled open, the lock busted, only to reveal an empty handgun case, some weed, and what looked like pirated porn DVDs. Ellery nodded at the missing gun. "Did the cops take that?"

"Don't know. We'll have to ask." He opened the closet to find a baseball bat, a bunch of clothes, and a ballcap with the Arrowmark Foods insignia on it. Reed patted down a leather jacket but it revealed only a cigarette lighter and some old movie stubs.

"Look at this," Ellery said as she pulled out a book from the desk drawer. "It's a Bible."

"Tommy didn't strike me as religious."

"Yeah, but there's underlined portions here. Take a look."

He moved to join her when a bit of white tape and red lettering caught his eye. It was stuck to the floor of the closet. He reached down to peel it free. It was an industrial sticker, the kind used to seal packages. *Biovix Labs,* it read. *Caution: Biohazard.*

"I think this one was in Coben's letters to Hope," Ellery said from where she was holding the Bible.

"Yes, I was looking at those again this morning. If the verse he quoted to me has significance, it's likely the ones he included in his letters are part of the code. I can't make the numbers fit anything yet."

"'If your enemy is hungry, give him bread to eat, and if he is thirsty, give him water to drink,'" Ellery read. "That was in the letters, yes?"

"Yes. Also verses about God's return to earth and revealing the unfaithful. Coben was big into Revelations, it seems."

She flipped through the Bible with a sigh. "Well, if it ever happens, Coben will be the first one to get smitten. I distinctly remember him screaming in my face, 'I'm your god now.'"

Reed froze. *I'm your god now.* Of course. "Jesus," he murmured.

Here was the key to cracking the code. Coben wasn't talking about God in those verses; he was talking about himself. "We have to get to the hospital right away," he said, striding for the door.

"Why? What's happened?"

He didn't answer. He paused in the kitchen where Darlene had lit another smoke. "Does Tommy's delivery route include the prison?"

"What?"

"Does Tommy deliver to the FCI in Terre Haute?"

A thin smile appeared at her lips. "Yes. He says he wishes when he drives in there that he could blow the place up."

Reed opened the door and headed to the car with Ellery close behind. "What is it? Do you know where Tommy is?"

"Never mind Tommy. It's Coben. He's planning to escape."

In the car, he tried to reach the warden but was told the warden was in a meeting. He next tried hospital security and got nowhere. Eventually, he reached head of nursing on the floor where Coben was being held and was told that the guard was still posted at his door and the heart monitor was hooked up. Coben hadn't gone anywhere. "Drive faster," Reed told Ellery anyway. The verses from Coben's letters lay strewn across his lap.

"I'm doing ninety. How do you know he's planning to escape?"

And if I go and prepare a place for you, I will come again and will take you to myself, that where I am you may be also.

"Hope isn't the only member of that family who has been in contact with Coben. The lawyer has been carrying correspondence from Tommy, too—maybe wittingly, maybe not."

"What's Tommy's angle then?"

"You heard his mother. Tommy wants to burn the place down. Absent any explosive device, poisoning the whole joint and helping Coben plot an escape would be a close second. That's the nonsense about giving food and drink to your enemy—to Tommy and Coben, the other inmates and the guards at the FCI are the enemy. The bits about the Son of Man returning are referencing Coben's return. He wanted Tommy and Hope to prepare a place for him to escape to once the food poisoning has created the opportunity."

"You think he's there now? At the hospital?"

"Who the hell knows. Whatever this plan is, it's been in the works for some time. Coben's been writing letters to Hope—and apparently, they are also meant for Tommy—for half a year."

He ran a search on his phone to confirm what he already suspected: Biovix Labs studied various pathogens, including *E. coli.* Somehow, Tommy had obtained the germ and sprayed it on the food meant for delivery at the prison. Reed doubted Tommy had the brains to pull off this operation by himself and Coben's communications were heavily monitored, meaning there was probably a middleman involved somewhere. Probably the same person who asked Hope for the "titty pictures" and maybe even the person who had murdered her.

Ellery drove double time and practically skidded into the parking lot of Mercy General Hospital. There was a car marked DEPARTMENT OF FEDERAL CORRECTIONS parked out front and a young blond guy drinking coffee from a paper cup sitting inside it. Reed flashed his ID. "We're here to check on Francis Coben."

"That's way above my pay grade. I'm watching the front door and I can promise you, he ain't come through it."

"Terrific," Reed muttered as he charged for the door. "We'll cross this one off the list." He stopped at the admitting desk. "Francis Coben is a patient here," he said as he once more showed off his FBI credentials. "I need to see him."

Two guys standing around from the Bureau of Prisons ambled over. "You're here to see Coben?"

"That's right."

"I don't think so. No one but medical staff and FCI personnel is allowed on that floor."

"Hey, I know you," said the nurse with a smile. "You're the FBI profiler who caught him. I've read your book."

"Yes," Reed said with relief. The two BOP goons looked him over with new curiosity. "That's me. I wrote the book on Francis Coben and I'm here to tell you he's planning to escape."

The BOP guy closest to Reed grunted. "He couldn't stand up when they brought him in here, let alone run off anywhere."

"Let's all go check together, shall we?" Reed said. "If there's nothing to worry about, we'll turn around and leave."

The nurse looked alarmed. "Yes, please check," she said to the guards. She caught sight of Ellery hanging back behind the men. "Oh, my God, you're her."

All the heads turned to look at Ellery. She cleared her throat and yanked up her sleeve, revealing the scars. "This is what he did the last time. He's spent the last seventeen years wishing to finish the job. If I'm standing here, you should know it's serious."

The BOP guards exchanged a look. "Okay," the older one relented. "We'll take a look."

They all rode the elevator up one floor to the wing that had been hastily converted to a prison ward. There was an armed guard at the nursing station and one standing in the hall. "Francis Coben," the BOP guy said at the nursing station. "Which room?"

"Two twelve," she answered with a curious look at Reed and Ellery.

Their little band traveled down the beige hall, dodging a laundry cart along the way. When they reached 212, Reed turned the handle. "It's locked. Why is it locked?" He jiggled it harder.

The BOP guy drew his gun and hollered back toward the nurses' station. "We need this door open. Now!" The woman they'd talked to came jogging down the hall with a set of keys.

"It's not supposed to be," she murmured as she slid an electronic key inside the lock.

"Look out," Reed said, brushing her out of the way. He pushed in first and sucked a breath at the bracing gust of cold on the other side. On the ground, naked, with tubing ringed around his neck, lay a dead guard. On the bed sat a cell phone that had been attached to the heart monitor, mimicking a normal rhythm. An IV needle dangled from the pole and a rumpled hospital gown lay discarded on the floor. The top sheet of the bed had been stripped, tied to a chair, and dangled out the open window.

Coben was gone.

20

For Ellery, the moment telescoped to the feel of the cold on her face and the sight of the open window, the white sheet from his escape flapping in the wind. She could still smell him in the room, his body fluids and dried skin cells, and she reacted with a dry heave, as if to expel even the atoms of him from her body. She heard shouts around her but couldn't make out any words. *He's out. He's out.* Her brain had rehearsed this scenario a thousand times in her dreams but she always woke up before he grabbed her. Alarms sounded throughout the hospital. Boots tromped in the hall. Outside, the helicopters mobilized like a swarm of hornets, rising into the sky. The place was going into lockdown. She gasped in fear as Reed took hold of her arm and he let go as if burned.

"We have to get you out of here," he said.

"Why?" She gestured at the gaping window. "This is the one place we know he isn't."

"He's wearing BOP gear and right now he could be anywhere. Come on." He took her arm again as they wove through the rising tide of prison cops filling up the hallway. He kept trying doors until he hit upon a small conference room with a table, six padded chairs, and a white board tacked to the far wall. No windows. Only one way in or out. He yanked her inside with him and locked the door behind them. "Get me Helen Fields," he said, already working the phone.

Ellery hugged herself as she looked around. The place was bigger than a closet, but with the towering bookshelves lined with medical journals and the crowded conference table, it didn't allow for free movement. Heat poured in from an overhead vent and she started to sweat. A beady, blank eye of a video camera stared down at her from the corner. "This place has security cameras," she said to Reed as he waited on hold. "We should pull the footage."

"Already on it."

She spun in a circle, frustrated. Of course. This was his turf, his show, hunting the animal. "I can't hide in here forever."

"He's still sick. The entire world knows what he looks like. Hopefully, we recapture him before he gets very far."

"And if we don't?"

He had no answer for her. His silence hung in the air for a few moments until his boss came on the line. Ellery turned her back to him and stared at the spines on the medical journals. Listening to him discuss her as though she weren't in the room was like being peeled alive. *Safehouse,* he suggested to his boss, like Ellery was the one who needed to be caged. *Protective custody.* Coben was free and she would be the one in jail.

"Helen is on her way over here," Reed said as he hung up the phone.

"Great, she can join the pointless party we've got going on." Coben might want to come for her, but he wasn't stupid. He'd be trying to get as far away from the hospital as possible right now and then lie low.

A sharp rap on the door made her jump. Reed held up a finger, ordering silence, and he went to the door. "Yes?"

"Agent Markham? It's Darren Michaud, SAC Indianapolis."

Reed cracked the door wide enough to examine their visitor and his credentials. He let the man inside. Michaud reminded her of a crane—white, tall, and thin, with angular features and a hunch in his shoulders that suggested a lifetime of fitting into spaces too small for him. He gave her an awkward nod as he produced a laptop. "I thought you would like to see the security footage from the hospital. You might be able to help us with an ID."

"I think we all know who escaped," Ellery said.

"Yes, but he wasn't alone. Just watch."

They gathered around the computer and he let the footage play.

"This is the rear parking lot. They have cameras at the back entrance. Nothing that looks at the building itself so you won't see him dropping down out of the window. But check this part." He stopped it and pointed to the left of the screen, where a figure appeared on foot. He had his back to the camera, walking away from it, but they could see he had dark hair and wore a BOP uniform. "This was four hours ago," Michaud said.

They continued watching as a black four-door sedan pulled up in the parking lot and the man got inside. The camera was too far away to catch anyone's faces or any plate on the car. "Any other camera angles?" Reed asked.

"We got the driver exiting. The passenger has put on a ballcap and pulled it down over his face." He clicked to the next video, which showed a woman leaving in a red SUV. She paused at the automated teller to pay her parking fee. When she pulled through, the same dark sedan appeared and the driver stuck out his arm to feed the machine his parking ticket. Michaud paused the video as it glimpsed the driver's face.

"That's Tommy Herndon," Ellery said.

"We found his sister, Hope, murdered and abandoned at Coben's farm," added Reed. "There's already a BOLO out on Tommy."

"The plates have been obscured," Michaud said. "But we can release details on the car. It's a Nissan Versa." He glanced at Ellery. "We've got everyone on this. It's our number-one priority and we won't quit until we get him."

She put a hand on her hip. "No offense, but the last time he killed at least seventeen girls before that happened."

"Ellery's right," Reed said, his voice like velvet-wrapped steel. "He'd like to get to her, yes, but he'll take advantage of the first warm target he can find."

"We're setting up checkpoints throughout the city. We've alerted bus depots, train stations, airports. But we need your help on this. You're the expert on Francis Coben. You tell us where we should look for him."

Reed's gaze flickered to the screen, where Tommy Herndon's face remained frozen at the moment of escape. "We know he had help, probably beyond Tommy Herndon, but Tommy is your weak point right now. Coben is a criminal mastermind. Tommy is a low-rent goon who probably relished the chance to infect a bunch of people in the prison with *E. coli*. He doesn't know what he's unleashed and he won't be as smart or as careful as Coben is."

"Meaning Coben will ditch him at the first opportunity," Ellery said as she caught on to Reed's point.

"We have to hope Herndon does something stupid to give away their location before that happens," replied Michaud. "We'll pull his electronic records and cell phone data, and see what turns up. Do you think Herndon killed his sister and put her on the farm?"

"He might have, if she somehow got in the way of the plan," Reed said.

"Then he should be considered as dangerous as Coben."

Reed ran a hand through his hair. "The most dangerous person or persons are the ones involved but we don't know about yet. Meanwhile, I suggest you take Coben at his word. His priority is finishing what he started with Ellery, and he's likely to be looking for her at locations where he thinks he might find her. This would include the hotel, obviously, so she can't go back there."

"My mother," Ellery blurted with sudden horror. "He knows where she lives." It made a terrible kind of sense that he'd look for her there, the place where he'd found her before.

"Where is that?" Michaud asked as he pulled out his phone. "We'll get people to her immediately."

"Chicago." Ellery took out her own phone. "I have to warn her." The line rang through to her mother's answering machine at home, and Ellery realized she would be at work. She tried the law office and exhaled with relief when her mother's voice came on the line. "Ma," she said. "It's me. You need to listen, okay?"

"Ellie. You caught me just as I'm packing up to leave for the day. Can I call you back from home? I don't want to miss my train."

"No, Ma. Stay there. We're going to send someone to get you."

"Get me? What on earth are you talking about?"

"He's out." She closed her eyes as she said the words. "Coben. He's escaped and we don't know where he is right now."

"What?" Her mother stopped moving around. "How is that possible?"

"We're working on that. Listen, you may need protective custody for a while, okay?"

"Protective custody? Does that mean lock me up? I can't. I have work. It's a busy time for the firm and Roger is counting on me to be here." Ellery heard her resume packing her tote bag to go home.

Roger, the head of the firm, had been kind to her mother during the years of Daniel's illness. She'd missed so many days back then, a debt she felt she was still repaying. "I'm sure he'll understand the circumstances, Ma. Just tell him to look at the news."

"It's nonsense. I'll be perfectly safe. He's not going to show up here at a law firm, for heaven's sake. At home, I won't open my door. It will be fine."

"Ma! It's not fine!"

The men turned their heads as Ellery shouted into the phone and she flushed at their silent rebuke. *Don't make noise. Don't make a fuss.* She lowered her voice.

"You can't make this go away by ignoring it," she said to her mother. "Coben is a violent predator. He's not out to keep the peace, you understand me? He's already killed one man and believe me when I tell you he'll come for you too if that's what he wants."

"He doesn't want me," her mother replied reasonably.

"You're right. Okay, you're right." Ellery sagged into the nearest chair, suddenly exhausted. "He wants me, but he may go through you to get it." She was poised to visit tragedy on her family again. She put her head down and hid her face against the smooth tabletop, the phone still pressed against her ear. For several long moments, she heard only the sound of her mother's heightened breathing.

"I hope he tries," Caroline Hathaway said at length. "I bought a gun fifteen years ago and I know how to use it."

"Ma, no," Ellery said, sitting up straight.

"Even if it didn't work," her mother continued steadily, "even if I didn't get him, he should know he could never use me to get you. It's insanity to think so. I would tell him nothing, make no appeals on his behalf. He would have to kill me."

Her mother would die for her but she wouldn't move apartments. She wouldn't board a plane. "That's what I'm trying to tell you," Ellery whispered. "He absolutely would."

Ellery stood behind the curtain in the new hotel room and regarded the darkened scene below her. From her vantage point, she could see a light snow falling, illuminated by the lamps at the front doors and the far-off streetlights. A squad car sat parked near the front. She knew a second one watched the rear entrance for any sign of Coben. She didn't worry that the occupants might nod off during surveillance. Everyone was on alert. Desperate to catch a glimpse of him, eager to play the hero. There would be new movies and maybe a future star to be born.

"You shouldn't stand by the window." Behind her, Reed sat propped up on the bed, working on his laptop, his phone at his side. The TV played a twenty-four-hour news station on mute, showing Coben's picture, footage from his trial, live hits from reporters outside the hospital where he had managed his escape. At one point, they had even interviewed Deanna Phillips, the young actress who had played Ellery in the latest adaptation. The girl looked nothing like her but it hardly mattered. Truth never entered into the story.

"I don't think he can strangle me from up here," Ellery replied to Reed. They had a third-floor suite.

"He has a gun," he reminded her, as if she'd forgotten that Coben took off with Ruben Alvarez's service revolver as well as his uniform.

She turned and shot him a look. "He's not hitting me with a nine-millimeter from this range. Besides, no one can see me from this angle." She returned her attention to the window and saw a figure emerge from the hotel and light up a cigarette. Jack Reeves. "The media team is here too?" she asked Reed. "Ben and Jack and Kate and the rest of them?"

"I heard Michaud wanted them moved. I didn't know they were here." He checked his phone again. "Where the hell is Helen already? She said she'd be here by now."

Jack turned to look up at the building and Ellery shrank back from the window. She regarded her half-eaten sandwich and empty bag of chips. Reed's dinner, a boxed tuna on wheat, sat unopened on the nightstand. Movement on the television caught her attention, and she looked over to see her own face staring back at her. "Reed," she said. "Look." It was the footage from the prison, the piece Ben swore would never air.

Reed glanced up and grabbed the remote. "What the hell?"

"You don't know anything about me," TV Ellery was saying to Coben.

"Oh, I do," he replied with a ghost of a smile. "I know you inside and out."

"Ben said they wouldn't do this," Ellery said. "This wasn't supposed to air."

"I know. I was there." He flipped the channel and there was Coben again. *You're holding back. Tit for tat, Abby.* Reed changed the channel again and found his own face this time, sweating under the bright lights. *And now?* he asked Coben on the television. *What does the beast say to you now?*

Coben took his time with the answer. *I miss you,* he said, and then he blew the camera a kiss.

Reed flipped around some more and found one channel showing Kate Hunter talking to the Trajans out in front of Coben's farm. The chyron at the bottom of the screen read: *Recovered remains may be Tracy Trajan.* "There's who's responsible," Reed said, gesturing at Kate with the remote. "You know it's her. But Helen was supposed to have final authorization on our end. I can't believe she'd go forward without telling me."

"That Helen?" Ellery pointed at the screen, where Reed's boss was being interviewed in a television studio. Her hair and makeup were perfect, her face appropriately serious. *FBI Assistant Director Helen Fields,* the text read.

"Son of a—" Reed swallowed the rest of the epithet as he collapsed back on the pillows. "What the hell does she think she's doing?"

"Francis Coben is a uniquely dangerous brand of predator," she was saying on the screen, "and one that the FBI is uniquely qualified to capture. We led the charge against him seventeen years ago and we have every available agent working on it now. We will find him."

"But do you have any leads?" The male anchor, his dark hair like a helmet, frowned on behalf of America.

"I can't discuss that," Helen answered. "He could be watching."

"Watching us? Now?" The anchor seemed to thrill at the idea.

"We know he's studied media coverage in the past."

"Agent Reed Markham is the one who broke the case years ago and he's been considered the Coben expert ever since. Tell me, is he involved in the current manhunt?"

"Involved?" Helen said. "He's leading the way."

Reed looked like a man who'd been fed to the wolves. "So if we don't get him right away, it's my fault," he said to the screen. "Thanks so much." A knock at the door made Reed mute the television again and get up from the bed. "Stay there," he told Ellery. She held up her hands in surrender. Cautiously, he approached the peephole and took a look. His head fell back as he looked to the ceiling in beseeching fashion.

"Well?" Ellery demanded. "Who is it?"

He opened the door in answer and Helen Fields stalked into the room, dressed in the same cream-colored suit she wore on the screen. She saw the television and halted, apparently rapt at her own appearance. Reed shut the door with authority and the noise jolted Helen from her trance. "I see you hurried right over," he said acidly with a glance at the television. "Right after you went to NBC for a little PR. Priorities, right?"

"If you must know, yes. Have you seen the nightly news these days? When the agency gets coverage, it's usually part of some scandal. This little disaster is all on the BOP, and now we get to mop up the mess. Someone had to do the interview. Like it or not, Reed, we are accountable to the public."

"Yes, the public that wants us to protect them from a madman."

"We're doing that." She looked around the room and then at Ellery. "I see this one even has her own personal security detail. We have dozens of personnel capable of babysitting her here at the hotel. We need you out in the field."

Ellery opened her mouth at the word "babysit" but Reed held up a hand to forestall any protest. "You know Ellery is at heightened risk. We can't be sure what Coben's next move is, but the safe money says he'll make some sort of play for her."

"Actually no." She had her phone out, scrolling through her messages. "Michaud has raised a signal from Tommy Herndon's phone. It's dead or deactivated at the moment but it last pinged in Shelbyville about two hours ago. We're headed there now and I stopped by to see if you wanted to tag along."

"Two hours ago means they could be long gone from there already," Reed replied.

"Perhaps. But Shelbyville PD has a missing persons report that could be of interest. Nineteen-year-old Melanie Doyle was having dinner with her boyfriend at a restaurant when she realized she'd left her cell phone in the car outside. She went out to retrieve it and did not return. As she left her purse inside with the boyfriend, local authorities are treating her disappearance as a possible abduction."

Reed looked to Ellery. "Can I see you a moment?"

She didn't have time to answer before he dragged her into the bathroom and shut the door. "You think it's Coben," she said.

"I think what I've thought since we saw that open window—one way to catch him is to follow the bodies."

"So, go then."

"I don't want to leave you here alone."

Her chin rose. "Then take me with you."

"You know I can't do that." He looked at her with such sympathy that she felt tears well up in her eyes. She blinked them back furiously.

"I'll be fine. Melanie Doyle needs you more than I do."

Still, he hesitated. "Do not leave this room. Do not even open the door unless you're sure it's me standing on the other side."

"Where would I go?" He gave her a meaningful look, and she spread her arms. "All the exits are being watched, right? Even if I tried to go anywhere, I'd have a black-and-white escort on my ass immediately."

"I mean it. This isn't your problem to fix. Don't be a hero."

"No," she shot back. "We all know that's your job."

The jab landed and he drew back. Regret flooded through her.

"I'm sorry," she said. "I don't mean it like that. We're all hoping for a replay, right? You find her before anything bad happens."

He met her gaze and held it. If Coben had Melanie, it was already too late for that. "I'll be in touch," he said as he prepared to leave.

"Wait." In her nightmares, the monster always came for her. She never wondered what might have happened if Coben had come home earlier and found Reed removing the nails from the closet door. They might both be dead. He paused at the door and she stretched out her hand to put a palm to his face. His skin was warm and she felt the underlying promise of tomorrow's beard. "Be careful," she said, her voice thick.

He put his hand over hers and squeezed briefly. Then he was gone.

Ellery went to the window again to try to catch sight of him, but he and Helen must have left through the rear. She was surprised to see Jack Reeves still standing outside in the snow, which was starting to accumulate. He had finished his cigarette and was now talking to someone, a woman in a red knit hat. The woman was smoking and Jack shifted from foot to foot, trying to keep warm as he talked to her. Farah, Ellery realized after a moment. Farah offered him another smoke and he accepted.

Ellery took out her phone and dialed Dorie, who answered before the first ring had completed. "Did they get him?" she asked.

"Not yet."

"Fuck," her partner replied, neatly summing up Ellery's feelings on the subject. "I don't like this. I don't like it at all. How are you feeling?"

"Like a goose on Christmas morning."

Dorie gave an uneasy chuckle. "You're being careful, right? You've got protection?"

"I'm staying with Reed." She fingered the curtain and watched the two figures below. Jack was laughing about something. Probably his own joke, Ellery thought. "Hey, I wanted to ask you if you'd looked into that name I gave you. Jack Reeves?"

"Yeah, hang on a sec." Ellery heard paper shuffling on the other end. "Ah, here we go. I was able to confirm at least three trips to Boston—one last April for a weekend, one in June where he stayed at the Four Seasons for ten days, and one visit two years ago in December for some theater benefit thing at Emerson. I'm not even sure he spent the night that time."

"Any record?"

"Busted in New York twice for possession when he was in his twenties. Nothing since. But I did a little extra research, and did you know he wrote that hit summer flick from five or six years ago, the one about the teenage kids who turn on each other when one of their group ends up murdered?"

"Must have missed that one." Ellery watched as Jack and Farah put out their butts and started inside together.

"The girl in the movie was strangled. Turns out her best friend's boyfriend was the killer."

"Okay. Why do we care?"

"I read a few interviews with Jack Reeves, and according to him, it's based on a true story. A girl at his high school was strangled in her home while the mom was out running errands or something. They never caught the guy who did it."

Jack opened the door for Farah. As she stepped through it, his arm slipped around her.

"Was Jack Reeves dating the girl's best friend?" she asked.

"No." Dorie paused for effect. "He was dating her sister."

21

Reed and Helen caught a helicopter to Shelbyville, and from the air, he could see the swirl of chaos on the ground. Squad cars massed near the restaurant, their red flashing lights like a giant alarm signal. Other units patrolled the surrounding streets with their high beams on. Off the main roads, patchy groups of searchers with flashlights blinked around like fireflies. The helicopter set them down in an empty parking lot half a block from the restaurant and they walked back through the freezing mist to find Michaud running point on the scene.

"What's the latest?" Helen demanded, even as he was on the radio with someone else.

"Copy that," Michaud said into the radio. "Try the next block." He nodded a greeting at Helen and Reed. "Thanks for coming. The shortest update I've got is that we have no sign of the girl. There's no evidence of abduction here at the scene—no blood, no hair, no broken glass. As you can see from the line of people over there, we're still interviewing potential witnesses, but so far, no one saw anything. It's like she walked outside and vanished into thin air."

"What about the boyfriend?" Reed wanted to know.

"Chase Mayfield. He seems like a solid kid, no history of trouble or fighting with Melanie. He and Melanie have been going together for more than a year, and he swears everything was fine between them—it was an ordinary date night. The local chief took him down to the station for a complete interview, but I heard his story personally, and I don't think there's any more to get out of him. He's as turned around as we are by all this. That's his white Ford pickup parked around back. We dusted it for prints before the rain hit, and those are being analyzed now. Who knows, maybe we'll get lucky."

While Helen quizzed Michaud about the possibility of exploiting nearby CCTV cameras, Reed walked to the pickup truck. He peered in the rain-slicked windows and saw a cell phone inside, still plugged into the charger. When he turned around, he noticed the truck had been parked in an opportune slot for an abduction, far from the front of the restaurant and its busy foot traffic. The rear showed a windowless service door and a large green dumpster with a heavy metal lid. He pushed the lid up and stood on tiptoe to peer inside, grateful for the near-freezing temps to keep the worst of the odors at bay. Too dark to see anything.

He heaved the lid back so it was fully open, and it landed with a reverberating crash. "What have you got there?" Helen called to him as he put on protective gloves.

"Nothing yet." He used his cell phone as a flashlight and examined the dumpster's contents. Bags of food waste and broken cardboard boxes. Helen materialized behind him holding an umbrella over her head.

"Reed, what are you doing? The Doyle girl isn't in the dumpster."

A flash of white caught his eye. Something was stuck to the inside front wall of the dumpster. He jumped up and balanced on his stomach so he could reach down far enough to pull the object free. Breathless, he dropped back to his feet and held up his prize. It was a medical bracelet from Mercy General Hospital. FRANCIS M. COBEN, it read.

Helen's eyes widened. "That's it, then. He's here."

Michaud joined them, and he frowned when Reed showed him the latest discovery. "I got the news back on the prints. They're Tommy Herndon's, not Coben's."

"Do you have a picture of Melanie Doyle?" Reed asked him as he bagged the medical bracelet as evidence.

"Her boyfriend gave us a couple." He used his phone to show Reed a picture of a honey-blond woman with brown eyes and a dimpled chin.

Reed shook his head at the picture. "I need something that shows her whole body."

Michaud gave him a funny look, but he swiped around until he found a second picture that showed Melanie with her boyfriend, Chase, taken from the waist up. They were outside somewhere with leafy trees and they had their arms around each other. "This is the best I can do."

Reed took the phone and zoomed in so he could see Melanie's hand where it curved around Chase's torso. She had unblemished skin, long slender fingers, pink-tipped nails, and a dainty wrist. He'd seen a dozen like them before, all severed from their owners and put on display. "Tommy Herndon didn't pick her," Reed said as he returned Michaud's phone. "Coben did."

"Then we have a pretty good idea of what he's doing to her," Helen said with disgust.

"Yes, but also where to look for him." He turned to Michaud. "Where's the nearest farm?"

Shelbyville and its environs did not have the sprawling farms of the Coben family estate, but it had multiple properties that would qualify as a farm, especially to the north of the city. They started with the ones closest to the restaurant where Melanie had disappeared and worked their way northward. Helen and Reed rode with Michaud while he kept in touch with the other teams that had started their search to the south. One by one, the reports came in over the radio: nothing, no movement, no sign of Melanie, Tommy, or Coben.

They circled various properties and looked for any sign of the black Nissan. They got out into the mud to look for tracks. They knocked on doors, where available, to ask the occupants if they had seen or heard anything. Through it all, Reed watched the clock. Six hours missing, then seven. Ellery had lasted three days, but she had been held alive the longest. Coben had murdered most of them within twenty-four hours.

Michaud pulled off the dark road into the parking lot for the latest farm. It was a commercial enterprise with a central building for sales of fruits and vegetables, flowers, soil, pots and tools. There was a large greenhouse visible in back but the store was dark and shut up tight. Helen shone a flashlight at the place as Michaud drove slowly alongside it. "I don't see any broken windows or other signs of forced entry."

"Moving on then," Michaud said, swinging the car around to exit the lot.

"Wait." Reed surged forward from the backseat as a flash of red appeared in their headlights. "Go back."

Michaud reversed the car. "What?"

"Back there by the tree line on the west side of the property. It looks like taillights."

Michaud aimed his lights where Reed pointed, and sure enough, the rear end of a car was visible. The front end seemed to be in a ditch. All three of them exited the vehicle and jogged down the path and through the muck to reach the car, which turned out to be a black Nissan. "This is it," Reed said when he saw the license plate had been obscured. "They've been here." He whipped his head around to look at the building, which sat in total darkness. Behind it, the fields stretched out under a blanket of half-melted snow. Reed could barely make out what was either a large shack or a small barn in the distance.

"I'll radio for backup," Michaud said, starting for their car.

"We can't wait for that." Reed charged up the hill toward the main building. Ellery would have died if he'd delayed his search by hours, maybe even by minutes. He slipped in the slushy mud. The icy rain slashed at his face, soaked his collar, and trickled down his neck. Dimly, he was aware that Helen followed along behind him.

He reached the main doors and found them locked. He shook hard but they did not yield. "Look at that," Helen said, and shone her beam on the pavement near his feet. "Does that look like blood?"

He knelt to examine the dark smear. "Yes." He cast his own light around. "There's another spot over there." They followed the drops around to the side of the building, where a second door appeared. It had been jimmied open and Reed pushed inside. He found himself among a cluster of rakes and shovels. The place smelled like damp cement and fertilizer. He listened but didn't hear anything but the sound of the rain on the roof. Behind him, Helen trained her flashlight beam around the perimeter of the large room. "Oh, God." The beam faltered and he heard her gag.

He flipped his own light up to where hers had been and felt his own stomach recoil. Tommy Herndon's head was affixed to the wall with an axe through his forehead. It hung up and to the right of the large counter where the cash register stood. Reed could not see behind the counter. He transferred his flashlight to his left hand and unholstered his gun with his right. He eased cautiously toward the macabre display, breathing through his mouth, leading with his weapon at the ready. He heard the door swing open and Michaud arrive on the scene but he didn't turn around. He crept closer to the counter. He could smell it now, the blood. Red and wet, it dripped down the wall like one of Tula's old finger paintings.

Reed held his breath and swung his gun to point behind the counter. No Coben. Just the remains of Tommy Herndon. His arms shook as he lowered his weapon. Michaud appeared behind him and gave a low whistle. "I guess Tommy outlived his usefulness," he said.

No, Reed thought, *Coben just didn't want to share.*

Helen joined them. "No sign of Coben or the girl?"

"Unless you want to count this as a sign," Reed replied as he flicked his flashlight beam over Herndon's body. Darlene would have a second child to bury. "Or this." He shone the beam at the wall next to Herndon's head, where different tools hung on hooks. GARDEN SPADE, read one tag. SMALL SHEARS, said the next one. There was one empty hook, and Reed halted the beam so it illuminated the tag: LARGE SHEARS.

Helen's expression said she remembered exactly what Coben used to do with the shears. "We've got to find him," she murmured.

"There's a big shed at the back of the property and I'm going to check it out," said Reed.

"I'll come with you," Michaud volunteered.

"Then I'll stay here with . . . him," Helen replied grimly. She raised her eyes to the front windows as flashing lights signaled the arrival of backup. "The cavalry is here in any case."

Reed didn't stay to greet them. He exited the same way he'd arrived, through the side door, and started down the slippery path toward the back of the fields. His flashlight beam danced along the ground in front of him. "I've got tracks," he said to Michaud. "Shoe prints and what looks like drag marks."

They both picked up speed, running now through the slush. Blood roared in his ears as his brain repeated a single word: *please, please, please.* Cold rain fell into his open mouth. He reached the wooden door and pulled on it. It shuddered but wouldn't open, swollen shut from the cold or the moisture. Michaud joined him and they yanked together until it fell open with such force that they were both momentarily thrown backward. Reed staggered forward. "FBI," he shouted as he breached the threshold. No reply. The barn held a small tractor and stunk like diesel fuel. He shown his light first one way and then the other. Lawn mowers, hoses, sacks of fertilizer.

He heard voices, the sounds of reinforcements arriving. *Come on, come on. Where are you?* He pushed deeper into the barn and his flashlight beam caught on one pale foot. "She's here!" he hollered, his heart seizing. He pushed a sack of soil out of the way with a furious shove and froze when he saw the full picture. Melanie Doyle lay unmoving on the floor, her hands removed. Reed swallowed painfully as he lowered himself to his knees next to her. He touched her neck and found no pulse. Her skin was cold. She'd been dead hours, probably even before he'd started searching for her. "She's gone," he whispered to Michaud, who hung back behind him. "Coben's not here."

Stiffly, Reed got to his feet. He wiped his face with one wet sleeve and put his gun away. He walked past the stricken Michaud and out into the rain, where Helen stood with a half dozen other officers. Her umbrella had vanished and the rain plastered her hair against her face. Her cream suit was muddied up to her knees. "Well?" she said, eyes wide with hope.

Reed shook his head just once. Her expression fell and the men around her looked at the ground. Overhead, the helicopters caught up to them, their bright lights shining down as if searching out a hero on the stage. Reed briefly turned his face up to them, his eyes shut. He did not look at Helen when he spoke to her. "I wonder," he shouted over the din of the blades, "who's going to give this interview?"

22

The call came at 5:11. She'd crashed, somehow, her body at the edge of the mattress like a car that had run out of gas on the side of the road. Wide awake at the first chirp, Ellery nonetheless kept her eyes screwed shut as she gripped the phone. "Did you find her?"

She had her reply in the long beat of silence. "Yes," Reed said at last. "We've recovered Melanie's body . . . and Tommy Herndon's as well. Coben's still in the wind."

She tightened her hold on the phone. "I'm sorry."

She heard his shuddering breath, felt the weight of his defeat. "Her boyfriend had to be taken to the hospital when he got the news. He started clawing at his own face, screaming that it was his fault for letting Melanie go out to the truck by herself."

She opened her eyes and stared at the ceiling. Melanie's boyfriend lived on the other side of tragedy now. He'd probably find another girl someday, get married and have a bunch of kids; maybe he'd grow so old that he could no longer recall what day of the week it had been or what he'd been eating when his girlfriend got up from the table for the last time. But that future wife, whoever she might be, would never go out to the car alone. "What about her hands?" she asked Reed.

Another pause. He cleared his throat. "Not recovered."

She curled into a ball, her scars itching against the sheets. At least Melanie's boyfriend got away clean. He would never have to look at his own body and see Coben.

"There's something else," Reed said, and her stomach knotted up in response.

"What is it?"

"There's a lot of blood here at the scene. Tommy's, obviously, and also Melanie's. They are both type O. But there's also a small patch in the trunk of the Nissan they were driving, and it came back type AB."

"What's Coben?"

"Type A."

"So, then he's got another one."

"We don't know it for sure yet, but we have to proceed as if it's true. We're checking with surrounding towns for any additional missing persons reports. So far, nothing promising, but it's early yet."

"And Coben? How did he escape if you've got the Nissan?"

"The farm where we recovered the car kept a white van on the premises for pickups and deliveries. Not surprisingly, it's missing. We've got alerts out on it and checkpoints set up on the highways."

"You can't stop and search every white van on the road."

"I don't care if I have to back up traffic into Canada—we're stopping the vans."

"What am I supposed to do? I can't just sit in this hotel room."

"For now, yeah, that's exactly what you do."

She sat up, prepared to argue. "Reed, I can take care of myself."

"I just watched them carry out a dead girl with her hands cut off," he replied harshly. "If Coben had his way, she would have been you."

She flung the phone across the bed and held her head in her hands. Maybe it should have been her. Maybe if she had died back then, Reed and the rest of them wouldn't be here now. She felt, in her core, the tension that remained with the original ending, the reason their story got retold a hundred times over.

Reed's voice called to her, tinny and far away, still arguing although she was no longer there to hear it. She took a shuddering breath and crawled across the bed to retrieve her phone. "If it's me he wants, then that's how you get him," she said, cutting Reed off. "String me up a flagpole or something and hide in the bushes until he comes back."

"No," Reed replied immediately. "You are not some bargaining chip. You are not bait. You should be back in Boston living your own life with the hound. You do not owe this man even one more second of your time."

Hot tears burned, unshed, in her eyes. She ached for her distant apartment, for her dog, for her small home in Woodbury and the simple life she'd had before Coben had come crashing back into it three years ago. She'd called up Reed because he was the only one she could think to help her. Now here was another dead girl and they both had to face the limits of his power. "I'm not that special," she confessed to Reed. "There's no reason for me to be here and Melanie not. Nor Tracy or Michelle or any of the others. The only reason I matter right now is because he wants me."

"He doesn't get to have you." His reply was fierce. "You're wrong, you know. You are special. Not because you are better than the others, because they deserved to live, too, but because you are worthy all on your own. It's not your fault you survived. It's not your fault they died. It's his, and he does not get to win." He ground out this last part, desperate and raw.

The tears spilled over at last, hot across her cheeks, and she swiped them away. "It's not your fault either. Don't try to be a hero, Reed. If he can't have me, he'd gladly take you."

"I'm not a hero. I never was. You showed me that."

She bit her lip so hard it bled. The world had pinned a medal on Reed for her rescue and elevated him to fame on the back of her suffering. For years, she'd felt he'd merely stopped her from dying. *You catch these guys and you get to go home,* she had told him, when her home had been forever taken away. But without Reed Markham, she wouldn't have the life she pined for now. "You are," she insisted to him, her voice full of emotion. "I shouldn't have made you doubt it."

She heard silence on the other end, and then a deep, sorrowful sigh. Her heart caught in her chest, confused by his pain. She thought this admission was what he'd always wanted.

"And that's why you ended it," he said. "Right? Because that's where we'll always be with this thing—you on one side, me on the other."

And him, Ellery thought, her gaze going to the window. *Right in the middle.*

Ellery paced the hotel room and checked her phone every ten seconds. As the world awoke and news of Coben's escape continued to filter across the airwaves and newspapers, her texts blew up. Her captain called. Then her dog-sitter. Her sister, Ashley, was positively panicked. "You need to go somewhere he can't find you," she ordered Ellery. "Like Norway or Antarctica."

"Somewhere cold, then," Ellery answered mildly.

"Somewhere safe," Ashley replied with emphasis. "Maybe you could come here? He doesn't know about us, right? You could share my room and I'd bake you chocolate chip cookies. They're not as good as Reed's but they're not bad." She lived with their father and her mother outside of Detroit. Ellery had never visited, mostly because she'd never been asked.

"Ash, that's really sweet of you, but I—"

Her father took over the phone at that point. "You're okay where you are. Right, El?"

Ellery looked around at the tired drapes, the paint-by-numbers art on the wall, and the gray laminate desk. "Yes," she murmured. Then more convincingly, "I'm fine."

"Hey, don't worry about it. They'll catch this psycho soon. The entire world knows what he looks like so he won't get far."

"Dad, he's already killed another girl."

John Hathaway grunted on the other end. Disagreement, maybe. Dismay. He'd run off years before Coben took Ellery and he hadn't come back in the wake of her return. She'd been afraid to ask him how much he'd known then about what had happened to her. She feared she already knew the answer. "You're staying safe, though," he said to her now. "You've got that FBI feller with you? Reed?"

She cast another look at the empty room. "Yes," she said. "He's here."

"Good, good. Like I said, they'll get him. Only a matter of time."

"Give me back to Ashley."

Ashley sounded tearful. "You promise you'll be okay?"

"I pinky swear."

Ashley laughed through her tears. "No one says that anymore."

"Oh, no? Sue me, I'm old. What do they say?"

"Um, maybe 'on life.' Like, you swear on your life?"

Ellery sobered. "Yes," she said. "Like that."

"I'm supposed to come to Boston to look at schools this fall."

"I'll be there," Ellery said. "I promise."

When the texts and calls continued—her mother wanted minute-to-minute updates—she silenced her phone except for Reed's number and flopped on the bed. She didn't want to watch the circus on television, which featured her face as often as not. The only reading material available was Ben Lerner's book, which Reed had left behind. She flipped it open and began reading. His father was an engineer for NASA back in the day. His mother was a movie star for about twenty minutes in the early 1970s. Skiing in Aspen, Broadway in New York City. The family seemed to have a home in every port. Then one summer day in Oregon it all went wrong when little Andy disappeared.

Jack Reeves was barely mentioned in the story, despite the fact that he'd been on the trip. She supposed this made sense for purposes of the memoir since an extra ten-year-old boy didn't seem to factor into the murder. Ben had told her he and Jack were out looking for lava rocks when they'd gotten separated in the woods. Andy had turned up later, murdered in the creek. Ellery sat up when she got to the details of the killing, which she hadn't known before. Andrew Lerner had been beaten over the head with a rock and then placed, unconscious but still breathing, into the creek, where he then drowned. Police found stones in the pockets of his pants and theorized these had been used to weight down the body.

She recalled Coben's description of the beast inside him: *He's always been with me. I don't remember a time when he wasn't there.* The nagging suspicion made her pull out her phone to do some internet snooping into Andy Lerner's death. There were hundreds of hits returned, including photos of the campsite and the Lerner family at the time Andy was killed. She even found one shot that included a scrawny kid with dark hair and glasses in the background. Could this be Jack? None of the searches answered her question about the rocks in Andy's pockets, but she did get the name of the investigating detective, William Moreno. A second search told her he had retired a dozen years ago and she found no current phone number for him. However, there was a listing for Cheryl Moreno, who owned a flower shop in Redmond, Oregon. Ellery started with her.

"Oh, yes, I should know a William Moreno," she said cheerfully when Ellery reached her. "I've been married to him for thirty-seven years."

"That's—that's great. The reason I'm calling is that I'm a police detective from Boston. I was hoping to talk to him about one of his old cases."

"Bill!" The woman didn't cover the phone as she shouted. "There's a lady detective on the phone who wants to speak to you."

Moments later, a gruff voice came on the line. "This is Bill Moreno."

"Detective Moreno, my name is Ellery Hathaway, and I—"

"I know who you are."

She felt herself flush, although he wasn't there to see it.

"You're all over the news right now," he continued with a touch of wonder in his tone. "The governor of Indiana is talking about calling in the National Guard to look for that guy. Coben."

"Yes, I know. But that's not why I'm calling. I'm interested in one of your old cases."

"Yeah? I've got to say I'm almost relieved. I was afraid you were going to say he was headed this way."

"I'm interested in the murder of Andrew Lerner."

"Oh." He sucked in a long breath and then blew it out. "That was a bad one. The worst I ever saw. Worse still that we didn't get the sonofabitch who did it."

"I read that the boy was found with rocks in his pants."

"That's right. A bunch of them shoved in all the pockets. They kept him submerged in the water so he never had a chance, the poor guy."

"Do you remember what kind of rocks they were? Or maybe you took photos?"

"Don't need any photos. Don't need any notes of any kind to remember that day. I can tell you for sure: they were dark and full of holes. Around here, we call them lava rocks."

Ellery watched out the window for the moment Jack Reeves stepped outside for a smoke break. Then she cracked the door to her room and peered down the hall to where the armed guard stood by the elevator. The bell dinged, grabbing his attention, and Ellery darted out from her room and to the stairwell that led to the emergency exits. She took the steps two at a time and arrived at the lobby just in time to see a family with four kids attempting to check into the hotel. The baby was screaming in its mother's arms while two of the older children shoved each other over whose turn it was to wheel their little suitcase. She couldn't have ordered up a better distraction if she'd tried. She approached the harried female clerk who was trying to navigate a conversation with the dad over the frantic yelling of the red-faced baby.

"My key card doesn't work," she said, slapping the piece of plastic on the counter. "I went to the gym and now I'm locked out of my room."

"One moment, ma'am," the woman replied without looking at her. She had the father's credit card in her hand.

"I really need to get in," Ellery insisted. "I'm expecting a call from work any minute now."

"Fine," the clerk said. "I'll get you another key. What's the room number?"

Ellery had traced Jack's return from an earlier nicotine hit. He was on her floor, six doors down. "Three fifteen," she said.

The clerk handed her a new key. Ellery palmed both of them with a thank-you and jogged back to the stairs. The guard at the end of the hall watched her emerge from the stairwell with interest, narrowing his eyes at her, and she acknowledged him with a curt nod. She hadn't left hotel property so there was nothing to tattle on to Reed. In reality, he couldn't force her to stay as she hadn't broken any laws. She was cooped up here voluntarily. She walked to Jack's room with authority, like it was her own, where she opened the door and slipped inside.

The place was tidy, mostly. The bed was made but the comforter had a Jack-shaped dent in it. The TV played on mute, tuned to a news channel that showed the scene in Shelbyville. Squad cars were stacked two deep outside of what looked like a farm stand. Jack had apparently been working on something before he went outside to smoke. His laptop sat open on the desk, the screen dark, and he had several folders spread nearby. A half-open bottle of whiskey stood next to a glass tumbler, which was empty with a wet ring around it, indicating it had recently been full. Ellery approached the workstation only to stop short as she discovered the tool standing up alongside the leg of the desk: long-handled garden shears.

With a hard swallow, she forced herself forward for a closer look. She crouched down and inspected the shears. They appeared shiny and new. Sharp. She rose on shaky legs and began riffling through the folders. She found printed pages with marked-up edits handwritten in red. *Michelle had a tattoo on her arm,* someone had written. *He cut it off.* She grabbed the next folder and a bunch of photos slid out, cascading to the floor like a waterfall. Coben's farmhouse. Severed hands. A girl with honey-blond hair sat slumped against the wall of the closet. Her face was obscured by the tangle of hair but Ellery recognized the green shorts. This was her.

Her mouth fell open in horror as she stared at the photo at her feet. The roar in her ears was so loud she didn't hear the lock unclick until it was too late. Jack Reeves stood in the room, his face full of fury. "What the fuck is this?"

She pulled out her gun. "Don't move."

"Don't move? You're the one who broke into my room." He took a step forward and she sighted the gun with the barrel between his eyes.

"I said don't move."

He put up his hands, his eyes glancing to the photos on the floor. "I can explain those. They're for a book I'm writing."

"I don't care what you're doing with them. I care how you got them. They're his pictures. He's the only one who could have taken them."

Jack rubbed his goatee with one hand. "Yeah, you'd be surprised what's out on the internet these days."

"Not these." She knew it in her bones. Pictures of her actual captivity had never surfaced. Reenactments, yes. Artists' renderings. Not the private mementos of the man who'd tortured her. She swallowed back her nausea and kept her weapon trained on Jack. "Coben must have given them to you."

"He doesn't even know I have them."

"That's impossible."

"It's the truth." He shrugged. "When you find him, you can ask him."

"Are you in touch with him? Did you help him escape?"

His eyes widened. "What the hell are you talking about? You think I want him running around killing people? I write this shit for entertainment. I don't want to live it."

"You said you're writing a book. This would make one hell of an advertisement."

He made a noise like he couldn't believe his good fortune. "Fuck yeah. We'll make bank for sure."

"We," she said, her voice hard. "So you are working with him. You have been all along."

He opened his mouth but didn't get a chance to reply before there was a loud knock at the door. Ben's voice called out. "Jack, I know you're in there."

Jack made a sarcastic gesture toward the door. "Are you going to get that, or should I?"

Ellery licked her lips. "Open it," she said. "No sudden moves."

She followed behind him, and when he opened the door, Ben stood there with Farah, Kate's assistant. "Have you seen Kate?" he asked Jack before noticing Ellery standing there with a gun. His hands flew up. "Whoa there."

"Before, I didn't believe the stories about her," Jack told him. "Turns out they're all true. She's a total crackpot."

"Get in here," Ellery told the new arrivals.

"What's going on?" Ben asked, his tone cautious as he eased deeper into the room.

"Your buddy has Coben's private collection of photos—not to mention a pair of garden shears."

Ben peered behind her to glimpse the photos on the floor. "Jack, what the hell?"

"I tried to explain to her that they're for a book I'm writing. A book on Coben." He looked Ben up and down. "No offense, but you were ready to dump this whole project to protect her feelings or some psychobabble shit like that. That's fine for you, maybe, but some of us don't have mommy and daddy's trust fund to fall back on."

"So that means you get to set up a side deal without even discussing it with me?"

"Shut up!" Farah hollered over both of them. "I don't give a fuck about your stupid book or TV show. Kate is missing."

"Missing?" Ellery asked. She'd lowered the gun but not reholstered it. "What do you mean?"

"I have been trying to call her all day. Since yesterday, even. We filed the piece from the local NBC affiliate yesterday afternoon, and she said she had another interview to do before we cut the next piece. She said I should start editing and she'd be back in two hours at the most. That was more than twenty-four hours ago now and I haven't heard from her since. I've texted her. I've emailed and called. No answer. Kate never takes more than a few minutes to get back to me. She's always working. Always."

"I can't raise her either," Ben said. "We tried her room and there was no answer. We came here to find Jack to see if he'd seen Kate recently."

"Don't look at me," he replied. "I haven't seen her since yesterday morning."

A thought occurred to Ellery and she turned to face Jack again. "You said 'we' were working on the book. Kate's the other one involved, isn't she?"

"Nah. She's as psycho as he is in her own way. I'd do all the work and she'd take all the credit."

"Who then?" Ellery demanded.

Jack looked at Ben like he didn't want to say. "Elliot Pritchett," he admitted finally. "Coben's lawyer. I mean, it's obvious, right?" He nodded his chin at the pictures. "Who else would have access to all that shit? He took the Coben case pro bono but he wants to get paid."

"Pritchett," she murmured, turning the possibility over in her mind. It fit. Out of all of them, Pritchett had the most opportunity to coordinate with Coben since their conversations in the prison had been privileged. "And where is he now?"

"Don't know. Haven't talked to him today."

Farah gave a sudden yelp. "That's the interview," she said. "The one Kate left to do yesterday before she disappeared. She was going to see Pritchett."

23

R eed staggered up to the hotel room like a zombie. His face felt cracked with fatigue. His spine ached from standing for six hours and then driving for three. He stood in the hall and regarded the computerized lock on his door like it was a riddle from the Sphinx. How to enter? Eventually, his muzzy brain supplied a picture of the key card, and he felt around in three separate pockets before he located it. The lock clicked open and he dragged himself over the threshold, steeling himself for a hundred questions from Ellery. Instead, he found a rumpled bed, a half dozen empty Coke cans, and no Ellery.

Panic jolted him, an electric current of fear. He had the fresh image of Melanie Doyle's body to remind him that he'd lost this fight more often than he'd won. He grabbed his cell phone and dialed Ellery, then sagged onto the bed when she answered. "Where the hell are you?" he shouted.

The door clicked open. "Right here," she replied into the phone and in front of him both at once.

"You're going to kill me," he said as he fell backward on the mattress. He was still wearing his boots and his overcoat.

"We have a new problem," she said in response.

He'd closed his eyes and couldn't make them open again. He

wasn't prepared for a new problem, not when the first one was still careening across the country with a pair of garden shears. "What is it?" he asked without moving.

"Kate Hunter is missing."

He peeked at her with one eye. "Missing?"

"Well, no one can reach her and she's not in her room. This is highly unusual according to Ben and Farah. The last they knew, Kate was heading to interview Elliot Pritchett. That was yesterday afternoon and no one's spoken to her since."

"She was on TV last night. We all saw it."

"Not live. Farah said they cut that piece yesterday."

He closed his eyes again. He wanted to sleep, to escape into a world where Coben didn't exist and wasn't his problem anymore. The FBI could slot in another profiler to do this job. Some other agent could be the one to play the hunch and beard the dragon in his den. He or she could do the interviews and write the book and have their story told over and over in movies and television specials; Reed would disappear into anonymity, back to an ordinary life.

"Reed?" Her voice had a note of concern in it, maybe even fear. Or perhaps he was projecting because he'd been stone-cold terrified since the moment he'd seen that open window at the hospital. He forced himself to sit up and look at her. Her gray eyes searched him, probing to see if he would help. Those eyes were the only part of her that remained the same since that night he'd found her on Coben's farm. Her hair was darker now, thanks to the chestnut-colored dye she maintained in it. Her body was strong, with a woman's hips, not a girl's. The black turtleneck she wore hid all the scars, but he could reach out and trace every one. She'd called him a hero and he took no joy from the word; he also knew there was no way he could walk away from her.

"Pritchett is probably involved in Coben's escape," he said at length. "Even if he was just a carrier pigeon for someone else's communications. The search of Tommy Herndon's place turned up a cache of letters from Coben that included instructions on how to use the bacteria from Biovix. Coben said a source would be providing the *E. coli*."

"You think Pritchett was the source?"

"Helen thinks so. She has a team drafting a search warrant for Pritchett's home and office now."

"He's not there. Or at least, he was not answering Jack Reeves when he tried to contact him."

"Jack Reeves?"

"They're writing a book together. At least that's what Jack says. Pritchett has not been available to provide any corroboration." She moved to sit next to him on the bed. "We have to find him."

Reed scrubbed his face with both hands and tried to think. Pritchett was fifty-seven, past the violent years in men who tended that way. He had a clean record and his worst sin appeared to be a bit of grandstanding, taking infamous clients and then doing little more than news interviews on their behalf. He'd convinced Coben to join up with the lawsuit filed by several members of death row, arguing that the treatment of inmates there was cruel and inhumane. "My guess is that Kate tipped him off to something in that interview—maybe that the FBI would be paying him a visit—and he's gone underground. As for Kate, if she found a juicy lead, she may be off following it. Every reporter in the country has parachuted in here like they're coming into battle. This was supposed to be her turf. If she thinks she's onto a fresh angle, she wouldn't want anyone else to get the scoop."

Ellery looked incredulous. "What, you think she's going to try to bust Coben with a microphone and a halo light?"

"Sure." He rolled his head around to look at her through bleary eyes. "And later she'd sell the rights and they'd make a musical about it." He gave her his best jazz hands and she almost smiled.

Ellery checked her phone again and scrolled through her messages. "I should let my mom know I'm still alive." She began texting and Reed shed his coat and shoes. He turned on the TV to see how the day was playing out on the airwaves. With any luck, they would spot Kate doing a live shot from Coben's elementary school. Instead, he found a group of men with automatic rifles being interviewed on a street corner.

"We're not going to wait for the cops or the FBI or whoever this time," the one with the beard was saying. "We're going to take care of Francis Coben ourselves. He won't have to worry about his unfair treatment on death row no more."

"The governor has instituted a nine p.m. curfew," the male reporter said.

"You think Coben punches a clock?" replied the bearded man. "The governor can sit inside his mansion tonight if he likes. We'll go back inside when Coben is strung up and gutted like the animal he is."

Ellery looked up from her phone. "Fabulous," she said, deadpan. "They're more likely to shoot each other or one of the search team looking for Coben."

"All the more reason for us to stay inside this hotel room."

He flipped the channel and found a different "man on the street" interview—this one inside a coffee shop. A middle-aged blond woman with big blue eyes held a mug in her hand as someone pointed a camera at her. "I'm not saying we should let him kill her. I'm just saying she's the one he's after, so maybe use that to get him. Put her on a corner somewhere and hide a bunch of cops in the bushes until he shows up."

"She's a cop," said the reporter's voice from off-screen. "She has her own gun now."

The woman nodded with obvious relief. "There you go. She's not fourteen anymore, right? Let him come for her and see what happens this time."

Reed snapped off the television. Ellery stood staring at it, her phone forgotten in her hands. He rose and took her by the shoulders. "Don't listen to her," he said firmly.

She regarded him. "Do you think it would work? Would he try it?"

"We're not going to find out. Look at all the knuckleheads out on the streets with guns already." He kissed her forehead. "I'm going to take a shower. You want to order a pizza?"

"Sure," she replied, sounding distant. "Whatever you want." Her phone buzzed in her hand and he heard her answer as he went to the bathroom. "Hey, Evan. Yes, I got your messages. Sorry, I haven't been in touch. Yes, I'm fine."

Reed closed the bathroom door and leaned against it, the horrors of the day weighing on him physically. He heard Ellery on the other side and knew he should leave her to her privacy but couldn't help torture himself with her end of the conversation. "No, you can't come get me," she was saying. "I'm okay, really. I've got half a dozen armed guards with me." He heard a pause. "Yes, Reed is here too." He heard another pause. Whatever truth she'd been keeping from Evan, it was all over the news now. "No, not anymore. We broke up last summer . . . I know. I miss you, too."

Enough, he thought, pushing away from the wall. *This is what she wanted. This is what you wanted for her. Let her be happy.* He turned the spray as hot as he could stand it and stepped beneath the rushing water. The hot needles washed over him, taking off the grime and dried sweat. He stood there half catatonic for several long minutes. He had the shampoo in his hand, ready to lather up, when Ellery came crashing into the room. She yanked back the glass, her expression wild-eyed.

"You have to see this."

He grabbed a towel and followed her, naked and dripping, back to the bedroom where the television played. On camera was Kate Hunter, smudged mascara rimming her eyes like a raccoon's, her shiny blond hair now a tangled mess. Duct tape silenced her mouth and she had a bloody wound on the left side of her head.

"It went dead for like thirty seconds and then this came on," Ellery said.

The camera moved again, pushing backward. Coben appeared in front of it, smiling. "I think it looks good, but you're the expert." He turned to where Kate sat tied to her chair. "What do you think?"

"Where is this coming from?" Reed asked, like Ellery would know the answer.

"It's not a TV studio. That's a living room. See the fireplace behind her?"

"Now then," Coben said on the screen. "We finally have time for that interview you promised me." He'd combed his hair and slicked it back, putting on a white collared shirt. He was pale, probably from his battle with the bacteria, but he seemed at home and in total control of the scene. He stood over Kate and leaned down so their faces were inches apart. "If I take the tape off, you won't start screaming again, will you?" He paused to glance at the camera. "Think of your fans. They believe you're a professional."

Kate shook her head slightly, her eyes round with fear.

"Good. There's no one around to hear it anyway. Just millions of at-home viewers . . . joining us in progress!" He yanked off the tape and Kate gasped from the pain but otherwise did not make a sound. He took the seat opposite her and gave a cheery wave to the camera. "Hello, out there, America! I'm Francis Coben, but you probably guessed that already. You probably even think you know me. Tonight, you'll get the chance. I'm here with renowned legal expert Kate Hunter, who promised me this exclusive interview." He glanced at Kate and then held up a knife in front of his face, squinting at it. "She tried to take it back, but luckily a window opened up and she has free time for me now. Let's get right to it, shall we?"

Reed's phone started ringing. He clutched the towel with one hand and answered it with the other. "Are you seeing this?" Helen demanded on the other end.

"We're watching now."

"We need to meet and figure out how he's doing this. How fast can you make it to the Indiana bureau?"

He glanced at the clock on the nightstand. "Forty-five minutes."

"Great. See you there."

On screen, Kate's voice quavered. "You've had six books written about you now. Three movies, and more than a dozen television specials. What's something about you that America doesn't know?"

Coben leaned back and scratched his chin with the point of the knife. "People think I was motivated by hatred when I chose those girls, but the opposite is true. I loved them. I still do. In another life, I think we could have been very happy together."

24

You're leaving?" Ellery said as Reed yanked on his clothes.

"We finally have a lead," he replied. "This guy's in someone's living room right now broadcasting his location for everyone to see. My guess? A summer home or a hunting lodge—somewhere not typically in use at the moment. But someone viewing may recognize it."

"I'm coming with you." She grabbed her coat.

"No."

"Reed, I can't stay in this room anymore, doing nothing. He's on live TV right now. It's not like he's lurking in the bushes outside, waiting to jump me. Like the woman said—I'm not fourteen. I'm armed, and so are you. There's no good reason why I shouldn't be there."

". . . Ellery Hathaway." At the sound of her name, they both turned to look at the TV. "You asked for her to visit you on death row and she complied. Why did you want to see her? Why do you think she came?"

Coben leaned in close to Kate. "Abby and I have unfinished business. They've told me all these years that she changed her name and ran away from me, that she thinks of me as a monster. I knew when I saw her I would know the truth." He reached out and dragged an empty chair forward so that it sat between them. "Soon we'll be to-gether again."

Reed shrugged into his overcoat. "That's why," he said. "Stay put. Don't answer the door. I'll call as soon as I know anything."

The door slammed with his hasty departure, making her jump. On screen, tears rolled down Kate's face and she said the words Co-ben must have heard a thousand times. "Please," she begged, "just let me go."

The broadcast turned to a test pattern and Coben disappeared. Kate's plea still hovered in the room, unanswered. *Just let me go.* At fourteen, Ellery had no choice but to lie on the closet floor and whisper those same words. At thirty-one, she had options and she planned to use them. She took out her phone and called Ben. "Coben has Kate," she said by way of greeting.

"I know. I caught the end of the show. What the hell are we going to do about it?"

"Where are you?" she asked. "What room?"

"One nineteen. Why?"

"I'm coming down." She took her phone and her gun and did not try to hide this time. The cop at the end of the hall looked surprised to see her when she hit the elevator button. "I'm going down to room one nineteen," she said. "You can come if you like."

He looked uneasy. "I'm not supposed to leave this post."

"Suit yourself," she said as she stepped in the car. At the last sec-ond, he joined her. They rode down and he trailed her to Ben Lerner's room. "This is as far as you go," she said to her escort when Ben answered.

He looked worse than she'd ever seen him. His hair stood on end, his shirttail was untucked. "I keep thinking of what he's doing to her," he said to Ellery as he paced the length of the carpet. He stopped short and looked at her. "I'm sorry, that probably sounds horrible to you. You know what he's doing, right?"

"We can't worry about that right now. Not if we're going to find him."

"Find him?" He looked confused.

"Coben interrupted the network broadcast somehow. How did he do that?"

"I'm not sure. If he has Kate, he may have some of her equipment. But he'd need a satellite to stream that kind of live segment—not to mention the access code."

"Would Kate know the code?"

His eyes widened. "Maybe. It's her old network."

"Okay, so that's how he's doing it. Now, the question is—can we trace him?"

"Uh, if I had access to the network, maybe."

She nodded at the laptop he had out on the desk. "So boot up and let's get him."

"No, not that network. I'd need to go to a station with a satellite link and use their setup." He paused, thinking. "I know the news director of the local access channel, Dan Weber. I could try him."

"Do it." She hesitated. "But don't mention me and don't tell him why you need access to the station."

She waited while he found Weber's number and made the call. He said he needed to cut together a piece on Coben right away and asked if Weber would let him use the station. When he finished, he wiped his palms on his jeans. "Dan said fine. He'll meet us there with the keys." He looked to the window. "I don't have a car here. You want to call an Uber or . . . ?"

"I'll find my own way. What's the address?"

"Uh . . ." He looked around for paper but instead came up with a promotional postcard for his book. He scribbled the address on the back and handed it to her. "You're sure you'll be all right? I don't think you should be out there on your own right now."

"I won't be alone." She was counting on her bodyguard in the hall to give her a ride. "Hey, the place we're going to . . . does it have the same capabilities as Coben's setup?"

"What do you mean?"

"I mean, could I do the same thing he did—make a broadcast."

He eyed her with interest. "Sure. What kind of broadcast are you thinking of?"

"I don't know yet. But if we can't trace him with the satellite link I'm wondering if I could get his attention some other way. I can't literally stand on the corner and wait for him, but maybe I could force him out of his hole somehow. He's had seventeen years to invent this plan, and so far, we're stuck working from his playbook. I just want to surprise him, shake him up a little."

He held up his hands. "Whatever you want. Whatever will bring Kate back alive."

Ellery didn't reply to this. She didn't want to lie. "I'll meet you there in twenty minutes," she said, holding up the card with the address. At the door, she hesitated and turned around. "Don't tell anyone, okay? Not even Jack."

"Jack left," he replied, not looking up from his phone.

"Left?"

"He said he needed a distraction from all this insanity. That usually means a bar." He glanced at her. "You don't need to worry about him. He'll probably come crawling back at closing time."

An uneasy feeling settled over her but she pushed it aside. Jack wasn't the priority problem right now. Coben was. "See you over there," she said. She returned to her room to get her jacket, and while there, she committed the address to memory. *All In,* read the title of Ben's book on the postcard. She squared her shoulders and committed to that as well. In the hall, her baby-faced escort, who was probably about twenty-two but looked like a high-schooler playing dress-up, stood up straighter at her return. "You have a car out there?" she asked him.

"Ma'am?"

"I need to run an errand . . ." She looked at his name tag. ". . . Officer Underwood. Do you have a car outside?"

"Ma'am, I'm supposed to be upstairs watching the hallway. Those are my orders."

"Do you know why you're watching that hallway?" She started walking for the rear exit. He hurried to keep up.

"Yes, ma'am. Francis Coben is at large and you may be a target."

"Right. So you see how the hallway isn't the key variable here?"

"Ma'am, you're not supposed to be off the property. . . ."

She pushed through the door and discovered it was snowing again. "Your car is here somewhere?"

He hesitated at the threshold, clearly torn. "If I could just radio my sergeant first . . ."

"No," she said, descending on him. "Are you out of your mind? The last thing you do right now is broadcast my location to everyone." When he still didn't budge, she softened her tone. "You know my story, don't you? How Coben took me off the streets and held me for three days on his farm? Meanwhile, the lead investigators interviewed Coben and let him go. Agent Markham followed his gut and ended up breaking the case."

His jaw worked back and forth. "I know it."

"That's what we're doing here, you and me. We're following a hunch."

Interest flickered in his eyes. "You know where he is?"

"Not yet. But we might have a way to get him. Now are you in or out?"

He considered some more. "Mine's the blue Toyota over there. I gotta warn you, though, it's kind of a wreck."

"I don't care," she said as she followed him through the snow to the car. True to his word, the passenger seat was covered in a bunch of fast-food bags, which he hurried to toss in the back.

"Where are we going?" Underwood asked as the wipers cleared off the powdery snow from the windshield. She gave him the address Ben had written on the postcard. "I know where that is," he told her. "It's a television station."

"That's right."

"You think you're going to find him on TV?"

He's been standing in the hallway all night, she realized. He hadn't seen the Coben Show. "Something like that."

His car fishtailed as they went around the corner and she gripped the side of the door. "Sorry about that. It's icy tonight." He slowed the car to a crawl and she sat forward in her seat, willing him to go faster. It felt like they hit every light in town. "Here we are," he said when they reached the lot for the station. It was a squat brick building that could have been any retail business in America, except for the large satellite dish on the roof. Ben had beaten them to the station, and he stood in the sparse light at the entrance, waving and holding the glass door open for them. The rest of the building was dark.

"What now?" Underwood asked her.

"You stay out here and watch the door. If you see anyone, and I mean anyone, try to get inside, you call my cell immediately. You got it?" She took his phone and programmed in her number.

"That's it?" He seemed disappointed.

"Hey, it's got to be more interesting than the hallway." She stepped out into the falling snow and jogged over to where Ben waited.

"Dan came by and opened the place up for us. He said to lock up behind us when we leave."

"Let's do that right now." She flipped the bolt on the front door. "Can't be too careful, right?"

"The control room is over this way," he said, leading her to a small antechamber with a bunch of screens and electronic equipment. "Let me boot up the computers and we'll see what's what." He flicked a few switches and Ellery wandered out to the studio, which consisted of a black cloth backdrop, a small stage, and two swiveling stools. A boom mic hung down over it, and she saw a rolling rack in the corner with more electronics in it. Various props stood stacked in one corner. Atop a tripod, a large camera trained its huge black eye on the whole scene.

Ben poked his head out of the control room. "Do you still want to do a recording? Because they definitely have the setup for that."

She had considered it on the ride over. Coben had been a creature of habit, almost compulsively so. Every single girl murdered in the same way, in the same place. She bet it was killing him that he couldn't go home again. But the farm was being watched and Coben was too smart to think otherwise. She had to activate those same impulses for him, to become the place he wanted to return to so bad he would damn the consequences. "Coben's an egomaniac," she called out to Ben as she circled the stage. "The first way to get his attention is to insult him. Maybe I'll point out that he's been too chicken to come after me. He made this big show of how 'I'm the one he needs' but then he grabs Melanie Doyle and Kate Hunter. Sounds like all talk, no action to me."

Ben had disappeared into the booth again. "I like it," he yelled out to her. "But what's the goal?"

"Anything to make him stick his head out of his hole and to keep him focused on me and not Kate." Ellery had lived for three days in part because Coben had been decompensating under the stress of appearing normal in public while the search for him had intensified. She wandered back to the control room where Ben studied a readout on the computer. "Any luck?"

"Not so far. I've got a couple other places to check."

She shivered. The heat was off and the room was cold. "Okay. I'm going to hit the bathroom, maybe comb my hair. Don't want to look like a serial killer just because I'm talking to one."

He grinned at her joke but didn't look up from his work. "I'll be right here."

She crossed the studio and went down the hall, where she saw a pair of shadowed offices, a micro-kitchen, and finally, a tiny unisex bathroom. She flicked on the bright bulb and winced as she caught her reflection in the mirror. Sallow skin from lack of food and sleep, lank hair, and dark rings under her eyes. She splashed some water on her face, combed her hair, and applied a coat of ChapStick to her lips. She frowned as she surveyed her handiwork in the mirror. *Still look like death warmed over,* she thought. *Only a serial murderer could love you now.*

She walked back down the shadowed hallway toward the lights in the studio. She noticed that Ben's head had disappeared from the big picture window in the control room, but she caught sight of him sitting on a stool on the stage. *Preparing the camera angles,* she thought as her stomach did a flip. She hated being on camera. "Did you find his satellite?" she called out.

The stool spun around and she realized it wasn't Ben sitting there. It was Coben and he had a gun. "Abby," he said, her name a happy sigh across his lips. "At last."

25

Ellery did what she hadn't been able to do at age fourteen—she ran. She bolted before he could say another word and took off running for the front door. Coben wouldn't want to shoot her. He'd been waiting more than seventeen years for the chance to stuff her back in a closet and slice off her hands, and her survival depended on not giving him that chance. Underwood sat in his car within twenty feet of the door. If she could just get to him, signal him somehow, this would all be over. "Abby!" Coben screamed her name, marching down the hall behind her, but she did not look back.

As if by magic, the front door opened with a swirl of snow and frosty air. Underwood appeared, followed by Ben. Ben! He was alive. She'd assumed he'd been left for dead on the control room floor. But no, he'd escaped and he'd gone for help. "It's him," she gasped, breathless as she ran toward them. "Coben's here. He followed us."

Underwood withdrew his weapon. It was the last thing he did. He gave a pained wheeze and then a gurgle as he collapsed to the floor. The sight was so shocking that it stopped her in her tracks. "What—?"

Ben said nothing, and she saw a knife in his hands, glistening with Underwood's blood. She had just enough time to realize her mistake, to reach for her gun before Coben seized her from behind. He hadn't followed them there. He'd been present the whole time. Ben smiled as Coben's forearm came across her neck, choking the air out of her. He stepped forward and held the knife flat against her face. "Oh," he told her as he slid the blade down her cheek, "it's going to be so good." Coben tightened his hold, dragging her backward and lifting her off her feet as her oxygen-starved brain fogged up and finally went blank.

She awoke to total darkness and the sensation of movement. The trunk of a car, she realized as she recognized the hum of the road beneath her and the smell of the engine. She had tape across her mouth. Her arms were pinned behind her. When she twisted her hands to loosen her bonds, her wrists came up against hard metal bracelets. Underwood's handcuffs. Her legs were tied at the ankle. Her head bumped up against some kind of bag that smelled like gym socks. She stretched her fingertips as far as she could reach, feeling around behind her. They touched a greasy, waxy paper, like the wrapper from a fast-food hamburger. Underwood's car.

They were moving at speed on a highway. She couldn't guess their destination and had no sense of the direction. The firm contact of her hip against the trunk told her that Coben had stripped her of her gun and holster. He'd no doubt taken her cell phone as well. Maybe he was stupid enough to leave it on so it could be traced by GPS but she rather doubted it. She wriggled hard to free her legs but her feet remained bound. All she'd managed to do was scrape up her wrists and set her lungs on fire from the effort. Panting through her nose, she let her head drop down on the hard bottom of the trunk in momentary defeat. He'd been planning this for years, whereas she had no warning and now no resources. She couldn't fight him like this, hog-tied in a trunk full of stale gym clothes and McDonald's wrappers.

The arm trapped beneath her started to go numb and she attempted to twist herself to relieve the pressure. Her fingertips tingled and throbbed. He could shoot her in the head and chop off her hands right here if he wanted, but she would bet he had something more elaborate in mind. This wasn't the fantasy. He'd want her to submit to him like before. The hands were no kind of trophy if they didn't come with the memory of her humiliation. No, he was taking her someplace they could be alone, someplace like his old farmhouse. She had to hope there was some detail he'd overlooked or miscalculated. One small mistake. Seventeen years ago, that mistake had been Reed. Did he even know she was missing now? He'd be furious when he found out she'd left the hotel room. If she lived through this, he might never speak to her again.

She continued her exploration of the coarse fabric covering the trunk. She grazed a paper bag, the rubbery toe of a sneaker, and finally, something small and metal. A paper clip, she realized as she turned it over in her fingers. She tucked it into the fleshy fold of her thumb. One small mistake.

26

He sent a text. He'd debated contacting Ellery at all since he had nothing substantive to report. They'd chased down six potential Coben sightings and every one was a dead end, so Reed was driving back to the hotel. When his text went unanswered, he told himself she was sleeping. It was still dark, the traffic sparse. He should let her rest. Five miles passed before he picked up the phone again. He would call and hear her voice, and then he could drive in peace. When he got her voicemail, he frowned at the phone like it was at fault for this unfortunate development. He did not leave a message.

He called again thirty seconds later. Then thirty seconds after that. She might have gone for a soda or even a swim, but his uneasiness grew and would not be ignored. He nudged the needle higher on the speedometer and dialed the police chief who was coordinating the officers protecting the hotel. "Who is watching Ellery's room?" Reed wanted to know.

The man on the other end had been sleeping. He grunted and told Reed to wait a minute while he checked the schedule. "Aaron Underwood. He rotates off in an hour."

"Can you contact him, please? I'd like him to lay eyes on Ellery. She's not answering my calls."

The second grunt suggested the chief wished he hadn't answered Reed's call either. "Sure, I will have dispatch call his radio. Sit tight."

Reed did not sit tight. He edged over the speed limit, scenery hurtling by on either side of him as he waited endless minutes for the chief to come back on the line. This time he sounded concerned. "Underwood is not responding on the radio. We sent another man up to check the hallway. It's clear, but Underwood is nowhere in sight."

Reed pushed the accelerator to the floor. "Check her room. Have them check her room."

"They did," the chief replied. "It's empty."

When Reed arrived at the hotel, he skidded into the icy parking lot and leaped from the SUV as soon as it stopped moving. Squad cars already clogged the access to the main door. He found Michaud on the scene, grim-faced and lacking answers. "We've learned that Underwood's car is gone from the lot. No one saw him leave and no one has seen Ellery either. Security camera footage has his car leaving the premises five hours ago. You can't see who is driving or if there is anyone else in the car, but we're thinking it's possible they left together."

"Where?" Reed demanded. "Where would they go?"

"We're working on that. We've got a BOLO out on his vehicle, a 2012 blue Toyota Camry. We've also contacted the cell provider to see if they can locate Ellery's phone."

"We don't have time to wait for that," Reed said as he stalked inside to the bank of elevators.

Michaud followed him. "If it's any consolation, we don't have any signs that she's in trouble. There's no blood, no evidence of a struggle."

"There wasn't anything last time," Reed replied as he stepped into the elevator car. "Coben took Ellery and her bike and it was half a day before anyone even knew she was missing. Coben is sneaky quick. You drop a glass and somehow he catches it before it hits the floor."

"I've looked at the security recordings myself," Michaud said as they reached Ellery's floor. "There's no sign that Coben has been here."

"Ellery's missing. That's the sign." Reed had his key card out and used it to open the door to their shared room. Even though he knew not to expect her, the emptiness hit him in the gut. Her jacket was missing, he noted. Her gun. This was the first bit of good news because it suggested she'd left under her own power.

He saw her roller bag open but undisturbed. The can of Coke on the bedside table was half-full but room temperature. At the desk, he shuffled through the hotel flyers for various services and local attractions. A postcard caught his attention. It was a promotion for Ben Lerner's book, calling him a *New York Times* bestseller. It showed the cover, his picture, and the different dates and locations for his book tour. At the bottom, in pen, someone had written an address. "What's this?" Reed asked Michaud, holding it up. "What's this place written here at the bottom?"

Michaud punched the address into his phone. "It's a TV studio. Local public access."

Reed tucked the postcard in the pocket of his overcoat. "We need to go there. Now."

Outside, the snow had stopped. The sky was beginning to brighten, reminding him of the passing hours. Michaud took the wheel and Reed tried Ellery's cell phone again. She'd ignored him before when it suited her, but he liked to imagine she'd answer him now. It went straight to voicemail. He clicked off with disgust only to startle when it rang in his hands. "Ellery," he breathed with relief.

"This is Dorie Bennett. I can't reach Ellery."

He let his head loll back in the seat and pinched the bridge of his nose. "No one can. She's been out of communication for hours now."

Dorie let out an epithet that succinctly captured how they were all feeling. "What about Coben?" she asked. "You get a line on him yet?"

"Negative. He's still at large."

"I don't like the feel of this."

"We're following a lead now," Reed told her. "I'll let you know if anything breaks."

"Do that. And if you find Ellery, tell her I've got news for her on Jack Reeves."

The fine hairs on the back of his neck stood up. "What about him?"

"After she told me he might have used local escort services, I passed his picture around to some of the girls I know. One of them recognized him as a client. She says he was in town in early December, which is still weeks removed from Maxine Frazier's murder, but he could have made a return trip."

"I'll relay the news. Thanks."

The mouth of the parking lot had been plowed and was blocked by several inches of hard-packed snow. Michaud had to take a couple of runs at it before the SUV surmounted the barrier and landed in the drift on the other side. The first thing Reed noticed was a lack of other cars in the lot. There was one space where the snow was indented, suggesting a vehicle had been parked there for a period of time, but its tracks had been obscured by the falling snow. The only other nearby car was a black Lexus SUV, parked not in the lot but on the street. Reed got out and sank his boots into the snow. He walked up to the glass front door and found it locked.

"We can get someone down here to open it," Michaud said from behind him as he pulled out his phone.

Reed cupped his hands around his face and peered into the glass, but it was dark inside and he couldn't see much. He took out his flashlight and shone it through the door. "There's a body," he said sharply. "Looks like a male."

Michaud came forward and they both yanked on the door. It held fast.

"Stand back," Reed ordered. He took out his gun and crouched down in the snow, shielding his face with one arm. He aimed the barrel toward the ceiling inside and fired. A shower of glass came back at him. He stood up and used his forearm to push enough of the glass out of the frame so that he could reach around and undo the dead bolt on the other side. The door opened, he rushed the ten feet down the hall to find a uniformed officer lying facedown, a pool of blood at his waist. Reed touched the man's neck and felt for a pulse. "He's alive," he murmured. "Call for help."

Michaud stayed with the fallen cop while Reed inched deeper into the studio. He walked with his back along the wall, his gun at the ready. He felt periodically for a light switch but could not locate one. His heart in his throat, he came around the corner ready to fire. Nothing. He could make out camera equipment, a stage, and stools. He located the light panel and turned on the studio overheads. No Ellery. No Coben. No further signs of a struggle.

He went down the back hall and checked the offices, the kitchen, and the bathroom. All were empty. When he doubled back to the studio, he found Michaud surveying the scene. "Anything?" he asked.

Reed shook his head.

"That's Underwood out in the hall. I checked his ID." He paused. "His gun is missing."

"So is his car." *So is Ellery,* he added silently.

A thump from across the room made Reed jump. He trained his gun in the direction of the noise, which appeared to be coming from the collection of props. "FBI," he called out. "Show yourself."

Another thump, louder this time. He heard a muffled reply and the costume trunk appeared to jump. "Someone's in there," Reed said to Michaud.

Michaud had his weapon ready. "I'll cover you."

Reed holstered his gun and approached with caution. "Who's in there?" he demanded.

The person answered but Reed couldn't make out any words. The voice was deep, male. Reed flicked open the metal catch on the trunk and stepped backward. "Come out now," he ordered.

The lid opened and Ben Lerner sat up, pale and sweaty. "Thank God," he breathed. "I thought I was going to die in there." He emerged on shaky legs. Reed could see a patch of dried blood at his temple.

"What happened?" he asked Ben. "Where's Ellery?"

"You tell me. I was in the control room over there when someone coldcocked me from behind." He winced as he touched the back of his head. "Ellery's not here?"

"No, she's not," Reed said. "We've got you in a trunk and an injured officer out in the hallway." On cue, Michaud left to greet the arriving EMTs.

"Injured?" Ben's face appeared troubled. "What happened to him?"

"I don't know. Shot maybe, or stabbed. He's lost a lot of blood. You really don't know who did this?"

Ben gave a helpless shrug. "Ellery wanted to come to the station to see if we could trace the satellite Coben was using to broadcast his interview. A buddy of mine let us in to use his network. I was working on it while Ellery went to use the bathroom. The cop was outside in the car. I was focused on what I was doing. I didn't hear or see anything until I felt someone whack me from behind. Then I woke up in the trunk. You think . . . you think Coben could have followed us here?"

"I don't know what to think." Reed paced a line in front of the stage. "Did you find Coben's satellite?"

"No," Ben said with disappointment. "I feel terrible. We never should have left the hotel. Ellery thought it would be safe with the cop to accompany us."

Reed walked to the control room. The only indication of a disturbance was a smear of blood on the edge of the desk. Presumably Ben's head had hit it on his way to the ground. "Did you hear anything while you were in the trunk?" he asked Ben.

"Nothing till you guys showed up."

Reed nodded like he'd expected that answer. Privately, he wanted to punch a wall. Instead he kept his voice neutral when he said, "You should get your head looked at. Probably go to the hospital."

"I'm fine." He touched it again lightly. "What's that they always say on TV? It's only a concussion?"

Michaud reappeared with his phone in his hand. "Markham," he said, beckoning Reed closer.

Reed about leaped across the room, his overcoat flapping like a cape behind him. "What is it?"

"There's been a development back at the hotel."

"What kind of development? Is it Ellery?"

"No, not Ellery. Details are sketchy but it involves Jack Reeves. I've got to hang here, but you check it out." He handed Reed his car keys. Reed dodged the pool of blood in the hall as he headed for the door. It was easier to get the SUV out of the lot now that the mound of packed snow at the entrance had been squashed by the arriving ambulance. He raced double time back to the hotel, where he found a young female agent from the Indiana Bureau had Jack Reeves hand-cuffed in the parking lot. His fevered brain couldn't remember her name.

"Brittany Vaughn," she said, and Reed felt every one of his forty-five years. People named Brittany were old enough to be federal agents now. She nodded at Reeves, who stood with his head hung low, reeking of alcohol. "We found this guy passed out in his vehicle in the parking lot right here."

"It's not a crime," Reeves mumbled, shivering in the cold. He did not have a jacket.

"This was on the seat next to him," she said as she held up a nearly empty bottle of whiskey.

"Okay, so Jackie was a very bad boy," Reeves said with a giggle as he swayed on his feet. Then he coughed and dry heaved.

"But the real piece of work is what we found under the driver's seat." She opened a paper bag and used one gloved hand to extract a knife. The blade was covered in blood.

Reed took one look at the knife and charged at Reeves, grabbing him by the front of his shirt. "Where," he shouted, "is Ellery?"

27

They drove for hours. It might have been in circles for all she knew. She'd nearly dislocated her shoulder trying to get the paper clip into her back pocket. The task took multiple attempts, with her wrists repeatedly straining against the metal handcuffs until she shredded her skin and started to bleed. Eventually, the paper clip slipped inside the pocket and she sagged against the floor of the trunk, spent. She may even have fainted because when she opened her eyes they had left the highway. The car moved at a slower speed and they hit an occasional traffic light. The pauses ceased as their journey continued, the road becoming more winding, then bumpy. When the car stopped at last, her whole body tensed in anticipation of his reappearance.

She heard him get out of the car, the crunch of his boots on the hard-packed snow. The trunk popped open and she squinted at the harsh bright light. He leaned in, grinning at her like a kid on Christmas morning. "I trust you had a nice—ah!" He broke off with a horrified yell, recoiling from her. "What the hell have you done?"

She couldn't reply with the tape over her mouth.

"Your hands. They're covered in blood!" He ran off and she seized the moment to try to get out of the trunk. With her hands behind her and her feet bound, it proved impossible. "Stop that!" he hollered when he returned to find her attempting to sit up. "Hold still while I assess the damage." He had a spray bottle of cleanser and a dish towel, which he used to wipe her hands. He surveyed his handiwork and breathed a relieved sigh. "Just the wrists are bleeding. The hands are fine. Don't move."

He disappeared momentarily and she gauged her surroundings. The air smelled cold and fresh. She could see pine trees looming overhead. Coben cut the view when he returned to remove her from the trunk. He tried to lift her and failed. She whimpered when he dropped her and the cuffs bit into her injured wrists. "You're something of a heifer now, aren't you," he told her with an angry frown.

I'm not fourteen, she thought. *And you've gone soft.* He'd always taken young women, most of them slight and easier to overpower.

"You leave me no choice," he said.

She thought he might shoot her right there in the trunk, but he vanished again, only to reappear with a long-handled tool that sent a current of terror down her spine. When he leaned into the car, she saw they were bolt cutters. He snipped the cuffs, and she groaned with relief as complete circulation returned to her hands. He used the cutters to snip the rope around her ankles. "Get out," he said.

Shaky from her confinement, she climbed over the edge and out into the cold. Her legs held her and she surveyed her new surroundings. Dense woods with only a small access road barely visible among them. She heard the call of a distant bird but otherwise the silence stretched for miles. "Turn around and walk." Coben had exchanged the bolt cutters for Underwood's 9mm.

She eyed the gun. If he shot her, at least it would be quick.

He followed her gaze and answered her with a thin smile. "I have many ways of ensuring your cooperation, Abby. Don't get cute with me."

She looked over her shoulder in the direction he wanted her to walk. A wood cabin, reminiscent of his old farmhouse, stood among the drifts of snow. With its broad porch and worn green shutters, it

could have been a hundred years old or more, except for the unusually large satellite dish on its roof. She wondered if this was where
he'd been holding Kate Hunter. Reluctantly, she turned and plunged
into the calf-deep snow, trudging up the hill toward the house. Coben
followed close enough to jab the back of her ribs with the gun barrel.
At the front door, he ordered her to open it and she braced herself for
what she would find on the other side.

Cold. The temperature inside the house wasn't much warmer
than the outside. Her memories of Coben were bound up with a
terrible, unrelenting heat, her tongue swollen in her mouth for lack
of water, that it felt surreal to be with him in this frigid landscape.
He pushed her forward and she stumbled from the front entryway
into a large living area. Right away, she saw Kate Hunter, bound to a
high-backed chair, slumped and motionless. Ellery froze in horror at
the sight and Coben shoved her again. "She's alive," he said. "At least
the last I checked. We need her to complete the interview."

He pushed her past Kate and beyond the kitchen into a shadowed
hallway. As they walked, Ellery looked around frantically for any
kind of clues as to where they were. The cabin had nice furnish-
ings but the decor was impersonal. The artwork on the walls showed
a painting of a brown bear at the river's edge and a fancy lettered
plaque that read, *A house is made with walls. A home is made with
love.* No photos or maps or homemade trinkets.

When they reached the hall closet, he grabbed her and shoved her
inside. "You'll wait here until it's time." He closed the door and she
heard a bolt slide into place on the other side. No way she could defeat that with a paper clip. Alone in the dark, she removed the tape
from her mouth and took several deep breaths. *Stay focused. Keep
calm.* Her skin started crawling even as she coached herself to calm
down. The smell of the wood, the dust, and her own sweat sent her
stomach roiling with nausea. She forced herself to ignore it and explored the narrow space around her. The solid wood panels did not
budge no matter how hard she pushed on them. No errant hangers or
any other contents were available to fashion into a weapon. The door

had no hooks. He'd even removed the bar that normally went across the top to hang the coats.

She fingered the hinges in the darkness, hoping to locate screws, but she found nails instead. The sensation of the hard metal heads against her fingertips sent a fresh wave of fear rippling across her body. She withdrew the paper clip from her pocket and straightened the metal. Coben had guns, rope, tape, and various sharp tools. She had no idea what he planned for his "interview" but her only hope was that he would be so caught up in his fantasy that he failed to notice reality. In the meantime, she braced her spine against the hard wall of the closet and stared at the thin crack of light visible at the base of the door. And she waited.

It felt like hours before she heard his footsteps in the hall. Her rear had gone numb from sitting on the hard floor. The wounds at her wrists throbbed with her uneven heartbeat, reminding her of the pain to come. When Coben stopped on the other side of the door, she slapped on the tape over her mouth and held her breath as he unbolted the door. His shadow fell over her. "I see you've behaved yourself," he said as she squinted up at him. "It's showtime," he declared in a singsong, yanking her from the closet and dragging her back to the living area. The fireplace had a roaring fire in it now. She could smell the wood burning even before she saw it. More heartening, Kate had raised her head and opened her eyes. They grew wider with fear when she saw Ellery.

Coben twisted one arm behind Ellery's back. "Don't make me regret this," he said as he removed the tape across her mouth. She gasped as it pulled free. He released her arm and pushed her at Kate. "Undo her arms. She needs them for the interview."

Ellery walked behind Kate's chair and began tugging at the knots in the nylon rope that held Kate's hands bound. Fear made her fingers clumsy. "Are you okay?" she asked in a low voice. "Did he injure you?" Up close, she could see blue fingermark bruises on Kate's neck. Blood caked to her temple.

"Shut up!" Coben shouted to them from where he fiddled with the camera. It was connected to a laptop, Ellery saw. "No one said you could talk."

Kate shook her head and tried to say something through the duct tape across her mouth. Ellery shushed her. She couldn't understand Kate's grunts and the noise would only set off Coben. "Just play along for now," she murmured near Kate's ear, her eyes on the door across the room. It was maybe twenty steps away.

Coben finished his work with the camera and he waved the gun barrel in Ellery's direction. "You. Sit." He pointed at the chair next to Kate.

Ellery wiped her palms on the rear of her jeans before complying. As she did so, she removed the unbent paper clip from her pocket, which she once again concealed in the folds of her thumb. She might get one chance, and if she failed, both she and Kate would be dead. Shakily, she took the seat next to Kate and Coben picked up the loose rope from the floor near Kate's feet. Kate remained tied around the waist but her hands and feet were now free. "Arms behind you," he told Ellery.

"I thought we needed our hands," she said.

"She does. Not you." He sniffed like an addict. "I have plans for you later."

Ellery complied, inhaling sharply at the pain when the rope made contact with her abraded wrists. Coben wound them together but didn't tie it off. He seemed distracted by his task. He knelt down behind her and she could feel his breath across her fingers. "Such beauty," he murmured to himself. "All mine." His lips met her skin and she tried not to flinch when she felt the wet slide of his tongue along her thumb. *This is it,* she thought. He was crouched awkwardly, licking up and down between her fingers. When he started to suck her thumb, she knew she had him. She jabbed backward toward his eye with the pointed piece of metal. When he cried out in pain and fell off-balance, she rose to her feet and went for the gun. He rolled away and shielded it with his body, still clutching his face with his free hand.

She wouldn't make it as far as the door. He would shoot her if he had to. Kate hopped around with the chair, trying to free herself. Any move Ellery made would leave Kate behind. She considered grabbing the chair and clubbing Coben with it, but he was already rising to his feet. Ellery, closer to the fire, ran for the flames. If there was one part of this fantasy he needed, this was it. She held her hand close to the flames.

Coben's mouth dropped open when he saw her intent and his hand fell away from his face, revealing a bloody, swelling eye. "Don't! Don't you dare!"

"I will." She inched her hand closer to the fire and heat seared her skin. "You'll kill me anyway."

"Get away from there." He swallowed visibly and took a step toward her. "Stop this right now!"

"Let her go." Ellery nodded in the direction of Kate. "Let her go and I'll back off."

He scowled and hunched his shoulders, the gun in his hand. "I should shoot you both."

"Fine. Do it." She shoved her hand into the fire and yanked it back out while Coben gave a soft cry.

"Okay, okay . . . just stop it. Okay? You win." He crossed to Kate and yanked with his free hand at the bindings around her waist until they came free. "You," he told Kate. "You can go. Get out of here."

Ellery kept her hand near the flames as Kate rose, swooned unsteadily, and staggered barefoot for the door. Where would she go? There was only an icy wilderness on the other side. Kate glanced back once, regret on her face, but she kept scrambling for the exit. Coben stalked after her but kept his eyes on Ellery. "Go and good luck," he said with mocking cheer as Kate dragged herself out the front door. "The mountain lions could use some company."

Ellery stood up, blood roaring in her ears. At least Kate was free.

She wouldn't have another body on her conscience. "Thank you," she said to Coben, who still stood near the door.

"I have your cooperation now?"

"Yes."

"Good."

He turned to the open door, sighted the gun, and fired off two shots in the direction Kate had gone. The noise ricocheted through the woods and pierced Ellery's heart. Coben grinned at her. "You didn't think I'd really let her leave, did you? Abby. It's like you don't know me at all."

"I can still burn them," she said, reaching for the fire again.

He shot her. The bullet nicked her shoulder and the force of it knocked her back against the stone fireplace. She fell to the ground and Coben was on her before she had a chance to recover. He pulled her to her feet. "You know what happens to bad girls, Abby. I tried to be nice. I showed you extra consideration because of our special relationship, but you've got no respect. You're trying to ruin everything."

He dragged her back down the hall and shoved her, bleeding and dazed, back into the closet. The bolt slammed shut and she let out an involuntary sob. She slid along the wall to the floor. As she pressed her hand to the searing wound on her shoulder, she knew there was no way she would last three days this time. She'd escaped death in the closet and felt it stalking her ever since, an unpaid debt. The bill had finally come due.

28

'I've told you a hundred times already. I don't know how the knife got in my car. I didn't stab anyone." Jack Reeves slumped over the table in the interrogation room, where Agent Michaud had been grilling him for the better part of two hours now. Reed stood on the outside looking in like a third cousin at the family reunion. He knew that effective interrogation comprised empathy, patience, and repeated questions, but he fantasized about storming in there and shoving the table so hard it pinned Jack against the wall.

"You say you don't remember anything past the Mongoose," Michaud said, naming the bar that Jack had been to the previous night. "Maybe you did go to the TV station."

Jack's reply was essentially a groan. "Man, I don't know what station you're talking about."

Helen materialized at Reed's side. "Anything?" she asked him.

"He's sticking to his story, which is that he somehow drove to the hotel from the bar, with no memory of how he got there, and then passed out in the parking lot. He has no idea where the knife came from."

"We got the tests back on the knife. Blood analysis is consistent with Underwood's. No prints."

"How is he holding up?"

"They sewed him back together but he's in critical condition. The blood loss apparently triggered kidney failure, among other problems." She frowned through the glass at Jack Reeves. "Camera footage from the Mongoose shows Reeves arrived about quarter to nine. There's no corresponding video to show when he left. The bar owner says there's an emergency exit by the restrooms that leads directly to the rear parking lot. The door carries a warning saying that it's alarmed but in truth there is no alarm. We're dusting it for prints to see if Reeves left any, but of course, that tells us nothing about the timing of his departure."

"What about his trips to Boston?" asked Reed. "Have you confirmed anything more there?"

"Hotel charges show the visits we know about, but there is one interesting anomaly. Previous hotel charges also coincide with charges at a bar called The Bukowski Tavern, which seems to be a favorite of his. So we searched the records for expenses run up at the tavern and found a bill for sixty-eight dollars and seventy-three cents on November seventeenth. No other indications that he was in Boston that day."

"Interesting." Reed's phone rang and he grabbed for it with eager hands, hopeful for news on Ellery. The caller was Farah Zardari, Kate's assistant. He almost let it go to voicemail but picked up at the last second. "Agent Markham."

"I know you're questioning Jack Reeves," she said, her speech pressured. "Has he confessed? Do you know where Kate is?"

"Ms. Zardari, I know you're concerned about Kate, but—"

"I have information for you. Something you should see." At his hesitation, she insisted. "It's important and relevant to Jack Reeves's involvement in this case."

He checked his watch. "Okay, I can meet you by the coffee stand in the hotel in twenty minutes. Will that do?"

"Yes, I'll be there."

Helen raised her eyebrows at him as he hung up the phone. "You have somewhere to be?"

"A quick errand. I don't imagine it will amount to much." He failed to see how a millennial production assistant would crack a case that a hundred FBI agents could not, but the passing hours had made him desperate. "I'll be back in under an hour. Call me if anything breaks."

Helen gave him a funny look. "You be sure to do the same."

At the coffee stand, Farah had a grande latte in one hand and a laptop in the other. "Do you want anything?" she asked, looking at the menu mounted on the wall.

"No, I'm fine. What have you got?"

She nodded to a table for two. "Let's sit down." When they sat, she opened her computer and tapped a few keys. "I knew I recognized that stone fireplace in the video that Coben has of Kate. It has a carved wooden mantel with scrollwork on the side and a big painting above it that has a stylized tree with various birds on the branches."

Reed leaned forward, intrigued. "You know this how?"

"The lodge was used as the setting for a teen horror flick seven years ago called *In the Woods*. The movie tanked but my little sister was obsessed with the actress playing the lead, so we watched it like a dozen times." She turned around the computer so he could see the screen. It showed a still capture of a CGI wolfman menacing a pair of teens, the fireplace behind him. "See the scrolls at the corner of the mantel? They're the same ones you can glimpse behind Kate." She brought up a screenshot to prove it to him. "And look here, you can see the edge of the picture frame, and even the orange-and-brown owl on the bottom branch of the painting."

"It does look similar. Where is this house?"

"I don't know. But Jack Reeves does. I checked the credits and he was the writer of the movie."

"We have to figure out where it is," he said, pulling out his phone. "Find the production team." At that moment, he caught sight of Ben Lerner walking through the lobby. "Was Ben involved in the movie?" he asked Farah.

"No, his name's not attached."

Still, Reed thought, the two were best buddies. Ben might know the location. He said a hurried thanks to Farah and chased after Ben, whom he found near the elevators. "Hey, there," Ben said, his expression concerned. He had a bandage on his temple from his earlier run-in with Coben. "I tried to call you but got your voicemail. Any word on Kate or Ellery?"

"Nothing yet. But you may be able to help me. Jack Reeves was the writer on a horror movie a few years ago called *In the Woods*. Do you know it?"

Ben gave a derisive snort and made a face. "A professional embarrassment, I think he called it. Jack likes to pretend it doesn't exist, and I've never seen it. Why?"

"Do you know where it was filmed?"

Ben moved to allow a trio of women to get into the elevator. "In the woods somewhere, like the title says." He considered a moment. "You know, I think it was somewhere in the Shawnee Forest."

"Where is that?" Reed asked as he consulted his phone. "Is it near here?"

"Not that close. It's in Illinois. Maybe three hours away, due south. Why?"

"It's possible that's where Coben is holding the women. We need to find the address of that cabin. Can you help me?"

"Sure, I can make some calls. . . ."

"Great, you can do it from the car." Reed put an arm around him and started marching him to the front doors.

"I don't understand. Where are we going?"

"Shawnee National Forest." Reed was not about to waste time waiting on the specific address when he could already be heading in the right direction. "When you get the address, we'll call for backup."

The sun had already sunk low in the sky, preparing for its early winter bedtime. Reed felt around for his keys in his overcoat and pulled out the promotional postcard for Ben's book he'd taken from the hotel room. Ben noticed. "You read my book?" he asked, pleased.

"I have, yes. But this is the card we found in Ellery's room."

"I know. I gave it to her."

Reed glanced at it before tucking it away as they reached the SUV. *Look again,* his brain told him. He yanked it out once more for a second look. Ben halted on the other side of the car.

"Something wrong?"

Reed stared at the card and tried to figure out why it bothered him. He saw the book tour dates and names of the bookstores like Harvard Book Store and Ballard Booksmith in Boston, Longfellow Books in Maine, The Strand in New York City. He saw Ben's head-shot. The book cover. Nothing strange stood out to him. "No, let's go," he muttered as he returned the card to his pocket.

Ben hesitated a long moment before climbing inside with Reed. "I can't be gone long. I have an important meeting I'm supposed to dial into at six p.m.," he said as Reed started the engine.

"More important than this?"

Ben's mouth snapped shut, his argument dying. "No, of course not. Let me see what I can find out about the location of that movie." He called his personal assistant first and put her on the trail of the address.

For his part, Reed phoned Helen and relayed the question about the filming location for Jack's movie. "See if you can get him to confirm an address," he told Helen. "If he does, get back to me immediately."

Reed drove while Ben made a few more calls. Mostly, he left messages. "I'm running out of contacts here," he told Reed.

"What about the actors? They might know."

"I vaguely know the guy who played the wolfman. We joke around on Twitter sometimes. But I don't think you want me putting this out over social media, right?"

"Right."

The sky darkened like a bruise. City lights faded away. Ben shifted in his seat. "So, my book . . . you didn't say what you thought of it."

Reed glanced away from the road where the headlights provided the only illumination. Benjamin Lerner had a shelf full of Emmy awards, millions of dollars, and a hot new book. If *The New York*

Times signed off on it, why should Reed's opinion matter? "It was interesting," he said eventually. "You've led a fascinating life."

"Maybe not as grand as yours. I've read your book too, you know."

"That's nice." Reed didn't care for book chitchat now. He wanted to find the address of that cabin. "What about the director for the movie? Did you try him or her?"

"The director died of a heart attack a few years back. Might've been the movie that killed him."

Reed tried to recall the other names he'd seen in the movie credits. "Casting director? Best boy? Someone's got to know where this cabin is located."

"Miranda is on it, and she's the best." He turned his head to look at Reed. "I read what wasn't included in your book, too. You were adopted. Your mother was a Latina teenager murdered in Las Vegas when you were a baby."

"That's right." Reed leaned forward to see the road better. Trees had cropped up around them on all sides. It was like driving through a tunnel. "We're going to need that address soon."

"Did you ever feel like you were in the wrong family?" Ben wanted to know.

Reed had a flash of standing on the streamer-draped dais with his three sisters in front of a crowd of Virginian voters, his father the carnival barker, inviting everyone to step right up and take a look. Always, there were whispers about him, the lone boy whose skin color didn't quite match the others. *That one's adopted.* But inside the Markham family home it had not mattered. There, he was just Reed, the baby of the family, the one who mucked for frogs in the creek with Kimmy and who swung on the porch swing with Suzanne. Lynette took them all for ice cream when she'd gotten her driver's license. His parents still had the resulting photo framed, the four kids with their cones sitting in a red convertible. In the pictures, in the stories his family told about themselves, Reed always belonged. "Not at all," he said to Ben. "I couldn't be happier where I ended up."

"Really?" He leaned back against the headrest. "Not me. I was nothing like my folks. My parents were active and outdoors people—always skiing, swimming, biking—but I wanted to stay in my room where I could draw and write. They accused me of always being somewhere else, in my own head, and I guess maybe they were correct on that one. I felt like if I could imagine the future I wanted clearly enough, it would come true."

Reed cast him a speculative look. "I guess it did."

Ben made a noncommittal reply. "Can you pull over? I need to take a leak."

"Can't it wait?"

"Hey, I've been mainlining coffee to stay awake after Coben shoved me in that costume trunk. Then you dragged me on this trip before I could hit the can."

"Okay, fine. Make it quick." Reed could use the break to check his own messages. While Ben got out of the car, Reed did the same. His phone had one bar, barely any signal. He texted Helen. *Anything from Jack?*

The reply came back immediately: *He says he can't remember where they filmed. In a forest somewhere.*

Reed cursed and turned in a circle, his head pointed at the sky. He felt tiny and completely lost under the blanket of brightening stars. He took his phone and looked up the movie *In the Woods* on the internet database. Maybe he could find some names Ben hadn't tried. As the page loaded, he looked up to see Ben heading toward him, waving his phone.

"Good news," he called out. "My assistant found the address."

"Great, let's go." The page froze partway loaded. He could only see the name of the movie, the poster, and the director and the writer. Jack Reeves was the writer. The director was listed as Jean Rennbimler. *I know that name,* Reed thought as he climbed in the car.

"I've got it programmed into my GPS," Ben said as he waved his phone at Reed. "We keep going up this road another seven miles, then turn left."

The wheels of the SUV skidded on a patch of ice as Reed maneuvered back onto the road. *Jean Rennbimler.* That was the name of Maxine Frazier's client, he recalled. The one who was with her before she died.

Thinking of Maxine caused another loose piece to snap into place in his head. Ballard Booksmith, the bookstore listed as one of Ben's Boston tour stops, was the same place that Maxine had purchased her used copy of Reed's book. Had they crossed paths? Maxine had been there in November. Reed made a furtive grab for the promotional card with his left hand and glanced down at it. Ben had been at the bookstore on November seventeenth. "The director who died," he said to Ben as he stuffed the card away. "Did you know him?"

Ben shrugged and stared at his phone. "Not well. He was a bit of a dick, if you want to know the truth. Slow down. We're coming up on the turn."

"His name was Jean?"

Ben's head jerked up and he looked at Reed in the semi-darkness. "That's right. Jean Rennbimler."

"Has he done any other movies? Something I might have seen?"

"I don't know. Does it matter? We have the address. Look, there's the turn."

Reed almost missed the narrow gap between the trees. *Jean Rennbimler.* Reed had always loved the word puzzles that came with the Sunday paper. His mother bought him books to keep him occupied on family trips. Word searches, crosswords, scrambled letters. It got so he could read forward and backward, seeing all possible letter combinations at once. As he drove, he slipped them around like letter tiles in a board game until the name came clear: *Jean Rennbimler* was an anagram for *Benjamin Lerner.*

Reed seized the wheel, his mind whirling at the possibility that Ben could have murdered Maxine Frazier. Ben was also at the station last night when Coben showed up. The two had probably been in contact before, Reed realized, negotiating the TV special. Here was the possible middleman they'd been looking for. If Ben had helped orchestrate Coben's escape and indeed was aiding him now, then he was either leading Reed into a trap or taking him on a wild goose chase. Ellery could be hundreds of miles away.

A buzz from his phone made him jump.

"You okay there, buddy?" Ben gave him a dubious look.

"Fine." The text was from Helen. It contained a link and instructions. *Watch this now.* He tried to make it open but his phone wouldn't load the link. Ben leaned over to observe.

"Want me to try?"

"No." Reed swerved to the side of the road and stopped the car. "It's my turn to use the facilities."

Ben seemed incredulous as he swiveled his head around to look at the dense forest. It was almost like a black curtain around the car. Low-lying fog emanated from the snow around them, cutting off the beams from the headlights. "Here?"

"When you've got to go . . ." Reed leaped from the driver's seat and hurried around the back of the car with his phone. His fingers flew as he texted Helen for help. *With Ben Lerner in Shawnee Forest. He may be working w/Coben. Send backup AS—.*

"Drop the phone."

Reed used his thumb to push send and prayed it would go through. He turned around slowly to find that Ben had produced a gun. "What's going on, Ben?"

"Please. All that Jean Rennbimler crap you were asking about. You obviously know what's going on. Give me credit for my intelligence and I'll do the same for you. Now drop the phone."

Reed did as he requested and his phone fell into a drift of snow. "You want kudos? You've got them. You're extremely intelligent, probably genius-level. You've been hiding who you really are for years now." He took a guess. "Even decades."

"I told you I didn't fit in with my family."

Reed nodded. "Coben. He's your people."

"That's what I've led him to believe, yes." He took a step closer.

"Use your left hand to unholster your weapon. Place it on the ground and kick it over here."

"Coben's been planning all this for a while," Reed observed as he complied with Ben's orders. "My guess is that you have, too. But I'm the monkey wrench, right? You can't have expected this."

An ironic smile twitched at Ben's lips. "Fitting, isn't it? You trying to play the spoiler again, just like old times. But Coben didn't see you coming until it was too late. I'm ahead of the game."

Reed spread his arms. "So, what's the plan, then? Shoot me and leave me by the side of the road like a deer carcass? People know we're together. They're going to ask questions."

"I'll have answers for them. Very believable ones. You see, you got to Coben at the cabin, only this time you weren't able to stage a rescue. He'll be pleased enough to end you and then I'll return the favor. The one who survives gets to write the history, or so they told me in school."

Reed felt a flicker of hope. "So Coben is nearby."

"I told you the address," Ben snarled, not pleased to be questioned. "Now get back in the car."

Reed considered his options. "What if I say no?"

Ben raised the gun. "You're going to the cabin. I don't give a shit if you're still breathing when you get there."

"Okay, I'm going." Reed took a tentative step toward the SUV, stalling for time to think. He could try crashing the vehicle with both of them in it. He could run sideways into the woods and disappear into the pitch-black forest. Ben might shoot him, but with all the trees and lack of light, he'd be liable to miss. Of course, then Reed would be lost in the woods.

The crack of the gun sounded like lightning as a bullet whizzed past him into the trees. "I said move it! We don't have time for this foot-dragging shit. Get in the car or I blow your brains out here in the road."

Reed saw a blur of motion. For a second, he thought it was a bear, or the wolfman from that terrible movie. Someone screamed and Ben fell to the ground. Reed scrambled to find the guns in the darkness, barely registering his rescuer. When his hand closed over his weapon, he rose and shone a light at the figure in the road.

Kate Hunter, sodden, bedraggled, and shivering, stood there with a bloodied log in her hands. "Is he dead?" she asked through ragged breaths. "Because I'd be happy to hit him again."

29

Ben wasn't dead. He lay unmoving but breathing on the cold, wet pavement. Reed ransacked the trunk for something that might secure him and cursed the fact that he had picked today to forgo a tie. He found only a flashlight, road flares, and a spare tire. He picked up the flashlight and aimed it at Kate. "You should get in the car." She looked half frozen to death.

"In . . . a sec . . ." She appeared to be struggling to take off her pants.

"What are you doing?" he asked, fearing madness had set in.

"I have . . . pantyhose," she replied through gritted teeth. "They're torn but should work." Her wet slacks clung to her frozen skin and her hands were red with frostbite, making the maneuver difficult. Reed glanced at his phone to see if his text to Helen had gone through, and he found a sudden burst of messages. *Coben is back on the air. We are tracing the signal and help is coming. Stay where you are and do not confront him.*

"Back on the air?" He went to his browser to see if he could bring up a link.

"Here." Kate staggered forward with a gasp and thrust the pantyhose at him. "I always knew they'd be good for something."

Reed split them in half and used one leg to secure Ben's hands and the other to tie his feet. As an afterthought, he removed the man's shoes and tossed them into the snowy forest. Then he dragged him across the gritty road and shoved him in the back of the car. Kate climbed into the passenger seat and held her hands in front of the heating vents. "Coben tried to kill me," she said as Reed took the seat next to her. "He shot in my direction and I just hit the ground, face-first in the snow. He didn't come to check if I'd been hit. He wanted to get back to Ellery."

"Where is she? Do you know?"

Kate looked vaguely around her. "It's so dark. I've been walking for hours. Maybe if you follow this road?"

The news browser finally finished buffering the video and flickered to life. Coben's face, now with one bloody eye, filled the screen. Kate yelped and clutched at Reed's arm. "Ellery did that to him. She stabbed him right in the eye. You should have seen her."

"Yes, but where is she?" Reed muttered at the screen.

"Here, let me have that. You drive." Kate took his phone, plugged it in, and then hit a few buttons on the dash. The video now played on the screen built into the car's console. Coben smoothed his black hair, which still bore the faint curl that drove all the girls wild. They'd lined up during his trial, eager for a glimpse of him. Reed wondered what they were thinking now. ". . . she's my mistake," he was saying on the screen. "My downfall. I know what the books have said. I know there have been movies. How stupid I was to let that FBI agent follow me. How I didn't kill Abby as quickly as the others because I was distracted. Not so!"

He stepped back from the camera to reveal Ellery tied to a table. Reed screeched to a halt in the middle of the road. "She's alive."

Kate leaned closer to the small screen. "The room didn't look like this when I was there. He didn't have a table."

Coben had run a rope around Ellery's midsection so that it also pinned her arms at her sides. Ellery appeared pale, her forehead sweaty and her eyes glazed as if with fever. Reed saw blood on her neck. "She's hurt," he said tersely as he started the car forward again. "We have to find them."

"I think it's to the left?" Kate's distress rose and she held her head in her hands. "I'm sorry I'm not sure."

"Who's mistaken this time?" Coben demanded, almost gleeful as he leaned down to push his face in Ellery's. "Didn't see this coming, did you?" He turned to admire the camera. "I've seen them, you know. The movies all have the same ending—I get trotted off to prison like a bad boy and the triumphant, swelling music plays. Abby is free. Hallelujah! All praise to the Lord Jesus Almighty and Special Agent Reed Markham!" He raised his arms to the sky and Reed saw he had a butcher knife. He crept in close to the camera again and gave a toothy grin. "Are you watching, Agent Markham? I hope you are. How special do you feel right now?"

"There's a turn!" Kate pointed at a break in the tree line and the car fishtailed as Reed swerved to take it. The terrain grew bumpy and he had to slow down or blow out the suspension.

"The movies don't tell the good parts," Coben was saying. "The makeup is terrible. Hollywood actors will only let you make them so ugly. Let's show them, shall we, Abby? Let's see what you're supposed to look like." He flicked the knifepoint across the buttons on her shirt one by one and then yanked it open. "Can you see it? Here, let me help you." He took the camera from its base and brought it in close to Ellery, who turned her head away.

Reed kept glancing back and forth between the video and the road. Blood. There was so much blood on her. The SUV bumped and jostled its way through the inky woods. "Is this the way?" he asked Kate. "Are we nearly there?"

"I don't know. I don't know!"

Coben zoomed in on Ellery's old scars and the fresh blood across her neck. "Are you getting this, Hollywood? Are you taking good notes?" He put the camera back on its tripod and returned to stand next to Ellery. "It's funny the parts they leave out. What's fit for American consumption and what goes too far. I take the hands, of course.

Everyone knows that." He paused to lean down and place a tender kiss on Ellery's hand. She curled her fingers in response but the ropes were too tight to escape his caress. "But did you know," Coben continued in a conversational tone, "did you know I also cut off the nipples?"

"Oh, my God," Kate said with horror.

"None of the movies talk about that part." He ran the knife blade across Ellery's chest, which heaved in fear. When he raised his gaze to the camera again, his eyes had turned dark and angry. "If you're going to tell the story, make it the truth. Here, I'll show you how it's done. Are you ready, Abby?"

The screen went blank, removing the light from inside the car. A test pattern appeared. "What happened?" Reed shouted. "Where did they go?"

Kate took his phone with shaking hands. "The station stopped broadcasting. Lord knows that's how it works in this country. You can show a woman hacked to pieces but God forbid anyone glimpses a nipple."

"There's nothing down this way," Reed said with frustration. He beat his hand on the wheel. The headlights revealed about eight feet of terrain at a time, all of it the same. A muddy, pockmarked road. Tree trunks and snow. "Where the hell are they?"

"Maybe we were supposed to turn right and not left," Kate said, distracted as she fiddled with his phone.

Reed cursed and turned the car around. In the backseat, Ben groaned as he awakened. Ben, Reed realized with a start. He had the address on his phone. He slammed on the brakes and Ben moaned again as he rolled off the seat.

"What are you doing?" Kate asked.

Reed ignored her. He opened the rear door on the driver's side and felt around in Ben's pockets. "Agent Markham," Ben mumbled. "I didn't know you cared."

Reed located the phone and then held it to various of Ben's fingers until it unlocked. The GPS had the address in its history. He had to hope it was real and not another piece of Ben's bullshit.

"Agent Markham!" Kate yelled from the front seat. "I found another stream. This one is internet-only." Reed climbed back into the driver's side and looked to the screen. The link again took time to load and Reed held his breath, afraid of what he would see when the camera came back online.

30

The knifepoint traced over her ribs, outlining each bone, and then trailed up between her breasts. "Plain cotton," he said with a sniff as he regarded her bra through heavy-lidded eyes. "So disappointing. But, like everything, it's removable." He tickled the center with his knife in a teasing fashion. "Would you like that, America?" He looked to the camera again. "Maybe we should have her take it all off."

Ellery's tongue darted out in nervous response, a timid slide that barely moistened the rough chap covering her lips. Pain radiated from her shoulder where she'd been shot. She felt hazy, her head filled with cotton. It would be easy to close her eyes and drift away.

"You haven't said a word to our audience," he scolded her, and she turned her gaze to the big black eye of the camera. He'd said they were broadcasting all over the country, maybe globally, but she wasn't sure she believed him anymore. Who would want to see this? "Don't you want to say hello to your mother? No last words for Agent Markham?"

She squeezed her eyes shut. She hoped they weren't watching. Not her mother or her sister. Definitely not Reed, who would wear this failure as heavily as he'd borne his earlier success. "You're off-script," she murmured. "I'm out of the closet."

"I'm giving them what they want. What they begged me for." He gestured at the camera with the knife. "We'll do a special just for you, they told me. America needs to hear from you in your own words." He walked to the camera and put his face down to the lens. "Are you listening now?" he screamed at it.

Ellery strained at the rope, steeling herself against the renewed pain from her injured wrists, but the struggle produced no results. Coben had strapped her tight to the table. Her fingers and hands started to go numb. Coben returned to stand over her and admire her helplessness. "If that thing is really on," she said, "the signal goes both ways. They're coming to find you."

He smiled faintly and stroked her hair. "Yes, they're coming to find me. Not you. I like that you've accepted your fate. But they will find you, won't they? Whatever remains. I could prop you up like a snowman outside for Agent Markham when he finally arrives. That would be funny, don't you think?"

"And where will you be?"

"Don't worry about me. I guarantee you I am never going back to that hole." He cupped his free hand to the side of her face like a lover might do and she jerked away. "Still got some spirit, eh? I like that."

He turned back to the camera. "If you're a longtime viewer, you probably know about the garden shears." He set aside the knife and picked up a pair of long-handled shears to illustrate. "They are a historical favorite, but I'm not averse to change. In my recent travels, I've picked up a new tool." He produced a small axe and displayed it for the camera. "I tested it once already and the blade goes through a human skull with amazing speed and precision. I think it will make quick work of the hands as well."

Ellery squirmed. "You'd better hurry then," she called to him.

He whirled around. "I'm in charge here, not you."

"I'm just saying . . . you tied the ropes so tight they are cutting off my circulation. I'm going to end up with gangrene here."

He crossed the room in two strides, his face contorted as he saw her hands were purple and swollen. "Why didn't you speak up sooner?" He set the axe on the table next to her legs and began tugging at the knots that held her to the table. "This is not how it happens," he muttered as he worked.

The ropes loosened and she held back a groan as circulation was restored.

"There," he said with relief, rising again as her hands returned to a normal color. He glanced away from her to retrieve his axe and that was her moment. When he turned his head around once more she drew her leg back and kicked him in the face. *Are you watching, America?*

He fell backward with a shout and she grabbed for the axe. She slid off the table but her legs collapsed out from under her and she dropped to her knees, the axe skittering away from her. Coben lunged for it but she was quicker. "That was very stupid," he growled at her. She swung the axe in his direction and missed. He retreated and she advanced, leading with the blade. He stepped sideways and fumbled behind him for something on the counter.

The knife, she remembered. He was going for the knife.

She threw herself at him to block his path and he knocked her down, the knife clattering to the floor behind him. "Stop it!" His face contorted with rage. The beast was fully in charge now. "You're not getting away, so just stop it right now."

She struggled to her feet, still swinging the axe at him. Her shoulder didn't work properly; she didn't have her usual strength and couldn't raise her arm above her head. She wasn't sure she could do more than wound him even if she managed to land a blow. They circled each other like boxers in the ring. She found the knife with her foot and kicked it away. He rewarded her with a tight smile. "This is harder than I thought. You aren't fourteen anymore, are you, Abby?"

"The last guy who tried this shit, I put him in the ground."

He hummed his approval, got a little bit closer. "My little hellion."

"I am not your anything. I never was." She made one ferocious swing at him. The momentum caused the axe to slip from her hand

and hurtle toward his neck. He jerked from its path and it caught his arm instead, opening up a gash that started gushing blood.

He cursed at her as she turned and ran. She found the front door but he'd nailed it shut while she was in the closet. He'd planned to die here along with her. "There's no way out," he yelled after her. "I told you that." A terrified sob ripped from her lungs and she ran for the stairs. Maybe she could get out through a window, jump down into the snow. He'd probably shoot her like he'd shot Kate but at least she'd have a chance. She heard his footfalls on the stairs behind her but did not look back. She raced into the first room she found, a bedroom, and slammed the door behind her, clicking the lock into place. "Abby!" He banged on the other side as she frantically pulled at the window sash. "It's no use, Abby. Don't you see the nails?"

She noticed them then and bit back a scream. She looked around for something she could use to break the glass, but the room was sparsely furnished, with a twin bed, a stout wooden dresser, and a picture of sailboats on the wall. There was also a closet. With a gulp, she turned the handle and looked inside. It held his cache, which included a rope, duct tape, a hammer and a box of nails . . . and a gun. Her fumbling fingers checked to see if it was loaded and found it had three bullets left in the clip. She tried to remember if he had more than one gun and concluded he probably had.

She jerked around to look at the door. He had stopped yelling. She listened and heard nothing, no noise at all from inside the house. Could he have left? Could he be somehow climbing up the outside of the house even now? She glanced between the window and the door, trying to decide the smartest move. If she jumped from here, she could hurt her legs and then he'd hunt her down for sure. She might also lose the gun in the fall. She crept closer to the door and held her breath to listen for him on the other side. Nothing.

She unlocked the door and cracked it wide enough to see out, all the while bracing herself for the possibility that he would rush in. She saw the shadowed hall and light coming up the stairs. There was no sign of Coben. Cautiously, she eased out of the bedroom and walked with her back to the wall as long as possible before heading for the stairs. Her shoulder left a blood trail behind her like a wounded animal in the woods. She halted again to listen but heard no sound except her own beating heart. Dizzy with fear, she started down the stairs.

At the bottom, she regarded the bar he'd nailed across the front door. She had no way to defeat it quickly. She had to hope there was a second way out in the back. As she came around the stairs into the living area, she found Coben standing there with a gun. He'd changed the camera so that it pointed in her direction. "Hello, Abby," he said. "We didn't finish our program." His left arm was soaked in blood, as was her right. They did, as he'd so often said, look made for each other.

"Tick, tock," he said with a gruesome smile. "America is waiting."

She aimed her gun at him and he raised his as well. "Police," she said unsteadily. "Freeze right there. Put down your weapon."

He laughed, darkly amused. "Oh, Abby. You think I'm afraid? Of you? You're nothing. You think you have a badge now that you're not the same worthless piece of crap left out on the streets at night. Who loves you now, hmm? Agent Markham? He only gives a shit about you because of me."

She fired and hit his right shoulder, causing him to shout and fall to the ground. His gun hit the hardwood floor and went spinning away. "I said freeze," she told him, advancing even as he struggled to his feet.

He panted, clutching his arm. "Go ahead and pull the trigger. You—you've earned it. Abby." He licked his lips and held his arms out to her in beseeching fashion. "Finish it."

Her finger felt the metal pull. So close. She could be rid of him forever. He wouldn't hurt her or anyone else again. "Stop right there. Get down on your knees."

He stumbled another step. "You're going to have to kill me."

"I said stop!"

"One bullet." He jabbed himself in the forehead with one finger, leaving a bloody mark. "Put it right between the eyes. America's still watching you, Abby. Show them who you really are."

Her gaze jerked to the camera and back again. "Go to hell."

"I'll see you there." He screamed in agony and rushed at her. She aimed her gun, narrowed her eyes, and fired.

31

W hat happened?" Reed shouted as he drove down another dark forest road. "Where did she go?"

"I think she shot the camera," Kate said. "I don't know what's happening now. I don't think anyone does." She sat forward in her seat and made an excited noise. "Look up there—that's it! See that light in the distance? Right beyond that huge tree is the house."

He'd seen a million trees by now and they all looked alike. But when the road curved he found the mouth of a driveway and at the end of it, he discovered Underwood's missing Toyota. Inside, the cabin was ablaze with light. *Lit up like Hollywood,* Reed thought as he stopped the car. He saw no movement and heard no sound. Helen's warning came back to him: *Do not confront Coben.* She must not have seen any of the movies. She'd failed to understand this was his life's purpose. "Wait here," he told Kate as he took out his gun.

"No fucking way. Not unless you want to leave that hunk of metal with me."

He didn't want to waste time arguing with her. He walked up to the front of the house and tried to see in the nearest window, but it was blocked off with a dark curtain. He tried the door and found it locked. With Kate trailing him, he tromped through the snow to the back of the house, where he found a second door. This one opened into a kitchen. He put a finger to his lips, silencing Kate. His heart thundered so loud he was sure it would give him away. He walked on the balls of his feet through the kitchen, down a short hall, pausing when he found a large blood smear on the wall. Kate turned green at the sight, a whimper escaping her, and he shushed her again. He advanced deeper into a disheveled living area, which he recognized immediately from the video. "Ellery," he blurted before he could stop himself.

"Here . . ." came the faint reply, and relief flooded through him.

He stumbled around the corner and found her sitting slumped in a chair, two guns in her lap. Francis Michael Coben lay on the floor, bleeding, hog-tied and gagged with a length of duct tape large enough to encircle his whole head. Reed reholstered his gun and stared down at Coben with satisfaction. "Someone made a mistake."

Ellery raised her bloodshot eyes to Reed's. "We were right," she murmured. "He was still expecting Abby."

"Ellery." He crossed to her and crouched down next to her chair to examine her injuries. "Are you okay? Help is coming."

"He wanted me to kill him," she said dully. "He wanted it on television for everyone to see."

"I know. I was watching."

She turned her head away. He'd found the wrong answer. Kate shuddered and hugged herself from where she stood back by the entry to the living room. "You should've blown him away when you had the chance. I would have."

"Let me look at you." Reed found the wound on her shoulder with gentle fingers. It was still oozing blood, and he cast around for anything to staunch the flow. "We need to get an ambulance here as soon as possible." As if on cue, blue lights started flashing outside. The help that Helen had promised was finally arriving.

"Ben Lerner is in on it," Ellery told him as she gritted her teeth under his examination. "He helped plan the escape."

"I know. I have him tied up in my rental car."

She twisted in surprise to look at him and then sucked in a breath as the pain hit her anew. "Good. Let him ride back in the trunk."

Helen and the arriving cavalry trooped in through the rear door, the same as Reed had, and his boss stopped short at the sight of Coben tied up and bleeding on the floor. "I'll be damned," she murmured. "Is this your handiwork, Markham?"

"No, ma'am, he was like that when I got here." He had found an armchair cover and was using it to apply pressure to Ellery's wound. He wished he could wrap his whole self around her. "We need an ambulance. I guess, if you count Coben, we need two of them."

Kate looked to the stone fireplace. "It's a shame that fire went out. Is anyone else c-cold?" Then she dropped to the floor.

Helen took out her phone. "I'll have them bring the whole fleet."

"That hurts," Ellery complained to Reed as she tried to pull away from his makeshift compress.

"I know. I'm sorry." He held tight to her shoulder but cupped the side of her face with his free hand. "Ellery. I'm so grateful you're okay."

"I had one bullet left. I could have done it."

He'd been standing there the night she'd made a different choice. "He would have deserved it."

"I think that was the plan all along. He said he was never going back to prison, but how could he remain free after this? The whole world would be looking for him. Everyone knows his face by now. No, he meant to die in a blaze of glory. He—he didn't want to spend the rest of his years rotting in a government cell while Hollywood told his story. He's the star. He wanted to control his own ending."

She had deprived him of the satisfaction. "I don't know how you fought him off with this shoulder wound."

"I fought him off with everything I have. But, turns out, he's not as strong as I remembered. Seems like prison made him soft." She raised her voice for the last words, leaning forward so Coben could be sure to hear.

"Maybe." He grazed her cheek with his thumb. "Or maybe you're just stronger."

The EMTs appeared with their medical gear, forcing Reed to step aside. "We're going to take you to the hospital now," said a woman with kind brown eyes.

"I'll go with you," Reed said.

Helen appeared, her phone to her ear. "Do I understand correctly that you have a Hollywood mogul tied up with pantyhose in the back of your rental car?"

"He's a murderer."

"Yeah? You're the only one right now who can prove that. As such, you're going to need to come with us to prepare the warrants and file the charges."

"But—"

"Otherwise we have to let him go."

"It's okay." Ellery stopped his protests from where she lay on the stretcher. They had already hooked up an IV. "I can go alone." The words made his heart hurt. She was always alone. She reached out with her untethered arm and touched his hand. "Hey . . . it's over, right?"

His chest tightened from the emotions he was holding back. He felt his eyes water. The crooked smile she gave him as they hauled her away signaled their private in-joke. The story was never over. Already, the cameras would be thronging outside, hungry for the latest chapter. He looked around the room at the bloodstains and ropes and the broken camera with a bullet through its lens. Coben had staged his exit on a literal Hollywood set. But he'd been right that the camera would never give the full story. It acted as a filter. It didn't capture the coppery scent of blood or the acrid traces of gunpowder in the air. It wouldn't show you the clumps of hair on the ground and the duct tape with visible pieces of skin.

Hollywood would be disappointed, Reed sensed, that Ellery hadn't killed Coben. Instead, the last reel would feature Coben in his drab prison jumpsuit, trotted off behind the high cement walls and disappeared from public view, despite a needy audience's pleas for *more, more,* always more. On the wall by the stairs, an insipid painting of a bear in a rowboat had a smattering of blood drops across the white frame. Reed bet it would eventually sell for more than ten thousand dollars.

Michaud arrived to survey the damage with a low whistle. "This looks like a scene out of one of those *Saw* movies. There's a guy back there bagging an axe."

"Coben's always loved his tools."

"I heard Ellery is going to be okay. That's great news." He clapped Reed on the shoulder and gave him a wry smile. "Also heard you don't get to burnish your credentials this time. The girl had to save herself."

Reed nodded without comment. He didn't bother to argue the truth, which was that he'd arrived too late last time. He didn't save Tracy or Michelle or Lauren or any of the others, for that matter. That the truth was Abigail Ellery Hathaway had done everything she could to stay alive long enough for Reed to show up, eking out precious hours through sheer strength of will, but this essential element never made it into any retelling of the Coben story, not even the version Reed had penned years ago. It took knowing Ellery and seeing how she carved out her own space in a world that had decided early on who she was and what her limits would be.

Ellery had always saved herself.

32

Her hospital room overflowed with flowers, like before, but this time the bouquets weren't sent by strangers or religious organizations. Dorie and her wife had somehow managed to find sunflowers in February, and they added a burst of cheer. Ashley had sent her balloons and a teddy bear, with an accompanying note that her bear, B.B., had gotten her through some long nights in the hospital. Her neighbor and pet sitter, Liz, sent freesias and a box of chocolates. Even Reed's sisters had sent a giant display. Behind them in the corner sat Evan's twilight-colored roses, an iridescent shade not found in nature, and she didn't wish to dwell on that symbolism. His card said he looked forward to seeing her when she returned home, and she tried not to think about that part either. Reed hadn't contacted her since the cabin. Since she and Coben had been hauled out of there on separate stretchers. *It's over,* she'd said to Reed. Maybe this time it really was.

Her shoulder ached from where Coben's bullet went through her, another scar for her collection. She had the grim satisfaction now that she'd left similar marks on him. After a blood transfusion, pain-killers, and eight hours of sleep, she had enough fortitude to phone her mother. As usual, her actions rendered Caroline perplexed. "I don't know why you didn't kill him," she said to Ellery. "I'd like to imagine him rotting in the ground."

"You are free to do so," Ellery replied. "I even recommend it."

"Instead the taxpayers shell out hard-earned money to feed and house him. Death row, what a racket! They don't execute them near quick enough. All those girls he carved up and killed, and the second he gets out, he starts after them again. If there was ever a walking argument for summary execution, it's him. I'd have blasted him into next Tuesday. He deserves it."

"It's not about what he deserves. It's about what I do."

"You? You're a hero," her mother said with certainty. "You deserve a parade."

Ellery pulled the sheet over her head at the very idea. "I just want to go home."

"Back to Massachusetts." Her mother sighed. "Always itching to get as far away as possible. I guess I can't blame you for that."

Someone had to be blamed. Chaos came for her mother in the form of a wayward husband, a dead son, and an angry, traumatized daughter. Her father and Danny were both gone, leaving Ellery as the surviving disappointment. *I didn't ask for this,* her mother had cried at her when Ellery had yet again snitched cash from her purse, skipped school, and shown herself around the city à la *Ferris Bueller's Day Off.*

I didn't ask for this either, Ellery had shouted back. It took her another fifteen years before she recognized this argument as common ground. Both of them were living lives they hadn't wanted.

"I should be there with you," her mother fretted. "There are reporters camped out by the entrance to our building, the same as last time. They must be wondering why I'm not with you."

"There are more reporters here. You couldn't get near the place."

"Still," her mother said with regret. "I wish I could take care of you."

The words made Ellery's eyes water, a lump sprung up in her throat. "Yes," she whispered. "I wish that too."

When the orderly brought her supper, Ellery poked at the well of orange mush in the corner and wondered if they were in cahoots with Coben, actively trying to kill her. Food made her think of Reed and she wanted more than anything to call him and hear his voice. But the case was over and they had no formal reason to be in touch. You didn't dump a guy and then mope when he failed to send you flowers. Still, she looked up eagerly every time the door opened.

Instead, it was Kate who visited. She hobbled in on crutches, dressed in red Gucci pajamas and a black satin robe. Ellery glanced down at her own drab hospital scrubs. "Aren't you a fancy banana," she said as Kate maneuvered a rolling chair to her bedside and collapsed into it. "What's with the crutches?"

"I lost two toes to frostbite," Kate declared with disgust. "So much for open sandals."

"Seriously? Wear whatever the hell you want." Ellery popped a grape from the fruit salad into her mouth.

"You mean like you do with your turtlenecks and long sleeves?" Kate replied archly, waving a hand at Ellery.

"I don't have my own TV show."

"No, but you could. Freakin' *France* has a news truck outside, hoping to get a look at you. I bet the Queen of England would take your call right now."

"Yeah, but what would we talk about?" Ellery replied, deadpan. Then she made a show of brightening, even snapping her fingers. "Oh, I know . . . dogs. She has corgis, and they're kind of like brothers from another mother for basset hounds. The long boys have to stick together, you know."

Kate shook her head, bemused. "You get an audience with the Queen and you'd talk about dogs."

"What would you talk to her about?"

"Girl, fashion." Kate flashed a smile. "The important stuff."

"Mmm." Ellery noticed they'd included a carton of chocolate milk on her tray, like she was five. She opened it and drank it down. "And what did you come to talk to me about? We know it's not fashion."

"Oh, I don't know. I just thought—" She faltered when Ellery looked at her dubiously. "There's two of us now. You know, who survived him."

Ellery put down her fork in surprise. She hadn't considered this angle, inured as she'd been to being the only one. Her eyes went to Kate's untouched hands, and Kate twisted them self-consciously in her lap. "I hoped he hadn't hurt you," Ellery murmured.

"He, uh, he assaulted me." Kate's gaze went to the ceiling. She licked her lips and tried again. "He raped me. With—with a hammer."

Ellery shut her eyes briefly. "I'm sorry."

Kate shrugged with an affected distance that Ellery recognized. No big deal. "Some people would say I deserved it," Kate said, a note of challenge in her voice. "They write me hate mail all the time, you know, saying I should be the victim for a change. Then I'd really understand."

"I don't know if you've noticed," Ellery replied seriously, "but there are a lot of idiots out there. Like, tons."

Kate answered with a watery laugh. "Those idiots are my viewers." She sniffed and wiped her eyes with her fingers. "I didn't come here for sympathy. Not from you. I came to say thank you for saving my butt and also to apologize."

"Apologize for what?"

Kate glanced at the window and back again. "The press is stacked ten deep out there. Bookers from the morning shows are blowing up my phone. It's the story of the century and I'm not outside with a camera. I'm in here, in pajamas, eating vanilla pudding and dodging my boyfriend's texts because I have no idea what to say to him. I'm where I always wanted to be, at the center of the story, but I know if I go under the lights and cameras they're going to ask everything."

"Yes." Ellery acknowledged her with a drop of her chin. "It's what you would have done."

"It's what you have to do," Kate said with a sudden fierceness. "If you want to be good at the job."

Ellery considered, thinking how she would approach it from Kate's perspective. "What I envy about your job," she said slowly, "is that you get to shape the story. You get to decide what parts are included. Who gets to talk and who doesn't . . . Which images get shown. You're reporting but you're also framing the story. No one else was in that cabin but us. The rest of the country might be beating down our doors right now, desperate for answers, but they will only ever know what you tell them."

"Or you." Kate gave her a pointed look. "You've never talked. Not once."

"Everyone else said plenty," said Ellery wearily, sinking back against the pillows. "If you're looking to me for some road map on how to live life as Francis Coben's victim, I'm afraid I don't have it for you. But you have the microphone and the camera. You call your own shots."

"I could, maybe. If you help me."

Ellery wrapped her fingers around the blanket's edge, wary now. "What do you mean?"

"Do an interview with me." She leaned forward in an impulsive gesture. "Time and place can be your decision. Content would be one hundred percent up to you. You want a chance to tell your story, your way? I'll give it to you."

"I don't want the camera. That's your thing."

"No, it was his." Kate scooted her chair closer to Ellery. "Coben understood the power of the lens and how to create a point of view. He set up that camera and put us on air tied up, dirty, bleeding. That's what he wanted everyone to see. But he's gone and the camera is ours now. He's where he never wanted to be—out of the picture."

Ellery smoothed the blanket by her hip. "I might be willing to do it," she said slowly, "with two conditions."

"Name them," Kate said swiftly. This was her element, bargaining for exclusives.

"First, the show has to be focused on all the victims, not just me. I get the attention because I lived and that's literally the only reason. I need you to learn all their names. I want a show about what made each of them special. I want—I want the world to understand everything he took away. That it's not just me and it's not just you. Each of these women had friends and family and people who loved them, people who die inside every time someone puts out a T-shirt with Coben's face on it that says 'Lady Killer' or there's an exhibit of his art or a comic book where he's the boogeyman. He gets movies, TV specials, and branded merchandise. What does Tracy Trajan get? Or Lauren McKenzie?"

She was breathing hard by the time she finished. Kate was taking notes on her phone and nodding. "You got it. Relatives with testimonials, baby pictures, talents and ambitions never realized. We'll give it the full treatment. What else?"

Ellery steeled herself. This was the important part. "I don't want him shown at all. Not once. You want to show the prison, fine. But no crime scene photos, no severed hands, no images of him preening in the courtroom like he's starring on *Law & Order*."

The phone sagged in Kate's hands. *Here it comes,* Ellery thought bitterly. *The rationalization why Coben drives ratings and how this country is one big starfucker for men who brutalize women and there's no way to change that, even if it means putting a spotlight on your own rapist.*

"I wish I could never see his face again," Kate whispered finally. "I mean, I'm totally fine with not putting him on the air. Let's do it. If the network wants to fight me, have at it. I've got experience knocking people out with a big log." She tried to smile. "But even if all the coverage stopped tomorrow, even if I somehow go the rest of my life without seeing his face, I'll never forget it. He's stuck inside my head forever and nothing will ever change that."

Ellery met her gaze and held it. "Yes," she said. "You see why I didn't kill him."

Kate's brows dipped in confusion. "Why?"

"Because even if he were dead, I'd still have to think about him the rest of my life. This way, he gets to sit behind a cement wall and think about me the rest of his."

33

Reed rubbed one hand over the stubble on his face. His vision blurred as he looked at the laptop screen, but he figured he'd typed out everything of importance for now. He longed for sleep, for a shower, and for Ellery. For her benefit, he might save her for last. He'd tried to call her at the hospital, but they had refused to put him through to her room and Coben had destroyed her cell phone. The person he'd spoken to at the hospital refused to say if she was a patient there. "I think the media circus in your parking lot rather gives that away," he had replied. "Look, I'm Reed Markham. I'm her—" He'd stopped abruptly when he realized he didn't know how to finish the sentence. "Her friend," he finished lamely.

"The lady seems to have a lot of friends right now," the woman had replied with a trace of humor. "At least twenty-five of them have called in the past hour. If she's as close to you as you say, I'm sure she'll be in touch. Have a nice day."

Helen entered the windowless conference room where he'd shut himself away to finish his work. "How's it going?"

"I'm about done here. Did you serve the warrants on Ben Lerner's properties?"

"Being done as we speak." She pulled out a chair next to him.

"You should know he's got an attorney and he's staging his own press conference. According to him, Coben did it all, including stabbing Aaron Underwood. Ben's just another victim."

"I think Ellery will counteract that narrative."

"We're going to need her. He's persuasive and he's got fifty million dollars behind him—not to mention a lot of powerful friends."

"Well, speaking of his friends, I had another chat with Jack Reeves. He claims total ignorance of any of this, of course, but he did point out that we never asked how they came to meet in the first place. It seems Ben transferred to public school where Jack attended from an expensive private institution in fourth grade, and the reason for the transfer is that someone had taken a live guinea pig in the science lab and placed it on one of the hot plates. The animal's feet were severely burned. A teacher saw Ben in the hallway right after the incident but he flatly denied any involvement. The parents withdrew him from the school rather than endure any further investigation."

"It fits. Sociopathic offenders often start with animals because they are the easiest prey."

"I don't think he stopped there."

She regarded him with mild surprise. "No, of course not. There's the matter of Maxine Frazier at a minimum. He can't pin that one on Coben because Coben was locked up at the time."

"We can't pin it on him either," Reed reminded her. "Not yet, anyway. But I'm thinking earlier. I suspect he may have murdered his brother, Andrew."

Helen drew back. "That was decades ago. He can't have been more than twelve at the time."

"Ten," Reed said softly. "I don't know that we'll ever be able to prove it since it was so long ago. But the boy was weighted down in the creek with lava rocks, the kind Ben said he'd been searching for in the woods. It would also explain how three dozen law enforcement personnel combed those woods and never found evidence of anyone else at the scene." Reed would bet money that Ben would never say a word. He'd already done a television series about the murder, given interviews as the poor grieving brother. This was the real thrill, to accept everyone's tears while knowing he was the cause of them. "Regardless, Ellery should be able to give us Lerner for the attack on Underwood, which is certainly enough to arrest him."

"Maybe. His attorney is already casting doubt on her potential statement. He's saying she's been through such trauma that she's not reliable on the subject of who did what to whom. With the nation having just viewed Coben's horrors in their own living rooms, it's going to be hard to convince anyone that pretty boy Hollywood is the same kind of monster underneath his designer clothes."

"I look forward to making the case," answered Reed as he snapped his laptop shut. "I've emailed you my full report."

"Where are you going?"

"I haven't showered in three days. I need to get out of here."

"Fine," she relented, swiveling her chair. "As long as you're back here by four this afternoon for the press conference."

He stopped packing up his things to stare at her. "Excuse me?"

"We have to tell them something," she said reasonably. "And for once, the news is good. This is a triumph, Markham. The good guys won this round. So go to the hotel, get some rest, and comb your hair. The victory lap starts at four."

"Victory lap? It was your decision to allow the interview that started this nightmare in the first place. I don't think we should be accepting any laurel wreaths for this one."

"Coben is back in a cell and we put him there. The rest of the world got a fresh reminder about why our work is so important. Coben's a known entity, but Ben Lerner has been flying under the radar for years. How many more of them are out there? And who's going to stop them? Some Podunk little police unit like they had in Woodbury? I recall that didn't work out so well for them."

"Nor for us."

"Dammit, Markham."

"You outrank me," he said harshly. "And it was your idea. You give the press conference. I don't have the stomach for it anymore."

Seventeen years ago, he'd been pumped to appear on the big stage. He'd done his first presser with his white shirt still stained down the front with Ellery's blood. The Smithsonian even held one of the original photographs from that distant night. He could picture himself, the sheen of sweat on his brow, his dark hair thicker but trimmed in the government-approved style, standing tall in front of the microphones and pretending like he hadn't been about ready to shit himself with fear only hours before. The intense lights of the cameras had hurt his eyes and when he'd stumbled away half-blind, the director at the time had clapped a hand on Reed's shoulder. *Son, tremendous job. Just tremendous. You've got a bright future here.* Reed hadn't been able to see a thing.

Helen put a hand on him now, her tone turning conciliatory. He looked down at where she touched him but did not pull away. "You'll feel better with some rest," she said. "We're all raw with exhaustion right now. But it can't be so bad, can it, being the poster boy for the greatest law enforcement agency in the world?" She smiled and ducked her head, trying to get him to smile back. "I'd do it myself but they want you, Reed. You're the Batman to Coben's Joker. Show them Gotham City is safe again."

Batman, he thought with some irony. *At least he got to take off the suit at the end of the day.* "You want a comic book? Hire an illustrator. I'm done here." He picked up his bag to leave but she blocked his path.

"It isn't optional. You'll do the conference." Her gaze was even, her words deceptively soft. "Don't pretend you're some naïf and I'm the recruitment officer begging you to join up. As long as there are monsters like Coben or Lerner roaming around, the country needs the FBI. Like it or not, Agent Markham, that's you."

"Not anymore." He glanced beyond her at the door, above which sat a red exit sign he hadn't noticed before. "I quit."

"What?" Helen's mouth fell open. "You can't just do that. Reed, wait a minute here . . ." She called something else as he walked out, but he couldn't have said what it was. He didn't have to listen anymore.

Reed tapped gently on her door before sticking his head inside. Ellery lay curled on her uninjured side and she broke into a broad smile when she saw him. "You came," she said, and the catch in her voice made him feel like a heel for not being there sooner.

"I was buried under a mountain of paperwork. The FBI files everything in triplicate."

"There was a lot to file this time," she agreed as she struggled to sit up.

He rolled up the chair as close to her as it would go and set the paper bag he carried on the bed by her hip. "How are you doing?"

"I'm all right. Still tired, but okay."

"You should be sleeping."

She tucked a lock of hair behind her ear and gave him a wry grin. "The story of my life, right there. 'She should be sleeping.' I just . . . can't."

He would offer to stay with her but he had learned his presence didn't make one bit of difference. The demons that kept her awake didn't come through the doors. "Well, as long as you're awake, you should have this." He took out a plastic food container filled with pasta. It was broad soft noodles with butter, lemon, capers, and two kinds of cheese.

"You cooked? How?" Her eyes grew round and she grabbed for the container with both hands before wincing and drawing back.

"Easy there, soldier. You have to train for that kind of heavy lifting." He fetched her a fork and a napkin from his bag. "I rented an Airbnb," he told her as she took off the lid and inhaled deeply. "I didn't know how long we'd be here."

She speared a forkful of noodles and shoved it in her mouth. "I don't know about you," she said as she chewed, "but I should be able to go home tomorrow."

"Tomorrow." He drew back, momentarily stunned. "That soon? That's . . . it's great." This was always how it ended, he knew, but he'd thought he'd have a few more days to get used to the idea.

Her eyes rolled back in her head as she groaned in pleasure. "How do you take a few ingredients and make something so amazing? When I try it, the pasta comes out all gluey, like kindergarten paste."

"I brought you a soda as well."

She accepted the can of Coke with a smile. "You know what I like."

"Yes, I do." Their eyes held and she set aside the half-eaten food so she could scoot closer to him on the bed. She took his hand.

He squeezed gently and marveled at the warm feel of her. Ellery had beautiful hands.

"I figured I would die this time," she confessed, her head bowed. "I thought about my mom and whether this would be the outcome she'd always expected. She's been mourning me for years now so maybe it would be easier if I were really gone. I thought about Ashley and how angry I was that I wouldn't get to see her grow up. And I thought about you." She raised her head to look at him. "How I ruined your happy ending."

He chuffed a reply and looked away. He'd always kept them separate in his head, the girl he'd rescued and the woman he'd come to love. She was the one who had made him see the folly in this dichotomy. "It's neither happy nor an ending, as you like to remind me."

"Your part is," she insisted, giving him a squeeze. "You stopped him when no else did. You deserve every accolade that comes your way. I'm here and so are all the other women he might have gotten if you hadn't followed him that day."

He let go of her hand and sat back in his chair. "The forensic analysis on the bones we found on Coben's farm has come back. One of the skulls belonged to Tracy Trajan. The others are yet unidentified." It would be someone else's case now, someone else's cause, but he would forever feel the weight of the dead. All the outcomes he could not change.

"At last Tracy gets to come home."

"I have to tell her parents before the media does." He checked his watch. "That means I have about two hours."

She shifted away from him. "What are you doing here, then? Go."

Time was slipping away. He'd said he loved her and she had made clear it wasn't enough. If he had a thousand more hours to sit with her, he couldn't find a better argument. He nodded to himself and took out one of his cards, where he scratched out a number on the back. "I hope to return before you're released, but in case I can't, here's a number where you can reach me."

She took the card and turned it over in her hand, puzzled. "What about your cell?"

"Well, now, that's FBI property, so I expect they're going to want it back."

Her brow wrinkled as she still didn't understand. "Reed?"

"I walked away. Whatever I am from here on out, it won't be the man from the FBI."

Her chin quivered, and for a hot second, he felt regret. Another part of their connection had just come undone. She looked at him with shining eyes. "You're leaving? Just like that?"

"It's time. Hell, it's past time."

She regarded the card in her hands. "Sarit will be thrilled. It's all she's ever wanted."

"Oh, I doubt she'll be throwing me any parades." His exit had come far too late to save his marriage. He hoped it was soon enough to save his future.

"But where will you go?" Ellery persisted. "What will you do now?"

"I don't know yet. I'll let you know when I pick a landing spot." He rose on creaky knees that were shot to hell from years of crouching over crime scenes. He reached out and touched her face. "In the meantime, you always know how to find me."

34

The deep blue of the Atlantic Ocean turned white with ice and snow at the shore, but Ellery welcomed the chilly view as her plane descended into Logan Airport. She had checked her bag because, with a gunshot wound to the shoulder, she couldn't lift the carry-on over her head into storage, and she damned sure wasn't going to ask someone for help and risk a conversation. Her head contained gunfire, her own screams, Coben's threats, and reporters shouting. It took all her energy to make it onto the plane and find her seat.

When the plane landed and she exited the gangway, she discovered Dorie Bennett waiting for her. Her brain would have to find reserves of energy strong enough to convince her partner to take her home and not to a second hospital. She forced a grimace. "I thought they didn't let people through without a ticket."

"Hello to you, too." Dorie probed her with kind eyes, crinkled with concern. "Turns out, the mayor can get you a backstage pass if you ask real nice."

"And did you? Ask real nice?"

"I did," Dorie said as she fell into step beside her. "I also promised you would stop by later to shake his hand. You know, when your bum wing is healed up."

"What a partner."

"Maybe you'll like this better." She pulled a platinum blond wig and a pair of tinted glasses out of her bag. "Here, put these on. The press is circling out there like flies on a turd so you're going to want to stay on the down low."

Ellery stopped walking to stare at the wig. "Wait. Am I the turd in this scenario?"

"Just put them on."

"Okay, I'm doing it," Ellery grumbled, fumbling the wig with one hand. Dorie stepped in to straighten the wig and assessed her handiwork with an affirmative nod. "I'm not sure I'm going to attract less attention looking like I'm cosplaying Marilyn Monroe—and badly, I might add."

"I've seen worse," Dorie said as they started again on the long walk to baggage claim. For a small airport, Logan operated like a labyrinth. The planes seemed to land in Rhode Island and taxi their way to Boston. Then, when you finally disembarked, you walked endlessly through beige hallways to find an exit.

"I have some good news for you. I would have called but I knew you were in the air."

"What's that?"

"I found a sales clerk at Ballard Booksmith named Melissa Jordan who can testify that Maxine Frazier and Ben Lerner were there at the same time. Melissa chatted with Maxine when she paid and remembers her because Melissa is a twin, and her sister is named Maxine. Ben, she remembers because the store was packed. Also, because he slapped her on the ass on his way out."

"Sounds like him."

As they waited for her bag to arrive, Ellery tried not to grind her teeth. The painkillers had worn off in the air and her whole right side had started throbbing. "You sure you're okay?" Dorie asked her. "You're as gray as the floor."

Her head swam and she feared she might be meeting the floor.

"I'm fine. There's my bag." She started forward but Dorie stopped her with one hand.

"Please. As if." She easily retrieved the roller and followed Ellery to the elevator that led to the moving sidewalks and the parking lot. By this time, Ellery was convinced Logan took up half the state. "Your bag will look cute next to mine in the trunk," Dorie said as they stood on the walkway.

"Are you going somewhere?"

"Yeah, your place. I'm bunking with you until you start to take on a human color."

"You don't have to do that."

"Too late," Dorie said as she hit the button on yet another elevator. "Michelle already signed off on my furlough. She saw the broadcast and she's as worried about you as I am." Ellery sagged against the nearest wall and Dorie looked at her with sympathy. "You know, it's okay to have someone take care of you sometimes. It doesn't mean you're weak. You keep your mother at arm's length, okay. I get that. But then you break it off with Reed. The new guy, what's his name?"

Her fuzzy brain took a long moment to come up with the name. "Evan."

"Right, him. Does he even have a chance with you? You keep your past a secret because you don't want to scare him off but the result is he has no idea who you really are. If you want people to show you their soft underbelly, Hathaway, you're going to have to let them get at least a flash of yours."

"I'm not flashing him anything," Ellery said as she pushed off from the wall. "And he's definitely not moving into my place to play nursemaid. I've never even kissed him. After this past week, I'm sure he's lost my number and wishes to forget he's ever met me."

"I wouldn't be so sure about that."

"Why?" Ellery stopped as a sudden thought sprung into her head. "Oh, God, you don't have him hiding in the car, do you?"

Dorie rolled her eyes. "Yeah—surprise! I hid your boyfriend in the trunk. No, I just meant that he obviously likes you a lot." She gestured with her chin at aisle P. "We're over here."

"You don't know he likes me." Dorie had never met him.

"I do know. Because you've been out on four dates and you've never even kissed. Here we are." She clicked open the trunk and at the beep, a familiar furry face appeared in the window, followed by two enormous paws.

"Speed Bump!" Ellery limped around to the side of the car so she could greet her dog. "You brought Bump."

"Yeah, I know which male you've really got it bad for."

Bump woofed and slobbered on her. She rubbed his floppy, velvety ears and accepted the hound kisses that came with any kind of reunion. "I missed you, boy."

Bump whined and rolled over on the backseat to show off his spotted belly. Ellery gave it a good rubbing as Dorie started the engine. "See?" she told Ellery with a pointed glance at the dog. "That's what you need to do. Maybe he can give you lessons."

"I'm not rolling around on the ground in front of Evan." She paused. "Or anyone else for that matter."

"Then Bump is it for you," Dorie told her with a sigh. "He's your man."

Bump stuck his huge head between them, his paws on the console, and Ellery hugged him around the neck. "We'll invite you to our commitment ceremony this summer."

Ellery let Dorie take her home to her loft apartment. She blinked, somehow surprised to see it looked as she had left it, down to the dishes in the sink. This part of her life had held still, awaiting her return, and now she had to see if she was the same person. She swallowed her pills and crashed in the bedroom with her dog at her side. The medicine worked its magic, filling up her head with cotton candy so she couldn't hear the noise. At last, she slept.

Ellery tolerated Dorie's presence for three days before she sent her back home to her wife. She was grateful, truly, for her partner's help in walking the dog, making the meals, and changing the bandage on her shoulder. She made a note to send her flowers. Or a case of beer. But she relished the total silence in her apartment as Dorie departed. For two days, she subsisted on takeout and prescription painkillers, emerging from her lair only to let Bump do his business in the chilly outside air.

On the sixth day, he leaped onto the couch next to her, but instead of curling at his end, he put his meaty paws on her lap and whined. "What?" she asked him, one eye on the television, where she was deep into a marathon session of *Veronica Mars*. "Have you seen this one already?"

Bump pawed her insistently and answered with a deep *woof*, his tail thumping against the cushions. He had tired of the couch potato routine. He wanted a real walk.

"Okay, okay," she grumbled. "Around the block and that's it."

She eased to her feet to change into something more presentable than sweatpants, only to stop when there was a knock at her door. She froze while Bump charged the entrance, barking vociferously, eager for some excitement. When she checked the peephole, she saw Evan standing on the other side with his Goldendoodle, Ollie. Ellery bit her lip. She could pretend not to be home. She could just not answer and he would get the message. Bump sensed her hesitation and pawed at the base of the door. He knew a friend waited on the other side.

Ellery undid the locks and cracked the door. Evan's face broadened, his blue eyes twinkling with his smile. "Hey," he said. "We were at the park down the street and thought we'd take a chance to say hello."

The dogs circled each other in the hall, wagging and sniffing. Ellery hung back. "Hello," she said cautiously.

"You haven't answered my texts." He paused. "I wasn't sure if you would want to see me."

"My phone is lost." She didn't say it had disappeared at the hands of a serial killer. Let him think she left it on the T. "I haven't gotten around to replacing it yet."

He nodded a little. "Ah, so it wasn't personal."

No, she hadn't wanted to talk to anyone. She heard Dorie in her head. *Gotta show your belly.* "Did you . . . want to come in?" She said the words but she still had the door opened only twelve inches, not especially welcoming. She hung onto the edge of it, unsure.

Evan cleared his throat. "Actually, I thought you might want to go for a walk. Bump seems like he could use it."

"We were just leaving," she said with relief. "Let me change and get my coat."

"Okay, but don't change too much." He flashed her a smile.

A flush went through her. He was flirting? After everything that had happened? He must have seen the news, if not Coben's broadcast itself. She slipped on jeans, boots, and a winter coat before grabbing Bump's leash and heading out into the hall. Bump surged forward toward the elevator and the motion yanked on her shoulder. "Bump, no," she said.

"Here, I can take him." Evan took over Bump's lead so that he held both dogs. "I know you're still recovering."

Ellery mumbled her thanks and they rode down in the elevator in awkward silence, the dogs' snuffling providing the only commentary. Outside, the afternoon was cold but sunny. The hulking snowbanks at the sidewalk's edge had dwindled to small piles with the promise of the coming spring. Ellery had enough room to walk side by side with Evan, and she found she didn't mind it. She'd expected heated questions from him, or maybe pity, but he mirrored her quiet and they walked companionably for a couple of blocks. "Look," she said finally, "I owe you an apology."

"No." He cut her off with a vehement shake of his head.

"I—I should have told you about my past." She squinted at a couple of kids chasing each other around in the park across the street. "To be honest, I assumed you knew. Then when I realized you didn't know my history, it was such a freeing experience to be with someone who had zero expectations. . . . I kept my mouth shut. I should have known better."

"Why?" He stopped walking and the dogs seized the opportunity to examine the base of a tree. "You should have known that Francis Coben would escape from death row and come after you again? I've been catching up on you, Ellie, and you're pretty damn badass, but you're not psychic."

Her jaw remained set. "I meant you should have known." She looked at the ground. "What you were getting into."

"Okay," he said easily as the dogs moved on. "So now I know."

It took her a second to parse his words and then catch up with him. "You don't know," she said, her voice still tight. "You don't know what I'm really like."

His nose wrinkled as he considered her words. "You don't really know me either, right? That's why we're spending time together. I don't expect you to declare all your baggage like we're passing customs or something."

An involuntary laugh escaped her at the absurd thought. "I'd be there for hours."

"Imagine the paperwork," he replied with his eyebrows raised, and she laughed again, lighter now. They walked on, and when his gloved hand slid into hers, she didn't pull away. "There's a coffee-house up around the corner that serves warm chocolate chip cookies," he said. "What do you say?"

Her cheeks felt pink with cold. "Maybe I was wrong. You do know me."

"I know enough for now," he replied, giving her a slight squeeze. She followed him around the corner and discovered he was right about the tiny coffee shop. Its windows were slightly steamed and the aroma of ground beans and chocolate wafted out as he opened the door. Ellery waited outside with the dogs, watching Evan through the windows and wondering how she had never been here before.

35

The last snow of the season came on March 11, but there was no way to know it at the time. Some things you only recognize from a distance. Ellery got a new phone and she emailed Reed the number, which he then entered into his new phone and it felt like they were starting over again. He had no new job but enough money that the situation caused him no particular anxiety. Still, Ellery sensed a restlessness to him, a searching for purpose, but for once, she did not share it. She was back at work, and except for the occasional lingering glance from Dorie, work was back to normal. DNA from a single hair found on Maxine Frazier's body came back to Ben Lerner and they formally charged him with her murder. He pled not guilty and Hollywood remained split in its popular verdict. It was a tired script Lerner himself would never have greenlit—a wealthy producer murdered a prostitute just to see if he could, to attract attention for his upcoming docuseries on the Coben murders.

Ellery had discussed it, off the record, with Kate Hunter when they did their interview. "Coben said Ben would always be a pale imitation, that he would never capture public imagination on his own the way that Coben did and that's why he tried to copy him."

"Ben's got all the headlines now," Kate had replied. "But Coben is right. It's the originals that get all the radio play—no one pays money to hear the cover band."

"There's going to be another movie."

Kate had grinned and held up her water bottle in triumph. "I know. I'm in it. I mean, I'll be playing myself."

Everyone copes differently, Ellery had reminded herself as she gritted her teeth. "How nice for you," she'd replied, trying to mean it.

Kate had shrugged. "Like you said . . . this way I control the story."

Ellery had filmed the special with Kate but not stayed home to watch it. Instead, she'd gone out to dinner with Evan at a new tapas bar, where they had enjoyed steamed mussels with spicy tomato and wine sauce served with crusty bread. The heady flavors made her think of Reed and how he would have been planning to re-create the meal at home. She did not think of him later when Evan took her home, his car idling outside her building as they kissed in the front seat. His mouth was warm and hungry, his hands on her body, sliding under her shirt, right past the scars and up to her breast. Her heartbeat fluttered at her neck and she realized with a start that she could take him inside with her. It would be fine. Maybe even good.

"I . . . I should get going," she said, breathless as she eased away from him.

"Too much?" The streetlight caught his mouth, wet and shining. She touched it with her fingertips. He really was so handsome. Sometimes when they were out, she felt eyes on them, and it had nothing to do with her or Coben. Other women watched Evan for his firm biceps, his strong chin and bright blue eyes. He radiated fitness and demonstrated kindness with every move he made. He had an easy smile, gentle hands, and a quick wit. He could have any woman he wanted and yet he was sitting in this car with her.

"No, it's perfect." She smiled and let her fingers linger on his lips. "You're perfect."

He caught her hand and kissed it. "Why does that sound like regret?"

"Because I have to go walk the dog."

He released her with a reluctant sigh. "But you'll call me?"

"I'll call you."

Inside, sixty pounds of hound came barreling over to meet her at the door. She rubbed him vigorously in greeting. "You're not fooling me," she said. "I can see your imprint on the couch." She gave him a quick walk and it was back inside to brush her teeth and ready for bed. Her head swam, dizzy from the sangria and Evan's kisses. She flipped on the television, where the late news played. They were showing excerpts from her interview with Kate and recapping the story.

With her toothbrush in her mouth, Ellery grabbed the remote to change the channel but stopped when she saw her own face in close-up. She had spent years avoiding looking at herself. Her house contained a single mirror that she glanced in every morning to make sure she was presentable. She had no photos. No selfies on her phone. Her physical self had belonged to Coben, and through him, to the rest of the world. That girl from the closet. It was all anyone thought about when they looked at her. It was how she'd seen herself.

Now here she was, looking regular, or maybe an enhanced regular thanks to the subtle makeup job performed by Kate's crew. Her brown hair shone under the lights. She'd worn a blue collared shirt, no turtleneck, and one of the scars was visible if you knew where to look. "I think about her sometimes," Ellery on screen was saying, "the girl on the bike. I think about who she was and the dreams she had that night before he took her."

"And what were those dreams?" Kate asked.

"Oh, she wanted money for a soda. She wanted her brother to get healthy again and her father to come home. She hoped she'd have homeroom with her best friend Krista in the fall. If you'd asked her what she wanted to be when she grew up, she'd have said a zookeeper or a veterinarian."

"Not a cop?"

Ellery on television gave a surprised laugh. "No. She'd never even met a cop or thought about them much at all. That's funny, right? In about thirty-six hours, they would all know her."

"You talk about Abby like she's a different person."

"She was," Ellery said with certainty.

"But she's you. She lives in you, yes?" Ellery didn't answer. Kate tried a different tack. "What would you say to her now, if you had the chance? What would you want for Abby?"

The camera didn't miss Ellery's eyes welling up. It recorded her every sniffle and her eventual smile. "I'd tell her I miss her. I'd tell her she did the hardest part and every mistake after is all on me. I'd wish . . . I'd wish for her to be happy."

"I have to ask this because even my hairdresser Nadine demands to know: what about you and Reed Markham?"

"We're friends."

"Friends? Is that all?"

"No. It's like . . . we've been shattered and put back together so many times that we probably contain pieces of each other by now. It's hard to put a label on that kind of relationship."

"Well, Nadine labels him sexy."

Ellery on TV gave an unguarded laugh. "She's not wrong."

"So then you're telling us there's hope," Kate said shrewdly.

"Hope for what?"

"A happy ending."

The newscasters cut back in for commentary and Ellery muted the television. She returned to the bathroom to spit and rinse, and while there, she stared at her reflection in the mirror. The woman looking back at her gave her a shy smile. Kate had suggested there could be a happy ending. Ellery always believed this option was taken from her years ago, that she had no control over the way her story got told or how it ended. But perhaps, like Kate said, you had to control the narrative. Seize the mic. Maybe happiness wasn't a state you were privileged to exist in or not. Maybe it was a choice.

Ellery left the bathroom and grabbed her phone, falling backward amid the pillows on her bed. She called Dorie, who grumped at her that she'd already been sleeping.

"Sorry," Ellery said. "I need to know if you can cover for me for a couple of days."

"Are you sick?"

"No, I have something I need to do."

"Tell me what the something is and then I'll decide whether I'll cover."

Ellery took a deep breath and relayed her plan. "I'm showing my belly," she finished. "Are you happy now?"

"I'll be happy when you stop calling me in the middle of the night. Go. Have fun. Call me at a normal hour to tell me all about it."

The next day, Ellery packed up Bump's bowl and bag of food along with her travel suitcase. "Road trip," she told him, and he wagged his white-tipped tail in answer. She put a pair of sunglasses on him and snapped a picture to send to Dorie. *He says thank you.* They drove straight through to their destination with only a quick pit stop for lunch and a bio break, so Bump was eager to get out of the car. She sent another few texts as she walked Bump around for exercise and then stopped at an outdoor café to enjoy an iced tea and the fading spring sunshine.

She waited, watching up the street to see if he'd show. Fifteen minutes later, he appeared, a familiar trim figure dressed unusually in jeans and a black T-shirt. He held up his phone with Bump's sunglasses picture on it. "I got a text from the hound saying I should meet him here."

Bump had risen to stamp his meaty paws, dancing an excited greeting for his long-lost pal. "He insisted we come," Ellery told him dryly. "It was an emergency. He's run out of your socks to carry around in his mouth."

"He can't have these," Reed said even as Bump ran his considerable nose over his feet. "They're cashmere."

"He's not picky."

"Yes, but I am." Reed pulled out the chair across from her. "It's good to see you. I caught your special last night and I think it was excellent."

"You're not put out she didn't interview you?"

He glanced up and murmured thanks to the arriving waiter, who furnished him a water glass. "It wasn't about me," he said to Ellery. "It never was."

"What are you doing with yourself now? I need details. I want to hear about the lifestyles of the sorta rich and semi-famous."

"Let's see. . . . I start my day with caviar and champagne, served on bone china. Then I've cleaned out my garage, chaperoned Tula's class trip to the science museum, and repainted the office. Twice."

She made a sympathetic face. "Misjudged the paint swatch the first time?"

"Morning mist made me feel like I was inside an aquarium." He took a sip of water. "Actually, I was thinking of going into business for myself, as a consultant. I'd get to control the cases and the hours, but I would still be doing the same work that has sustained me all these years."

"That's perfect for you," she declared happily, with private relief. She breathed easier with Reed Markham on the job.

"What about you?" he asked. "What brings you to town?"

"I told you. Bump wanted to see you." She paused. *Here we go,* she thought. "So did I."

"Yeah? I'm glad. I'd hoped we would still be friends."

Friends. She glanced away. "I made a mistake," she said and swallowed hard. "I've made lots of them, but I made a big one years ago and it's affected everything ever since. I stopped thinking I had choices. I left home and dropped the name that Coben called me but it didn't change anything. He still owned me. I was That Girl. Whoever I was going to be before he took me, she didn't matter anymore. I was as he made me."

"Ellery . . ."

She held up a hand, forestalling him. "Just let me finish, okay?" she said, her voice raw. "And who would ever love that girl? She was covered in scars and broken inside from where he'd stuck tools in her. She couldn't have children. She couldn't sleep at night. Everywhere she went, people stared and reminded her who she was. Frankenstein's monster. Well, Frankenstein got a bride, one made especially for him. For a while, I thought that was you. You're the only one who knew my past and understood how I came to be. If Coben made me, he also made you. Your life and mine, they were joined a long time ago. We didn't have a choice in the matter."

It was Reed's turn to look away. "I see. You didn't pick me. He did."

"I thought that," she confessed with tears in her eyes. For once, she didn't hide them or swat them away. "I thought you were the only man I could be open with, the only one who would ever accept me, but it turns out I was wrong."

He worked his jaw back and forth. "Ah. The new guy. He's sticking, is he?"

"Evan is sweet. I like him and he seems to like me." She searched herself for the right words. "I realized I could be with him. I realized I had a choice. And that's when I realized how badly I'd screwed up, because if I have a choice, then I can choose you."

His head jerked up and he looked at her. She gave him a tiny nod. "What are you saying?" he asked.

"I want to be with you. Because of you. Not because of Coben."

He held her stare. "He's not going anywhere. That hasn't changed. The government may never get around to executing him, and Hollywood is going to keep right on making movies. Sure, I've retired from the FBI now, but I can't change the past or control who recognizes us on the street. When we're together, people are going to ask the same questions. Always."

"Always," she repeated with a nod, liking the sound of it. "Got it."

He leaned back in his seat, shaking his head, clearly not sure whether he could trust her. "You like this other guy. He's way less complicated and lives in the same city as you. If you have a choice, pick him. Go. Be happy."

"I would," she said, reaching across the table for his hand, "but every time I go out with him, I keep wanting to call you up and tell you about it. I like him because he reminds me of you. I'm happiest with you. Why should I settle for an imitation when I could have the genuine article?" She hesitated, suddenly unsure. "Unless. Unless you're already seeing someone less complicated."

"Well, now," he said thoughtfully, "as a matter of fact, I do have a date tonight, someone I've been seeing regularly, and she is a fair bit less complicated than you are."

"Oh." Heat flooded her face, the result, she was sure, of her heart breaking open. She tried to play nice because she owed it to him. "That's . . . that's great. Do you love her?"

"To the moon and back." He paused. "Except when I step on her LEGO blocks in the middle of the night. Then I have some choice words for her."

"It's Tula," she realized with a wave of relief. "You're having dinner with Tula."

"It's my weekend with her," he agreed. "I dropped her off at a friend's house when I got your text message. Or rather, the hound's message. But I should be getting back by now." He pushed back his chair but stopped to look at her when she didn't follow suit. "Are you coming?"

"Am I?"

"We're having baked ziti tonight. I recall that's one of your favorites."

"You're my favorite. I don't care what we eat." She laid some money on the table. Bump jumped up, eager for his new adventure.

"Liar," Reed said affectionately, taking her hand.

"Is there cake?" she asked.

"That depends. Are you willing to help me make it?"

"You know I don't know how to cook," she said, stopping on the sidewalk. He turned and looked at her, shielding his eyes from the sun. She squared her shoulders with determination. "But you know what? I'm ready to learn."

Epilogue

Ellery and Reed lounged on a bench in Boston Common, watching Tula splash around in the Frog Pond. She'd made friends with another girl about the same age and the two of them stood in the calf-deep water, inventing a secret handshake. "The Red Sox players exchange less complex greetings after a home run," Ellery observed.

"She'll teach it to you later," Reed replied. He had one arm around her over the back of the bench and the other held a fresh-squeezed lemonade. His shorts showed off lean, tawny legs that she regarded with a mixture of hunger and envy.

"You turn this gorgeous brown color in the summer," she said as she held her pale leg next to his. "If I get any sun, I become a lobster."

"But lobster is tasty," he said as he leaned in to bite her neck.

She laughed and pulled away. "There's a meet-cute story we haven't tried. We both showed up at the deli looking to buy a lobster, but the last two in the tank turned out to be a bonded pair. Our lobsters fell in love before we did."

"Could work." He leaned his head against hers as he considered. This was a game they played with each other now, making up potential stories of how they met that did not involve a serial killer. In real life, if they got the question from someone who genuinely didn't know the Coben story, they just said the truth: they met through work. "Or try this for size. One day, your hound starts bringing home stray objects. A tennis shoe. A newspaper. A baseball cap. You don't know how he's getting out of the yard, so you put a camera on his collar and discover he's learned how to unlatch the gate. The camera shows he goes out of your yard and down the block to my house, where he makes his home in Tula's kiddie pool. When you investigate, you find I'm missing one shoe, one sock, and one baseball cap. It's fate."

She reached down and scratched Bump behind the ears. "It does have an element of truth to it."

"The best lies always do."

Bump raised his head for her rubbing, and in doing so, spotted a fat squirrel waddling nearby. He took off in pursuit before she had time to grab the leash. She called after him but he galumphed at top speed in the rodent's direction, ears flying in the wind. Even a rotund squirrel fattened on tourists' hot dog buns could outrun a basset hound, so she caught up with him when he abandoned his prey and fell to the ground to let a pair of young men shower him with affection. "Bump, you're embarrassing us both," she said to him.

The blonder kid looked up from where he was rubbing Bump's belly. "Great dog you have here."

"I like him."

"My aunt had a dog like this when I was a kid. Basset, right?" The second kid wore glasses and a Boston University T-shirt. He glanced at her and then stood up. "Hey, you're that girl."

His friend stopped petting Bump to give her a second look. The BU kid pointed at her. "You took down that serial killer. What's his name? Coben." He elbowed his buddy. "I saw the movie on TV last month. He kidnapped her and then she got free and blew him away right on camera."

"No way," the other one said with admiration.

"Yeah, it's totally a true story." He looked to her for confirmation.

"Oh, sure," she said at length. "True story." Hollywood had

written her a different, more dramatic ending, and she channeled this other Ellery, if only for a moment. She imitated a gun with her hand and pretended to shoot the BU kid. When he paled, she grinned and turned around. "Come on, boy." The dog jumped up and Ellery walked back with him in the sunshine to where her life was waiting.

Acknowledgments

Huge thanks to the many people who helped me turn a bunch of words into a real book! I am honored to work with the great team at Minotaur Books, especially my wise and essential editor, Daniela Rapp, who provides such valuable feedback and advice, and Cassidy Graham, for her good humor and attention to detail. If you've heard of this book and found it somewhere, that's probably due to the amazing efforts of Kayla Janas and Mac Nicholas.

Thanks also to my terrific agent, Jill Marsal, who cheerfully answers all my pesky questions.

I am especially grateful to readers whose comments, questions, and concerns are always a joy. I love that a shared passion for the written word connects us all. Special thanks to Maureen Carden and Jay Roberts, who found Ellery and Reed early and have cheered them on ever since.

As ever, I would be nowhere without my #TeamBump. Thank you to my crackerjack beta squad, for your feedback and encouragement. I am grateful and indebted to Katie Bradley, Stacie Brooks, Rony Camille, Ethan Cusick, Rayshell Reddick Daniels, Rebecca DaSilva, Jason Grenier, Shannon Howl, Robbie McGraw, Michelle Kiefer,

Rebecca LeBlanc, Suzanne Magnuson, Jill Svihovec, Dawn Volkart, and Paula Woolman.

Grateful as always to my wonderful family, especially Brian and Stephanie Schaffhausen and Larry and Cherry Rooney, for love and support.

Home is where the heart is, and mine is always full because of Garrett Rooney and our daughter, Eleanor. Alas, home is also always covered in fur and half-chewed dog toys because of our basset hound, Winston. I wouldn't have it any other way.